NEW YORK REVIEW BOOKS
CLASSICS

D0355551

BELCHAMBER

HOWARD OVERING STURGIS (1855–1920) was born in London to a rich and well-connected New England merchant family. Russell Sturgis, Howard's father, was a partner at Barings Bank in London, where he and his wife, Julia, were noted figures in society, entertaining such guests as Henry Adams, William Makepeace Thackeray, and Henry James, who became an intimate friend and mentor to Howard. Sturgis was a delicate child, closely attached to his mother, and fond of such girlish hobbies as needlepoint and knitting, which he continued to practice throughout his life. He attended Eton and Cambridge, and, after the death of his parents, purchased a house in the country, Queen's Acre, called Qu'acre, where Howdie (as Sturgis was known to his intimates) and his presumed lover William Haynes-Smith (called "the Babe") frequently and happily entertained a wide circle of friends, among them James and Edith Wharton. In 1891 Sturgis published his first novel, *Tim: A Story of School Life*, based on his unhappy days at Eton, which was followed, in 1895, by *All That Was Possible*, an epistolary novel written from the perspective of a retired actress. Both books went into several printings. Nearly ten years passed before Sturgis published his masterpiece, *Belchamber*, which was successful neither with the public nor with his friends. He was not to write again.

EDMUND WHITE has written biographies of Jean Genet, Marcel Proust, and Arthur Rimbaud. He has also written several novels, travel books, and a memoir. He teaches writing at Princeton and lives in New York City.

BELCHAMBER

HOWARD STURGIS

Introduction by
EDMUND WHITE

Afterword by
E. M. FORSTER

NEW YORK REVIEW BOOKS

New York

THIS IS A NEW YORK REVIEW BOOK
PUBLISHED BY THE NEW YORK REVIEW OF BOOKS
1755 Broadway, New York, NY 10019
www.nyrb.com

Library of Congress Cataloging-in-Publication Data
Sturgis, Howard Overing, 1855–1920.
  Belchamber / by Howard Sturgis ; introduction by Edmund White ; afterword by
E. M. Forster.
      p. cm. — (New York Review Books classics)
  ISBN-13: 978-1-59017-266-7 (alk. paper)
  ISBN-10: 1-59017-266-3 (alk. paper)
  1. Aristocracy (Social class)—England—Fiction. 2. Nobility—England—Fiction.
I. Title.
  PR5499.S242B45 2008
  823'.8—dc22

                                         2007038829

ISBN 978-1-59017-266-7

Printed in the United States of America on acid-free paper.
10 9 8 7 6 5 4 3 2 1

CONTENTS

INTRODUCTION

Belchamber, first published in 1904, is the portrait of a sissy and was initially disliked by everyone, including Henry James and Edith Wharton, who should have known better. Curiously, the author, Howard Sturgis, was a beloved, amiable sissy who made no effort to hide his embroidery frame and the basket of silk thread he kept beside him at all times. Just as "Sainty," the hero of his novel, finds the only happiness of his boyhood in his "work," so Sturgis plied his needles with modest contentment and unremitting application.

Sturgis, however, had arranged his life much more satisfactorily than did his miserable character. Sainty has to give up his sewing. As Sainty's boisterous, athletic younger brother Arthur blurts out, "You're jolly bad at games, and you like to sit and suck up to an old governess, and do needlework with her, like a beastly girl." Whereas Sainty has no friends of his own and must submit to the wishes of his iron-willed Scottish evangelist of a mother, in real life Howard Sturgis surrounded himself with a family of distinguished and scintillating friends who adored him.

Sturgis was an American from a rich Boston family. His father, Russell Sturgis, had made money in the Philippines, but when he returned to Boston to enjoy his success he found the cost of living had become dauntingly high. He decided to go back to Asia with his family, but in transit they all stopped in London for several weeks—and never left. A bank, Baring Brothers, offered to make him a partner. Russell Sturgis accepted and soon was successful enough to maintain three houses, including a big country place, Givons Grove at Walton-on-Thames. He was wonderfully hospitable and Russell was soon known as the "entertaining partner" at Baring's (just as a character in Ford Madox Ford's

No More Parades is called "Breakfast Duchemin" after his splendid morning spreads).

Through his parents little Howard met such American luminaries as Charles Francis Adams and Edward Boit (a Boston artist who'd settled in Paris and whose daughters were painted by John Singer Sargent in one of the most technically astonishing canvases of all time). Howard also met writers such as Thackeray (to whose fiction his own "caste-ridden" *Belchamber* has been compared) and Henry James, who was introduced to the family in the 1870s.

Howard was extremely attached to his parents, especially his mother. As a child he made his mother's boudoir into his playroom, and she refused to correct him for his effeminacy. She murmured that he was "sweeter as he was." As Howard's cousin, the philosopher George Santayana, remarked,

> As if by miracle, for he was wonderfully imitative, he became save for the accident of sex, which was not yet a serious encumbrance, a perfect young lady of the Victorian type.

For instance, when he would step over a puddle he'd automatically lift the edge of his coat "as the ladies in those days picked up their trailing skirts."

He attended Eton and Cambridge (like Sainty), but unlike his character he courageously affirmed his effeminacy before his jeering classmates. His brothers had hoped Eton would make a man of Howard, but the plan came to nothing. Santayana praised Howard's "inimitable honest mixture of effeminacy and courage, sensibility and wit, mockery and devoted love."

Howard also attended art school but soon was entirely occupied with nursing his father and then his mother through long illnesses. Russell Sturgis died in 1887, when Howard was thirty-two, and Howard's mother died the following year.

Suddenly Howard was in possession of a large fortune—and had no direction in his life. As his friend A. C. Benson recalled, "He was almost in the condition of a nervous invalid, suffering from the long strain as well as from the shock of the double bereavement." He made a yearlong trip to America, where he met Edith Wharton and Santayana. He returned to England the following year, in 1889. He then sold a remote country house in Wales and bought a much more accessible and commodious one in Windsor, right next to Windsor Great Park and not far from Eton. It was called Queen's Acre, which was always abbreviated to "Qu'Acre." It had been built only twenty years earlier and was cozy and comfortable with its wide verandas, vermillion brick walls, oeil-de-boeuf windows, and its single acre of rather frowsy gardens.

Inside, however, everything was perfectly tended—small rooms with deep chintz-covered armchairs and couches and little side tables and coal fires glowing in every grate. It was the height of comfort and Howard, who disliked exercise, would leave it only for the occasional "toddle" with Misery, his dog, into Windsor Park. Howard was envied for Mrs. Lees, his cook, and for his expert, attentive butler. Perhaps he was even envied for his stolid, pleasant lover, William Haynes-Smith, known simply as "the Babe," a man's man who preferred cigars and the racing results in "the Pink 'Un" to literary chat and *The Golden Bowl*. Eventually the Babe inherited what was left of Howard's sadly depleted estate—and moved a wife in.

But for years and years Howard and the Babe received Howard's many friends in such an unending stream that Howard confessed, "I feel at times like the unctuous manager of a smart hotel!" Most of the friends were male, many of them younger homosexuals, often from Eton, and they gathered in adulation around Henry James (after all, they had literary careers of their own to launch). They included Percy Lubbock, who would go on to enshrine James's and

Wharton's ideas about the novel in *The Craft of Fiction*—he also wrote book-length portraits of James and Wharton. Another was the good-looking portly young writer Hugh Walpole (who purportedly once made an—unsuccessful—pass at the elderly and virginal James. Staggered by the initiative, James blubbered, "I can't, I can't").

Arthur Benson, Edmund Gosse, and Gaillard Lapsley were all regular guests (Lapsley shared Edith Wharton's enthusiasm for A. E. Housman and Proust). Wharton was one of the few women in the inner circle. She would travel with her fairly crazy husband, Teddy, over from France in her chauffeur-driven motorcar and swoop down on James in Sussex and whirl him off to Qu'Acre. She called the habitués of the house her "male wives."

Everyone seems to have been happy there with the lively conversation, the alternate currents of stylish bitchiness and genuine affection, and the studied luxuries. Some of the guests would go on outings to nearby stately homes. They all loved reading aloud; James put aside his habitual stammer to cry forth with eloquence the rolling periods of Walt Whitman. James called Qu'Acre "a sybaritic sea." Wharton was happy enough to leave behind the "anxious frugality" of James's Lamb House for the "cheerful lavishness" of Qu'Acre. Santayana called Sturgis "host and hostess in one" and dubbed him a "universal mother." Sometimes, of course, there were complaints in such a close-knit circle. As Hermione Lee puts it in her biography of Edith Wharton, "Hugging and yearning went along with satire and malice."

Many of the guests were transplanted New Englanders or New Yorkers who were delighted to affirm among themselves their very American form of exclusiveness. It was a relief for them, who were so often condescended to by the superior English, to mock the king as an emperor of India who lived at neighboring Frogmore. They liked calling Edward VII an arch-vulgarian (the great French chef Escoffier claimed that the king—then Prince of Wales—liked to have caviar scattered over every dish, a preparation known as "à la Prince de Galles"). As fellow expatriates, Wharton and Lapsley would swap clippings from American papers on their favorite headlines about adultery, murder, and felony.

These New Englanders at Qu'Acre included Walter Berry (Wharton's best friend and mentor), Morton Fullerton (a bisexual who became her lover—perhaps her first, since her marriage may have been sexless), Henry James, Lapsley, and Sturgis himself. As Percy Lubbock remarked, it was the only house in England where James was completely at home. In *A Backward Glance*, her memoir, Wharton writes that Sturgis sat next to the fire in a chaise longue,

> his legs covered by a thick shawl, his hands occupied with knitting-needles or embroidery silks, a sturdily-built handsome man with brilliantly white wavy hair, a girlishly clear complexion, a black moustache, and tender mocking eyes under the bold arch of his black brows.
>
> Such was Howard Sturgis, perfect host, matchless friend, drollest, kindest and strangest of men, as he appeared to the startled eyes of newcomers on their first introduction to Queen's Acre.

The contrast of tenderness and mockery was noticed by all his friends, who remarked on his almost tearful kindness; after Sturgis's first visit to Lamb House James asked him to live with him and years later Sturgis asked James the same thing—both unsuccessful bids. James once compared Sturgis to a big sugar cake that everyone—all his friends—feasted on. But Sturgis could also waspishly imitate his friends, especially James, including his maddening way of stammering as he groped after *le mot juste*. Just as Marcel Proust could reduce everyone to helpless laughter with his mimicry of *his* mentor,

Robert de Montesquiou, in the same way Sturgis could "do" James—and perhaps this art of mimicry was linked to both men's novel-writing talents.

In 1903 Sturgis passed along to James the first 160 pages of the proofs of *Belchamber*, his third—and as it turned out his last—novel. His first, *Tim*, had been the tale of a schoolboy crush at Eton. In his second, *All That Was Possible*, an epistolary novel, Sturgis had impersonated an actress who flees London for the peace and authenticity of Wales only to discover that Welsh men are as caddish as those in the capital.

Belchamber was altogether more ambitious. Sturgis worked on it intermittently for more than ten years. In it he draws the portrait of an English marquis who is also Baron St. Edmund and is nicknamed "Sainty," a diminutive that is at once trivializing and an acknowledgment of his basic goodness. Just when Sainty is about to be sent to Eton and pushed on the brutal playing fields, he is providentially injured in a riding accident. Lame and feeble, a partial invalid anchored to a raised shoe, Sainty is unable to participate in ordinary male games and the gentlemanly rites of hunting, much to his relief. From the beginning he was effeminate (more feminine than his bossy, controlling mother), but now he has an excuse for it.

Sainty is a complete contrast to his macho younger brother Arthur. When Arthur enters Eton he

> took the place by storm with his frank and friendly manners, hatred of books, love of games, and perfectly obvious and understandable type of beauty.

Arthur remains uppermost in Sainty's thoughts throughout the novel, first as an endearing but easily corrupted and brainless boy whom Sainty must look out for, then as someone who has been corrupted by his feline French cousin Claude

Morland, who has introduced him to gambling and actresses. Claude—well-mannered and penniless—is suspiciously polite, a Gallic smooth operator:

> Claude's smile was a caress, the grasp of his hand an embrace; in later years a lady once said of him, that she always felt as if he had said something she ought to resent when he asked her how she did.

Whereas Henry James worked out his "international theme" of Americans versus Europeans, Sturgis pitted his supersubtle, suave, and immoral French characters (Claude against his grandmother, who was Lady Belchamber and now, *en secondes noces*, the Duchess of Sunborough) against his English elite, who are either puritanical (Sainty and his mother) or selfish and unbridled in their lust, covetousness, and capriciousness (Arthur and the woman who will become Sainty's wife, Cissy Eccleston).

Sturgis brings up his big guns to satirize these English profligates. When Sainty attends one of his brother's routs he thinks,

> If this was the sort of entertainment Tannhäuser found in Venusberg, he thought the pilgrimage to Rome must have been an exhilarating change.

Elsewhere Arthur is supposed to be cramming in order to be admitted to the army but he keeps being lured away by the pleasures of the hunt. As Sturgis puts it,

> It might be all very necessary that he should help to slaughter his fellow-men by and by, but the immediate duty was the destruction of pheasants. . . .

If Sainty's mother is a zealous evangelist whose faith is

at odds with what English society expects of such a wealthy, titled woman, Sainty's uncle is not troubled by his brand of Christianity:

> His religion was of that comfortable, rational kind in which there is more state than church, and which is first cousin to agnosticism, but infinitely more respectable.

Perhaps because Howard Sturgis was so androgynous and such a keen observer and impersonator of women, he could be most unchivalrous in his descriptions of them:

> She presented him to her mother, a terrible warning of what she was on the high road to become. This lady was a shorter and twenty years' older edition of Lady Arthur, more coarsely painted, more frankly vulgar, more consentingly fat, and she wore an olive green wig of Brutus curls.

Sainty is the incarnation of everything the English gentleman was not supposed to be. He is bookish and is happiest during his years at Cambridge. He dislikes sports and hunting but adores gardening and interior decoration. He accuses himself of being a coward though the reader is not so sure; often he seems quite daring in espousing his eccentric beliefs. He is a great landowner who faints when he's meant to address his tenant farmers. He admires boys, especially thoughtless, rugged ones like his brother, but he is hoodwinked into marrying a fortune-hunting girl remarkable for her acting abilities before the wedding and her cruelty after it. He is, worst of all, a virgin and a cuckold who does not take punitive action when his wife becomes pregnant by another man.

Sainty's spinelessness, and his refusal to fight back against his dictatorial mother and his mocking, abusive wife are what James and Wharton both objected to. Perhaps if Sainty had been provided with Sturgis's own acerbic wit or literary friends or stolid Babe they would have forgiven him. But even if Sainty has a satirical eye he keeps his own counsel and seldom translates his thoughts into speech.

Wharton was kinder than James. She reviewed the book favorably and in her memoirs she allowed how Sturgis had chosen a "difficult" subject and that this unfortunate choice revealed his "relative inexperience as a novelist." Then, in a more ambivalent vein, she went on to say,

> He has shown us, in firm, clear strokes the tragedy of the trivial, has shown us how the susceptibilities of a tender and serious spirit...may be crushed and trampled underfoot in the mad social race for luxury and amusement.

The modern reader takes exception. Maybe because of our own gender explorations we ask why the problems faced by an effeminate man constitute "the tragedy of the trivial." Why is Sainty a "difficult" subject except insofar as he isn't conventionally masculine? Nor can we quite see how Sainty is crushed by the race for luxury, since he himself is rich enough to absorb his losses and quite indifferent to all his possessions and, at least initially, eager to hand them over to his brother, who he's sure will make a more suitable Lord Belchamber. Sainty's great disappointment is not with his beautiful wife, whose superficiality he recognizes from the beginning though he hopes that somehow, miraculously, she might love him in spite of his ugliness. He thinks:

> Jewels, clothes, a house in town, the means to feed the thankless rich, the power to walk out of the room before older women—if these things could make her

happy, as far as they were his to give, let her take them
in full measure. They were freely hers. He had no particular use for them himself.

No, Sainty's real disenchantment comes when he discovers
that his Cambridge mentor Newby is an unconscious hyp-
ocrite. Although Newby presents himself as an idealist tend-
ing toward socialism, he turns out to be overimpressed with
Sainty's wealth and lands as well as with the titles of the
guests who attend Sainty's coming-of-age festivities (one of
the best sections of the book).

James wasn't quite sure that Sturgis, as a mere American
and commoner, had mastered all the details of the milieu of
an English marquis and wondered if he shouldn't have lowered everyone's rank a notch or two; which was strange since
Sturgis's brother-in-law was a marquis (but maybe James had
forgotten that). Then James found the end terribly rushed
since (according to him) what is interesting in a novel are
not the events (and the end of *Belchamber* is very eventful)
but how they strike the governing central intelligence. To
James, one gathers, Sainty was not sufficiently alive to his
circumstances. No, he was nothing but a "poor rat."

James's objections are for the most part cryptic, as if he
didn't want to assault Sturgis too directly, but he seems to
want Sainty to be more a man, even a sexually performing
man:

You *keep up* the whole thing bravely—and I recognize
the great difficulty involved in giving conceivability to
your young man's marriage. I am not sure you have
taken *all* the precautions necessary—but one feels, in
general, that Sainty's physiology, as it were, ought to be
definitely and authoritatively established and focussed:
one wants in it a *positive* side—all his own—so that he
shall not be *all* passivity and nullity.

Elsewhere James, commenting on a scene where Cissy halfheartedly attempts to seduce Sainty so that she'll have an excuse for being pregnant,

> I wish [Sainty's] failure to conjoin with [his wife] about 2 a.m. that night on the drawingroom sofa, could for his sake have been a stand-off *determined* by some particular interposing, disconcerting, *adequate* positive fact . . . something not so merely *negative* for him. . . .

In another letter James elaborates: "Suffice it for the present that I am perhaps just a wee bit disappointed in the breadth of the celebrated nuptial night scene. . . ." Does he mean it's too long or too short? Too detailed or not specific enough?

Would James have been happier if Sainty had insisted on his conjugal rights? If, improbably, he had raped Cissy? But that would have been another novel and another character. It seems almost ludicrous that Wharton and James, who may have both been virgins at this point, should be bullying Sturgis about his lack of heterosexual expertise.

Amazingly, James writes in a later letter, "Start next year *another* book and let me anonymously collaborate." This is the same strange offer he made to several other writer friends, so certain was James that he alone knew how to write a proper novel. Still, in spite of all his objections, James predicts that the book, which was "never for a moment dull," would be a roaring success—a dubious compliment since James was certain that the public was ignorant ("no one notices or understands *any*thing, and no one will make a single intelligent or intelligible observation about your work"). But even so James can't resist adding that Sainty lacks a self and that as a result the reader keeps asking, "To whom *is* it happening?"

This criticism was sufficiently damning that Sturgis threatened to withdraw the book from publication. James shrieked,

If you *think* of anything so insane you will break my
heart and bring my grey hairs, the few that are left me,
in sorrow and shame to the grave.

Repeatedly James assures him that the book would be very
successful with the British Public (which he calls "the BP").

It wasn't. Typically *The Times Literary Supplement* wrote that
Belchamber "is a literary work rather than a work of literature," which presumably means it was uninspired and un-
persuasive if carefully elaborated. The other critics were
equally harsh, objecting to Cissy as a disagreeable woman
and Sainty as a weakling, and the book sank quickly out of
sight. It had to wait until the 1930s, a decade and more after
Sturgis's death, to be hailed as a classic by E. M. Forster in an
essay he collected in *Abinger Harvest*. One critic, George
Thomson, even argues that Sturgis may have influenced
Forster's earliest fiction. Thomson points out that *Belchamber* is intimate (in its direct access to the pathos of Sainty's
feelings) and ironic (in its satirical portraiture of most of the
other characters). Thomson argues that Forster adopted the
ironic tone but rejected being on an intimate footing with
the main characters—what we might call "doting." Forster
never dotes on his characters but rather treats them all with a
bracing dose of ironic distance.

Santayana was clearly influenced by *Belchamber* in *The
Last Puritan*, "a memoir in the form of a novel" that he took
forty years to write. By 1966 the anonymous reviewer of the
TLS was calling a reissue of *Belchamber* "a remarkable book."
The supporting cast, the reviewer wrote, "was a collection of
deplorable though intensely lifelike characters, which in-
clude some of the most appalling women to be encountered
in all fiction." In fact they seem no worse than the women in
the slightly later *Guermantes Way*.

After *Belchamber* Sturgis wrote almost nothing except a
short story in which a younger writer is severely criticized by

his imperious mentor and commits suicide. In the story, "The China Pot," a stand-in for James called John Throckmorton lets slip several half-uttered but damning criticisms of an unfinished novel by Sturgis's double, Jimmy. Mortally wounded, Jimmy withdraws from society. He cannot go on living while knowing that his hero, Throckmorton, thinks he is talentless. He kills himself. At the funeral Throckmorton pretends that he can't fathom why Jimmy, who had "everything," would have committed suicide. Jimmy's best friend out of politeness also pretends to be mystified.

In real life Sturgis was much more sanguine about giving up his writing career. His friend A. C. Benson said that he thought Sturgis had all the makings of a great writer except the drive. Perhaps he was right. Even though Sturgis ran through his fortune and fell on hard times toward the end of his life (he went so far as to propose that Santayana live with him as a paying guest), he still seemed to be enjoying himself. He told Wharton after he underwent unsuccessful surgery for cancer, "I'm enjoying dying very much."

—EDMUND WHITE

BELCHAMBER

CHAPTER I

BELCHAMBER is one of the most beautiful places in England. The name, if not the house, dates from days when Norman-French was the polite language of our kings; the reigning monarch, some early Henry or Edward, alighting for the night, as was the habit of reigning monarchs, at the house of his vassal, and having been especially pleased with something about the apartment prepared for his use, is said to have remarked in high good humour, '*Pardie! tu as là une belle chambre.*' Something of old-world scandal hung about the legend (which in its authorised form is just a little bare and dull for the nucleus round which gathered the fortunes of a noble family), tales of frail beauty not insensible to a royal lover, of feudal complaisance, not to be more overtly acknowledged than by this gracious allusion to the *belle chambre*, from which the domain was to take its name.

The house, as the humblest tourist may see for himself on certain days of the week, is an exquisite Jacobean structure borrowing largely from the Renaissance palaces of Italy, yet with a certain solid British homeliness about it that specially fits it for its surroundings, the green undulations of an English park. The view from the front is sufficiently extended, and behind it, the various Dutch and Italian gardens are interspersed with water-works and statues like a miniature Versailles. Great oaks and ashes and Spanish chestnuts stand in the park, and four large avenues of elms draw their straight lines across it to the four points of the compass. The little river, which in the woods and meadows is a natural shallow trout-stream with loosestrife and ragged robin fringing its banks, is pressed in the gardens into many curious uses—fountains and cascades, and oblong rectangular fish-ponds, where old carp and goldfish circle in and out among the stalks of foreign water-lilies sunk in hampers. The huge lawn behind the house is shaded by cedars of Lebanon, that are such a characteristic feature of Restoration places,

and there is one that disputes with the famous tree at
Addington, and I dare say with half a dozen others, the
doubtful glory of being the oldest cedar in England.

Of the thousands of acres of which the property con-
sists, the farms and manorial rights, the livings in the gift
of the owner, it is not necessary that I should give a catalogue; it is not the business of the novelist to value for
probate, but if possible to convey a vague but imposing
impression of wealth and position. Suffice it that the
Lord of Belchamber is ground-landlord of the greater
part of three large parishes, and that in the county of his
residence alone no less than three beneficed clergymen sit
in their comfortable rectories by the grace of a sickly
young man of no very definite religious beliefs, without
counting his lordship's domestic chaplain, who ministers
to the spiritual needs of a small army of in- and out-door
servants and their families in the little tame church that
is, so to speak, tethered on the lawn.

Belchamber has suffered but little at the hands of
restorers; the family have always taken a sort of lazy pride
in the beautiful house, which luckily seldom rose to the
point of desiring to improve it. The third marquis, to be
sure, had some formidable projects for remodelling the
building, of which the plans remain in a great Italian
cabinet in the hall; but his two favourite pursuits combined to save his home, for he lost so much money at cards
that even he drew back before the large expense involved,
and while he still hesitated, a bad fall out hunting cut
short his building projects with his life. That was more
than a hundred years ago, when gambling and unpaid
debts were indispensable parts of the ideal of a gentleman.

If Charles James, third Marquis and eighth Earl of Belchamber, lost large sums at the club gaming-tables when
he came up to the House of Lords, and died as he had
lived, in the hunting-field, his successor, George Fred-
erick Augustus, the fourth marquis, in no way fell short
of his respected parent's example. He played as high,
drank as deep, and rode as hard as his father, while he
imported into his excesses just that flavour of vulgarity
which the bucks of the Regency copied so successfully

from their master and pattern. He kept two packs of hounds, and several establishments in addition to his acknowledged and legitimate residence; and if he did not break his own neck, he at least broke his wife's heart, not to mention such unconsidered trifles as his word, and a large quantity of beautiful old china, when in liquor. Belchamber saw him but little; he preferred London and Brighton, and one of his smaller places which was in a better hunting-country; and here once more the very vices of its owners seemed to conduce to the preservation of the beautiful house and its treasures. The books, the celebrated Vandykes, and the painted ceilings suffered somewhat from want of fires; but neglect has never been so fatal to works of art as attention, and if the pictures cracked and faded a little, at least they were not burnt, or repainted, or buried under a deposit of coachbuilder's varnish.

To the poor lady, who was occasionally brought from the seclusion of her lord's hunting-quarters to be exhibited at a drawing-room in the family emeralds and diamonds, a son and heir was born, who received, in common with so many of the children of that date, the names of Arthur Wellesley. This was the fifth marquis and tenth earl, and the grandfather of the hero of this book. Marquis Arthur differed from his father and grandfather only in his mode of getting rid of money. If he played less, he made up for it by losing large sums on the turf, and by a generally luxurious and extravagant style of living. He was a notorious beauty, and had a straight nose and an immense bushy pair of whiskers which were fatal to the peace of mind of great numbers of the fair sex; he was inordinately vain, and a woman had only to tell him she was in love with him, and that she had never seen a man with such small feet, to get anything she wanted out of him. He frittered away more money over bouquets and scent and ugly jewellery than his father and grandfather had lost in their longest nights at Crockford's. His triumphs over female virtue were so numerous and notorious that many thought he would never give a hostage to fortune in the shape of a wife of his own. But when the nets of the fowler had been spread for many years in the sight of this volatile bird of gay plumage, he surprised every one by bringing home a bride from across the Channel.

If report said true, this beautiful young woman revenged the wrongs of her sex, and of many husbands, most thoroughly on her whiskered lord, who was not her master. At first it was impossible to Lord Charmington (as he then was) to believe that any woman he honoured with his affection could fail to be madly in love with him; then as the conviction grew upon him (and ideas came to him slowly), there were furious scenes of recrimination, anger, and jealousy on his side, and cold contempt and indifference on hers. More than once they were within a short distance of the divorce court; but his vanity never could be reconciled to the thought of appearing *coram populo* in the character which to him seemed always the most ludicrous and humiliating possible. His wife soon discovered this weakness, and traded on it freely. If she was not a very clever woman, he was a more than ordinarily stupid man, so that he learned to dread her tongue almost as much as the ridicule that must attach to him in case of a scandal. He also began to take a certain pride in her position both in London and Paris. She was certainly for many years one of the most conspicuous figures in the society of both capitals; and if the more particular and old-fashioned ladies held up their hands in horror at the stories told of her, she had a large share in introducing a different standard of morals for the younger set, in which she was always a leader. When no longer in her first youth, she was one of the galaxy of beautiful women who adorned the Second Empire, and though at the severer Court of St. James she was less smiled upon, there were not wanting circles in the land of her adoption hardly less august, and infinitely more congenial, where she was not only received but highly popular.

Through long years which converted her contemporaries into invalids or grandmothers, in which her husband grew fat and coarse, and took to drink and low company,

in which children were born to her, two of whom died
in infancy, in which her eldest son and one daughter grew
up and married, in which her grandsons were born, and
her son died, she remained always 'the beautiful Lady
Belchamber,' always in the world, and of the world,
immutably 'gay,' and fast, and frivolous, following the
same dreary round of fashionable existence year in and
year out, bedizened in jewels not always virtuously come
by, dressed and head-dressed in the latest mode, and
absorbed in the newest craze or pastime with women who
might have been her daughters and men who were sometimes the sons of her early lovers. As her natural charms
faded, they were, of course, replaced by art; the raven
locks that had been admired by Louis Philippe at first
only took on an inkier black, then grew a little brown,
and passed through dull burnished copper to a rich
golden red, while the cream-white skin grew more and
more rosy in sympathy. Gradually, as fashion artfully
disarranged the hair of its votaries, and the wig-makers'
art developed and improved, so much of her ladyship's
elaborate coiffure came to be false that it could be
almost any colour she chose without inconvenience, and
was even known to vary with her gowns.

As for her husband, the flattery of women being as the
breath of his nostrils, it was only natural that the older
and less attractive he became, the lower he went in the
social scale in search of it. The poor little feet that had
stepped so nimbly on the hearts of many frail ones, began
to spread in the vain attempt to support the Silenus-like
body, and, cramped in tight boots, carried their tottering
owner into very queer byways indeed. The beautiful
nose swelled and grew purple, the Hyperean curls, much
thinned at the temples, were still carefully oiled and
arranged, and with the famous whiskers became more
hyacinthine in hue with each advancing year. When I
was a young man, this poor, foolish, wicked old marquis
was still strutting about Pall Mall, and ogling the women,
with a few other bucks of his own generation, padded,
laced, and dyed. I dare say there are bad old men still,
but they are bald, and have grey beards, and are some-

how not so ridiculous as Lord Belchamber and his peers were. He and his wife met but seldom, and though he sometimes grew quite eloquent over the way she treated him, he was not really unhappy; after all, he was leading just the same life he always had, and if his companions were coarser and commoner, his taste had coarsened too, and the dull, bloodshot eyes had lost their keenness of vision and grown less critical. He outlived his son, and did not die till after the Franco-Prussian war. Almost the only remark of a purely sentimental nature he was ever known to make was on the subject of the siege of Paris and the fall of the Empire. 'Poor old Paris!' he said. 'I've had many a good time in Paris, though I did meet my wife there, damn her! but I shouldn't care to go there again, hanged if I should, with everything so changed, and all that——'

We shall have nothing more to do with him in this work, except to bury him, which, by and by, we will do with befitting pomp. Of direct influence he never had the smallest on any living creature, but who shall say what mysterious legacy of evil tendencies he may have bequeathed to his descendants? The question of heredity is very fashionable just now, but remains not a little obscure; and perhaps it is safer in the interests of morality that we should not know too exactly how little responsibility we have for our bad actions, and how much we can shuffle off on to our grandfathers and grandmothers. Whether it was the result of heredity or education, or a mixture of the two, the children of such a couple did not start in life with the best chance of being quiet, reputable people, and the two who survived the disorders of infancy were left to bring themselves up very much as fortune willed. Lady Eva was a very pretty girl who seldom saw her mother, left entirely to French maids and governesses, and mainly educated on the novels of that country, which she abstracted from her mother's boudoir and read on the sly, generally with the connivance of her instructress, on condition that she passed them on to her. Lady Belchamber used sometimes to see this official, when she thought of it, for five minutes while her hair was being done.

'Lady Eva se comporte bien?'

'Parfaitement, ma'm la marquise.'

'Qu'est-ce qu'elle apprend? voyons.'

'Lady Eva étudie, en ce moment, comme géographie, l'Asie orientale, la Chine, le Japon; comme histoire, le dix-septième siècle, les guerres de Louis XIV, la guerre civile en Angleterre, la restauration de Charles II; comme langues, Italien, *I Promessi Sposi*, Allemand, la *Maria Stuart* de Schiller, Français, *Le Cid* de Corneille; comme mathé atique——'

'Assez, assez! ne faites pas trop étudier cette p'tite, vous en ferez un bas bleu. Elle va bien?'

'Parfaitement, milady. Désirez-vouz voir Lady Eva?'

'Pas ce soir; je n'ai pas le temps.'

Once some one asked the little girl to give her mother a message. 'I will write to her,' the child said, 'it will be quicker.' They were living in the same house.

When in due course she was presented and made her appearance in the world, she was very much admired. At nineteen she was engaged to two men simultaneously, and got out of the difficulty by running away with a third, a rather shady hanger-on of her father, called Captain Morland, who not long afterwards had to disappear from society, owing to an unfortunate difficulty that he experienced in confining himself to the strict laws of the game at cards. Thenceforth they lived mostly abroad, and little was heard of them. Lady Belchamber, who was not an unkind woman, used to write to her daughter sometimes, and send her old dresses and hats; and the old lord, when on the continent, would have the couple to live with him, and give them money. He had a sneaking kindness for Morland, which he never quite got over, finding him a congenial companion; and his son-in-law was very patient in listening to his tender confidences. Lord Charmington, who was two years older than his sister, had the better chance that comes to boys of being sent away to school. Unfortunately for him, the one thing he did not inherit from his parents was the naturally strong constitution that was common to them both. Lady Belchamber, though herself a marvel of strength and vitality, came of an extremely old family, of which the blood, enfeebled by much marrying of cousins, had had time to run very thin indeed; and though the Chambers stock was originally strong and healthy, the excesses of the last three bearers of the title had not tended to the transmission of a fine physique to their descendants.

From his childhood poor Charmington was a rickety, feeble lad, and more than once came within a tittle of sharing the fate of his younger brothers, instead of surviving to be the father of our hero, in which case this book would never have been written. If he could have stayed out his time at Eton, it might have done much for him, for he was not without some naturally kindly qualities, though he was as stupid as an owl, and never could learn to spell the simplest words. In those days there existed no ruthless law of superannuation, and he might have remained contentedly in fourth form till he was nineteen, had it not been for his unfortunate health: he was always ill, and always having to be taken away and sent to the seaside, or abroad, in the care of any one who could be got to go and look after him. This employment fell as often as not to his future brother-in-law, Captain Morland, than whom a worse companion for a growing lad could hardly be found, and where he could be, Morland found him, and introduced him to his charge. By the time he was twenty, the lad was an accomplished little rip, gambler, and spendthrift, and had materially impaired his already feeble constitution. He was bought a commission in the household cavalry, but at the end of a few years, having come to the end of everything—health, money, credit, and the limits of his father's patience—he was thenceforward lost to the service of his country.

After a severe hæmorrhage of the lungs, he was ordered to winter abroad, and by way of retrenching and building up his strength, he selected Nice as a quiet, inexpensive winter resort, with the chance of a little congenial amusement in the nearness of the tables at Monte Carlo. Here he found his sister and her husband (whose little trouble at the club had befallen the year before) hanging on to the fringe of society. But here, too, he encountered that veteran statesman, the Earl of Firth, who, with his wife and two daughters, was recruiting his strength, after his retirement from public life, at a villa in the neighbourhood. The Morlands were established at Monaco, where the Firth party never set foot, so Charmington had no difficulty in keeping his disreputable brother-in-law out of sight of his new acquaintances. He began to frequent the villa of the old Scottish peer with quite surprising assiduity. Just what there was in either Lady Sarah Pagley or her surroundings to attract a man like Charmington will always remain a mystery. Perhaps the jaded, invalid young man found something of the home atmosphere he had never known among these prosy folk; perhaps the blameless dulness of their lives was rather restful to him; or it may be that he took refuge with them from Morland's incessant appeals for the money of which he himself was so sorely in need. It has been suggested that he paid court to Lady Sarah from mercenary motives, but to a man of his tastes and traditions her modest £15,000 would have seemed a very trifling price to receive for the surrender of his liberty; and if a rich marriage had been his object, there were wealthier maidens scattered along the Mediterranean shore who would not have despised the suit of a marquis's only son. He himself explained his choice to a wondering friend by saying that she was the woman most unlike his mother that he had ever met.

With mere carnal charms the Ladies Pagley were somewhat scantily equipped. They were both fairly well-grown young women, healthy and vigorous; Lady Sarah, as she was the elder, was also slightly the taller of the two. Both wore their smooth brown hair divided in the centre and brushed plainly down behind their ears, a fashion from which Sarah has never departed to this day. Both were badly dressed, and either, in whatever part of the world she was met, would unhesitatingly be pronounced to hail from the British Isles by people who had never seen an Englishwoman before. Sarah was religious, Susan political, each following the bent of one parent, for Lord Firth had been a member of several Cabinets, and divided his time between nursing his gout and studying blue-books, whereas Lady Firth dosed her body with quack medicines and her soul with evangelical theology. But the old lord had the ingratitude to prefer the daughter who reflected her mother's tastes. 'They are both dour women to tackle, my daughters,' he would say; 'but Sally's not unkindly in matters where religion is not in question, whereas Susie has no bowels, none at all.' Lady Susan was a great talker, and loved argument for its own sake; but Lady Sarah was reserved, silent, and really very shy for all the grimness of her aspect. If it did not seem profane to think of beauty in connection with either of them, who considered it so little, I should say that Susan was the prettier of the two, having a better complexion than her sister, and hair of a brighter, redder shade of brown.

There never were two girls more predestined by nature for old maids, or better fitted to meet the cold world single-handed; and yet they both married, and married what is called 'well,' while many of their fairer and more eager sisters were left ungathered on the stem. Susan was led to the altar by a West Country baronet and M.P., Sir Charles Trafford, while Sarah, to every one's surprise, became in due time Lady Charmington. If it will remain a puzzle what drew her husband to her, it is still more insoluble what attraction she found in him. Old Lady Firth, for all her piety and her sermons, was not above a little worldly gratification that her plain elder daughter at seven-and-twenty should marry the heir to a marquisate and a historic house; but I honestly think Lady Sarah was little swayed by these considerations. She may have felt a thrill at the thought of the power her position would one day put into her hands, but for its own sake she valued that position very lightly. Perhaps poor Char's weakness appealed to her strength, and his wretched state of health stirred that pity that was so carefully concealed in her proud heart. Perhaps her missionary zeal awoke at the thought of plucking from the fire a brand that was already little more than an ember. No doubt both these feelings worked for him, but I am inclined to think that his most potent advocate was the fact that he was the

first man who had ever made love to her. No woman
hears those magic accents for the first time unmoved, and
if she has reached Lady Sarah's age without the faintest
breath from the wing of Romance, the effect of them is not
thereby lessened. Be that as it may, this sick, dissipated
boy, who was three years her junior, and whose past
life had been made up of everything of which she most
disapproved, succeeded where a better man might have
been very likely to fail, and they were married with great
splendour during the ensuing season in London, the
occasion being one of the few on which her husband's
parents were ever seen together in public. Lord Firth
and his son, Lord Corstorphine, looked very sulky at the
wedding, but Lady Firth was all tears and benedictions,
and old Belchamber, after much champagne at the
breakfast, became quite maudlin over the consideration
of his son's respectable connections. 'It'll be the making
of Char,' he hiccoughed into the ear of the sympathetic
Lady Firth. 'Ah, if I'd had such a chance, now! if I'd
married a different kind of woman, she might have done
anything with me——' The lady with whom he had just
been celebrating his silver wedding was radiant in sky-
blue silk and white lace flounces and a Paris bonnet all
Marabout feathers and humming-birds. 'I don't envy
Char,' she wrote to her daughter, who did not come over
for the wedding. '*Dieu!* what people those Firths! *Heureuse-
ment*, they won't want to see much of *me*.'

Very likely Lord Belchamber was right, and Sarah
might have made something out of the unlikely material
she had taken in hand. Her influence over Charmington
was enormous, and he both loved and feared her. She
nursed him, ruled him, and generally watched over him,
protecting him alike from the scorn of her kinsfolk and
the bad influence of his own; she rigorously kept both
wine and money from him, doling them out in infinitesi-
mal doses. If she allowed no questioning of her authority,
she accomplished the miracle of awakening some glimmerings of self-respect in him, and she bolstered up his
shattered constitution so that he lived four years with her,
during which she bore him two sons; but his lungs were

too seriously affected for the imperfect science of the
sixties to heal, and in spite of all her care he did not live
to be thirty, dying, as has already been said, while that
elderly Adonis, his father, was still figuratively wearing
the family coronet.

CHAPTER II

THE world is like a huge theatrical company in which
half the actors and actresses have been cast for the wrong
parts. There are heavy fathers who ought to be playing
the lover, and young men on whose downy chins one
seems to see the spectre of the grey beard that would be
suitable to their natures. Perhaps the hardest case is
theirs who by their sex are called upon to 'have a
swaggering and martial outside,' 'a gallant curtle-axe
upon their thigh,' and yet, like Rosalind in her boy's
dress, start and turn faint at the sight of blood. The right
to be a coward is one of the dearest prerogatives of
woman. No man may be one with impunity, and it is
precisely the women who are the first to despise him if he
be. Those who are born with the gift of personal courage
(and they are happily the greater number) have no
adequate idea of their blessing. To be in harmony with
one's environment, to like the things one ought to like—
that surely is the supreme good. If that be so, then few
people have come into the arena of life less suitably
equipped for the part they had to play than the subject
of this history.

Charles Edwin William Augustus Chambers, Marquis
and Earl of Belchamber, Viscount Charmington, and
Baron St. Edmunds and Chambers, for all his imposing list of names and titles, started in life without that
crowning gift—wanting which all effort is paralysed—
a good conceit of himself. And in fact, except for the
gewgaw of his rank, which sat on him as uneasily as a
suit of his ancestral armour, he had not much that would
win him consideration from the people among whom his
lot was cast. From his father he inherited his feeble

constitution, his irresolution and want of moral courage, from his mother her sallow complexion and lack of charm, her reserve and shyness, and the rigid conscience which a long line of Covenanting ancestors had passed down to her, and which in him, who had none of their counterbalancing force of character, tended always to become morbid. In his babyhood he had been called Lord St. Edmunds, as was the custom in the family for the eldest son's eldest son; his father in half derisive affection had abbreviated the title into 'Sainty,' and Sainty he always continued to be to all who were intimate enough, and to many who were not. He was only three when his father died, and his baby brother, Arthur, was not yet two. Even in those early days the contrast was strongly marked between the brothers. Sainty was a pale, nervous child who cried if spoken to suddenly, while Arthur was as fine a pink and white fat baby as you could see in a picture-book, who crowed and gurgled and clapped his hands and liked his bath and took kindly to his food, so that the nurses adored him. When he had a stomach-ache or was thwarted in his wishes he roared lustily for a minute or two and then returned to his usual placidity, whereas poor Sainty, if anything 'put him out,' as his nurse would say, whined and fretted, and kept up a little, sad, bleating cry for hours.

He could not remember his father, but with the help of the large coloured portrait in uniform that stood on a gilt easel in the corner of his mother's room he had built up for himself a shadowy heroic figure, strangely unlike poor Charmington, which in his imagination did duty for this departed parent. He never spoke of him to any one but Arthur, but to him he talked with such conviction of 'Papa,' that the child, not very attentive and perhaps not greatly interested, gathered an impression that the elder boy was drawing on his memory for his facts, and indeed he almost thought so himself, until one day Lady Charmington, hearing some such talk between the two, sharply rebuked poor Sainty for telling falsehoods to his little brother. His earliest impression of his mother was in her black dress with the gleaming white on head and throat and wrists, a dress that lent a dignity to Lady Charmington's somewhat commonplace figure. When she left off her cap, it was of the nature of a blow to him. Though he could not have described his sensations, she seemed somehow discrowned with her sleek, bare head.

Grandpapa's funeral was a different matter from these early fleeting impressions. That he remembered clearly, for he was seven when it happened, and had a little black suit of knickerbockers and black stockings and gloves, and led Arthur by the hand similarly attired. Every incident of that frightening, gloomy, yet strangely fascinating and exciting day, remained engraved in his recollection. He remembered the crowd in the churchyard, the murmur that greeted his own appearance, the staggering of the bearers under that long, heavy burthen, the gloom of the church full of people in black, and the great yawning hole in the chancel pavement. What he did not grasp until very long afterwards, and then only most imperfectly and by degrees, was the difference the event of that day made in his own position; but his mother realised it fully, and indeed it made much more difference to her than to the meek little boy accustomed from earliest infancy to swallow distasteful puddings and nauseous drugs at her command, and anxiously to examine his conscience, if some remnant of the old Adam ever led him to question her decrees. Henceforth Lady Charmington entered into her kingdom, and it must be confessed that on the whole she ruled it well and wisely, and entirely in the interests of her children. Almost the only sensible thing the old lord had ever done was to appoint her and her brother the guardians of his grandchildren, and under the careful management of his daughter-in-law, aided by the wise advice of Lord Corstorphine, the property was nursed through his grandson's long minority back to a tolerably healthy condition.

As to Lady Belchamber, nothing would have bored her more than being cumbered in any way with the guardianship of her grandchildren. She carried off what her daughter-in-law declared to be a most ridiculously disproportionate jointure, and the furniture of her private apartments, in which some valuable china and cabinets, that she had certainly not brought into the family, somehow found themselves included at the time of the move. She even showed a decided inclination to keep the famous emeralds which, as Lady Charmington said, everybody knew were heirlooms; but these she was made to send back by her second husband, the Duke of Sunborough, one of the oldest and most faithful of her admirers, whom she married just a year after her lord's death. On the other hand, she generously abandoned all claim to a damp and mouldy dower-house in which she had a right to reside for life, which, considering that the duke had a palace in London and five country seats, was very handsome of her. Three generations of gambling and extravagance leave their mark on the most imposing fortunes, and if the Belchamber estates did not come to the hammer, it was due to the action of the last person who might have been expected to save them, in marrying a hardheaded Scotswoman and dying before his father. To get the estate into order was Lady Charmington's prime object in life. To this end she inaugurated a rigid system of economy, and made a clean sweep of the heads of almost every department under the old régime, toiling early and late to make herself mistress of many details of which she was ignorant; for this, she endured the dislike of the poor, whom she benefited in her own autocratic manner, and much hostile comment from her equals. She was rigidly just, and generous, too, in her own way; only prodigality and waste she would not tolerate, nor look with a lenient eye on the small peculations which those who serve the great come to regard as quite within the pale of honesty.

If the mother spared neither time nor labour that she might be able to hand over his property to her son free of encumbrances when he came of age, she was not less eager and indefatigable in her efforts to fit him for the position she was making for him; and this task she found incomparably the harder of the two. It was not that he was naughty or insubordinate. A meeker, more obedient child did not live. The difficulty was far more intangible;

it is easier to drive a slightly pulling horse in crowded
thoroughfares than one with so light a mouth that he never
will go properly up to his bit; and Lady Charmington
had not the blessed gift of light hands in conducting the
education of a child, whatever she might have on horseback. As a girl she had ridden a good deal, and even
hunted; and though she gave that up after her marriage,
she still found it possible to keep a more effectual eye on
all corners of the huge estate from her square seat on the
back of a substantial cob than from any other coign of
vantage. No farmer ever rode more diligently and
thoroughly about his fields; and on these excursions it was
her pleasure that the boys, and especially Sainty, should
accompany her. Arthur had a natural seat, took to
horses from the first, and wanted to gallop his pony and
make him jump before the family coachman had thought
fit to abandon the leading-rein. With poor Sainty it was
far otherwise. He rode, as he ate rice pudding, because
he was told to; but he was cold for an hour beforehand,
and he sat his pony, as his mother remarked, like a sack
of potatoes. The smallest thing unseated him; he was
always rolling ignominiously off.

On this and similar shortcomings, he received many
admonitions from his mother and uncle, from which the
chief impression he derived was a rooted belief in the immense superiority of his younger brother. 'At the worst
there will always be Arthur.' When and under what circumstances had he overheard that remark? He never was
quite sure that he had not formulated it for himself. Be
that as it might, it early became the burthen to which
his life set itself. Far from resenting the point of view, he
drew from it a certain consolation under his abiding
sense of his many imperfections. He was still quite a small
boy when he decided that his *rôle* in life would be to die
young, and make way for the younger brother who was
so eminently fitted for the position that suited himself so
ill; and he found a certain gloomy satisfaction in settling
the details of pathetic deathbed scenes. I fear an element
in these imaginings which was not without attraction for
him, was the thought of exhorting Arthur with his latest

breath on matters in which his brother's conduct did not always square with his own more evangelical standard, such as a certain looseness of statement, and somewhat lax ideas of property. If Arthur could not find his own cap, or bat, or riding-whip (and his things were generally tossed about the great house wherever he happened to be when he last used them), it was always less trouble to take Sainty's, which were sure to be in the right place, than to go and look for his own. He also on occasion carried the juvenile habit of untruth rather further than mere thoughtlessness warranted; but he told his stories with so open a countenance, and such a fearless gaze, that he was invariably believed, as against poor Sainty, whose knitted brow and downcast eyes, while he sought in his mind for the exact truth, had all the appearance of an effort after invention. 'Arthur is very thoughtless and tiresome,' Lady Charmington would say, 'but there's one comfort about him, I can always depend on his telling me the truth if I ask him. I wish I could say the same for Sainty; I am sometimes afraid he is rather sly. I try not to be hard on him, for he is timid, and I don't want to frighten him into telling untruths; but I do wish he was a little more straightforward, and would look one in the face when he talks.'

Many such hints, all showing a like perspicacious insight into the characters of her sons, were given by this conscientious lady to the governess she had engaged to assist her in moulding their dispositions. Alice Meakins was the daughter of the rector of Great Charmington, and had the prime recommendation in her employer's eyes of being her humble slave and completely under her orders. Had she been a little less in awe of Lady Charmington, and less impressed with the enormity of differing from her, she might perhaps have enlightened her on many matters concerning the little boys. Her mild rule, while it galled his more spirited brother, sat very lightly on Sainty, who worshipped the governess as the most talented and accomplished of mortals. 'But I like her, I'm fond of her; I don't *want* to do what she tells me not,' he pleaded to the indignant Arthur, as usual

incensed by his brother's want of pluck in refusing to join
in some plot against the authority of their instructress.
'Ho, ho, Miss Moddlecoddle, you can't ride, you've got
no seat and no hands; Bell said so. You're jolly bad at
games, and you like to sit and suck up to an old governess,
and do needlework with her, like a beastly girl. I'm a
man, and I shan't do what she tells me. What business
has she to order me about? she is only a servant like the
others.'

Sainty was shocked. 'O Arthur! you do say *horrid*
things,' he said. It was true that he did like sitting with
the gentle Meakins, and acquiring the modest arts of
which she was the mistress. She had many little manual
dexterities such as governesses impart to children,
whereby the world is filled with innocent horrors, kettleholders in cross-stitch, penwipers faintly resembling old
women with cloth cloaks and petticoats, and little black
seeds for faces, and book-markers in the shape of crosses
with many steps, plaited of strips of gilt and coloured
paper. In all these manufactures Sainty soon became
proficient. He also illuminated texts, 'Be thou faithful
unto death,' and 'The greatest of these is Charity,' which
were presented to Lady Charmington on her birthday.
On the subject of the texts and the little plaited crosses
Lady Charmington had a word to say to Miss Meakins
in private, as being rather too papistical in tendency;
but she was not displeased with the simple presents, on
the whole, until her anxious maternal eye was led to
detect the danger that might lurk in cross-stitch by some
petulant remarks of Arthur's, who wanted Sainty to
come out and play Red Indians in the long shrubbery.
'Muvver,' he cried, bursting into the boudoir, where his
mother was busy with some farm accounts, 'isn't Sainty
howid? He won't come out, though he's done his lessons,
'cos he will stick in and do beastly woolwork.' One of
Arthur's many charms was a babyish imperfection of
speech. He never could pronounce 'th' or 'r,' even when
quite grown up.

'What is it he's doing?' asked Lady Charmington.

'Oh, beastly woolwork; he's got two-fwee fings he's

makin', and he likes to sit like a girl, instead of coming out and playing.'

A shade of annoyance crossed the mother's face. 'I wish you wouldn't use such words as "beastly," Arthur,' she said severely, but the severity was really addressed to the absent first-born and the effeminacy of his tastes; and the schoolroom was presently visited by the mistress of the house, and Sainty duly turned out to distasteful recreation. When he had gone forth to be scalped by the fraternal savage, his mother turned to the instructress. 'I think, Alice,' she said, holding up the offending kettle-holder, 'that it is a pity, on the whole, to teach Sainty to work; he's quite sufficiently effeminate by nature, without having that side of him encouraged. I will speak to him about it. I shall tell him I don't approve of his working; it's not manly.' She was surprised, when she carried out this intention, by meeting with passionate tears and protestations.

'O mother, I love my work; it's the only thing I do enjoy, except botany, and reading, and some lessons (not 'rithmetic or spelling); and I have to do so many things I *don't* like, cricket and riding, and—and—all the dreadful things that men and gentlemen have to do,' the little boy concluded, quoting a formula frequently used for his encouragement.

Though not habitually distrustful of her own judgment, nothing so confirmed Lady Charmington in a view she adopted as any opposition to it; and the kettleholders became taboo from that day forward. Poor Sainty's confession of dislike for the manlier sports that, as he said, were considered a necessary part of the education of a gentleman, was perhaps the most unfortunate argument he could have chosen, for it naturally convinced his mother that the mischief lay deeper than she supposed, and suggested to her the advisability of transferring the boys from petticoat government altogether; that is, of course, as far as the subordinate powers were concerned. The particular petticoat that typified her own sway remained in undisturbed possession of the throne in all her plans for the future.

'I think the boys are getting too much for poor Miss Meakins,' she said to her brother, on his next visit. 'She is an excellent girl, though a little inclined to be high church; but they ought to be under a man, I feel sure.'

'Don't tell me that Sainty is becoming insubordinate?' said Lord Corstorphine.

'No; but Arthur hasn't the smallest respect for her. With Sainty the danger is of a different kind; he is perhaps *too* fond of women's society.'

'Not a precocious passion for the governess! I can't believe that.'

Lady Charmington looked resigned. 'I don't deny, Corstorphine,' she said, 'that you have been a great help to me in the management of my fatherless boys; that is why I am consulting you on the present occasion. But it is no help to be flippant and funny. What I mean is that Sainty is quite sufficiently inclined by nature to be a milksop, without living perpetually with women, and adopting their ways. He likes better than any game to sit indoors with Miss Meakins on fine days, and do wool-work.'

'Have him out, Sarah, by all means,' returned her brother. 'I can't help being a little pleased at his liking reading. A Chambers who occasionally opens a book, and is tolerably well behaved, will be an agreeable variation of the type. But it's bad his not wanting to be out and playing games; it isn't natural.'

Lord Corstorphine felt that he was as near normal as it was possible to be, without becoming commonplace, and that those whose tastes differed widely from his own must always be more or less blamably eccentric. Still, his greater commerce with the world had given him a wider toleration than either of his sisters, who had been known to call him a Laodicean, and Sarah once went so far as to draw a parallel between her brother and Gallio. But though she affected to be shocked at the looseness of his views, his known moderation made her lean the more confidently on his judgment. The know-ledge that her opinion was backed by one whom the world praised for common-sense gave a pleasing security that her own noble zeal was not hurrying her into extremes. It was invariably she who initiated every change in the education of her sons. But, though it may be doubted how she would have borne opposition from her fellow-guardian, his agreement was always a comfort to her.

So Alice Meakins, with her little crosses and penwipers, returned to the paternal rectory, with the highest testimonials from her dear Lady Charmington, to look out for another situation.

Poor Sainty could not be comforted. To be sure, no one tried much to comfort him. For the first time he felt a rebellious bitterness towards his mother. Though he could imagine nothing so dashing as active disobedience, he cherished a dark determination to be very cold and reserved towards the new tutor, with the natural result that Miss Meakins's successor, a youth fresh from Oxford, and also of the children of the clergy, conceived a great liking for Arthur, and favoured him prodigiously.

This young man, who had been selected mainly for his reputation as a cricketer, left Lady Charmington nothing to desire in the matter of sport, and was quite ready to ride any horse in her limited stable; nor need she feel anxiety as to his holding extreme views in religious matters. It is true he attended family prayers with exemplary punctuality, and accompanied his charges to service twice on Sundays; but she could detect no sign of the interest in matters ecclesiastical which she looked for in a son of the Church, and his waistcoats and riding-boots had a decidedly worldly air.

Under Mr. Kirkpatrick, Sainty early proved the cynical dictum that life were endurable but for its pleasures, the hated pastimes in which his sex and position in life inexorably demanded that he should find enjoyment. He stood like a martyr at the stake, to be bowled at with the Englishman's fetish, that terrible disc of solid leather which he knew he should not hit, but which not infrequently hit him; and he would unhesitatingly have indorsed Mr. Pinchbold's remark that 'the horse was a fearful animal.' He was so painstaking, however, and anxious to do what was expected of him, that he might possibly have attained in time to some sort of proficiency in these alien arts, had his efforts been greeted with a little more encouragement, and a little less ridicule; but the race is not yet extinct of those who hold that the best way to teach a child to swim is to throw him into the water.

Meanwhile, a new terror arose on Sainty's horizon. When Mr. Kirkpatrick had been at Belchamber eighteen months, he one day intimated to Lady Charmington that he had been offered a mastership in a public school, and could not afford to remain much longer with his pupils. It was therefore suggested that, as they were both presently to go to Eton, a few years at a private school would not be undesirable as a preparation. Even Arthur was a little daunted at the prospect, while rather fascinated by it; but to Sainty it loomed black as the final end of all brightness, closing in the vista of his life and blotting out the sun. It seemed to him that each step in the *via dolorosa* of his existence was fated to be more awful than the last. When his beloved Miss Meakins had been replaced by the hated Kirkpatrick, he thought to have tasted the dregs of bitterness; but now a new prospect had come to make life in the familiar places that he loved with a catlike fidelity appear the one thing desirable, even shadowed by the tutor and his cricket-ball. I suppose it seemed a hard thing to our first parents when the Serpent was introduced into Eden; but life in Paradise, even with a snake in the garden, was a very different thing from the flaming sword that drove them out into an unknown world of work and briars. Sainty said little to earthly ears, but he prayed nightly with intense fervour that he might die before the day came to go to school, which seemed the only escape to his poor little hunted mind.

But there was another way, which, if he could have foreseen it, would have taxed his courage with a far more genuine fright than that vague abstraction, death, for which we all cry aloud so readily in our youth when things do not go as we wish. Arthur went to school alone when the time arrived, and this was how it came about.

It was a beautiful day at the end of March. Mr.

Kirkpatrick was to leave at Easter, and the dreaded exodus was only a month away. It was a late spring, and the snow still lay on the north side of the hedgerows. But it had rained in the night, and there was that indefinable sense of spring in the air that sometimes comes quite suddenly. The primroses were beginning to gem the coppices, the birds to sing late in the long twilights. Daffodils waved in the fields where the young lambs were bleating.

'What are you and the boys going to do this afternoon, Mr. Kirkpatrick?' asked Lady Charmington at lunch.

The tutor looked inquiringly at the boys. 'I'll do whatever they wish, Lady Charmington. What should you like?' he asked of Sainty.

'I should like to go to One-tree Wood, and get primroses,' Sainty answered, after the usual slight struggle that it always cost him to express a wish or an opinion.

'Get Gwanmuvvers!' burst in Arthur. 'Bovver pwimwoses; you don't care about 'em, do you, Mr. Kirkpatrick? I want to wide; Bell says the gwound's in quite good order to-day, after the wain. We've hardly widden at all lately, 'cos it's been so hard.'

As usual Arthur had his way, and poor Sainty was condemned to ride. Generally he gained confidence when he had been out a little while, but to-day, somehow, everything went wrong. He began by rolling off at the hall door, because his stirrups were too long, and the pony moved on unexpectedly while they were being taken up. He was much chaffed for this misadventure by his companions, and he did not like chaff. Then the pony was fresh and inclined to shy, after the inaction of the long frost, so that he had a bad time of it altogether; but he managed to stick on somehow until they were on their way home.

They had been round by Little Charmington, and their way lay through one of the high woods. When they came to the gate that led into the park, they found it locked.

'I never knew this gate locked before,' said Kirkpatrick, pulling feebly at it with his whip. 'I don't suppose either of you have got the key by any chance?'

'Jaggins must have locked it. He's got some young

pheasants further up the wood,' said Arthur; 'he told me so.'

'I suppose we must go back,' said Kirkpatrick, 'but it's an awful long way round. We shall be late for tea, which your mother doesn't like, and you've got some more work to do afterwards. There's a gap in the hedge a little way along here,' he added more hopefully. 'I suppose you couldn't jump the ditch? It would save us a good two miles, and it's really nothing of a jump.'

'Of course we can jump the ditch. Hurray! what fun!' cried Arthur, and without more words he wheeled his pony, put him at the gap, and the next moment was careering about on the turf beyond, in a great state of excitement and jubilation.

'You see, it's quite easy,' the tutor said, turning to Sainty, whose pony was already beginning to fidget, excited by the trampling about on snapping twigs and the rush past of the other. Sainty was very white.

'You know I can't jump, Mr. Kirkpatrick,' he said, gulping tears. 'I'm sure to fall off if I try; I always do.'

'Not you,' the young man replied encouragingly. 'You see your little brother has done it. I should be ashamed to have him ride so much better than me, if I were you.' The poor man was rather in a fix, with one pupil already across the obstacle and the other resolutely declining to follow.

'See,' he said, 'I'll give you a lead. It's as easy as easy; you've only to sit well back, and give him his head.' And so saying, he put his horse at the gap, and followed Arthur into the park. 'Come on,' he called.

'Jump, Sainty, jump,' piped Arthur. 'I wouldn't be such a funk.'

Whether Sainty would ever have found the courage to attempt the jump is doubtful, if the pony at this stage of the proceedings had not decided matters by bolting at the gap. But bothered and bewildered by the tugging of his rider's despairing hands, he swerved just at the jump, and, slipping on the trodden earth where Kirkpatrick's horse had taken off, he came to the ground; then, struggling to his feet, galloped off through the wood by the road they had come.

The young man was horror-stricken when he saw the accident; he was off his horse and by the side of the fallen boy in a second. Sainty was unconscious, that was all he could tell.

'Now, Arthur,' he cried to the younger boy, who was beginning to tremble and cry, 'this is the moment to show the stuff you're made of. I must stay here with Sainty, but you must get home across the park as hard as you can go, so as to tell your mother what's happened, and save her the shock of seeing Donald come home without his rider. And then send people here to carry Sainty in; he may be more hurt than we think.'

Arthur waited for no more, but galloped off in the direction of the house, glad to have something definite to do, instead of staring at poor Sainty.

Lady Charmington had come home sooner than she expected, and was taking off her hat when she saw Arthur come galloping across the park alone. She looked with pride at the boy, thinking how well he sat his pony; and she gave a little sigh at the half-formed thought that just crossed her mind, 'What a pity he wasn't the elder!' The next minute her heart stood still; she had caught sight in the far distance of a speck, which as it drew nearer she recognised with sickening terror as Sainty's pony, riderless, and with his saddle turned under his belly. 'Not *that* way, my God! I did not mean *that*.' Was it possible that God was punishing her for her rebellious thought? could He have thought that she desired the death of her first-born? And she prayed with all the intensity of her soul that whatever had happened her boy might not die. 'Maimed, crippled, or an idiot, if so it must be; only let him live.' This was the cry of her heart, again and again repeated, as, guided by the child, she stumbled across the park with the men who were to bring him home. Arthur could tell her little, except that Sainty had had a fall and was hurt. Perhaps even then her child was lying dead, while she was wishing in her sinful heart that his brother had his heritage.

But Sainty was not dead, and did not die. The pony had kicked him in its struggles to rise, and he had fainted.

There were long nights and days of pain to be borne, and he bore it as nervous people often do, who can stand anything but anticipation.

At first he made sure that the death he had asked for had come to him, and even, one day, when he was a little better, attempted to bring off one of the beautiful scenes with Arthur which he had so often rehearsed. But somehow it was not a great success. Arthur did not do his part at all nicely. He only said, 'Oh! bovver, dear old Sainty. You ain't going to die; what's 've good of jawing?' and went off to more congenial pursuits.

Though his life was not in danger, Sainty's injury was a grave one; the hip was broken, and the great London surgeon who was called down did not conceal from Lady Charmington that the boy would probably always be more or less lame.

On one of his visits, Sainty astonished the great man not a little.

'Sir John,' he said, 'I want you to tell me something. Shall I ever be able to walk and run again?'

The famous surgeon had boys of his own, and his heart smote him at the pathetic question. 'Yes, my boy, yes,' he said; 'certainly to walk. As to running, oh! well, you won't be very good at running, not for some time; we mustn't go too fast, not too fast, you know. Walking comes first; we must get you on your legs first.'

'But I shan't ever be able to play games, shall I? not like other boys, I mean.'

'Oh! well, never 's a long word. I can't say, I'm sure. Not for a long while, I fear. But we never know, we never know——'

'Well, at any rate, I shan't be able to ride, shall I?' persisted the patient.

Poor Sir John hated to extinguish hope; but thus pushed into a corner, he admitted, 'Oh! well, ride, you know—I don't know. I doubt if *riding* would be advisable. My poor little man, if you must know, I'm afraid you mustn't count on riding again.'

To his surprise, the boy heaved a sigh of unmistakable relief. 'Ah! well, that 's a comfort, anyhow,' he said.

CHAPTER III

PROBABLY nothing is less calculated to make a man feel at home in another's society than the knowledge that he owes him a debt which he cannot pay. Custom enables a number of people to support this awkwardness with tolerable equanimity, but I suspect that even the habitual debtor feels a certain nameless uneasiness under his equable shirtfront; while to a person whose boast has always been that directness of gaze celebrated in the Village Blacksmith, to have to look shiftily before the eye of a creditor must be peculiarly galling.

Something of this consciousness had become the daily burthen of poor Lady Charmington with regard to her first-born son. Certainly nothing was further from claiming damages than Sainty's attitude, for it never entered his head to hold his mother in any way responsible for his accident. But in the long weeks in which he lay so uncomplainingly bearing pain, and the inaction which to young creatures is worse than pain, she could not look at him without a very distinct twinge of remorse. She was even glad to see the once forbidden needlework cheating the weary hours of some of their dulness. Once when he thanked her for the withdrawal of the interdict on this pastime, her breath caught in her throat like a sob.

'You must find the time very heavy,' she said, smoothing back the boy's hair with an unusually tender touch.

'Oh no!' Sainty said, 'I don't. I can't help thinking what a good thing it was it happened to me and not to Arthur. Think how *he* would have hated it. I've never minded keeping quiet. And then it'll always be such a good excuse for not doing things. Before, when people said "Why can't he be like other boys?" there wasn't anything to say. Now you can say "Well, you see, poor boy, he's lame; he met with an accident." '

He delivered this piece of consolation quite seriously, and with no ironic intention, but it may be doubted if it cheered his mother as much as he intended.

Poor Kirkpatrick, overwhelmed with remorse, had wished to give up his public school mastership and devote himself to Sainty's education, but the sacrifice had not been accepted. Lady Charmington, who, in spite of her hard head, was not without some very feminine weaknesses, could not bear the sight of the young man who was incurably associated with the most awful hour of her life.

In her compunction, she made an attempt at regaining the services of Miss Meakins, but the governess had without difficulty obtained a situation in the household of one of those gorgeously dressed little dark women who drive about the north side of Hyde Park in such well-appointed carriages. They are of Lancaster Gate to-day, but who knows if to-morrow they may not be giving laws to fashion from a palace in Park Lane? Miss Meakins, with the stamp of the aristocracy upon her, was quite an important person in this opulent Tyburnian mansion and the beautiful villa at Roehampton, with its velvet lawns and blazing parterres.

'Tell us about the little marquis and his brother, and the big park at Belchamber, and the deer,' her little charges would ask of her, as they walked on Wimbledon Common. They had large eyes, and beautiful gentle manners, and that look of ineffable world-weariness that is common to the children of their race. Sainty would have been astonished to know what an object of interest he was to these other children.

It must have been her uneasy desire for compensation that made Lady Charmington give to a suggestion of her sister-in-law that she and her 'fatherless boy' should pay Belchamber a visit, a very different reception from that which she would otherwise have accorded to it. Lady Eva had lost the embarrassing Morland, and was inclined to return to her native land and see what she could get out of her kinsfolk. She went first to her mother, who received her very graciously, and was really pleased to see her. Her daughter brought the duchess a whiff of her beloved Paris, and entertained her immensely with anecdotes of a world quite unlike that in which she herself had formerly figured. The younger lady, finding her noble relatives in the Faubourg rather inclined to cold-shoulder her, had gone in for being a sort of Muse, and surrounded herself with all the youngest and most modern of the new school of poets and painters. She wore indecent clothes, with a rope of turquoises round her waist, and lay on a white bearskin, smoking a narghilé, while they recited their verses to her. They spoke of her as 'la petite Morland' and 'la belle Ève.' Her portrait by a young American of genius had been the great *clou* of the salon, she told her astonished step-father. 'It really was *épatant*; he painted me at full length on the sofa in straight perspective, my feet away from you, and my head hanging over the end, so that my face looks out at you upside down. I have my turquoises in my teeth, and the whole is lit by Chinese lanterns. It is amazing *de vérité*, and will make his reputation.'

'And what about yours?' asked the duke, who thought he was rather a wit.

The duchess was much amused with this talk, and all went well until she and her daughter happened unfortunately to fix their affections on the same young man, who was a good deal the junior of either, when a violent quarrel ensued, and Sunborough House having become much too hot to hold her, Lady Eva was seized with a sentimental desire to 'show the home of her childhood to her boy,' and wrote intimating this wish to her sister-in-law. Lady Charmington knew very little of the lady, beyond the fact that she had made an unfortunate marriage and was now a widow with an only son. The early surroundings of this boy must have been deplorable; but while she trembled for the effect he might have upon her sons, she licked her lips at the thought of the influence she might be privileged to acquire over him. Lady Eva's cleverly insinuated hint that she did not find the atmosphere of her mother's house congenial, did much to open the doors of Belchamber to her; but perhaps her best ally was the thought that his cousin might be a companion to Sainty during Arthur's absence. Sainty at least was not likely to get any harm from unfortunate lads who had been brought up in an atmosphere of papistry or atheism—the two words meant much the same to Lady Charmington—and then who could tell what they might be able to do for *him*!

Claude Morland was between two and three years older than Sainty and extraordinarily grown up for his age. He was a handsome boy, but of quite a different type of beauty from Arthur, who had the fair curls and florid complexion of the Chambers family, whereas Claude had inherited his colourless white skin, thick, straight black hair, and large, dreamy eyes from his French ancestors. He was not unlike what his grandmother had been as a girl, but with a certain heaviness of make and feature that came from his lamented father, and might easily become coarseness as he grew older. He seemed to Sainty like some strongly scented hothouse flower, white with a whiteness in which there was no purity, and sweet with a strong sweetness that already suggested some subtle hint of decay. As the flowers which his cousin recalled to him were among the things he did not like, his first feeling towards him had been one of vague repulsion; but to a naturally shy and silent person, any one with Claude's ready flow of talk and perfect self-possession must prove attractive in the long-run. Then Claude had charming manners when he chose. To Sainty, accustomed to Arthur's scornful affection and undisguised contempt, the little attentions and deferential politeness of this older boy were bewildering, but strangely pleasant. Claude's smile was a caress, the grasp of his hand an embrace; in later years a lady once said of him that she always felt as if he had said something she ought to resent when he asked her how she did. But at thirteen this latent sensuality only made him like some charming feline creature that liked to be stroked and well fed, to lie in the sun and purr. A boy who spoke French as easily as English, and German and Italian a little, and read mysterious foreign books for pleasure, could not fail to be impressive to a small, home-grown cousin; while the discovery that this gifted creature had never played cricket in his life, and, though an excellent rider, had not the smallest wish to hunt, made him at once sympathetic and puzzling.

'Uncle Cor hunts,' Sainty said, 'and Arthur is dying to, as soon as ever he is allowed. *I* can't, of course; but then I shall never ride any more. But all the men I know hunt—our neighbours, Mr. Hawley at Hawley Park and Sir Watkin Potkin at the Grange, and everybody, even the farmers, when they can afford to. I thought all men who rode wanted to hunt as a matter of course.'

'Well, *I* don't want to,' Claude answered. 'I like riding, and the *manège*, and all that; a gentleman should of course be a good horseman. But to get up early, and gallop all day across country after a wretched little vermin, *merci, cela ne me dit rien.*'

'Ah! you're sorry for the poor fox; I'm glad of that,' said Sainty. 'I can't help feeling it's cruel. I think of all it must feel when it hears the dogs getting nearer and knows it is out of breath and can't run much farther. And yet very good men hunt, even clergymen. None of our own clergy, because mother doesn't approve of it; but some of those from the other side of the county, who, I believe, are quite good men. I asked Uncle Cor, who is very kind to animals, about it, but he said if it were not for hunting, the foxes would all have been exterminated long ago, and he didn't suppose they'd have liked that any better.'

'There is certainly something in that,' replied his cousin gravely; 'but I'm afraid I wasn't considering the matter from the fox's point of view. I hate getting tired, and wet, and muddy, and to kill a wretched little yellow animal doesn't seem worth so much fuss and trouble. *Voilà tout.* In France, if the foxes eat the poultry, they shoot them; it is much more simple.'

'Then what do you like to do in the way of exercise and games and that?' asked Sainty.

'I like the lawn tennis fairly well,' said Claude. 'It is not such a good game as the real tennis, the *jeu de paume.* I have played that a little, but not much; it was too expensive; but lawn tennis is very well. That, and riding, and fencing have been my principal amusements. But we have moved about so much; my mother is very restless. We have never stayed anywhere long enough for me to settle down and really take to anything seriously.'

'And cricket?' asked Sainty, almost under his breath; 'have you never played cricket?'

'*Mon Dieu!* no. A game that takes three days to play! Those stupid stepsons of grandmamma took me to see a match at—what do you call it?—"Lords," when I was in London. It went on all day, and nothing happened. I yawned myself hoarse. I can never do anything for more than two hours at a time.'

Here was some one who was not apologetic or ashamed that he could not play cricket, who spoke of it even with contempt, as of a pastime for fools. Sainty was dumbfounded. He wondered what Arthur would say to such heresy. What Arthur did say when presently he came home, was that his cousin was a 'bounder,' and 'like a beastly foreigner.' It was a curious fact that though Claude acquired a considerable influence for harm over Arthur, the latter always continued to speak slightingly of him, and never really liked him; whereas Sainty, who was not influenced by him in the least, and after the first discoveries of superficial agreement found that they differed essentially in their views on almost every subject, cherished a sneaking regard for his cousin, which died hard even when Claude had done his best to kill it. Arthur's mind could accept nothing that was not traditional; and this surprising outcome of shady foreign watering-places and Parisian *ateliers* lay altogether outside of his traditions.

Their aunt was as much of a surprise to the boys as their cousin. Lady Eva modified herself considerably, with a view to conciliating her pious sister-in-law; but in spite of extra tuckers, the first sight of her when dressed for dinner was a severe shock to Sainty, accustomed to the modest *décolletages* of the neighbouring clergywomen who dined from time to time with Lady Charmington, and the little square of his mother's neck, which barely accommodated the large oblong locket of black enamel, like a baby's coffin, with which she decorated herself for these festive occasions.

Luckily for Lady Eva, Lady Charmington was not of the intimate order of women, and never invaded a guest's bedroom, or she might have been a little scandalised by the tone of some of the literature she found there; but she would probably have been still more bewildered, as she had kept up scarcely a bowing acquaintance with even ordinary French. 'I have read Madame Craven's *Récit d'une sœur*,' she said, 'but I read few novels in any language; it does not seem to me very profitable. I was once recommended Feuillet's *Histoire de Sibylle* as quite unobjectionable, but I found it very papistical. It did *me* no harm, but I shouldn't have given it to any young person to read in whom I was interested.'

'I don't remember to have read either of the *romans* you mention,' said her sister-in-law wearily.

The two women found it increasingly difficult to talk to each other; neither of them seemed to take the faintest interest in anything which occupied the other. Lady Eva dwelt much on the disadvantages of her bringing-up, finding that a subject on which her hostess was much inclined to be sympathetic, and also on her maternal anxieties about her boy's future. She and Claude laughed a great deal at the good lady behind her back, and smoked a great many cigarettes together in the long shrubbery, when Sainty was having his daily drive, and Lady Charmington was busy about her farms. Arthur caught them at it one day, but was bribed to silence by being lured into participation in the crime.

'Tell me, Eva,' said Lady Charmington, when the ladies were sitting alone together, 'you are not, I trust, a Catholic, are you?'

'No; oh no!' answered her sister-in-law, with perfect truth; though she might have added that she had at one time been a very devout one, and had since tried several other *cultes*, of which the last had been some queer Parisian form of esoteric Buddhism. 'Oh no! I have seen too much of Romanism; I have lived abroad too much.'

Lady Charmington was delighted. 'I have no doubt they tried to pervert you,' she said, fairly beaming on this martyr to the faith.

'Tried!' repeated Lady Eva, with an eloquent gesture.

'And your boy?' continued Lady Charmington. 'He must have been much exposed in those countries. I trust you have managed to keep his faith untouched?'

'I have done my best,' said Lady Eva meekly. 'Poor boy! he has had to knock about the world very young, and to see and hear much that he should not. I have felt that he had only his poor weak mother to stand between him and—and—well—all sorts of things. He has not had the advantages of your dear boys, Sarah—a good home and peaceful, virtuous surroundings, nor such a good mother, I'm afraid.' And Lady Eva cast down her fine eyes, on the lids of which she had not been able to deny herself a faint tinge of blue, on learning that Lord Corstorphine was expected, though she had been trying not to paint at Belchamber. 'You know how my own youth was neglected,' she added presently. 'But I had rather not talk of that. After all, the duchess is my mother, and in her own way has meant to be kind to me, I think. Only, I have dreamt of something very different for my Claude. Such influences as he finds here are exactly what I have wished for him, and what I have all too seldom been able to give him.'

'Well, now we have got him here, we must try and keep him, and see what we can do for him,' said Lady Charmington, much gratified. 'Have you thought at all what you are going to do with him? You are not going back to France?'

'Oh no! I want to stay in England—*at home*'; and Lady Eva gazed tenderly at her surroundings in a manner which hinted plainly that an invitation to consider Belchamber in that light might not be unwelcome. Lady Charmington, however, was in no hurry to give it, but she debated in her own mind many plans for the benefit of her nephew. She got but little encouragement from her brother, who by no means seemed inclined to take a friendly view of these interlopers.

'That's a horrible woman,' he remarked, with brutal frankness, of the 'belle Morland,' 'and just the sort I should have thought you would have hated, Sarah.'

'I can't honestly say I exactly like her, Cor,' his sister answered, 'but I'm sorry for her and for the boy. Think of her deplorable bringing-up; think what a mother she has had, and what a husband! The poor body seems to have some glimmerings of a desire for better things, if she had any one to take her by the hand; and I must say it's to her credit to have kept by her faith, exposed as she has been to the darts of the enemy. But what touches me most about her is that she evidently wants to do well by her boy. She's not a bad mother, whatever else she may be; and, after all, she's poor Char's sister, you know.'

Lady Charmington very seldom delivered herself of so long a speech, and still more rarely made any allusion to her dead husband. Corstorphine was surprised and touched. Perhaps some likeness to her brother in Lady Eva, some trick of speech, or expression that recalled him, had gone to the not very accessible heart of her sister-in-law, and reinforced the adroit flattery which had been offered to her pet prejudices. Perhaps mother's heart really spoke to mother's heart in some language he did not understand; the woman, with all her faults, might have a genuine wish to do the best for her brat. He could have checked his sister's nascent inclination to befriend her husband's kinsfolk with a word, but it seemed an ungracious task. After all, Sarah was not too often in a melting mood, and if she could do something for this wretched lad, whose best chance was that he was fatherless, why should he seek to restrain her?

'I don't like the boy either,' he couldn't help saying; 'he's a deal too smooth and civil spoken. He's no business to have such finished manners at thirteen, and be such an accomplished little man of the world. But if you think you can do anything to prevent his turning out such a blackguard as his deceased parent, pray do; it's a Christian act. All I say is, consider whether he is likely to harm your own boys in any way.'

'I've thought very much of that. Do you suppose it wasn't my first thought?' his sister answered. 'But one mustn't let anxiety for one's own stand in the way of snatching a brand from the burning. Something tells me this boy has not been sent here for nothing.'

'Well,' said Corstorphine, 'and what particular form of charity do you think he was sent for?'

Lady Charmington ignored the scoff. 'I was thinking whether I mightn't offer to send him to Eton, if he could be got in,' she said; 'he won't be fourteen till November. I know his mother can't afford it. Then he is very gentle with Sainty, and the child seems to like him; and I thought if later on Sir John thought Sainty could go to Eton, it might be a help to him to have a cousin who had been there a year or two, and could look after him a little. He can never be quite like other boys, you know.'

Corstorphine smiled grimly. It tickled his not unkindly cynicism to find his pious sister had so human a thought for her own offspring nestled under her zeal for her nephew's soul.

'Well, I agree,' he said, 'that the best chance the youth can have is to see as little as possible of his mother and grandmother. Perhaps if he gets well kicked at Eton, and you have him here mostly for his holidays, he may not turn out so ill. It would take an 18-horse power profligate to corrupt Sainty, it is true; but how about Arthur?'

'Arthur doesn't like Claude; he makes no secret of it; so I don't think he can do *him* any harm. Besides, when the boys are at home I have them so constantly under my own eye, I should know in a minute; and by the time Arthur goes to Eton, Claude will be almost leaving.'

'Or if he turns out badly, he may even have left,' said Lord Corstorphine.

So the matter was broached to Lady Eva, who, you may be sure, was profuse in a mother's blessings and tears. She was fond of her son in a way, and honestly wanted the best that was to be had for him in life. She had been ruefully reflecting that she would never be able to send him to a good school, except at the cost of decided privations to herself; and there was no doubt he would be dreadfully in her way in London.

Lord Corstorphine proposed himself for a Sunday to a great friend among the Eton masters, and found that his host, having an unexpected vacancy for the next half, was delighted to do a good turn to any one in whom he was interested. The duchess, when she heard what was on foot, suddenly insisted on helping, and promised to pay half of her grandson's expenses; and though her contribution was frequently several terms in arrear, she generally paid up in the end, unless she had been unusually unlucky at cards.

So, though Lady Eva had failed to extract from her sister-in-law that general invitation to regard Belchamber as her country-home which she had hoped for, she left for town with a comfortable feeling that her visit had not been wasted. Claude was practically off her hands; he would go to Eton at no expense to her, and spend most of his holidays at Belchamber. 'Dear Belchamber, where poor Char and I spent our happy childhood, and of which I have always carried the picture in my heart, through all my wanderings,' she said to Lady Charmington the day before her departure.

'Indeed,' said Sarah, with a little dry cough, 'I always understood from poor Char that he had hardly ever been here as a child. He said, when we first came here in the old lord's time, that he hoped his son wouldn't feel such a stranger here as he did, when he grew up.'

'Ah well,' said Lady Eva hurriedly, 'my happiest times, almost the *only* happy ones of my neglected childhood, were here, so I suppose they bulk large in my memory. I have so little reason to remember most of my youth with pleasure.'

'You said, Aunt Eva,' Arthur burst in, 'vat you wemembered every corner of ve place, blindfold, but you soon lost your way even in ve shrubbery, and you thought One-tree Wood was the other side of the village.'

'Ah, traitor!' cried his aunt, playfully embracing him, 'have you so little gallantry as to try to convict a lady of making mistakes?'

'You were a little rash, dear mamma,' Claude said to her afterwards, 'in remembering your happy childhood at Belchamber so well, unless you took a little more trouble to get up the subject.' Claude, for his part, was quite willing

to go to Eton and try how he liked it. Almost the only principle that had been early instilled into him was that it
was always worth while to accept anything expensive
that could be enjoyed at another person's expense. It was
rather absurd, no doubt, for so finished a gentleman to
go to school; but experience had taught him that it was
always quite easy to get sent away from educational establishments, if one did not happen to like them; and what
was the use of his precocious knowledge of the world if it
did not insure him an easy victory over such simple people
as schoolmasters and schoolboys? As a matter of fact, his
astuteness did save him from paying the extreme penalty
for many peccadilloes that would have cut short the career
of less sophisticated youths under 'Henry's holy shade.'
His tutor's attitude towards him was a curious alternation
of attraction and distrust. But though never cordially
liked by either boys or masters, he was still there, as an
overgrown youth in 'lower division,' when Sainty hobbled into the school, a pale, gloomy little boy with an iron
boot and a stick, and was even keeping a precarious footing when Arthur appeared a year later, and, of course,
took the place by storm with his frank and friendly manners, hatred of books, love of games, and perfectly obvious
and understandable type of beauty.

Whether Claude really did much for his cousins on their
arrival at Eton may be doubted, but he certainly managed
to impress Sainty with the belief that he had been of
incalculable service to him. To Claude, Sainty meant
Belchamber with all its comforts, horses to ride, pheasants
to shoot, good food, luxurious quarters, and presents at
Christmas; things his shelterless childhood had taught
him to consider in a way that boys to whom they had
always been matters of course could not understand. It
never occurred to Sainty that his cousin's attentions proceeded from anything but a naturally kind heart com-
passionating the limitations of a cripple and an invalid.
He soon learned to disapprove of Claude, and to dread
his influence over Arthur, and on several occasions
screwed himself up almost with torture to the point of
speaking very plainly to his senior, a thing especially diffi-

cult among boys; and the indulgent good nature with
which his strictures were received, where they might
easily have been resented, gave him an uncomfortable
sense of obligation towards one to whom his conscience
forced him to say such disagreeable things in return for
uniform kindness and affection.

'Dear Sainty,' Claude would say, 'you do look so sweet
when you're angry and solemn, for all the world like an
old hen with all her feathers up in defence of her chick.
Of course I'm a wicked, unprincipled hawk, but I promise
not to devour your bantling.' He generally managed to
refer again to these conversations when Arthur was present, knowing that nothing enraged the younger brother
so much as the idea that Sainty, for whom he always
entertained the sublimest contempt, had dared to give
himself the airs of looking after him.

It early dawned on Sainty that a loving heart was not
an unmixed blessing, unless one had the gift of imposing
one's views on the object of one's affection. Had he not
been fond of Claude, it would be nothing to him that he
disapproved of him; if he did not love Arthur, it would
not have been a daily grief to him to see so clearly what
his brother ought and ought not to do, while he was desti-
tute of the smallest shred of influence over his actions.

'You know, dear,' Claude said to him once, 'there is
nothing so easy as to get rid of me. I am horribly *mal vu*
by the authorities. If tutor hadn't stuck up for me like a
brick, I should have been sacked long ago; he has told
me pretty plainly that if there are any more rows he shall
say he thinks they had better take me away. A hint to
him that I am corrupting his pet lamb, and a word to
your mother, and neither Eton nor Belchamber will be
troubled with me much longer.'

Such a speech hurt Sainty like a lash. 'Don't you see,'
he cried, 'that it is just the knowledge of what you say
that makes it impossible for me to do anything? I am
helpless.'

See? Of course Claude saw; no one better. 'Dear,
generous old boy!' he said, with one of his sudden pretty
changes of manner, throwing an arm lightly round his

cousin's shoulder; 'who should know what an angel you are, so well as your poor scamp of a cousin, who owes everything to you?'

'Don't,' Sainty said, wincing; 'you do things you know I hate, and teach Arthur to do them, and then you manage to make me feel a brute, and put me in the wrong.'

Claude shrugged his shoulders, almost the last of his little foreign tricks of manner that he had not lost at Eton. 'You are impossible, dear Saint,' he said, and went his way, quite secure that what he had let fall of the ease with which his cousin could get rid of him would effectually tie his hands.

The day came, however, when without any intervention of a schoolfellow, the measure of Claude Morland's ill-fame overflowed, and the College of the Blessed Mary numbered him no longer among her children.

That summer half was 'long remembered' at Eton (almost eighteen months) for what Claude called a 'great massacre of the innocents.' We are not concerned at this distance of time to inquire into the nature of this old story. As usual, it was not the most guilty who were sent away; there were angry mothers in many counties of England who declared their darlings had been most unjustly used, and that 'there was a boy called Morland who was much worse than poor Tom, Dick, or Harry, who had only had to leave at the end of the half, and with no blame attached to him.' 'Claude was more or less mixed up in rather a painful affair,' his tutor wrote to Lord Corstorphine. 'He did not know how much he was to blame, but it would be best for the boy himself if his friends were to remove him. Personally he liked him, but . . . '; and Sainty tried hard not to feel a certain relief at his cousin's departure. He atoned for this unchristian want of sympathy by making the best of the matter to his mother and guardian, and begging that it should make no difference in the culprit's footing at Belchamber. What he never mentioned at home was that Arthur had come very near being implicated, and that he, Sainty, had strained his conscience to the utmost in solemnly pledging his word to his tutor for his brother's innocence. Arthur accepted this as he did everything else from Sainty. 'What is vere to make a fuss about?' he said. 'I'd have done as much for you, or for vat matter, for any over chap who wasn't my bwover. You jaw about your conscience, and not being sure, and tell me to see what I've made you do. I don't call that lying. Of course, if a fellow's asked point-blank if anover fellow's done a fing, he's *got* to say he hasn't. Don't be such a pwig.'

Sainty did not stay very long at Eton himself. In spite of constant staying out, and much sick-leave, he really was not strong enough for the life there; nor was it a great grief to him to go. He did not make friends easily; his shy, reserved manner, his studious habits, and inability for athletics, not less than his austerely high standard of ethics which his minor found so unnecessary, were not calculated to make him popular with his schoolfellows; and he resented their familiar abbreviation of his title into 'Belcher.' He stayed long enough to see Arthur launched on a course of prosperity, and in a fair way to become a 'swell,' and then sang his *Nunc dimittis*. Arthur remained, alone of the three, and flourished like a green bay-tree. He did just enough work to get through his various examinations with a little cribbing, and found plenty of people ready to do all the rest for him. He was quite selfish, self-indulgent, easy-going, good-natured, and happy, and was as popular with the masters as with the boys. The elastic code of schoolboy honour fitted him like a glove, and he had the makings in him of a first-rate cricketer.

CHAPTER IV

LORD CORSTORPHINE had been an Oxford man, but some curious lingering dread of Puseyism made Lady Charmington send Sainty to Cambridge. She gave a moment's anxious thought to the vicinity of Newmarket, but, as she truly said, that hardly seemed a danger to Sainty; and as Arthur was to read for the army when he left Eton, there was no question of the University for him.

Sainty went to college, as he did most things, from the habit of obedience, but with no great hope of personal enjoyment. Anticipation to him was rarely pleasurable; he had not the sanguine temperament. He looked on Cambridge as a larger Eton, a new field for unpopularity and isolation in the midst of a crowd, but he soon began to be aware of an atmosphere of wider toleration than he had known at school.

It is true he was a dreary failure among his peers, the gilded youth who went to Newmarket, kept hunters, and spent their evenings at the card-table; and he was ignominiously blackballed for a certain fashionable dining-club for which someone was so ill-advised as to put him up. His college, however, was large enough to contain men of all sorts, and among some of the more thoughtful he found congenial society and kindly appreciation, especially in the little knot of undergraduates who gathered round a young don called Gerald Newby.

Sainty was just ripe for some one to worship, and Newby supplied the object beautifully. In all his reserved, unhappy boyhood, he had never known the joy of that falling in friendship, so to speak, which is one of youth's happiest prerogatives. The only two companions for whom he had felt much affection, his cousin and his brother, had certainly given him more pain than pleasure. The generous delights of an enthusiastic admiration had hitherto been withheld from him. This young man, sufficiently his senior to speak to his troubled soul with a certain authority, yet near enough to his own age for discussion on equal terms, excited such a feeling in the highest degree.

It is difficult for older people not to smile at very young men's estimates of themselves or of one another. Newby had opinions, splendid opinions, on all sorts of subjects, which his disciple imbibed with rapture. Sainty took his young mentor quite seriously, and Gerald, it need hardly be said, took himself quite seriously; and between them they were sublimely earnest and high-toned, and perhaps, if the truth must be told, just a trifle priggish.

For one thing, of course, Sainty had 'doubts.' It is not

to be supposed that a youth with a morbid conscience, a tender heart, a keen mind, and delicate health, reared in Lady Charmington's school of extreme Calvinistic theology, should have reached the age of eighteen without many searchings of heart.

Little as this profane page may seem the place for the discussion of such subjects, it would be impossible to give an adequate notion of Sainty's life at Cambridge, or his relations with Gerald Newby, without a passing reference to the topics that kept them from their beds far into the small hours of many a chilly morning.

Young men of Gerald Newby's stamp can conceive of nothing that is not the better for being 'threshed out,' as he would have called it. He held that if the old creeds were 'outworn,' it was no reason for abandoning faith— that there was to be evolution in belief as in other things; and he had dreams of an universal Church freed from strangling dogmas, in which all sincere seekers after truth should meet in a common brotherhood. Perhaps he was a little vague as to what was to be left as the object of belief when everything had been eliminated in which the controversially inclined could find matter for discussion, but that did not trouble him in the least.

'What we want,' he said to Sainty, 'is more light. All churches in all ages have been alike in the mistake of endeavouring to stifle discussion of their doctrines. Discussion is the breath of life; unquestioning acceptance is death.'

'But once one begins questioning things, one is so apt to find one doesn't believe them——'

'Then let them go. Depend upon it, what won't bear the investigation of reason cannot be worth keeping. The truth, and the truth only, must emerge clearer and purer from every test to which it is submitted; and it is the truth we want. Why, when in all other departments of knowledge our understanding becomes truer and stronger every year, should we seek to stultify ourselves and shrink from all growth in the highest science of all, that which deals with the fount of all knowledge, and the spring of all conduct?'

'But suppose,' Sainty asked, 'one should find in the end that one believes nothing?'

'Then believe nothing,' said Newby grandly. 'But I won't, I can't, suppose any such thing; it is belief that comes of inquiry, not the negation of belief.'

Sainty was very much impressed. He had never before had any one to whom he could unburthen himself on these subjects. His mother, he knew well, would have revolted in horror from any questioning of the doctrines she herself accepted, and his uncle would not have approached the discussion in that serious spirit which alone he thought befitting. But the lads who assembled evening after evening in Newby's rooms had no angelic fear of treading on anything, and talked everlastingly on all subjects, religious doubt or belief among the rest. If they found the world out of joint they by no means shared Hamlet's distress at being 'born to set it right,' or doubted for a moment their perfect ability to do so. These boys who so confidently settled the affairs of the nation, the world, the universe, are getting middle-aged men now, hard-working public officials, clergymen, schoolmasters, and would probably smile at their own youthful enthusiasms. Many of them are married and fathers of families. Newby himself is senior dean of the college, and a very different person from the ardent apostle of universal belief and brotherhood to whom Sainty brought so many of his perplexities.

Belchamber spent an immense amount of time in the young don's comfortable rooms. A kind of sensual austerity marked the place, something cloistral and monastic, yet with a touch of art and luxury. Pale autumnal sunlight, or the soft glow of shaded lamps, lingered lovingly on the backs of well-bound books, some large framed photographs of early Italian Madonnas, and a reproduction of a Neapolitan bronze. A great many teacups reflected the fire, while a permanent faint smell of tobacco just gave a masculine character to the mellow warmth of the atmosphere. Several armchairs and a huge sofa seemed always trying, by the sad colour and severe pattern of their coverings, to conceal the fact of their depth and softness, just as their owner, who had a handsome refined face and a well-knit frame, affected a slouch and wore shabby clothes to show he was not vain.

If Sainty poured himself out to Gerald when they were alone, he took but little share in the general discussions when other people were present. To express himself was always a difficulty to him; he lay, as it were, on the margin of the pool of talk, into which one eager speaker after another dashed past him while he was still trying to summon courage for the plunge. It would sometimes happen that at the end of a long evening he had not opened his mouth, and he was taken to task more than once on the subject by his friend. 'You really should try and talk more; men take your silence for ungraciousness. It looks as if you didn't think them even worth disagreeing with, you know. Locke asked me to-day if you weren't very proud; he said you sat all the time he was talking about the essential Christianity of Shelley's point of view, the other night, with a little supercilious expression which said plainer than words that you thought him a fool.'

'Oh dear! and I was so much interested,' Sainty cried. 'I had nothing particular to say about it; to tell the truth, I had never thought of Shelley exactly from that point of view, but I liked it all so much.'

'Well, you should have told him so; you see, you didn't convey that impression to Locke.'

Gerald was by no means always tender with his proselyte. He had great belief in his own powers of sympathy —('I understand,' he used to say in a meaning way to those who laid bare their difficulties to him)—but he was quite capable of 'smiting friendly and reproving' when the occasion seemed to demand it. 'I shouldn't be your friend if I didn't say . . .' was a favourite formula with him, and he constantly invited an equal frankness in others, though it is doubtful how he would have liked the invitation to be accepted.

'I have been thinking a good deal,' he said, pausing in the act of making tea, and turning to Sainty with the kettle in one hand, 'about what you said the other day of shunning uncongenial society. Of course there is a great deal of truth in it, and nothing obliges one to live habitually with people with whom one has nothing in common, but one has a duty to the outside world as well as to oneself.'

'I can no more be myself with certain people,' Sainty objected, 'than I can write my own handwriting on paper I don't like.'

'Of course we all feel that,' responded Gerald rather brutally, 'but there are two things to consider: in the first place, there's the danger to one's own character of getting narrow and cliquey; and in the second, unless you have something to do with men who are your inferiors in aim or culture, how are you to influence them for better things?'

'I don't say they are my inferiors,' said Sainty humbly; 'I only say they are so unlike me in their habits and point of view that I can't talk to them. They may be quite as good fellows as I am; probably they think themselves much better——'

'Yes, but *you* don't think so; you know you don't,' insisted his mentor sternly. 'Ah! you are looking at that Giotto; it's from the Arena Chapel at Padua; it's a jolly thing, isn't it? The meekness of the Virgin's expression is so wonderful. Those fellows lost so much of the religious feeling when they ceased to be archaic. Probably you don't cordially like or approve even of all the fellows you meet here. I don't altogether myself. But it is one of my principles to welcome all sorts of men. It is not only that I think they may get good from us, but they teach us too. We must try to be broad, to keep our sympathies open on all sides, to be in touch with every kind of person, if we hope to do any good.'

'You are like St. Paul,' said Sainty quite seriously; 'it is very wonderful of you. I wish I was more adaptable, but people shut me up so.'

Newby smilingly deprecated the likeness to St. Paul, but in his heart he thought it quite true. 'Take Parsons, for instance,' he said; 'do you suppose I am not often shocked by things he says? Yet I think he keeps us fresh, as it were; he is bracing, stimulating, useful, if only as keeping alive in us the wholesome reprobation of some of the views he thinks it necessary to advocate. And look at the matter from his point of view. It is far better he should come here, and find his own level, and meet with wholesome disagreement, than be driven into thinking himself a social pariah persecuted for his opinions, or surround himself with a little set of duller men, who would take what he says for gospel, and on whom his influence would be wholly bad.'

'I don't like Ned Parsons,' said Sainty simply. 'I know he's clever and amusing and all that, but I think he's rather a beast.'

They were interrupted by the arrival of several undergraduates, including the subject of their discussion, the pursuit of which had therefore to be postponed to a more fitting opportunity.

'Yes, Newby,' said Parsons, settling himself luxuriously in the deepest armchair, 'I will take a cup of tea, though I should prefer a whisky and soda. And what might we be going to improve ourselves with to-night? the religious opinions of Swinburne, or the relation of the Ego to the non-Ego?'

'You are incurably flippant, Ned,' said Gerald, with an indulgent smile.

'Here we all are, burning to be enlightened,' continued Parsons. 'Pray don't deny us the tonic of stimulating conversation.'

'I've been wondering,' innocently struck in a large rowing man, whom Ned described as having 'aspirations after higher things,' 'what it is that keeps us all together, when we've so little in common, and I've come to the conclusion it must be our sense of humour.'

'Quite right, Og; no doubt it is,' said Parsons approvingly. 'And you and Newby are specially rich in it; and so is Sainty over there in the corner, though he is funny by stealth and blushes to find it fame.'

The room was growing full of smoke and of the buzz of voices; Newby was holding forth to a small knot of admirers. 'The Radicalism of Mill,' he was saying, 'is as dead as the dodo; all the things that were vital to his generation have been attained——'

'How about female suffrage?' Parsons asked.

'But there is a newer Radicalism,' Gerald went on, without paying any attention, 'which is not incompatible with Imperialism in its best forms——'

'All Radicalism,' said the rowing man sententiously, with the air of making a valuable contribution to contemporary thought, 'tends to Socialism——'

'Well, yes, in a way you may say it does,' assented Newby politely; 'but that in my mind is not altogether an objection. The word Socialism used to be a bugbear to frighten children with; but there is a new Socialism as there is a new Radicalism. If you come to think of it, all interference by the State is a form of Socialism; it is the community at work for the good of the community, instead of the individual making weak and isolated effort for his own good——'

'Poor dear Mill!' interjected Ringwood, a young man who in these days would have been called 'æsthetic,' 'it is a pity he is so *vieux jeu*; he had such a nice, refined face, and learned Greek as a baby, and it was so nice and unconventional of him to want women in parliament. Perhaps in time parliament may come to be all women, and men be free to look after things that really matter.'

'Such as old china,' said Parsons.

'Women,' said the rowing man, 'should stick to woman's province; her home and children should be enough for any woman.'

'And suppose she hasn't got any?' asked Ned.

'But I see what Ringwood means,' said the rowing man. 'Of course politics are very important and all that; far be it from me to deny it. For my part I'm a Conservative, and I don't care who knows it. But the thing that really matters is no doubt the intellectual life.'

Even Newby smiled discreetly.

'No doubt, no doubt,' he said. 'There is a great deal in what you say; but it is essential that politics should not be left to inferior men, or what becomes of the nation? Look at America with her venal professional politicians, and see what it has brought her to. Depend upon it, it is the intellectual element in parliament that leavens the lump.'

Our thinkers must not shut themselves up from public life; we must go down into the arena and put the result of our thought into action, if we hope to do any good in our generation.'

This magnificent sentiment was applauded as it deserved to be, but Newby had not nearly had his innings. He had much more to say about the new Radicalism and the new Socialism, and he talked so beautifully of the wickedness of being a hermit that Sainty resolved to widen his horizon by asking Ned Parsons to lunch next day, and proceeded at once to 'put the result of his thought into action.'

It was not often that he indulged in the luxury of entertaining. He had none of that genial desire for presiding which to many a man makes the top of his own table such an exciting position; moreover, he had been trained in the practice of the most careful economy, and had been accustomed to hear his mother condemn unnecessary profusion as hardly less sinful than irreligion.

The question of his allowance had been carefully discussed between his guardians, and the sum eventually decided on, although it would have been treated as quite inadequate by most young men of his position, seemed to him so ridiculously large that he was always endeavouring to conceal the amount of it from his poorer companions. He did so entirely from a feeling of delicacy; but it need hardly be said that his motives were frequently misconstrued, and he was firmly believed by many to be of a penurious and miserly disposition. As a matter of fact, if little of it went in ostentatious hospitality, he spent still less upon himself. Arthur early discovered that his brother was 'a safer draw for cash than the mater,' and Claude, if he asked for help less often and with more circumlocution, also found Sainty a convenient banker. Lady Eva's son was studying with a well-known coach for diplomacy, and though he lived with his mamma, 'found life in London,' as he wrote to his cousin, 'horribly expensive.' 'I wear my gloves till people look sympathetic when they shake hands with me, thinking I am in mourning, and should as soon think of taking a hansom as a coach

and four. But cigarettes I must have; they are literally
the breath of my nostrils, and no matter how skilfully I
hide them, mamma will find them and smoke them when
I'm out. If it were not for Sunborough House, I believe
I should starve. How, when, and where my revered
parent feeds I am wholly unable to discover; but there is
never anything to eat at home. Luckily, I am in high
favour with grandmamma. I tell her she is the most
beautiful woman in London, and that if I wasn't her grandson I should be frantically in love with her, and she
swallows it all. We are the best of friends, but I don't get
much out of her, except food and an occasional back seat
in her opera-box; and of course I have to make her little
presents *de temps en temps*. I ask myself, my dear Saint,
how on earth all the young men I see about, smiling and
spruce, contrive to live in this wicked, costly place. They
can't *all* be millionaires.' This was the burthen of many
letters. Belchamber smiled indulgently; he couldn't help
being amused by them; they were certainly better reading
than the ill-spelt scrawls in which Arthur announced he
was 'infernal hard-up.' 'What with subscriptions, and one
thing and another, a fellow had such lots of expenses at
Eton, it was perfectly beastly, and the mater kept him so
precious tight, and always seemed to think because you
were at school you were a kid, and had no need of money.'
Unlike as were their styles, the upshot of all the letters was
the same: the youthful writer was in pressing need of funds,
and would 'dear old Sainty' kindly supply the deficiency?
And 'dear old Sainty' usually did.

It is no doubt a very bad thing to be in want of money,
but it is almost worse to be the quarry at which the impecunious let fly all their shafts; to know when you see a
beloved handwriting on an envelope that it is hunger and
not love that has set the pen travelling, and dictated the
letter that lies within. It is an experience that only comes
to most of us later in life; boys of Sainty's age are not often
called upon to taste that half humorous bitterness. This
was one of the few troubles about which Sainty did not
consult Gerald Newby. He knew instinctively that his
virtuous friend would have little sympathy with his sup-

plying the funds of luxury and extravagance. The double drain, of which neither the amount nor the recurrence could ever be accurately foretold, kept the boy perpetually anxious about money matters. Perhaps it really did tend to make him, as people thought, unduly careful in his daily expenditure; and, though he took infinite pains to conceal the fact, he liked to be able to help humbler unfortunates than his brother or cousin.

Another eccentricity which showed his unfitness for the state of life to which he had the misfortune to be born, was his exaggerated propensity for work; he had a real aptitude for scholarship, a love of erudition for its own sake. No pains seemed too great to him, no research too profound, for the illustration of a curious expression or the elucidation of an obscure passage. There was a danger that his health, never robust, might suffer from such close application. 'If you were a poor student,' Newby said to him, 'with your way to make in the world, having come up from Glasgow with a bag of oatmeal, I should think it most meritorious of you to peg away as you do, but for *you* to go injuring your health by overwork is worse than unnecessary—it's wrong.'

'My health does not seem to me such an unusually fine specimen that all risk of injury to it must be avoided at any cost,' Sainty answered. 'Besides, what am I to do, if I don't work? I know few people, and the men I do know are all busy. I can't play games or ride; when I am not working I loaf, and you are always inveighing against loafing as the root of all evil.'

'You should come out more, have more air,' persisted Gerald.

'In the summer I am out a good deal, as you know,' Sainty answered, 'but at this time of year I can't sit out, and I can only do a very moderate amount of walking without getting tired.'

'Why don't you start a cart and pony?' his friend asked.

Sainty looked scared. 'It costs such a lot to keep a cart and pony,' he said. 'I do hire one sometimes.'

'What nonsense!' Newby protested. 'In your position

it's absurd to talk as if you couldn't afford a trifling thing
like that. That's the sort of thing that makes fellows say
you are screwy——' He stopped rather abruptly, having
said more than he intended.

Sainty froze instantly. 'Oh! they say that, do they?' he
said, with an expression which would have recalled Lady
Charmington to Newby, had he enjoyed the privilege of
her acquaintance. 'Perhaps I am the best judge of what
I can afford.'

Like many people who are theoretically in favour of
independence, Gerald resented it in his disciples. 'For
all your false air of humility,' he said, 'one has only to
scratch you to find the aristocrat.'

It seemed to Sainty one more proof of the irony of fate
that even such qualities as his application to study and
careful ordering of life's economy, which would have been
held as highest virtues in many of his fellow-students, by a
curious process of inversion became almost faults in him,
faults too for which he must be rebuked by the mouth of
Gerald Newby, the great apostle of industry and frugality,
and the one person in the University whose praise would
have been sweet and valuable to him.

'The things you reproach me with are hardly aristocratic vices,' he said, with a sad little smile; 'but are you
quite consistent? You lecture Parsons on his laziness, and
Ringwood on his extravagance, and then you come and
try to drive me into being an idler and a spendthrift, who
have no gifts in those directions.'

'Of course, if you resent advice,' Newby said, 'I'm
sorry; I have no business to *lecture* you at all.'

'Ah Gerald!' said Sainty, stretching a protesting hand;
but Mentor was nettled and would not immediately be
mollified. It was on the tip of Sainty's tongue to explain
his need of economy, but the story of his mother's long
struggle to restore its solvency to their house seemed too
sacred and intimate to be told even to his dearest friend.
The unveiling of his own soul was only a personal im-
modesty, but his mother's thrift and Arthur's premature
dissipation could not be touched upon without a sense of
disloyalty to them from which he shrank.

'Let us go and get a trap and have a drive,' he said.

'Thanks; I'm busy; I'm afraid I haven't time,' Newby said stiffly. 'Did you think I was hinting that I wanted to be taken out driving?' and the offended sage strode across the court to his own rooms. Sainty heard the man in the rooms below him, to whom a scholarship was a dire necessity, being dragged forth to football by clamorous companions who would take no denial. 'Well, I won't go and drive in an east wind and get neuralgia all alone,' he concluded, as he turned again to his table piled up with learned commentaries.

CHAPTER V

IN spite of his untoward mania for study, or rather because of it, the years spent at Cambridge were the happiest of Sainty's life. He allowed himself to be dissuaded from going in for a scholarship, which he had much wished to do, on the ground that, as he would certainly have got it, it was grossly unfair to men to whom it was of real importance. Balked in this ambition, he concentrated his efforts on his degree, but here he encountered a new difficulty.

It happened that his second year at the University was also the twenty-first of his life, a coincidence which to most of his fellow-students would have been productive of no derangement; but it became apparent that in the very middle of the long vacation, just when he hoped to go up to Cambridge and do his most valuable and undisturbed work for the tripos, he had got to be present at a horrible function known as 'coming of age.'

Nothing like serious hospitality on a large scale had been attempted at Belchamber during the two-thirds of his life in which he had been the nominal head of his family, but Lady Charmington was conscientiously anxious that this event should lack no befitting pomp and ceremony. Unfortunately, fourteen years of ceaseless watchfulness and economy are not a good training for lavish display when the time demands it; so the poor lady found herself much exercised in mind over many details, and not a little perturbed at the thought of what it was all going to cost. By no means a diffuse or prolific correspondent at ordinary times, she began early in the May term to rain letters upon her son about the selection of the house party for the great occasion. 'Your Uncle Cor,' she would write one week, 'says that we must ask your grandmother and the duke. Of course I am only anxious to do what is right, and I suppose we must have them, though the duchess has never shown any particular interest in you or Arthur. Tell me what *you* think about it.' The next it would be, 'I am told there must be a ball, that there has always been a coming-of-age ball; the county will expect it. Such things are not much in my line, as you know, but I shouldn't like anything to be wanting that ought to be done, or that people expect.'

To Sainty the whole thing loomed an unmitigated horror. What pleasing anticipations, for instance, could the prospect of a ball awaken in a young man one of whose legs was shorter than the other, and to whom a highly polished floor was nothing but a danger? He came to dread these letters of his mother, each one of which contained some new detail of the approaching martyrdom; such alarming obligations as the necessity of a speech at the tenants' dinner sprang suddenly on him at the turn of a page, and left him gasping.

'You have rather a cold nature,' his mother wrote, 'not very imaginative, so I don't feel I need fear your being carried off your balance by all this fuss. If you were excitable and emotional like Arthur, I should feel more anxious. In your case the danger is more that you will take the whole thing as a matter of course, and not realise fully the importance of this epoch in your life, and all the new responsibilities it entails on you.' Characteristic passages like the above, scattered up and down the letters, seemed to give Sainty the measure of his exact knowledge of his mother, and cast a flickering light into the depths of her abysmal ignorance of him. The sense of a somewhat unfair advantage bred in him by these revelations of his superior insight brought into his love for her an element of almost pitying tenderness which alone was wanting to rivet the chains of his early acquired habit of obedience to her will.

'Are you afraid of your mother?' Gerald Newby asked him once, with some scorn, in reply to his repeated assertion of the impossibility of going counter to her wishes.

'I am very fond of her,' Sainty answered, with gentle dignity. He had an almost painful intuition of her sacrifices, her hopes, her frustrate ambitions for him, and of the disappointment he must inevitably be to her; he probably read into her not very complex emotions fine shades of sensibility from his own consciousness, after the manner of tender-hearted ladies with their dogs, which made his sympathy for her a little exaggerated. It was this habit of deference to her lightest wish that sent him forth sorely against his will to make a solemn call on a youth whom Lady Charmington had indicated for this attention. 'My friend Lady Eccleston has been staying here,' she wrote, 'with her daughter, and I have asked them to come in August for your coming of age. She tells me her son Thomas is at Cambridge. I didn't know he had left Harrow, but it seems he has been at the University two terms. She said it would be very kind of you to call on him, and I hope you will, as his mother is a friend of mine. If you find the young man agreeable, you might ask him to come with his mother and sister in the vacation. *A propos*, of course you will ask any of your own friends you would like; we shall want some young men; there will be Cissy Eccleston and the two de Lissac girls—only let me know in good time how many you ask.'

On his way to show a grudging civility to Tommy Eccleston, Belchamber revolved in his mind his mother's parting injunction to provide a band of youths for the feast. Luckily, here lay one ready indicated to his hand, but as he ran over the restricted roll-call of his intimates, they did not strike him as ornamental. Young Lord Springald and Sir Vaux Hunter and their friends would have been the very people for the occasion. They would have been voted 'nice, gentlemanly young fellows,' or 'fine, high-spirited lads,' according as they were shy and dull, or noisy and rowdy; but then, unfortunately, he did not know them. He could not ask men whom he had spent two years in avoiding, and who had blackballed him for their club, but his terrible habit of appreciating other people's points of view showed him how unsuitable his own friends would seem in the eyes of the duke and duchess. Gerald of course he wanted, and Gerald would be at home and imposing anywhere. His uncle Corstorphine at least, who had many friends among the intelligent obscure, could be trusted to appreciate Gerald; but he inwardly hoped that his friend might not select Lady Charmington as the recipient of his views on revealed religion. Apart from Newby, his progress towards the compilation of a list had been purely one of elimination up to the time of his arrival at Mr. Eccleston's lodgings. In response to his knock, the voice of some one who evidently spoke with a jersey over his head made muffled answer from an inner apartment.

'All right, damn you, wait a sec., there's no hurry. I'm changing,' and a moment after the owner of the rooms appeared, a pleasant, commonplace pink youth struggling into a college blazer, with one shoe on and the other dangling by its strings from his teeth.

'Hulloa! beg pardon,' he remarked; 'I thought you were Johnson, who was coming to go down to the river with me. I thought as he was so quiet he was probably smashing something,' and he held out a blistered palm of welcome.

'Oh! er—how d'ye do,' said Sainty, laying his own in it with no unnecessary cordiality. 'My name's Belchamber. My mother asked me to call on you; she knows your mother, don't you know. I should have come sooner, but I didn't know you were up.'

'Oh, it doesn't matter; awfully good of you,' answered Tommy. 'Sit down, won't you; have some lunch?' A piece of cold pressed beef and a boxed tongue, with a pot of marmalade, showed that the host had himself recently partaken of that meal.

'No thanks, I've had lunch,' said Sainty. 'But I oughtn't to keep you; you are just going out.'

'Oh no, not at all; there's no hurry; I haven't got to be at the river for half an hour. Besides, I'm waiting for Johnson; he said he'd come and go down with me.'

Then there was a moment of uneasy silence, broken with an effort by Sainty.

'Your mother and sister have been staying with my mother,' he remarked.

'No, really?' said Tommy, with the faintest possible show of interest. 'My mother stays about a lot; she's awfully popular.'

There was another pause, during which he finished putting on his shoes.

'I say, are you *sure* you won't have some lunch?' he cried suddenly, with quite a show of eagerness. 'Do. I'm afraid I haven't got any cake or anything, 'cos I'm in training. Have a whisky and soda, won't you?'

'No thanks, really not; I've just lunched. But I'm sure I'm keeping you in.'

'Oh, that's all right,' Tommy responded genially, and added, not very consistently, 'I can't think where that ass can be?'

The conversation seemed in danger of collapsing altogether, when the long-looked-for appearance of Johnson came as a welcome relief to both.

'Tommy, you brute, why ain't you ready?'

'Well, I like that, when I've been waiting half an hour for you.'

Sainty got up.

'Well, I mustn't keep you', he said.

'Beg pardon; didn't know you'd got any one here,' said Johnson.

'Oh! Lord Belchamber—Mr. Johnson,' said Eccleston, getting very red over the fearful embarrassment of an introduction. Then to Sainty, who remained standing, 'Must you go? Awfully good of you to come; wish you'd have had some lunch.'

'Good-bye,' Sainty said. 'I hope you'll come and see me—D, Old Court. Come to lunch or tea or something; or look me up in the evening if it suits you better.'

Sainty reported this conversation verbatim to Newby.

'You see,' he said, 'how hopeless it is for me to try and be gracious to people with whom I have nothing in common. If you could have seen how hard that poor boy struggled to look pleased to see me, and the grimness with which I sat and scowled upon him, you would have felt sorry for us both; you couldn't have helped it.'

'Of course, if your idea of being gracious is to sit and scowl at people——' Newby said.

'I didn't mean to; I wanted to wreathe my unfortunate features in smiles, but it was not a success. I am sure I feel as kindly towards my fellow-creatures as most people do; but I approach them with invincible terror; and there is no such sure way of making a dog bite you as to think he is going to.'

'Then don't think so,' Newby said. 'Have you *no* control over your apprehensions? Strengthen yourself in any way you like. If you can do it in no other way, say to yourself that you are a great personage and that most men will be only too glad of your attentions.'

'Oh! but *that* is a way that I should *not* like,' Sainty cried in horror; 'the one thing that finishes me completely is any idea that people may think *I* think they could want to know me for such a reason.'

' "The idea that people may think that you think," ' Gerald repeated. 'My dear Belchamber, this is very morbid. Do try and be simple.' Like all elaborately synthetical people, Newby was always preaching simplicity and a return to nature.

'And the sad part of this individual failure,' Sainty continued, 'is that I particularly wanted it to be a success. I had a purpose in calling.'

'And what dark designs had you on this innocent fresher?'

'My mother told me to ask him to the horrible business in August; his people are coming. By the way, she suggests that I should provide other victims, and I can't think of any one who would not be hopelessly inappropriate and bored to death. None of our friends *could* take the thing seriously, except, perhaps, Og.'

'Well, he's no use to you, as Providence having un-

kindly made him nearly your twin, he has got, in a small
way, the same business on at home, and *he* takes it seriously enough, I promise you. I happen to know, because
he has done me the honour to ask me to stay for it.'

Sainty gave the cry of a thing in pain. 'You haven't
accepted?'

'Well, I didn't commit myself; I'm really not quite sure
yet where I shall be this Long. I rather want to go abroad,
and perhaps do some climbing. Holmes and Collinson
want me to coach them part of the time, and I thought
we might combine the reading and the exercise, and drop
down to the Italian lakes in the autumn.'

'And I had so counted on your being there, Gerald,'
Sainty said. 'You are just the one person I did want. I
felt there would be something human about it all if I had
you with me.'

'You never said so, you know,' Newby interjected.

Sainty felt the hot, pricking sensation at the back of his
eyes which was the nearest he ever got to tears. He had so
intensely desired that Gerald should be at Belchamber in
August, that it had not occurred to him to put his desire
into words; they had talked the subject over so often that
he took it for granted his friend would know that he looked
for his help on the occasion.

'I thought—' he began, 'I hoped—I suppose you would
feel——' He couldn't express just what he meant at the
moment.

'You see, you didn't ask me,' Newby persisted, 'whereas
Og did.'

'Oh! go to Og, or Switzerland, or Hell, as far as I'm
concerned,' Sainty broke out.

Gerald laid a kind restraining hand upon his shoulder.
'My dear boy, you needn't lose your temper and swear
at me,' he said; 'I haven't said I wouldn't come. I only
said you hadn't asked me, and I couldn't be expected to
assume that I was invited to your coming of age, unless
you said something about it.'

Sainty was trembling all over; his little gust of passion
had passed and left him humbled and ashamed. How
could he have spoken so to his friend?

'Oh! forgive me,' he cried. 'I suppose I felt in my heart such a need of you that I couldn't but fancy you would know it.'

Newby coughed uneasily. 'For Heaven's sake, don't let us be sentimental,' he said, in his little, prim, dry manner.

'My mother says I am cold and unimaginative,' Sainty answered sadly, 'and you accuse me of hysteria. You can't both be right; but anyway, I suppose *I'm* wrong. After all, why should I assume that just because I wanted you I was certain to get you? I haven't so often got what I wanted in life. I should have remembered that though you are nearly everything to me, I am to you only one of a hundred men your kindness has helped.'

Gerald smiled. Like all Englishmen he had been frightened by the indecency of a glimpse of naked emotion, but he was always prepared to accept any amount of solid adulation soberly offered.

'You make too much of anything I may have been able to do for you,' he said graciously. 'And affection is a great gift; I'm sure I'm very proud that you like me and feel I have been of some use to you. I have no doubt I can manage to make it fit in.'

Sainty was profusely grateful; he really felt that Gerald had conferred a tremendous favour on him, which is probably what Newby meant he should feel.

His other invitations were less successful. Even Ringwood, whom at last he decided to ask, though he knew his mother and Arthur would say he was an affected ass, had pledged himself to the rival celebration.

Tommy Eccleston, to be sure, accepted. 'Oh, thanks!' he said, 'very good of you; I shall like it awfully.'

So Sainty wrote and announced this meagre harvest to Lady Charmington, who forthwith responded: 'Do you mean to say that out of all the young men you must know at Cambridge, you can only get two? Try and find two more, or we shall be more women than men. Johnny Trafford is coming, and I have asked Algy Montgomery, and of course there will be Claude, but none of the other Trafford boys can come, and I know so few young men. You see, we are such a lot of women. There is grand-

mamma (my mother, I mean), and your Aunt Susie, and
Lady Eccleston and her daughter, and Alice de Lissac
writes that her husband, she is sure, won't come, so there
are three more women. And now the duchess insists on
my asking Lady Deans, whom I don't know, and your
Aunt Eva wants to bring a friend of hers. I counted on
your having lots of friends you would want asked, or I
should not have agreed.'

At last, in despair, Sainty had recourse to Tommy
Eccleston again, who seemed sociable and friendly, and
was the only person who had accepted with anything like
cordiality. 'You haven't got any friend you'd like to
bring, have you?' Sainty asked.

'I think Johnson would come, if he was asked,' said
Tommy thoughtfully. 'You see, between you and me,
he's rather sweet on my sister.'

It only wanted two days to the end of the term, when
the list was finally completed in the most unexpected
manner.

Sainty was hobbling disconsolately across the court one
evening, when he almost ran into Parsons. Since he had
invited this gentleman to lunch as an attempt at greater
catholicity, they had frequently met, and something like
friendship might by a little stretch of imagination be said
to exist between them. Sainty, feeling how very little
strain their intercourse would bear, was always careful
not to tighten it unduly.

'I hear you are coming of age,' Ned remarked, 'and
have got a regular corroboree in honour of the event at
the family fried-fish shop. I can't think why you haven't
asked me.'

The intention was evidently humorous, but Sainty was
a little taken aback. The fact was that Parsons was the
only man of whom he saw anything like as much, whom
he had not tried as the possible fourth demanded by the
necessity for sexual symmetry.

'Should you care about it?' he asked, a little doubtfully.

'My dear fellow,' Ned answered candidly, 'don't ask a
poor devil like me to a place like Belchamber; I should be

ludicrously out of place. Besides, you know, you don't
really like me. Of course I was only joking.'

Sainty was touched. Perhaps he had done Ned injustice. He certainly had never been very civil to him, and
Parsons had borne no malice.

'Will you come?' he said.

'Do you mean it?' said Ned. 'Of course I will.'

As Sainty wrote to announce this last recruit to Lady
Charmington, he could not help smiling at the thought of
three out of the four who were to represent his chosen
intimates and cronies on the great occasion.

CHAPTER VI

DURING the long years of Sainty's minority there had been
but a moderate establishment kept at Belchamber. Lady
Charmington had been anxious the boys should be
brought up there, and have the early associations which
alone make a place a home, though it would have been
simpler and much more comfortable to have lived in the
dower-house, and some of her relations had blamed her
for not doing so.

Sainty had hardly ever been into the great central body
of the house, where what were called the State Apartments seemed only to exist to be shown to tourists by the
housekeeper. A whole wing of guests' and servants' rooms
had been permanently closed, and was only occasionally
aired and inspected. Sometimes, when the boys were
little, they had played at hide-and-seek in the long vista
of empty chambers; but for the most part the family lived
entirely in the west wing, much like royal pensioners to
whom a set of apartments had been granted in some un-
used palace. Sainty had exactly the intense love for the
place, not unmixed with awe, which might have been felt
by the child of a custodian. His mother's long habit of
unquestioned and unquestioning authority, not less than
her constant inculcation of a sense of stewardship and
responsibility to a certain abstraction known as 'the

estate,' had combined with his natural modesty and self-effacement to eliminate all sensation of personal ownership.

In the stable one pair of carriage horses, Lady Charmington's cobs and favourite hack, the boys' old ponies, and a riding horse or two, had sufficed for all their needs; and old Bell the coachman had never wanted more than the groom and a couple of stable-lads under him, cheerfully doing much of the work himself. The butler, who had been with them fourteen years, was perhaps rather practical than ornamental, but could turn his hand to anything, and the two footmen were lads from Lady Charmington's own Bible-class in the village, released by their proficiency in the scriptures from the necessity of following the plough, to wear the badge of servitude upon their shining buttons. The housekeeper and her ladyship's maid held sound evangelical views, and the morals and health of the under-servants were looked after with equal care and sternness. Lady Charmington was thoroughly versed in the spiritual state of the odd man, and could have told without a moment's hesitation the date of the third housemaid's confirmation, or when the scullery-maid last had a quinsy.

Now, however, all was to be changed. Sainty came home to an atmosphere of expansion and innovation. He found his uncle, Lord Corstorphine—whom in future we must remember to call Lord Firth, the old earl having been dead some years at the date of his grandson's majority —in constant consultation with his mother, consultations in which, to his extreme embarrassment, he was expected to take part. He discovered that he had absolutely no views as to the proper functions of a groom of the chambers, or the relative undesirability of keeping a lot of young men unemployed when you were alone, or having extra liveries into which, on the occasion of a large party, temporary hirelings could be hastily inducted; about whom, as Lady Charmington truly remarked, you could know nothing, and who might steal the spoons and flirt with the maids. Old carriages that had not seen the light of day for years were dragged from their retirement and unveiled before him, while all the horse-dealers in the county brought animals for his inspection of every shade of unfitness for the duty of drawing them. Lord Firth's political engagements made his presence necessarily intermittent; he could but seldom be there; and in his absence Lady Charmington would look anxiously at her son, hoping for some expression of opinion from him, but Sainty's ignorance was only equalled by his indifference. He tried in vain to care whether, supposing the carriages were worth doing up at all, they should be sent to London or confided to a provincial renovator.

As to the horses, as Bell scornfully told him, he 'had never knowed one end of a 'oss from the other.' On general principles he was on the side of the least expenditure. If he had said what he really felt, it would have been 'Why need we live any differently because I shall be twenty-one next month than we did when I was twenty? We have always had all we wanted; why spend all this money on things that are not going to give me the smallest pleasure—rather the reverse?' But these are the things one must not say. He looked at his mother's wistful face and strove manfully to show the interest in all these questions which was expected of him.

Arthur, when presently he came home, having just left Eton for good, flung himself into the whole business with very different gusto. The spending of money, either his own or other people's, was always a genuine pleasure to this young man, and the horse-coping afforded opportunities for displaying to an admiring audience a knowingness quite amazing in one so young, and a pair of irreproachable riding-breeches. Once when Sainty was walking in the shrubbery that masked the stable-yard he overheard the dealer from Great Charmington expressing himself to Bell with a freedom in which he would not have indulged had he known who was behind the wall.

'I'd a deal rather have to do with Lord Arthur,' he was saying, 'than with either my lord or my lady. His lordship, he don't want no horse at all; Lady Charmington, she knows a good horse when she sees 'im, but she don't want to pay for 'im; but Lord Arthur, he wants a good article, and he's willing to pay a good price. He's a gentleman, he is.'

'Ah!' answered Bell, 'it's a pity 'e wasn't the eldest; 'e'd 'ave made something like a markis, 'e would.'

It was the old, old story; the one thing poor Sainty seemed able to do was to stand between his younger brother and the position for which the very stablemen saw his superior fitness.

Arthur had been allowed to stay at Eton over his nineteenth birthday that he might once more represent his school at Lord's. A finer-looking young fellow it would have been hard to find at this time, tall and fair and ruddy, of athletic proportions and agreeable manners, a most attractive personality, and, as Sainty felt sadly, admiringly, but without a touch of envy, a most complete contrast to his elder brother. No one but Sainty, and he only imperfectly, knew the selfishness, the carnal appetites, the imperious need of enjoyment, the lack of moral sense, that lay beneath that smiling surface, or suspected the rock of primitive obstinacy above which the floating growth of apparent pliability waved so prettily in the tides of circumstance. Arthur had not been at home a week before the usual demand for money made its appearance. There is no doubt the younger brother had been extremely useful to the elder just then; his happy presence had eased the strain between Lady Charmington's strenuous eagerness and Sainty's incompetence, and lent quite a spice of amusement to the fearful upheaval in house and stable. The boys were together in what had been their common sitting-room ever since it had been their schoolroom. Sainty had had thoughts of asking for a study of his own, having much need of somewhere to work undisturbed; but it seemed ungracious to ask for the one thing that would have added to his comfort, when so much was being done for him that gave him no pleasure whatever.

Arthur, arrayed in a new pair of yellow boots, spotless white 'flannels,' and a lovely pink shirt, was whistling the airs from the latest musical farce while oiling his favourite bat and sadly shaking the table at which Sainty was trying to write a treatise on Epictetus.

'I don't suppose, dear old boy,' he said suavely, 'that you could oblige your little bwuvver with a small sum of money?'

Sainty looked up quickly. 'Why, Arthur,' he said, rather sternly, 'I heard you tell mother you didn't owe a penny now. You know she offered to pay any debts you had at Eton when you left, and you said you had given her a complete list.'

'So I did, poor dear, and it made her hair curl. I even took my bill and sat down quickly and wrote fifty, which was a hint I had got from the passage of scripture she had read to us at prayers, so as to have a little to go on with; but the fact is, dear boy, I've been cursedly un-lucky——'

'Arthur! you haven't been betting?'

'Yes; you see that's just what I have been doing. Damn it all, Sainty, don't look as if I'd been robbing a church. Every fellow has a little something on his favourite horse: it's not a crime.'

Sainty stared aghast. He had often wondered how Arthur managed to get rid of so much money at Eton, where, as he knew, though the boys were absurdly ex-travagant, the opportunities for spending were not un-limited. Now he understood, and a bottomless gulf seemed to open at his feet.

'Of course it's only a temporary thing,' Arthur went on. 'I made a good thing over Ascot, but I've been unlucky with the Eclipse; one can't always win, you know. Un-fortunately these things have to be paid up, don't yer know. My bookie's a very good sort of chap, but he's got to pay his losses, and he naturally wants his money. You can call it a loan, if you like. I've got a splendid tip for the Leger——'

Sainty looked down at his paper. Epictetus seemed to have gone a long way off and become suddenly very un-important since he had looked up from it. He knew how useless it would be to expostulate; but he wanted time to adjust his mind to this new terror.

'How did you come to know *how* to bet?' he asked; 'I mean the machinery of the thing. Who introduced you to a bookmaker?'

Arthur laughed aloud. 'Upon my word I don't remember,' he said; 'but I assure you it's not difficult. Half the fellows I know have a book on all the meetings. I rather think it was Claude told me of this chap; he's a very good sort. The man I went to before when I won a pony over the Derby wrote and said my telegram had come too late. I wasn't going to stand that kind of thing, so I cut him, naturally——'

Of course Arthur got what he wanted; it wasn't, as it happened, a very large sum. But Sainty was left with an abiding dread. He wondered sometimes how it was that he saw so clearly the dangers that menaced his brother, while Arthur himself remained so sublimely unconscious and untroubled. The mention of Claude's name in the matter, too, had reawakened an old anxiety. He had supposed that after his cousin left Eton Arthur would not be likely to have much to do with him except at Belchamber, and under his own eye. Claude's was an influence he particularly dreaded for his brother, and it was evident that they had at least been corresponding. He wondered if he ought to say anything to his cousin about it, but he remembered the small effect such interference on his part had always produced.

The Morlands were among the first to arrive for the coming-of-age festivities. Lady Eva had said, when she proposed it, that there must be heaps of things to attend to, and she should love to be of use. It need hardly be said that she was not. Her notion of offering assistance was to look in when Lady Charmington was busy, and say, 'Dear Sarah, I see I should be dreadfully in the way just now; you will do much better without poor silly me. I will take a book out under the trees.'

Claude, on the other hand, was extraordinarily helpful. He was capable, when it suited him, of taking immense pains, and he had a genius for order and detail which was of incalculable service to his aunt and cousin. He helped Lady Charmington and the housekeeper to arrange the long disused rooms, he settled who should occupy each, and wrote out lists of every kind of thing and person in a beautiful, neat, clear little handwriting. He was gay, tactful, amusing, good-humoured. Sainty was overcome with gratitude, and felt it more than ever impossible to take this smiling, affectionate person to task for such a little thing as introducing Arthur to a bookmaker. After all, it was not his *first* introduction to a gentleman of that profession, and apparently all his cousin had done was to substitute an honest for a dishonest member of the ring.

Claude's attentions to his grandmother had not proved fruitless, for when he failed, no one quite knew why, to pass his examinations for diplomacy, she had persuaded the duke to take him as his private secretary; and his experiences in that capacity made him now of incalculable use in coping with the new groom of the chambers, a young man of Olympian beauty, with a sepulchral voice and manner, who had been the duchess's footman, and in keeping the peace between him and the butler, who regarded this recent acquisition with unconcealed distrust and aversion. The establishment was now more or less on its new footing, the unwieldy machine beginning to act, with much creaking and groaning and a need of all the oil that Claude and Sainty could supply between them.

Old Lady Firth had been for some time installed in the warmest spare bedroom in the family wing, with her maid next door to her, and her son came down as soon as the session was over, giving up the 'Twelfth' with a sad heart, but promising himself to fly to the golf-links and moors of his native land as soon as he had done this last duty for his ward. Sainty appreciated the sacrifice his uncle was making for him, and much wanted to thank him for it, but only succeeded in feeling and looking embarrassed.

'I'm sure it's very good-natured of you coming here for this boring business, Uncle Cor,' he said suddenly one evening. 'I feel sure you'd rather be in the north.'

'I don't know, my dear boy,' answered his uncle patronisingly, 'why you should not give me credit for a natural interest in being present on what is really rather a big occasion in your life.'

'It is so ungracious of Sainty,' said Lady Charmington,

'to persist in looking on the whole thing merely as a bore, when we are all doing our utmost to mark our sense of the event.'

'My dear mother,' Sainty cried, 'don't think I don't appreciate——'

'Oh, I don't want to be thanked,' his mother made haste to interrupt; 'nor, I'm sure, does your uncle. We are only doing what we feel is our duty; but it would be pleasant to know you took a little interest. I believe no one takes so little interest in your coming of age as you do yourself.'

'It does sometimes seem about the worst thing I could have done,' Sainty said bitterly, a remark not calculated to soothe his mother's susceptibilities. He wondered why, whenever he tried to express any kindly feeling, it always appeared that he had said something disagreeable, with the result that by the end of the conversation he generally had actually done so.

'Who comes to-morrow, Aunt Sarah?' inquired Claude tactfully. 'I declare I've forgotten, though we went through them only this morning.'

'Let me see,' said Lady Charmington, swiftly reabsorbed in her duties as mistress of the house; 'Ecclestons, three; de Lissacs, three; my sister Susan and Johnny, two; and a young man Firth has asked, Mr. Pryor. Algy Montgomery has written that he can't come till Monday; he will come with his father and the duchess and the Rugbies. When do your Cambridge friends come, Sainty?'

'Johnson comes to-morrow with the Ecclestons, mother: he's Tommy Eccleston's friend more than mine; Parsons on Monday; Gerald Newby, I'm afraid not till Tuesday.'

It will be seen that a tolerably large party was being gathered together. The actual festivities were to occupy two days—Wednesday, which was Sainty's birthday, and the following day; and not only was Belchamber being once more filled with guests, but Hawley and the Grange, and even some bigger houses further afield were preparing to bring over large contingents for the garden party and ball.

'Do you think we had better dine in the big dining-room to-morrow night?' Lady Charmington asked.

'Oh, not till Monday,' Sainty pleaded; 'surely that'll be time enough, mother. This room is quite big enough for to-morrow's dinner.'

Lady Firth, who was dreading the draughts in the great banqueting-hall, and secretly wondering if she would not dine upstairs the first night it was used, and let the rest of the party air it for her, was strongly of Sainty's opinion.

'Do let's stay a family party as long as we can,' said Lady Eva. 'With mamma's advent on Monday we shall inevitably become very *mondain*. Who are all these smart people she has insisted on adding to the party?'

'The Nonsuches are cousins and old friends,' Lady Charmington answered grimly; 'but your mother wished Lord and Lady Dalsany asked, and Lady Deans; I confess I don't quite see why. I suppose she thought she would be bored here unless she provided her own company.'

Lady Eva laughed as if her sister-in-law had said something witty.

'Oh! is Vere Deans coming? That will be nice!' exclaimed a young lady who had come with Lady Eva. Amy Winston dabbled in literature, and spelt her name Aimée. She always wore black, white, or yellow, and still looked remarkably handsome in the evening. 'She is a dear, and *so* clever,' Lady Eva had said of her; 'writes, you know, and dresses so well on simply nothing. You would love her.'

If Lady Charmington did love Miss Winston, she disguised the feeling with perfect success. 'Is Lady Deans a friend of yours?' she asked coldly.

'Oh no!' said Miss Winston; 'but I'm simply dying to know her. She's so handsome, and has such splendid jewels, and they say she's so wicked.'

'I hope not,' Lady Charmington returned, with an increase of severity; 'but if she were, it seems a strange reason for wishing to know her.'

Every day now some of the renovated carriages rolled up from the station, bringing recruits to the house party, in one of whom the reader will be pleased to recognise an old friend. The Mrs. de Lissac, of whom mention has several times been made, was no other than Sainty's former governess, Miss Meakins. Outwardly in rustle of silks and flash of diamonds, and the deference with which the world treated her, Alice de Lissac was a very different person from Alice Meakins, but inwardly she was just the same kindly, tender, sentimental creature as ever. Riches, which have such a corroding effect on some people, had left that shy, gentle heart quite untouched; they represented to her only delightful means of doing good to her less fortunate brethren, and she was still wondering why all the great ones of the earth were so kind to a poor, humble little creature like herself. It has been related in a former chapter how this kind lady had entered the service of a Jewish family, when she left Belchamber, as governess to two little girls.

Mrs. Isaacs, her new employer, was a little, fiery, black-eyed woman of immense social ambition, which grew with the steady growth of her husband's carefully accumulated wealth. She would have been the Napoleon of London society, had she only lived, so instinctively did she grasp the market value of her possessions in the exchange to which she brought them. She had already effected the removal of the family from Lancaster Gate to Grosvenor Square, and the metamorphosis of Isaacs into de Lissac, when Death, who, alas! is no respecter of even the largest fortunes, put a term to all her hopes. It seemed as though the very energy that spurred her to ever fresh exertions was a fever burning in her blood, and sapping while it stimulated her vital forces. Poor Madame de Lissac!—as she insisted on being called—she died within sight of the goal. To the end she fought her illness, and would stand with trembling limbs and head aching under the weight of a huge tiara, while the names of half the peerage shouted in her staircase gave her strength to bear the pain that was killing her. Her widower remarked truly, between his sobs, that it 'would have been a comfort to Rachel' to have seen the cards that snowed on the hall table for days after the funeral.

He, poor man, cared little for all this. He had been glad Rachel should have it, just as he liked to give her superb presents on her birthday, and anything else his money could buy for her. Personally, his interest was in his work; he did not like the great people who had eaten his food and been rude to him. After a hard day in the city, he wanted his carpet slippers, a big strong cigar, and a volume of Schiller by the fire, or perhaps a sonata by Mozart or Beethoven.

Alice Meakins was an angel in the bereaved household; the little girls adored her, and gradually Mr. de Lissac found that he could not do without her. The girls were just coming to an age when most of all they needed the care of a mother; if she, of whom they were all so fond, abandoned them, what would become of them? Poor Alice had a terrible struggle. She was sincerely attached to the good man who had been the most generous and considerate of employers, and she loved her charges with all her heart. The great, luxurious, easy house had been the kindest home to her. How could she turn away from all this warmth and affection? 'You know—you know how I respect, how I love you, if I may say so,' cried the poor girl, with tears in her eyes; 'and I'd lay down my life for the children. But oh! Mr. de Lissac, feeling as I do about things, I couldn't marry any one who wasn't a Christian.'

And now the most wonderful thing came to pass. Her principles inspired this shyest and humblest of human beings, who blushed if she had to correct a pupil's mistake and to whom a difference of opinion was almost a physical pain, with something of the spirit of the early martyrs. She herself always considered that she had been miraculously aided; perhaps a certain pagan divinity, whose assistance she would have made haste to repudiate, counted for something in the matter. But certain it is that she was the means of leading a whole family after her into the fold, and it may be imagined the excitement she was to Lady Charmington under the circumstances. Mr. de Lissac had not been a very fervent Jew, and he made a most unenthusiastic Christian; but he was nominally converted. Instead of not attending the synagogue, he now stayed away from church, and that satisfied his not very exacting helpmate, to whom the permission to bring up her stepdaughters in her own faith gave the last brimming happiness in her cup of blessing. They at least supplied all the warmth and devotion she demanded. An eminent co-religionist of her husband's, in the city, remarked to a friend: 'Isaacs can shanshe his name, and shanshe his religion, but he cannot shanshe his nose.' Neither could he change his habits. He accompanied his wife once to the rectory, and once to Belchamber, where the rejoicing of the angels embarrassed him to the point of regretting that he had not stayed in the wilderness; but his wife mostly made her excursions to the scenes of her youth without him, and the present occasion was no exception to the rule.

Mrs. de Lissac was always fluttered and excited when she came to Belchamber, and Sainty's coming of age was just the sort of occasion to appeal to her imagination. The young ladies were fine-looking girls: the eldest, Gemma, whose biblical name Jemima had been thus abbreviated about the time of the removal to Mayfair, was tall and slight, with a clear, olive paleness and almond eyes. Nora was more like her father, shorter, and with more pronounced features, but with her mother's brilliant colour and black, burning orbs. They were both a marked contrast to Cissy Eccleston, who was the fairest, pinkest, and whitest creature imaginable, with a little button of a nose, a more refined, etherealised edition of her brother Thomas. Lady Eccleston, too, had been fair, but had grown a little red and wrinkled with time. She had an astonishingly slight and youthful figure, with rather an elderly face. Her hair, having a choice in the matter, had very naturally elected to stay young with her waist rather than grow old with her countenance; indeed, its adherence to the party of youth seemed to become more marked with each succeeding year.

This lady was slightly known to Sainty as a rather unlikely friend of his mother; she was, in point of fact, of the nature of a favourite sin to Lady Charmington. Her late

husband, Sir Thomas Eccleston, K.C.B., had been a permanent official in one of the Government offices, and had
left her with a moderate competence, and a colossal
visiting-list. She was essentially in and of London, a Bel-
gravian to the marrow of her bones. Nothing but insuffi-
ciency of income could have prevented her living in Eaton
Square. As it was, she worshipped at its temple, the
church of St. Peter, and lived as immediately round the
corner as her means permitted. She shopped in Sloane
Street, she had her books from Westerton's, she visited a
ward in St. George's Hospital; she also took a fashionable
interest in a poor East-end parish. In short, she mingled
religion and philanthropy with the punctual performance
of her immense social duties in exactly the proportion
demanded by the society of which she was a living, breath-
ing, integral part. Much in so mundane a personage was
at first rather alarming to Lady Charmington; but they
met in the committee rooms of charity, who, among the
multitude of sins she covers, could surely spare a corner
of her mantle for the few venial transgressions of such a
respectable devotee as Lady Eccleston. The very worldliness of her relations made her a powerful factor for good
works. She might always be confidently relied upon for
a duchess or minor royalty to head a list of patronesses,
or a rich friend ready to lend a big house for drawing-
room meetings; and even her deplorable habit of asking
theatrical people to dinner on Sundays had been proved
to have its good side, the professional gentlemen and
ladies being very useful in giving their services in aid of
many deserving funds. No one was a more practical hand
at organising bazaars, concerts, tableaux, the various
conduits which brought to the objects of her own interest
the fertilising stream of other people's money. She and
Mrs. de Lissac and their families had travelled from town
together. Alice was made for Lady Eccleston, who feasted
at her expense, used her carriage, copied her bonnets,
directed her charities, and revised her visiting-list. They
were allies in many good works. The girls adored Cissy
as only dark girls can adore a creature composed of rose-
leaves and sunlight, though they were a little shocked at

the triviality of her ideals, and the way she occasionally spoke of her mother.

The visitors arrived about tea-time. Five o'clock tea had never been the institution at Belchamber that it is in most country-houses, the domestic altar where the high priestess makes her little daily sacrifice of blue spirit flame and fragrant herb. Lady Charmington did not drink tea as an everyday thing; being a rigid abstainer, she kept it for a stimulant when she was tired, which was not often. When there was company, a tray of half-cold cups ready poured out used to be handed round by one of the footmen, the other following with cream and sugar, and the butler bringing up the rear with a plate of bread and butter, and some sponge-cakes in a silver basket.

For the present party, the wonderful Claude had brought about a charming revolution. A pleasant table with its white cloth and gleaming silver was spread under the cedars, at which he and Arthur and Aimée Winston dispensed good things to the tired and dusty travellers.

'How good tea is after a journey,' Lady Eccleston remarked, beaming on the company.

'I never touch it,' said Lady Firth, with a shudder; 'it is destruction to the nerves. This habit of five o'clock tea is having the most deplorable effect on the younger generation. My maid, who has been with me five-and-twenty years, always brings me a glass of taraxacum and hops at half-past four; it is wonderfully strengthening.'

'Oh dear! it is very dreadful of me to like tea so much,' cried poor Lady Eccleston. 'And I so agree with you, dear Lady Firth; we do all live on our nerves so much, too much, nowadays. I declare now you put it like that, I shall be quite afraid to drink it; but taraxacum——'

'Let me send for some for you,' said Lady Firth earnestly; 'you can't think the good it does you. I gave some to the dear bishop of Griqualand, after that drawing-room meeting at my house, when he spoke for two hours and a half, and was quite exhausted.'

Hardly was Lady Eccleston able to escape the proffered refreshment by tender and well-timed inquiries after the dear bishop and his mission.

Sainty, by reason of his lameness, was not expected to hand about eatables. He sat, as he usually did, a little drawn back from the circle about the table, talking little, noticing everything—Lady Eccleston's striving after cheap popularity, Mrs. de Lissac's parted lips as she listened to his mother, for whom she had retained all her old reverential admiration, his uncle Firth's bored expression as his Aunt Susan Trafford held forth on some small bill that had been too hastily passed at the end of the session, and the easy grace with which Claude moved about among the groups, dispensing sugar or fruit, and saying little laughing nothings to every one. 'Really, he is marvellous,' Sainty thought; 'it is impossible not to love him.' Claude was solemn, brief, and official with Sir John Trafford, the young M.P., knowing and mysterious with Austin Pryor of the Stock Exchange, playful with Arthur, *empressé* with the young ladies, and kindly civil to Tommy Eccleston and Johnson, who were very shy, while always ready to fill the teapot for Miss Winston, or hand a third cup to Lady Susan, who, like all great talkers, was a thirsty soul.

But something else seemed vaguely perceptible to Sainty, watching from his low chair under the cedars, a sense of some secret bond or understanding between his cousin and the tea-maker. What gives these sudden intuitions? What silent, mysterious voice speaks to what inner sense, when with all our outward senses we are receiving quite different impressions? Claude failed in no shade of pretty deferential politeness to Miss Winston; his manner had just that touch of insolence which it had to all women, and which many of them take as a compliment. They were the centre of a large party, and bathed in the clear golden light of a summer afternoon. Sainty intercepted no meaning glance between them, no contact of monitory fingers, yet he felt as if a curtain had been momentarily withdrawn from some secret thing that he should not have seen.

He roused himself with a start that was almost guilty, to find that Miss Eccleston, who was sitting near him, had addressed a remark to him which he had not heard.

'I beg your pardon,' he said; 'I didn't know you were speaking to me.' Cissy laughed a little, clear, bubbling laugh.

'You were a thousand miles away,' she said. 'I wonder what you were thinking of; but I am not so indiscreet as to ask; it was evidently none of the present company. I hope I haven't broken into some important thing you were thinking out. I'm told you're awfully clever and deep, and read a lot.'

'You mustn't believe all the harm you hear of people,' Sainty said, with a weak attempt at persiflage. He was thinking how pretty this fresh young creature was, the childish face shaded by a great hat, the small head rising flower-like from among the laces at her throat. No young monk in his cloister had had less to do with girls than Sainty; it was a curious fact that in his generation there were none in the family. Lady Susan Trafford, like her sister and Lady Macbeth, had 'brought forth men children only.' No early intimacy with sisters or girl cousins had taught him any of their ways.

'You must have had a hot journey down,' he remarked politely.

'Oh! it was unbearable,' cried Cissy; 'the carriage was like a furnace. You can't think how fresh and sweet it all seems here, after London.'

'We were on the Montagues' yacht for Cowes, and did Goodwood from it; you can't think how delightful it was,' said Lady Eccleston in a slightly raised voice to Lady Eva. 'They wanted us to go on a cruise with them afterwards, but there were so many things I had to see to, I was obliged to go back to town for a day or two before coming here, and I wouldn't have missed *this* visit for anything.'

Cissy drew her chair a little nearer to Sainty, and dropped her voice to a confidential whisper. 'Isn't that like mamma? She heard me say we had come from London, and all that was put in for fear you should think we had stayed in town after the season was over.'

'For fear *I* should think?' Sainty repeated, slightly bewildered.

'Oh! you or any one else,' said Cissy. 'Mamma would die if any one thought she hadn't more invitations than she could accept. I do wish she wouldn't listen to me when I'm talking to men; it makes me furious.'

'I'm sure you never say anything you would mind her hearing,' said Sainty rather priggishly.

'I wouldn't answer for that, you know,' rejoined Cissy, with an arch expression of something not unlike contempt.

If Sainty had been old Lady Firth, he could not have felt himself more outside the sphere of the ordinary attraction of man to maid. When his eye rested with admiration on Cissy Eccleston, his first thought had been what a charming couple she and Arthur would make. He thought it very kind of this pretty young lady to take pity on his disabilities, but he felt that it was hard on her to be left to talk to him; he didn't want to monopolise her, and he looked round to see if some more suitable companion were not within reach. As if in answer to his thought, Claude came towards them at the moment.

'It is cooler now, Miss Eccleston,' he said. 'Some of us are going to the kitchen-garden in search of gooseberries; do you care to come, or do you despise gooseberries?'

Cissy rose with alacrity. 'I love 'em,' she said simply.

Sainty was quite inconsistently annoyed at the sight of the two standing there before him. Had Arthur or one of the other boys come for her, he would have been glad, but he felt on a sudden that in the light of what he had half surprised between his cousin and Miss Winston, Claude had no right to come making eyes at this fair young creature. An impulse stirred in him to snatch her away, to save her from he did not quite know what. He rose too. 'I am sure Miss Eccleston is tired,' he said; 'it's a long way to the kitchen-garden; she had much better come in and rest.'

'Oh, I'm never tired, except when I'm bored,' said Cissy.

'I know who *is* tired,' said Claude, with affectionate solicitude. 'You look quite done up, old chap; you ought to lie down before dinner. Remember you've a lot before you.' Sainty saw in a second how silly and unreasonable he was being.

'Yes, you're right,' he said; 'I am tired. I'll go in.'

Claude and Cissy moved off in the rear of the little procession of young people that was beginning to stream across the lawn, and Sainty stood a moment watching them. As he turned towards the house, he saw Miss Winston, who had not gone with the others, also looking after the retreating couple.

CHAPTER VII

THE Duchess of Sunborough had not revisited her former home since she left it after the death of her first husband. Sainty had paid one or two duty visits to his grandmother on the rare occasions of his being in London, sometimes with his mother, sometimes alone. He had always found the duchess smiling and debonair, very civil, and entirely indifferent, a most mysterious personality, both in her strange spurious youthfulness and her entire detachment from family ties. She returned on the present occasion as cheerful, as amiable, and as unembarrassed as though she were paying a first visit to some distant acquaintances, in a place that was entirely new to her. She was accompanied by her husband, his eldest son and daughter-in-law, Lord and Lady Rugby, and one of his younger sons, Algernon Montgomery, a young officer in the Life Guards. The duke was a well-preserved, clean-shaven, spick-and-span old gentleman, whom people were fond of citing as a typical nobleman, and indeed among the dukes he made a very creditable appearance. Had he been the senior partner of some large commercial house he would have passed unobserved in a crowd of equally respectable-looking contemporaries on any suburban railway. In his youth he had been a gambler and a rake, and had made his first wife (the mother of his children) thoroughly unhappy by his devotion to many ladies, chief among whom had been his present duchess; but having at seventy outgrown his taste for youthful pleasures, he was spoken of as a pillar of the State and a model of all the virtues. In the year of Belchamber's majority, a Tory government, of which his grace was an inconspicuous ornament, was busy making Great Britain what she is among the nations. The Chamberses, as far as they had a political creed, belonged, it is needless to say, to the same party. Lord Firth's family, on the other hand, had always been Whigs, and the old lord, as well as the present one, had been a member of more than one Liberal cabinet. It was Lady Susan in her younger days who had given vent to the sentiment that she would as soon have married the foot-man as a Conservative; but a recent cataclysm among the Liberals had driven this ardent lady as well as her cooler brother into antagonism to their own party, though they had not as yet been absorbed into the other. There was a political flirtation going on between the duke and Lord Firth, who found themselves in novel agreement as to the line their young relative ought to take in politics. 'When the Union is threatened, all minor differences must be sunk,' the duke said graciously; 'when the ship has sprung a leak, no matter what are our views of the way she should be sailed, we must all take a hand at the pumps'; which made Claude call his revered chief the 'Pompier.'

The guests were assembled before dinner in the great saloon, which even in August had a chilly suggestion of not being habitually used.

'I hope,' Lord Firth said, with an inviting side glance at his nephew, 'that Belchamber will be able to help Hawley's election. I don't know exactly what his views are——' and here he paused long enough to give Sainty an opportunity of making a profession of faith if he were so minded. Nothing, however, was further from Sainty's intention.

'I think Mr. Hawley's election quite safe,' he said; 'it is fifty years since the county returned anything but a Con-servative,' and he moved away to take Ned Parsons, who had arrived since the other guests had gone to dress, and present him to Lady Charmington.

Sainty had been a little apprehensive how Ned would fit into the picture. Parsons had grafted on to the sloven-

liness that was either natural or affected at Cambridge a
rather aggressive splendour; though a rebel tuft waved
defiance on his crown, and his shirt-front was a little
crumpled, his collar and tie were of the moment, his
pumps were new and glossy, and he wore a gardenia in
his buttonhole. Lady Charmington was talking to Lord
and Lady Rugby. Lord Rugby was explaining with
tactful grace that it was lucky Sainty had been born in the
summer, otherwise he, as a M.F.H., could not possibly
have been present on the occasion. From Easter to the
beginning of the cub-hunting he was, so to speak, at
leisure, and had nothing to do but talk of last winter's
hunting. Lady Rugby, though also a keen sportswoman,
was capable of other forms of amusement, and said for
her part she liked a 'bit of season,' but 'poor Rug was so
bored in London it was a terror to see him.' She was
dressed with the uncompromising neatness affected by
hunting-ladies; her complexion had that bricky tint that
results from much exposure to the weather at the covert
side, and fashion decreeing undulation, her naturally
straight brown hair was crimped into a series of little
ridges and furrows, whose hardness of outline and
mathematical regularity suggested corrugated iron.
Somewhat to Sainty's surprise, Ned fell into easy conversation with this horsey person, rather suggesting, though
he did not actually say it, that he spent his life in the
saddle.

But now the duchess appeared in all her glory, and
dinner being announced, Sainty offered his arm to his
grandmother and headed the long procession to the
dining-hall.

'Well, my dear boy,' she began, when they were seated,
'and how have you been lately? You don't look strong;
you must take care of yourself. What do you drink? you
look as if you wanted red wine. My doctor has put me
upon whisky. I hate it, but he says I am *goutteuse*. They
call everything gout nowadays; too silly, isn't it?'

'I am sorry you haven't been well, gr——'

Sainty paused, and 'grandmother' died in his throat.
It seemed so ludicrously inappropriate to this festive

apparition at his side. He glanced with quite a new tenderness to where old Lady Firth sat huddled in shawls and
then back to the lady on his right. Above the thick frizzle
of sherry-coloured chestnut that descended to the carefully pencilled brows shone one of the duchess's smaller
tiaras—the great Sunborough family crown was being
kept for the ball on Thursday—the little nose gleamed
unnaturally white between the tired eyes heavily rimmed
with paint and the puffy cushions beneath them that
merged into the vivid carmine of the cheeks. The wrinkles
under the chin were gathered tightly into a great collar
of diamonds and pearls sewn on a broad black velvet.
Below it the shoulders sloped away in their still beautiful curves, displaying to the world with the indifference
of long habit their great expanse of lustreless pallor. The
little of her grace's dress that was visible above the line
of the table-cloth was of a delicate peach colour embroidered in silver, and a huge bunch of purple orchids
cut with an almost brutal contrast against the excessive
whiteness of the flesh. She sat erect, placid, exhaling a
faint sweetness, not unlike the idol of some monstrous
worship.

'Do you like the smell of my *verveine*?' she asked. 'I
think every woman should have her own *parfum*. I have
it sewn into all my *corsages*. I never could bear strong,
coarse scents. My daughter has rather brutalised herself,
and is quite capable of using patchouli. Horror!'

'I'm afraid I don't like scent at all,' Sainty avowed
penitently; 'it makes me feel rather sick always.'

'And now, tell me who every one is,' continued the
duchess affably. 'Who is the champagne blonde with the
iridescent perlage trimming next your brother?'

'That is Lady Eccleston,' said Sainty.

'Oh! of course, she has been at Sunborough House at
parties; one sees her everywhere. I ought to have remembered her'; and the duchess sent a gracious smile towards
Lady Eccleston. 'And the pretty girl that Claude is flirt-
ing with is her daughter—one can see the likeness. *Elle
est très bien, la jeune fille*; charming. Madame de Lissac I
know: she is *richissime* and very generous; and your

mother tells me she was your governess once; that is very romantic. The black girls are not her daughters, *n'est-ce pas?*'

'Her step-daughters.'

'Ah yes. And the men? Pryor I know; they say he is making money and will get on. The pink boy is *encore* a (what did you say?) Eccleston. They resemble each other like peas, that family. And the untidy young man who is amusing Aimée Winston so much? By the way, how came *she* here? With your Aunt Eva, of course. She is not a nice girl.'

The duchess delivered this condemnation with a most majestic air of virtue. 'I do not like a girl to be talked about,' she continued; 'afterwards, *je ne dis pas*; but before marriage a girl cannot be too careful. She always succeeds with men, however. The duke declares she is very clever; and one can see she is pleasing Mr.—— Who did you say he was?'

'He is a Cambridge friend of mine; his name is Parsons.'

'He seems a nice fellow,' Lady Rugby cut in from the other side of Sainty. 'I wonder if he is anything to do with the Leicestershire Parsonses. My old uncle, Sir Tom Whittaker, who hunted the Scratchley for years, married a widow, and one of her daughters married a Parsons. I know it used to be a great joke in the family because he *was* a Parson, don't yer know.'

'I couldn't say, I'm sure,' Sainty answered; 'you will have to ask him.' Really, Ned was fitting in beautifully, and if only his relationship to Lady Whittaker could be established, he felt he need trouble no more about him.

The duchess yawned. 'They are all charming, no doubt,' she said; 'but, my dear boy, none of these people give much *éclat* to your coming of age. I felt you must have a few people whose names people would know, just to put into the *Morning Post*. And your mother has lived so long out of the world she knows no one—but no one. I believe she is angry with me for insisting on the Dalsanies and Vere Deans; but I am used to that; she has always been angry with me.' This was getting on dangerous ground.

'It is very good of you to take an interest,' Sainty said in his stiffest manner; but the duchess did not in the least wish to be treated as family; she thought it *was* good of her.

'Oh! *du tout,*' she said suavely. 'Besides, it was not all unselfish. Ella Dalsany plays piquet with me, and Dalsany takes a very good hand in the duke's whist. I suppose,' she added tentatively, 'your mother would not allow a baccarat?'

'Good gracious!' cried Sainty, much alarmed, 'I don't suppose there is a card in the house.'

'Oh, I always travel with my little box,' said his grandmother. 'But we must respect the prejudices of the *châtelaine*; we will only play whist.' This was before the days of the tyranny of bridge.

The duchess glanced at Sir John Trafford, who was sitting at her right, and seeing his attention engaged by the lady whom he had taken in, she leaned a little towards her grandson, and sinking her voice confidentially, she murmured, 'When I knew that your cousin here was coming, I felt it was only kind to ask the Dalsanies; and if Ella had her cavalier, then poor Dalsany must have *la belle comtesse* to amuse him; he couldn't be left out in the cold, poor dear.'

'Scandal, Hélo,' Lady Rugby called out—(the duchess liked the younger members of her family to call her by her Christian name). 'When you have on that expression, and I can't hear what you say, I always know you are taking away some one's character.'

'Whose character is the duchess taking away?' asked Sir John; 'not mine, I hope'; and this struck her grace as so humorous that she almost choked.

Sainty sat bewildered and vaguely pained. In the mouth of an old woman, and that old woman his dead father's mother, the playful innuendoes, which to the duchess seemed only the ordinary small change of dinner-table talk, struck him as signs of a monstrous depravity. He glanced round the great room with its ceiling by La Guerre, and heavy gilt decorations, and the rows of portraits by Vandyke and Lely, down the long table with its lights and flowers and massive plate, at the two rows of flushed, eagerly talking people stretching away on either hand, and his heart failed him. He wondered sadly why Ned Parsons, who was one of six children in a little shabby rectory, and the de Lissac girls, whose grandfather was said to have been a rag and bone merchant, should seem perfectly at home among all these splendours, while he, the founder of the feast, the owner of the house, who had been born and bred in it, felt so curiously ill at ease at the head of his own table. Arthur, just fresh from school, was chattering away to Lady Eccleston and Nora de Lissac, between whom he sat, with the ease and assurance of an old London diner-out. It was neither birth, breeding, nor custom, then, which made people feel at home in society. Whence came this horrible sensation of being out of place? After all, these people, who together produced such a dazzling effect of glittering festivity, were individually nothing but relations, old friends, undergraduates, schoolboys. His mother, his grandmother, his uncle Cor, his aunts, his former governess, his cousins, his brother; he had sat down with each and all of them to a score of meals without feeling like the lady in *Comus*. He feared it was very snobbish of him to be so disagreeably affected by dining in an unaccustomed room and with an unusual number of guests. Perhaps it was the duchess, with her shocking old shoulders and naughty hints, and the little scent bags sewn into her bodice, who brought such a disturbing atmosphere of the great world into his life. If so, how much worse was it going to be next day, when she would be reinforced by these threatened strangers of her own undoubted fashion and loose morality? The thought of all these guilty married people, cynically invited 'for' each other, filled him with horror. No doubt he exaggerated, and took the whole matter more tragically than the circumstances warranted, but he was very young and very unsophisticated, and things that were not right appeared to him terribly and portentously wrong. He felt as though the home of his mother, of his own innocent childhood, were being turned into a house of ill fame.

But Tuesday, if it brought this last brimming influx of

unwelcome strangers, brought with them one supreme compensation in the person of Gerald Newby. Gerald, who was making a cross-country journey, was arriving at a different station from the other guests, several miles in an opposite direction, and Sainty decided to drive his own confidential pony to meet his friend. His mother looked grave when she heard of it, and asked if he did not think it would be more civil for him to be there to receive the Dalsanies and Lady Deans. 'Oh no, mother; the last person they would care to see is their host,' Sainty said. 'You will be here, and Uncle Cor has promised to be about; he knows them all. I shan't be missed.'

For once Sainty had his way, and drove off rejoicing in his escape. He was generally nervous of driving alone, his lameness making him so helpless in case of an accident; but to-day, that his conversation with his friend might be quite free, he would not even take a groom with him. He had so much to say to Gerald, so much which he could say to no one else, that he wanted to pour it all out unchecked by fear of listening ears. As he drove to the roadside station in the shimmering heat of the August afternoon, by great fields of waving corn, and under the thick, sleepy woods knee-deep in fern where he could hear the pheasants scuttling and clucking, he felt a weight lifted off his heart; now at last he would have some one to talk to, some one who understood. The train was late, and the flies bothered the pony dreadfully, but at last the long wait came to an end, and Newby, bronzed by foreign suns and very cindery and dusty, emerged smiling from the station, and climbed into the cart beside him.

'Oh! you have come yourself,' he said; 'that was very kind. Where's your man?'

'I came alone,' Sainty answered; 'I wanted to talk. I wanted you all to myself, and your portmanteau must sit behind; there was no room for the groom.' Something in Gerald's face made him add playfully, 'Did you expect a coach and four? Am I not receiving you with sufficient ceremony?'

'Oh, *me!*' said Newby, with a little deprecating gesture of quite false humility.

Sainty wanted to hear all that his friend had been doing, of the countries he had visited, the walks he had taken, the peaks he had climbed; but for once Newby did not seem to be inclined to talk about himself. He leaned back, beaming lazily on the passing landscape.

'After all,' he said, 'one may go where one will, to the grandest of Swiss peaks, or the sunlight and flowers of Italy, but there is nothing like this English country in the summer; it is so prosperous, so established, at once home-like and ineffably high-bred, like the best of our old landed aristocracy.'

'O Lord!' Sainty cried. 'That same landed aristocracy is smothering *me*. Wait till you see the awful specimens who have come together to rejoice in a new recruit to their ranks.' And he launched out into a tirade, as enthusiastic young people will, on the barbarism of the English upper classes, their want of education and refinement, their inability to appreciate intellectual pleasures, their low standard of morality, and, above all, their entire self-satisfaction and conviction of their own perfect rightness.

'Look at the duke,' he said; 'there's a man who owns the finest private library in England. I don't believe he knows even its chief treasures by name. If it was sold to-morrow, and the shelves fronted with sham book-backs, like the doors in the library at Belchamber, it wouldn't make the smallest difference to him. Rugby could keep his collection of riding and driving-whips in them; I am told it is unique. He is a kind of centaur; he can, and will, recount to you every run of last winter, without omitting a fence or a ditch; but if you ask him the simplest question about the history or archæology of the country he hunts over, he will stare at you as if you were a mad-man. What have I in common with such people? By what curious freak of nature have I been born among them?'

'Lord Rugby is the Duke of Sunborough's eldest son, isn't he?' asked Newby. 'And the present duchess, if I'm not mistaken, is your grandmother. I like to know who the people are that I'm going to meet.'

'My grandmother!' said Sainty tragically. 'Well, she's

my father's mother, and I mustn't say how she affects
me; but oh! heavens, Gerald, wait till you see her! And
she has asked some other people, whom I don't even
know, but who all seem to be in love with each other's
wives, and to have to be asked to meet each other as you
would engaged couples. It sickens me, I tell you. It's an
atmosphere I can't breathe.'

Somehow Newby, whom he had often heard give vent
to sentiments of a lofty and republican purity, and in
whose mouth a favourite phrase was 'the aristocracy of
intellect,' did not seem to enter as sympathetically into
his feelings as he had hoped. He continued smiling peace-
fully on the prospect around him.

'And where do you begin?' he asked presently, a little
inconsequently.

'Where do I begin? How do you mean?' Sainty stammered.

'I mean your property, your land. When do we come
to your boundary?'

'Oh! the property,' Sainty answered. 'It's pretty well
all Belchamber all the way, except just for a bit on the
left of the road soon after we started, where the Hawley
woods cut in, in a sort of wedge.'

Gerald nodded placidly, as if the thought gave him
pleasure.

'I expect you're tired after your journey, this hot
weather,' Sainty said, finding his friend so languid. 'Shall
we shirk all the crowd, and go and have some tea in the
schoolroom when we get in?'

'Whatever you say, my dear boy,' Newby agreed. 'I
am entirely in your hands.'

Sainty was aware of the slightest, most impalpable
change in his friend's manner towards himself, just the
faintest tinge of something that might almost be called
deferential in a person so naturally authoritative as
Newby; and this seemed to accentuate itself with every
acre of Chambers land across which they drove. It made
him vaguely uncomfortable; his denunciation of his peers
seemed somehow to dwindle and lose force in such an
unfostering atmosphere. He had still a great deal on his

heart of which he longed to unburthen himself, but Gerald was perversely interested in the size of the park and the number of deer, and paid but a polite and perfunctory attention to his host's exposition of the sins of the British aristocracy. Later on, when they joined the rest of the party, and Sainty, having been himself presented to the newcomers, proceeded to perform the same office for Newby, he noted with terror something that in any one else he would almost have called obsequious in his friend's attitude. He resolutely shut his eyes to it; it was of course out of the question that a person of Newby's commanding intellect and noble independence of character could be in any way affected by the mere baubles of wealth or rank in the people with whom he came in contact. He wondered he could be so snobbish as to think of such a thing, even to deny it; but he couldn't help seeing that Gerald's manner to the duke and even his uncle Firth and Lord Dalsany was not absolutely frank and unembarrassed.

'He is trying to make himself agreeable for my sake,' Sainty thought. 'A man whose whole life has been spent in a bracing atmosphere of noble thought cannot feel *at home* in the exhausted receiver that is called "society"; but if he only knew how much better he appears with his own natural manner, though it *is* a little dictatorial, he would not try and soften it even for the sake of being civil to my guests.' What with trying not to observe that Newby smiled and bowed too much, and not to watch for indications of the good understanding at which his grandmother had hinted as existing between certain members of the party, Sainty spent an even more miserable evening than he had done the night before.

When the duke and Lord Nonsuch had smoked their elderly cigars and gone to bed, he succeeded in persuading Newby that he was tired, and leaving the rest of the party listening to Lord Dalsany's Irish stories, he accompanied his friend to his room, bent on having out the rest of the talk of which he had been defrauded in the afternoon.

'It is awful, simply awful!' he burst out, as he shut the door, 'all this horrible display and waste of money! I feel

like Nero, sitting 'through these long steamy dinners with
too much to eat and too much to drink, and thinking of
the thousands of starving people who could be fed for
months on the money we waste on a meal.'

'That is very good of you, my dear lad,' Newby
answered, stretching himself luxuriously in the armchair
which he wheeled up to the open window, 'but not at all
what Nero would have felt.'

'Don't laugh at me, Gerald,' Sainty said piteously. 'I
know it 's absurd to rant and be high-flown; but it nause-
ated me to hear Lady Deans talking about these new
clubs and restaurants and saying what a mercy it was to
have some place where one could get decent food. I
thought of that woman never spending less than a pound
on her dinner, and thinking it was a merit, while people
were starving a few streets off. My bookseller told me he
wanted her to buy a six-shilling book the other day, and
she said she couldn't afford it, she should get it from the
library.'

'That tall lady on your left with the black pearls *was*
the Countess Deans then, whom one hears so much
about,' said Newby. 'I didn't catch her name when you
introduced me, but I thought it was she from her photographs, though they don't do her justice.'

'Grandmamma says she and Lord Dalsany are *au
mieux*. Good God! what does she mean? And that Lady
Dalsany——Faugh! I can't stir about this dirt. Is this just
their silly way of talking, or are they all really people
whom decent folk oughtn't to ask into their houses?'

'Oh, you exaggerate,' said Gerald, waving his hand
gently. 'You have lived the life of an anchorite. These
Londoners have their shibboleths, and understand each
other; the badinage of a great city is not meant to be
taken literally.'

'What *you* must think of it all!' cried Sainty affectionately. He had an uneasy feeling that Newby was not as
much horrified as he ought to be. 'I hoped,' he went on,
'that you might have found some congenial companionship in my uncle; but Uncle Cor disappoints me. When
he gets with all these smart people, he seems to sink to

their level. I can't make him out. Seeing him to-night you would never guess what real convictions he has. I have looked up to him all my life, but this evening he appeared frivolous and cynical; I could hardly believe it was he talking.'

'I thought Lord Firth charming,' Gerald replied, with real conviction. 'His talk seemed to me in just the right tone of easy playfulness for light social intercourse, with ladies present. He was not in his place in the House of Lords; nothing called for a profession of faith.'

'And I hate all this Unionist business,' Sainty continued. 'I never thought I should live to see Uncle Cor, who has always been a Liberal, and from whom I imbibed all my own politics till I met you, making up to that old Tory duke. They tried to get some expression of agreement out of me last night, but I wouldn't say what was expected of me. You know I'm a Radical, and a Home Ruler.'

'That is all very well for *me*,' Gerald answered, 'but, my dear child, doesn't it seem a little absurd in *your* position? Oh, don't mistake me. I don't want you to deny your convictions, but there are so many things one believes without flourishing them in the face of the public. You wouldn't, for instance, care to tell your mother just how you feel about the doctrines of revealed religion——'

Sainty drooped with discouragement. 'It is true; it is hideously true,' he said. 'One is tied and bound with the chain of a hundred shams. Shall I never be able to say what I really think? To-morrow, for instance, nothing would content my mother but that the performances should begin with a sort of thanksgiving service at Great Charmington. It is meant as a solemn dedication of me. If I were really brave and honest, I should refuse, but I think it would break my mother's heart.'

'You are quite right, quite right; and why *should* you refuse? I am sure you *do* dedicate yourself to the principle of good which rules the universe. What more do you mean, what more need you mean?'

'My mother will take it as meaning much more, and I know that she does, and so will Mrs. de Lissac and her dear old father; they will look on it as giving in a solemn adherence to all their doctrines.'

'You take things too seriously, my Sainty,' said Gerald, with an indulgent smile.

'But it is you who have always exhorted me to take things seriously; I have heard you inveigh a hundred times against the careless flippancy that is the curse of our generation.'

'Good heavens!' said Newby, suppressing a yawn; 'have I invented a Frankenstein monster, who is going to turn and devour me?'

'I don't know you to-night, Gerald,' Sainty said reproachfully. 'You are like my uncle; you seem changed somehow. Surely if there is ever a time for serious thought and serious talk, it is the vigil of one's twenty-first birthday.'

'Ah yes,' said Newby solemnly. 'Don't think I minimise the importance of all to-morrow means to you. You are coming into your kingdom, and must rule it wisely and well; but I don't want you to make your first appearance in arms tilting at windmills, my dear fellow, and alienating all the people who are your natural allies.'

'I wanted to consult you,' Sainty said, 'about my speech to the tenants, but you are tired and sleepy; it is a shame to keep you up.'

'Not at all, not at all,' said Newby politely, with the most transparent effort at interest.

'I was going to show you some heads I had put together, but I think I won't bother you; there is only just one thing I want to ask you. Ought I to tell them what I really think and feel about things, about Home Rule, for instance? Some sort of utterance will be expected of me about politics, I feel sure.'

'Your uncle was talking most sensibly to me after dinner about that very thing. "My family," he said, "have always been Liberals, but this is a Conservative county, and the agricultural population is always Conservative. I have had, as you know, to differ from the chiefs of my own party. It is a painful position. Luckily for Belchamber, he has not been required to make the choice that I have found so hard; he inherits his politics as he inherits his estate, both, I flatter myself, the better for a little enlightened handling by his mother and myself. He will not be a worse statesman for having come under some Liberal influences in his youth." It struck me as admirable.'

'Then you would have me be merely colourless, indulge in a few platitudes, instead of saying what I think?'

'What good could you effect by starting in to preach Radicalism to a tentful of Conservative farmers merry with beef and ale, supported on one side by a duke who is a member of a Tory government, and on the other by a Unionist earl?'

Sainty sighed. 'You know it is always fatally easy to me to hold my tongue and let people think that I agree with them,' he said bitterly; 'courage has never been my strong point.' He had looked to his friend for counsel, for support, for the strength to tell the truth in the face of all the world, the strength in which he felt himself so sadly lacking. He left him baffled and discouraged, and all at sea as to what he would do and say on the morrow.

As he passed down the long corridor of bedrooms, he saw the last door before the staircase open noiselessly a very little way, as if some one were looking out. When he came quite near to it, it was swiftly, but still silently, closed again. The hinted scandals that had oppressed him came crowding to his mind, thoughts of shameful, illicit things being done in the great silent, dark house. He could not resist the curiosity that made him lift his candle and read the name on the little ticket on the door; it was Miss Winston's.

Sainty and Arthur still kept the rooms they had occupied as boys, which, with the old schoolroom and another that had once been the tutor's and was now Claude's, formed a small pavilion adjoining the west wing, and consequently at the opposite extremity of the house from the guest chambers. To regain his own room he had to cross the whole great central part, now black and quiet as the grave. Just as he reached the door that shut off the family wing, he heard some one behind it. No doubt the tapping of his stick had warned whoever it was of his approach, for as he opened it he saw a figure swiftly vanish into the room on the right. His first impulse was to pass on and take no notice; then it struck him that it might be a thief, and with the sudden courage of nervous people he went into the room, holding his light high, and cried 'Who's there?' He found himself face to face with his cousin. The stable clock struck two at the moment.

'Good heavens! Sainty,' said Claude, with an uneasy laugh, 'who expected to find *you* prowling about the house at this unearthly hour?'

'I have been sitting up talking to Newby,' Sainty said rather sternly. 'What are *you* doing dodging into rooms in the dark?'

'We have only just left the smoking-room. I came in here to get a book to take up to your friend Parsons; he said he should like to see it.'

'Your candle is out; shall I give you a light?' said Sainty.

'So it is,' said Claude; 'the draught from the door, no doubt. How lucky I met you. Good-night, dear old man.'

'Good-night,' said Sainty.

CHAPTER VIII

WHETHER or not there was truth in what Lady Charmington had said, that no one took so little interest in the festivities of his coming of age as Sainty himself, it certainly came about that hardly any one took so little part in them.

The memory of his birthday remained with him as a shifting phantasmagoria of painful images that partook of the nature of a nightmare. To be the principal figure in any pageant must always have a charm for the imagination of youth, if combined with the ability to play the part becomingly; but it is a very different matter for one conscious in every nerve of his own inadequacy to be set up a butt for disappointment and a peep-show for ridicule.

The day had begun with a message from his mother that she would like to see him before prayers. He found her in her private sitting-room, where the picture of his father which he had worshipped as a child was enthroned on its gilt easel in the corner. Lady Charmington was clean and cool from her morning toilet, her hair even smoother and tighter than usual. She was dressed in her Sunday black silk, and seated in a high-backed chair beside a little table, with the air of a priestess at the altar. Her large, serviceable hands were crossed on the Bible on her lap. They had big knuckles and many rings, some of which, having been her late husband's, were more massive than is usual in a woman's. Sainty's quick eye noticed that a signet she habitually wore was not among them. He also saw that on the table beside her was an imposing pile of ledgers, a small morocco box, and a book which, from its being bound in black with depressing-looking soft flaps folding over the edges of the leaves, he rightly conjectured to be a work of devotion.

Lady Charmington was not a demonstrative woman, and she was a very shy one. She drew her son towards her, and gravely kissed him on the brow, by no means a daily occurrence or matter of course between them; then she plunged rather nervously into a little speech she had prepared for the occasion.

'This is a solemn day for both you and me, Belchamber' (he noticed that she did not call him by the familiar nickname), 'and one to which I have long looked forward. I have worked hard,' and she glanced at the pile of account-books beside her, 'in your interests. God forgive me if it is wrong, but I fear it is not without pride that I come to you to-day to give an account of my stewardship.'

Sainty gently pressed his mother's hand, which he still held. 'Dearest mother,' he said, 'I know well how hard you have worked, and all you have done for me. I assure you I appreciate——' But Lady Charmington withdrew her hand, and held it up in deprecation.

'I do not wish to boast or to be thanked,' she said, 'but I think I may truly say I have spared neither time nor

labour. It has been my object to be able to hand over the
estate to you free of debt and unencumbered, and I can
do so. To-day my stewardship ends.'

'But oh, mother!' Sainty broke in, 'it mustn't end
to-day, nor, I hope, for many days to come. You know
how utterly inexperienced I am, and then I have got to go
back to Cambridge till I have taken my degree. You won't
refuse to go on looking after everything just as you have
always done, will you?'

Lady Charmington had lost the thread of her discourse;
she looked rather anxiously at her son.

'We have no time to-day to go into accounts,' she said;
'but some day, when all these people have gone, you
must give me an hour or two, and we will go through
everything.'

'Very well,' said Sainty.

'Before we go down,' his mother went on, 'I must wish
you many happy returns, which I haven't done yet, and
give you my little presents. The new set of harness for
your cart is with the other things; you saw that: Arthur
says your old one is a disgrace; but, besides that, here is
your father's signet-ring, which I want you to wear,' and
she produced from the morocco case the ring he had
missed from her finger. 'And this is a little book I want you
to use every morning and evening; you will find it very
helpful.'

Sainty just touched the ring with his lips before he
slipped it on his finger, and glanced with passionate
tenderness at the simpering image in the corner. Then he
began turning over the leaves of the little book with its
limp cover that reminded him of French plums. He was
wondering if honesty obliged him to say that he did not
use such aids to devotion, did not, in fact, very often pray
at all. Finally, he decided that he had not the courage
to say anything of the sort, so he accepted the volume
without much enthusiasm, and put it in his pocket. Then,
detaining his mother as she was preparing to leave the
room, 'I want to tell you, mother,' he said, 'that, though I
don't *say* much, I do really value all you have done for me,
and been to me, and Uncle Cor too. Between you, you

have almost done away with the disadvantage that every boy must be under who has no father.'

Lady Charmington was faintly stirred—probably she was pleased.

'There are many things, my son, that I should like different about you,' she said, 'and especially I wish you stronger. But no one can say you have ever been anything but a good boy.' They went downstairs, both a little moved by having performed the operation so difficult to the British race, of displaying feeling.

At breakfast the question had arisen of which of the party would attend the service at Great Charmington parish church. This part of the proceedings did not seem to find favour among most of the company, and Lady Charmington's brow grew dark as one after another excused himself. The duchess was of course out of the question, as she seldom appeared before lunch, her elaborate construction being a thing of time and caution. To Lord Nonsuch, communion after breakfast was nothing short of sacrilege; he was a leading light in the High Church party, and this was his first appearance at Belchamber since a memorable occasion many years before, when he had said Lady Charmington was an Erastian, and she had called him a Jesuit.

'*I* should *love* it, dear Sarah,' said Lady Eva, 'but a poor literary hack's time is not her own. I *must* work this morning, to be free this afternoon.'

'What has your mother got to do?' asked Cissy of Claude. 'Is she writing a book?'

'Didn't you know mamma was "Maidie," who does "the girls' tea-table" in the *Looking-glass*? She has very nearly got the sack because she never gets her article ready in time; but she takes herself very seriously as a journalist, I assure you.'

The Dalsanies were Roman Catholics, and Lady Deans nothing in particular; and Gerald Newby, when he found that the people of higher rank were shirking, discovered that he had letters to write which could not be put off; but the climax of Lady Charmington's displeasure was reached when Arthur announced he would rather stay

at home and play lawn-tennis with Parsons. Lord Firth
had not intended to go, but he sacrificed himself to
mollify his sister. His religion was of that comfortable,
rational kind in which there is more state than church,
and which is first cousin to agnosticism, but infinitely more
respectable. He took a great interest in the distribution of
bishoprics and the proper conduct of the service, which,
however, he rarely felt called on to attend, except in such
cathedrals and college chapels as gratified his fastidious
taste and fondness for sacred music.

Finally, a dozen people had been got together, and
made a sufficiently imposing appearance. Old Lady
Firth, Mrs. de Lissac and the girls, and Lady Eccleston
went as a matter of course. Claude went to please his
aunt, Cissy because Claude did, Johnson because Cissy
did, and Tommy because his mother told him to. 'I
never have *any* trouble about church with my boys,'
Lady Eccleston said. 'I never have *made* them go, even
when they were little. I let them play tennis or do whatever they like, till the time comes; if I've time I play with
them. Then I just cheerfully say "Now, boys, who's for
church?" and they nearly always say, "All right, mother,
we'll go," unless they're ill.'

Lady Charmington, sore over Arthur's defection, was
in no mood to admire the success of this plan. 'Do you
mean to say you play lawn-tennis on Sunday?' she asked
frigidly; and Lady Eccleston discovered she 'must fly and
put her bonnet on, or she'd be late.'

Through the service in the church, and the subsequent
ceremony of presenting him with a silver salver and an
address from the tradesmen of Great Charmington, the
headache with which Sainty had most inopportunely
begun the day grew steadily worse. The thought of all
these poor men putting their hard-earned pounds together to give a great, ugly, useless thing to him, who had
already so much more than he wanted, unmanned him;
the tears were in his eyes as he tried to thank them. Nor
was he less cruelly embarrassed by the discovery that the
guests in the house had all thought it necessary to come
laden with gifts. In his life no one but his mother and

uncle had ever given him anything; he was not accustomed to presents, and received them with an awkward sense of obligation.

Belchamber being peculiarly rich in beautiful old plate, Arthur presented him with a huge heraldic claret-jug of monumental hideousness, for which long afterwards he paid the bill, when settling his brother's debts. The duchess gave him a cabinet inlaid after the manner of Sheraton, in which a whole army of tumblers and soda-water-bottles, lemon-squeezers, spirit-cases, and cigar-boxes rose and sank and manœuvred with incredible ingenuity on innumerable springs. Down to Lady Eccleston, who brought the latest fashionable invention for tearing the leaves of his beloved books, no one was missing from the list; even Lady Deans and the Dalsanies contributed their tale of paper-knives and cigarette-cases.

The only person whose gift showed any care or knowledge of Sainty's tastes and wants was Claude, who had taken the trouble to get from Paris a really beautiful cane, a true Malacca, strong enough to be a support, with tortoiseshell crutch encrusted with little gold stars, and an indiarubber shoe to prevent its slipping on the floors of the house. Sainty flushed with pleasure at sight of the charming thing, which seemed to adorn his lameness with a certain elegance. He wondered why his cousin, who was full of such pretty little cares and tendernesses, should be so wanting in moral sense. His heart yearned over him. 'Ah Claude,' he said, and could say no more.

'Dear old boy,' said Claude, pressing his hand, 'what do I not owe you? There is nothing that a pauper like me can give to *you*; but such as it is my little present brings real affection and heartfelt wishes for your happiness.'

Sainty's head was by this time aching cruelly, his temples throbbing like sledge-hammers; he was feeling worn out mentally and physically, ravaged by conflicting emotions. Having what was very rare with him, a slight flush, he looked less ill than usual, and nobody thought of his being tired; but it was at the tenants' dinner that he set the seal on the ignominy of his failure.

In consideration of the fact that this was a long and crowded day for one who was not robust, it had been settled that he should not preside at the meal, but merely come in and take the chair for the healths and speeches, when the solid business of feeding had been satisfactorily disposed of. It was between three and four o'clock, the hottest part of the afternoon; and though the sides of the tent had been opened here and there, the atmosphere was stifling, heavy with the odours of meat and drink and the acrid exhalations of humanity. Sainty almost reeled on entering, and had to steady himself by Arthur's arm. There were some seventy or eighty men present of all ages and degrees of stoutness, all very hot, and mostly somewhat red in the face. Many of them were intimately known to Arthur, who stopped several times in the progress up the tables to shake hands right and left. He met them at the covert-side, he shot over their farms, he played in cricket matches with them. Sainty would have given anything for a touch of that happy graciousness, that power of being hail-fellow-well-met. Circumstances had combined to make him almost a stranger to the men who were on such friendly terms with his younger brother. He knew that in his heart he had far more real brotherhood with these sons of the soil, a much more jealous respect for their manhood and independence; but his very sense of equality made him feel the falseness of his position, whereas Arthur's easy familiarity sprang from a firm conviction of his own unquestionable superiority. Sainty was only too well aware, as he took his seat in gloomy silence, that his grave bow in answer to their friendly greetings, would be set down to pride by most of the people present. When, after loyally drinking the Queen's health, the guests were once more seated and their glasses filled, the oldest tenant rose to propose the toast of the occasion. He began by complimenting the young man on attaining his majority, spoke shortly of his attachment to the place and the family, and at great length on the badness of times and the difficulties of the agriculturist, which he seemed in some mysterious way to attribute to Mr. Gladstone. The voice went droning on, monotonous by reason of its very emphasis, until Sainty felt almost hypnotised by it and by the buzzing of the numberless wasps and flies that were hovering over the remnants of food and drops of beer on the table-cloths. Sainty had quite ceased to attach any meaning to the sounds, when suddenly the voice stopped; the old man was sitting down; the audience, which had been dozing, shook itself and sat up alert, and all eyes were turned on the hero of the occasion. For weeks past Sainty had given anxious thought to what he should say to his tenants. He had never before had to make a speech, and he had rehearsed many alternative utterances in the privacy of his chamber. He had felt somehow that this was going to be his opportunity, the electrical moment when he was to make himself known to those for whom it was of such importance what manner of man he was. He would let them see that he was not an indifferent invalid, still less a selfish pleasure-seeker, a careless eater of the produce and neglecter of the producer; he would tell them how much he had their welfare at heart. In carefully prepared sentences he would allude to his great obligations (which incidentally were theirs also), to his mother's long, laborious steward-ship, his uncle's enlightened economic teaching. He had devoted hours to the consideration of just how much it would be well to hint at his political convictions; some-times he had been pleased to fancy himself electrifying his hearers by a militant profession of faith, but in calmer moments more moderate counsels prevailed.

Now the time so anxiously anticipated had actually arrived. With a great shuffling of feet the company got to its legs; some one started 'For he's a jolly good fellow' rather shakily, which was promptly taken up and cheer-fully shouted in a great variety of keys, and then all settled down to await the answering speech.

Sainty rose unsteadily and passed his hand across his forehead; for a second he stood silent, while the guests greeted his rising by drumming on the tables with their knife-handles. Then it seemed as though a crushing weight descended through the top of his head to his brain, the hum of the insects swelled to an organ roar in his ears, the hundred faces before him seemed to float and swim in a mist, and with a kind of gasping cry he sank back unconscious in Lord Firth's arms.

After this there could be no question of his appearing at the monster fête and garden-party which had been organised for the afternoon. The distant braying of a band, the sounds of many voices and laughter, and the scrunching of innumerable wheels upon the gravel were borne to him on the summer breeze, as he lay prostrate upon his bed. He had not yet come back to any sense of shame or distress; for the moment, pure physical pain was almost a relief, a restful half-consciousness that, with no effort of his, a solution had been found, a way out of all difficulties and disagreeables.

Not till late next day did he crawl downstairs, feeling very weak and battered, to receive the hollow sympathy and polite inquiries of his guests, and apologise with what grace he might for having failed so lamentably in his duties as a host.

Arthur had got up a cricket match. 'You needn't worry, old man,' he said cheerfully, as he carried out his bat and found Sainty among the group of spectators. 'You weren't missed a bit. The duke made a speech after dinner, and proposed your health, and I returned thanks for you, and said all sorts of nice things about you, which you never could have said for yourself. I did it much better than you could have done, because I was rather drunk, which you would never have been.'

'O Lord Arthur! how *can* you say Lord Belchamber wasn't missed?' cried Lady Eccleston. 'We all missed you dreadfully, didn't we, Cissy? But your brother did do his best to supply your place, and really made a delightful speech; and I do hope your head is better; it was too bad your breaking down, and we were all quite miserable about you.'

'I wanted to send you some really wonderful nerve tonic Dr. Haslam gave me,' said Lady Firth. 'I'm sure it would have done you good, but your mother said you had everything you wanted.'

Sainty insisted on showing himself at the 'treat' for the

children and the labourers; this was the one part of the 'rejoicings' in which he took a personal interest; but after a very brief appearance he was forced to go and lie down again till dinner, if he hoped to receive the guests at the great ball which was to wind up the proceedings of the second day.

The ball was a very grand affair indeed; there must have been over five hundred people present. Every woman there had put on her most gorgeous raiment, and the best of her jewellery. The duchess positively shone in white and gold brocade, hung in ropes of pearls, and with a great crown upon her head. Even Lady Charmington had had what she considered a low-necked dress made for the occasion, and had withdrawn the Belchamber emeralds from their twenty years' seclusion at the bank for the pleasure of wearing them before her mother-in-law. Sainty's share in the entertainment was strictly limited to standing by his mother, under the portrait of his great-great-grandfather, leaning with his left hand on the crutch stick which his cousin had given him, while his right was shaken by a long procession of people, who all one after the other said: 'I must—er—congratulate you, Lord Belchamber, on this auspicious occasion. Sorry to hear you weren't well yesterday; hope you're all right again.' To which he had to reply, 'Thanks awfully, very good of you; so glad you could come; you'll find the dancing through that next room, straight on.'

By the time he had repeated this phrase between three and four hundred times, and the guests had all defiled before him, he felt so sick and giddy that he had to be helped to bed by his valet, where he lay awake hour after hour, listening to the distant strains of the dance music, and picturing the scene in the great saloon to himself. He thought how nice it would be to be an ordinary, normal, healthy, courageous young man. He did not desire to be exceptionally gifted, strong, or beautiful, only just like any one of a hundred youths who were at that moment whirling in his ballroom, or eating his supper. Surely, he thought, no one had ever got so little fun out of his own coming-of-age ball before. He thought how pretty Cissy

Eccleston had looked, all in delicate pale green, with a sort of white butterfly of some shimmering stuff just poised on her bright curls for only ornament—not a jewel on her beautiful neck or arms. He fancied her, aglow with dancing, sitting to rest under the great palms and banana-trees of the winter-garden, and perhaps Claude ensconced beside her in one of those nooks that he had watched his cousin arranging, 'for flirtations,' as he said.

It was in these sleepless hours of the early morning that he decided to say something to Claude Morland which he had had on his mind for two days, and the first time he got him alone, he put his head down, dug his nails into his palms, and said, 'Claude, may I ask you something?'

'Of course; what is it?'

Sainty gulped and was silent. He had made up his mind to speak the first time he got an opportunity, but he had been genuinely relieved by every interruption, and was conscious that he had even purposely avoided being alone with his cousin.

'It is rather a queer question,' he said, 'and one which you may resent.'

Claude was lolling in a deep chair with a book; his hat tilted over his eyes left little of his face visible but his moustache and the soft curve of his chin.

'How could I resent anything from you, old chap?' he said sweetly, but without looking up. 'For which of my many sins am I to be taken to task? Fire away.'

'I know I've no right to ask such a question, but I wish you would tell me if there is anything between you and Miss Winston.'

Claude gave an almost imperceptible start, and sank lower into the deep chair. Sainty was conscious that under his air of supreme nonchalance he was suddenly tensely on his guard. 'Between us?' he murmured interrogatively.

If Sainty were going to be indiscreet, his cousin obviously did not intend to make it easy for him.

'I mean, are you in love with each other, or engaged, or anything?' Sainty persisted. Claude gave a little laugh;

he was evidently trying to keep a certain relief out of his voice as he answered in his usual soft tones, 'I would not be so rude to our dear Aimée as to say I was not in love with her; I have been in love with her any time these two years; as to being *engaged*, you really do ask the most simple-minded questions. Will you tell me just what you think I have to marry on? Am I in a position to think of marrying, especially another pauper like myself?'

'That's just what I was coming to,' said Sainty eagerly. 'I didn't ask from mere idle curiosity. But if you are in love with Miss Winston, of course you *want* to marry her, and you think you ought not to propose, because you are not in a position to support a wife—isn't that so?'

'Well—no, dear boy,' answered Claude slowly; 'to be honest, I don't exactly know that it is. Aimée and I understand one another perfectly,' he added, after a little pause.

'Do you think she *does* understand? Don't you think you may have given her the impression that you mean more than you do?'

'I am not the first man Miss Winston has met,' said Claude, turning rather an ugly grin upon his cousin; 'the dear creature was having her little flirtations before I went to Eton.'

'Of course, if you don't want to, and you are sure she doesn't want to, there is no more to be said. I only wanted to say that if you were being held back by want of money, perhaps I—perhaps we—you know—I mean, that part might be arranged, don't you know,' and Sainty blushed hotly.

Claude reached out a long, white hand, and very gently pressed Sainty's knee. 'You really are more kinds of an angel than any one I know,' he said, laughing softly, 'but you need not worry about Aimée Winston; she has no vocation for matrimony; if she ever makes up her mind to marry it will be some one who can give her a far larger share of this world's goods than even you could spare for my dot. And as for me, if I should ever find myself, either through your kindness or in any other way, in a position to take to myself a wife, she would be a very different person from *la belle Aimée; elle n'est pas de celles que l'on épouse*'; and Claude turned again to his book in such a way as to intimate that the subject was closed.

By the time that the opportunity for this singularly abortive conversation presented itself the house-party had dwindled sensibly. Those who came to please the duchess, to meet each other, and to lend the support of names well known to the chronicles of fashion, had fled the day after the ball. They had come for an 'occasion,' and the moment existence at Belchamber threatened to resume a course remotely resembling home life, they departed to other 'occasions,' with all their baggage and camp-followers. Lord Nonsuch could not spend a Sunday where the services were conducted according to the ideas of Lady Charmington; and by the Monday all had gone except old Lady Firth, the Morlands, the Traffords, and the Ecclestons, who somehow or other contrived to stay on till they should be due at another country house.

Lord Firth, ere he departed for Scotland, had a talk with his nephew. 'It has all gone off very well, my boy, on the whole,' he said, 'considering how new you and your mother were to anything of the sort. Your breakdown was unfortunate, of course, but it couldn't be helped. You had better come up to Fours for a bit next month; it'll do you good; and in November you ought to have another party here, for the covert shooting. You will have to live suitably in the place in future; all these new servants will get lazy and demoralised unless you give them something to do.'

'But I shan't be here in November,' said Sainty, 'I shall be back at Cambridge, you know.'

'Your mother and I were thinking that perhaps you wouldn't want to go back to Cambridge now you are of age,' said his uncle.

'Not go back to Cambridge!' Sainty interrupted, with unfeigned horror; 'not take my degree!'

'Many people don't, you know; and in your case, though it was no doubt right for you to have a little taste of university life, there seem to be claims which call for you more urgently elsewhere.'

'Don't ask this of me, Uncle Cor,' Sainty said earnestly. 'You and I have both been workers; in my way I have worked as hard as you. You can understand what it must be to be told when one is in sight of one's goal that one must give it up and not try for it. I gave up the scholarship because I saw that it was a shame to take it from men who needed it; but this is different. I stand no chance with Cook; he deserves to be senior classic, and is safe to be; he has nothing to fear from me, or any one; and if I beat any of the men who come next, well, it won't hurt them; they will have their first class all the same, and it makes no difference to a man if he is second, third, or fourth.'

'Do you care as much as all that?' asked Lord Firth.

'Yes, I do,' said Sainty.

His uncle appeared to consider. 'Well,' he said, after a pause, 'I don't see, if you want to go back and take your degree, why you shouldn't; but couldn't you come down for a week, say, for the pheasants?'

'Uncle Cor,' said Sainty, 'why *should* I come down, just in the middle of my work, and idle away a whole week, in order that other people should shoot pheasants? I don't shoot, myself; I hate the sound and sight of shooting.'

'Don't you think you could get to like it? Of course it's out of the question for you to hunt, but you could quite well shoot, with a quiet pony and little cart, or even from a camp-stool, if you couldn't walk.'

'I don't *want* to shoot; I should hate it. And in my case, the one excuse, the tramping, the manly exercise, would be wanting. I should seem to myself a kind of monster, dragged out to the work of slaughter in some form of machine; sitting down to butchery, like Charles IX firing on Huguenots out of a window.'

'Well, I only thought it would give you something more in common with your fellow-men, make you more like other people.'

'Oh yes, I know; it's the old story, my unlikeness to

other people, my hopeless, incurable unfitness for my position in life. I do so hate my position in life.'

'Many people would be glad to change with you, my boy,' said his uncle gently.

'I wish they could, with all my heart,' said Sainty. 'Oh, I fully realise, no one more, what an anomaly I am. If only some one of the hundreds of nice, impecunious young men with a public school education and no taste for work could have it all instead of me! Arthur, for instance, would be ideal. He would hunt, shoot, play cricket, captain the Yeomanry, be popular, successful, suitable, and enjoy the whole thing immensely into the bargain.'

'My dear boy,' said Lord Firth, taking refuge behind Providence with a simple piety worthy of his sister, 'does it never occur to you that if it had been intended that Arthur should have your birthright, he would have had it?'

'Oh, if you come to what was "intended," ' Sainty answered, 'I give up. I don't pretend to understand.'

'It comes down to the simple old rule that you learned in your catechism,' said Firth, in a more natural manner; ' "to do my duty in that state of life unto which it shall please God to call me." (I quote from memory.) You can surely understand *that*?'

'Oh yes,' said Sainty, 'I can understand *that* right enough, as a principle; but it is when you come to the question of just what *is* one's duty that the difficulty comes in. For instance, I don't believe that it is a duty incumbent on me from any religious point of view to sit in a chair and shoot tame pheasants, nor to waste money in expensively feeding a whole tribe of people with whom I have no sympathy whatever.'

'We must "use hospitality," ' quoted Lord Firth a little half-heartedly.

'Oh, if you quote Scripture on that matter,' said Sainty, not without malice, 'I think you would find I was enjoined to entertain a very different class of person from the duke, or Lady Deans, or the Dalsanies. Indeed, I am not without the highest authority for selling all I have and giving to the poor; I sometimes think it would be the best solution, as it would certainly be the simplest.'

'And how about the entail?' asked his uncle.

The wholesale disposal of his property being thus declared out of the question, Belchamber had to try and find some other answer to the riddle of life. For the present he was contented to have carried his point about going back to Cambridge; the terrible coming of age was safely past, and the danger of his university career being cut short averted. As he had not gone up till he was nineteen, he had still a year of happy college life before him, a year of peaceful study, of stimulating discussions, of congenial society, a year of hard work for a definite object. With a sigh of relief he found himself once more in his old rooms, surrounded by the dear familiar shabbinesses, his accommodation a bedroom, sitting-room, and Gyp-closet bounded by a battered 'oak'; his establishment the tenth part of an old woman in a sat-upon black bonnet, and a twenty-fifth share in the services of a Gyp, but lord of his own soul, and free to follow his own bent, an undergraduate among undergraduates, and not the slave of a cumbrous estate and an unwieldy palace.

CHAPTER IX

SAINTY did not think it necessary to go home for the covert shooting, and it is doubtful if he was much missed. Young Traffords and Montgomeries came as usual, Lord Firth brought an older man or two, and Arthur acted as host, not without a few skirmishes with his uncle, who had been accustomed to appear in that capacity on such occasions. Arthur was now at a crammer's preparing for the army, but he had none of Sainty's objection to breaking in on his studies for a little sport, and every one thought it quite right and natural that he should do so. It might be all very necessary that he should help to slaughter his fellow-men by and by, but the immediate duty was the destruction of pheasants; and whatever might be the shortcomings of the absent lord of the mansion, Arthur and the guests assembled at Belchamber had a proper sense of their responsibilities in this respect.

Sainty only wished that his brother would take his other duties in life as seriously; there was permanently at the back of his mind an anxiety about Arthur, which, like some latent poison in the blood, might lie dormant for months, but was liable to stir up and give pain at any moment. A certain sense that his own existence, unreasonably prolonged, was, as it were, keeping his brother out of his inheritance, added poignancy to all Sainty's feelings about him. But for the unfortunate accident of his own eighteen months' seniority, Arthur would have stepped naturally into his appropriate position, and found congenial occupations, duties, pleasures, ready to his hand. He felt that anything that might go wrong with his brother before his own death made tardy restitution, would be almost his fault. It did not occur to his morbid apprehension that with superior means at his command all Arthur's vicious tendencies would have increased a hundredfold; he only saw the boy who had no aptitude for study obliged by circumstances to work that he might pass examinations, and driven from healthy and innocent recreations at Belchamber into a world of dangerous companions and temptations which he lacked self-control to resist. Sainty appeared to himself as an unwilling Jacob, who by no act or fraud of his own stood possessed of the birthright which was only a burthen to him, and who yet had no appetite for the pottage for which a younger Esau's full red mouth watered so hungrily. As in the nursery days when he had decided to die young that his brother might succeed him, he still cherished an undefined feeling that he was only occupying for a time. He would never marry; all must eventually go to Arthur and to Arthur's children; but he was possessed of an ever-growing terror lest meanwhile, before this desirable end should be reached, his brother might steer the frail bark of his good behaviour to some irreparable shipwreck, commit himself irrevocably in some way that should disqualify him for the position ere it should come to him.

Sainty mused much on abdications, on men who had cast aside rank and wealth for the peace and seclusion

of the cloister; the monastic calm of his beloved courts
drew him like a spell; had he been born in the turbulent
times of his fighting ancestors he would probably have
been violently dispossessed and immured in some convent
of holy monks. He began to wonder whether in spite of
all the boasted progress of the centuries they had not
managed things in a simpler and more effectual manner
in the middle ages. He even went so far as secretly to
consult a solicitor as to whether a peer could legally renounce his title and estates in favour of the next heir
entail, with the discouraging result that he learned that
while he lived no act of his, short of high treason, could
make him other than Marquis of Belchamber in the eye
of the law, or bestow that title on any other human being.

'It seems hard,' he said to Newby one day, 'that a man
can be born into a position with no act or consent of his
own and bound in it for life; struggle as he will he cannot
free himself.'

'Are we not all alike in that respect?' asked Gerald.
'Are not circumstances, as they are called, the fetters
that each man wears? We delude ourselves with a
phantom of free-will, but I suspect that men are really
born as irrevocably parsons, doctors, politicians, as you
are a peer. Who shall free himself from the bonds of
fate?'

'You are strangely inconsistent, Gerald. I can fancy
no one less of a fatalist than yourself.'

'The doctor varies his medicines according to the
disease of the patient,' said Newby sententiously. 'When
men come prating to me of fatality as an excuse from all
effort and responsibility, I have a very different word to
say to them; but in your case, when you complain of
being fettered by your position, I wonder whether some of
those who perhaps think they would like their path thus
plainly marked for them, may not really, by inherited
tendencies and a hundred other intangible threads, be
as truly constrained in their life choice as yourself.'

' "All men are born free," ' quoted Sainty. 'There
never was a more deplorable fallacy; for my part, I feel
like the ghost in Dickens's story, who had to drag that

chain of cash-boxes and keys and deposit-safes wherever he went. Perhaps it is my lameness which accentuates this sense of being hobbled. I can't take a step without feeling the pull of the whole Belchamber estate; it is hung round my neck like the Ancient Mariner's albatross.'

'You certainly have a most deplorable trick of mixing your metaphors,' said Newby. 'But,' he added, with the mild awe of which Sainty had been so disagreeably sensible at Belchamber, 'yours is certainly a great position, a grave responsibility.'

'If I might have gone in for a scholarship, like you, and stayed and got work in the college till I could try for a fellowship!' Sainty sighed. 'The life would have suited me down to the ground.'

'There are many leading that life who would be glad to change with you,' Gerald answered with conviction.

'That is just what my uncle says, "many people would be glad to change with you." It is the old saying of our nursery days—"Many a poor man in the street would be glad of that nice pudding." Do you think it makes unpalatable food more savoury to feel that one is keeping what one does not like from some one to whom it would perhaps be an escape from starvation? It is the strangest doctrine.'

'Nevertheless Lord Firth is a very sensible man,' said Newby; 'and I don't feel disposed to pity you overmuch.'

'I don't think I want pity,' said Sainty, 'I want help. It seems too deplorable that there should be no way out of an undesirable position. I think it is this sense of being shut in that drives men to suicide far more than great grief. Is any situation really hopeless, unalterable by human effort? If any one were once persuaded of that, he *must* go mad. I suppose the pistol or the overdose of chloral is the last supreme refusal to accept such a belief. "What!" you say, "no way out of this *impasse*? Well, there is always this." '

'How theatrical!' said Newby. 'You are talking claptrap. Who ever heard of a man committing suicide to avoid a marquisate and £50,000 a year?' and he resolutely led the talk into other channels.

Arthur hadn't been a month at his crammer's before he began to justify his brother's anxiety. Of course he broke all the rules of the establishment, came and went as he pleased, drove tandem, and hunted several days a week. Then there were complications about dogs, of which he kept a perfect kennel of all sorts and sizes, which raided the reverend gentleman's poultry-yard, killed his cat and his children's pet rabbits, and harried his wife's old pig. Sainty had always wanted a dog, but had never been able to have one because Arthur's perpetually changing menagerie had kept Lady Charmington's powers of endurance stretched to their easily reached limit.

In the Christmas vacation Arthur had already stigmatised the establishment to his brother as a 'damned hole,' where a gentleman couldn't live, and obliged him with graphic accounts of his many differences of opinion with its principal.

'But doesn't he *mind* your setting your dogs on his pig?' Sainty asked.

'Mind? of course he minds; it makes him wild. But you should see the old woman; she gets twice as mad as he does. She's always telling us we are "no gentlemen," and that we shouldn't do the things at home, and why don't we treat her as we would any other lady.'

'And why don't you?' asked Sainty, with delicate irony.

'What, *her!*' with fine contempt; 'the fellows say she was the old man's cook, and that he *had* to marry her, 'cos he'd got her into trouble. You should see her in the evening in a greasy old black satin and a sham diamond locket; she's awfully particular about our dressing for dinner, so Wood came in the other evening in muddy shooting-boots. She asked if he wanted to insult her, but he said he was awfully sorry but he couldn't find his pumps, and glanced significantly at her toes that were sticking out of her gown: she has enormous beetle-crushers, and had sported a brand-new pair of patent-leather shoes. She fairly cried with rage.'

Sainty saw the futility of trying to suggest the poor lady's side of the question; Arthur was never very quick at seeing other people's point of view.

'I just don't pay 'em any attention,' he said; 'the old 'un is always at me about not working. Says I shall never pass my prelim., and objects to my hunting. I tell him it's necessary for my health.'

'And how often *do* you hunt?'

'Oh, well, not more than two days a week mostly, never more than three. You see, I've only got two hunters there; it's so infernally expensive keeping 'em at livery, and I have to pay for the man's keep too. It runs into a devil of a lot of money.'

After several such conversations, Sainty was not altogether surprised to hear from his mother that a three days' absence without leave to attend a race meeting had brought matters to a crisis, and that the care of his brother's education had been transferred from the church to the army. Arthur went to this new place with only a pony cart and a bicycle, promising great things; the hunters had been suppressed and the kennel cut down to two fox-terriers and a bob-tailed sheep-dog. Sainty was rather surprised at hearing nothing from him for several weeks—not even the familiar demand for money had broken the silence between them—and the day he came home for the Easter vacation he made haste to ask for news.

He was sitting in Lady Charmington's sitting-room, where she had conceded a cup of tea to his fatigue after a journey, but was rigorously abstaining from refreshment herself. Sainty was drinking his tea and eating cake, while his mother hastily ran through some farm accounts she was going to submit to him.

'How does Arthur get on at Colonel Humby's?' Sainty asked.

Lady Charmington looked up from her ledger with an abstracted air and her mouth full of figures. 'Thirty-even, forty-two, fifty, fifty-six, fifty-six pounds, seven and fourpence halfpenny,' she murmured. 'Didn't I tell you he'd moved?' and she noted the sum at the bottom of the page and turned over.

'What! again?' cried Sainty in dismay.

'He said he couldn't get on there; he felt he wasn't

making any progress, and he didn't seem to like the men there; apparently they weren't a very nice set.'

'He'll never pass his exams. if he keeps chopping about like this, a month in one place, a month in another. I'm afraid as long as he's expected to do any work, he'll never find a coach who quite suits his views. Where has he gone now?'

'His friend, young Hunter, who was with him at Oxbourne, had gone to that man in London they say is so wonderful——'

'Mother! you *haven't* let him go to London?'

'Why not? The boy seemed to think he should do better at Monkton's; it is such a new thing, as you say yourself, for Arthur to want to work, that it seemed a pity to balk his good intentions.'

'But surely you must see—London! Dear mother, won't there be many more distractions there for a boy of Arthur's temperament than at a dull place like Hog's Hill?'

'He said that was one trouble with Colonel Humby's place, that it *was* so dull; there was never anything to do there. If he wanted any amusement, he always had to go away for it, and this broke into his work, interfered terribly with it, in fact.'

'And so you think he'll be likely to do more work when the things that break into it are under his hand? Oh! why didn't you ask me before agreeing to this?' cried Sainty in genuine distress.

This being his first day at home, Lady Charmington only smiled indulgently at the suggestion. She was not in the habit of consulting other people before making up her mind, and least of all Sainty. 'My dear boy,' she said, 'you are scarcely older than your brother, and in some ways have really seen less of the world. Why should you think you can settle things for him so much better than he can for himself? or, for that matter, than I, who have been accustomed for years to arrange your lives for both of you?'

Sainty felt despairingly that there was nothing to be done with his mother in that direction. He had come to know the signals, and to recognise Lady Charmington's 'no thoroughfare expression' as though it were written on a notice-board. He wondered sometimes if she were really as much at ease about her younger son as she seemed, but he never dared try to find out, for fear of awakening in her heart the uneasiness that oppressed his own. It was incredible that a woman so shrewd and far-seeing in most of the relations of life as his mother, should really feel a restful confidence about Arthur. To be sure, she was ignorant of many things that he knew only too well, such as the younger boy's habit of betting and constant appeals to his elder for money; on the other hand, Arthur took but little pains to conceal his views of life, and occasionally delivered himself in his mother's presence of remarks which, it seemed to Sainty, could not fail to enlighten a much more obtuse intelligence than Lady Charmington's.

When he came to breakfast next morning he found her entrenched behind the zareba of teapots and kettles, under the shelter of which she habitually partook of that meal. She looked up from her letters with a certain air of triumph to say, 'I have a letter from Arthur; he is working so hard that he will not even come home for Easter; he says he might run down just for the Sunday and Monday, but he thinks it would only break into his work, and that on the whole it is best for him not to come away at all.' That was all the voice said, but the eyes said quite plainly, 'You see!'

Sainty said nothing. He went and peeped into the dishes on the sideboard, and picked himself out a poached egg, with no great appetite. This habit of his of saying nothing when he had nothing to say was called 'rudeness' by some people, by others 'pride' or 'indifference.' If he had spoken out his real thought to his mother she would have told him he was suspicious and could never believe any good of his brother, and would probably have exhorted him to watch against such an unamiable disposition.

The breakfast, the day, the weeks passed in this silence between the two, a silence eloquent of disagreement, yet broken only by a few words on indifferent subjects, except when the presence of guests made necessary some form of conversational rattling of peas in a bladder.

Whether it was duty or pleasure that kept Arthur away, the house seemed strangely empty and silent without him, even when some of the inevitable family party were gathered together in it—perhaps most so then, for though Arthur put himself out for no man, the mere fact that his pursuits were those of the normal young Englishman made him an important help in the entertainment of cousins. Sainty took endless trouble, but sent the men after rabbits who were secretly pining for the last meet of the season, and mounted the only Trafford who hated horses and had come down burning to throw the first fly of spring. Claude made things easier when he arrived a little later, but now that he was the duke's private secretary, his presence was generally required at one of his grace's numerous country-houses on the festivals of the Church, so that he was much less at Belchamber than formerly.

'I'm worried about Arthur,' Sainty said to him the first time they were alone. 'You know he's left the second place he went to, and my mother has let him go to London to read at Monkton's. They don't even board there, you know; he has rooms somewhere near.'

Claude's eyebrows arched themselves, and he gave vent to a low but expressive whistle.

'Yes,' said Sainty, 'that's what *I* think; I feel sure he must be in mischief, he's keeping so quiet. He wouldn't even come home for Easter; it's incredible that a woman of mother's cleverness should really believe that it springs from excessive devotion to work.'

'Have you told your mother what you think?'

'I've tried, but there's the difficulty. She thinks it is only my base jealousy and suspicion. I wonder why she so readily believes all good of him, and never gives me credit for even decent feelings. I've tried all my life to please her, studied her, thought what she'd like, and I don't believe Arthur has ever done or given up one single thing for her sake; yet she cares more for his little finger than for my whole body.'

'Oh, the secret of Arthur's favour is not hard to guess. In the first place, he's got nothing, and you've got everything. On the face of it, that seems like an injustice to him; so, with true woman's logic, she takes it out by being thoroughly unjust to you.'

'Got everything! Heavens! Do you suppose I wouldn't rather be tall and strong and straight like Arthur, be liked by men and admired by women, than own half England and be fifty Lord Belchambers?'

'Very likely; though a woman of my aunt Sarah's respect for "plenishing" is not likely to appreciate that point of view. But the real reason of her partiality is that Arthur is just the one person in the world who isn't afraid of her. Oh yes, you are afraid of her; it's not the least use your saying you're not, and so am I, and so's every one about the place. Whereas Arthur doesn't care a damn *what* she thinks; he does jolly well what he pleases, and, *maîtresse femme* as she is, she can't help admiring him for it.'

'Well, never mind about that; I didn't mean to complain; that any one should prefer Arthur to me is not a phenomenon that needs explanation. I only deplore this particular result of her devotion to him for *his* sake. What am I to do about it?'

'It's a good thing you mentioned it to me; I must see what I can do. Perhaps I shall be able to keep an eye on Master Arthur to a certain extent.'

It is true that his cousin's influence had hitherto been unmixedly bad, yet he seemed so sympathetic, so anxious to help, so entirely at one with him in his desire to keep Arthur from making an ass of himself, that Sainty went back to Cambridge vaguely consoled, and with a feeling that Claude, being on the spot, might really perhaps be able to exercise some kind of check on the object of their common solicitude.

This was his ninth and last term, the term of his tripos exam. and his degree, and he was so busy that he had but little time for thinking of his brother. Lady Charmington mentioned him but rarely in her letters, beyond a casual observation that Arthur was as hard at work as ever.

Arthur himself wrote even less than usual, but he did vouchsafe a few brief notes, saying he was 'all right,' and 'sapping like the devil,' and ending with the usual demands. In spite of his close attention to business, London seemed by no means an economical place of residence. 'His landlady robbed him shamefully; he was told they all did; and though he was sure of the fact, he knew too little about such things to be able to spot her.'

One day Sainty showed one of these epistles to Newby, and hinted at his uneasiness. 'You remember my brother Arthur?' he added, seeing Gerald look a little vague.

'Remember him? of course I do. A nice lad, a very jolly lad; an awfully charming type of healthy English boyhood.'

'Oh yes, he's all that,' Sainty assented; 'but I wish he wasn't knocking about in lodgings in London by himself. He's very young, and awfully fond of pleasure, and hasn't a great deal of self-control.'

'Let him alone, my dear boy,' returned Newby airily. 'He must sow his wild oats, like another; but he won't go far astray. *Bon sang ne peut mentir.*'

'Oh, can't it?' groaned Sainty; but his friend wouldn't hear of any danger.

'That kind of healthy, well-bred English lad always comes out all right in the end,' he said. 'You can't ride a thoroughbred with a curb.'

'Dear me, how sporting you've become; you're as horsey as Ned Parsons when he talked to Lady Rugby.'

'Talking of Ned, have you heard about his book?'

'No—what book?'

'Why, he's written a book which they say is going to be the success of the year; it ought to be out by now. I saw some of the proofs, and thought it deplorably flippant and vulgar, as anything by him was sure to be, but undeniably clever in a way.'

'Is it a novel?'

'Yes, a novel of society—as if Ned knew anything about society!'

'How came you to see the proofs? Did he show them to you?'

Newby's pale cheek took on a faint flush. 'Well, some one told me he had put *me* into it; there is a young don in the story, and of course some one who wanted to be clever immediately decided it was meant for me, so I just taxed Parsons with it the first time I met him. "I hear you've been putting me into your book," I said.'

'And what did he say?'

'At first I thought he looked a little queer, then he laughed one of those irritating, insolent laughs of his and said he'd send me the proof-sheets of the chapter where his young don was described, and I could judge for myself.'

'Well?'

'Oh, of course, as soon as he offered to show it to me I knew it must be all right, and directly I saw it I found as I expected the character wasn't the least like me. The fellow was a most egregious prig, and not only that, but a snob; and whatever my faults, *that's* a thing my worst enemy couldn't say I was, could he?'

'I'm glad it was all right,' said Sainty. 'It would have been too caddish of him to return all your kindness in that way, and somehow I don't think Ned's a bad sort at bottom.'

As the tripos drew nearer Sainty had less and less time for anything outside his work. It may be said at once that he took a very good degree. In country rectories and cheerful middle-class households from which the clever son of the family had been sent to college at the cost of some privation and not a little grumbling, a place among the first six in the Classical Tripos would have been acclaimed with grateful pride and rejoicing. In Sainty it was accounted an innocent eccentricity to care what degree he took, or whether he took one at all. Lord Firth, who was the most understanding among his kinsfolk, wrote a kind little note of congratulation. Lady Charmington was mildly gratified to find that her boy had brains and the grit to work for a desired end, but she frankly acknowledged that she could see no use his first class would be to him in after life, nor how it would help him to manage his estates. Arthur said 'his brother was

the rummest devil he ever came across, he was hanged
if he could understand him.' They would all have been
infinitely better pleased had Sainty taken his uncle's
advice, bought a gun and gone shooting in some form
of movable go-cart. It was the more remarkable that he
should do so well, as he was always more and more preoccupied about Arthur. Once the examination was over,
and his mind at ease on that score, the old anxieties
came crowding back upon him, and he decided to go to
London and try and find out for himself what his brother
was about. He would come up again for his degree.
Meanwhile, his work was done and he had kept his term,
so there was no difficulty about getting an exeat for a day
or two, and he wrote to his uncle to ask if he could put
him up.

After old Lord Firth's death his widow had given up
the house in Bryanston Square and retired to Roehampton with an elderly companion, an elderly maid, and an
elderly Blenheim spaniel; and the present peer had
bachelor quarters somewhere near Whitehall, close to the
House of Lords, and with a sidelong squint at the river
if you got very close to the windows.

Having arrived and ascertained that his uncle would
probably not be in till dinner-time, Sainty went west-
wards in search of his brother. The educational establishment, familiarly known to candidates for the army
as 'Monkton's,' was situated in the wilds of South Kensing-
ton, and in order to be handy for his place of study Arthur
had taken rooms in the same respectable region. But
neither at the crammer's nor his lodgings did Sainty find
trace of him. At the former he heard that his brother had
been there in the morning, but had not returned since
lunch, and his rooms seemed an even more unlikely place
to obtain tidings of the studious youth. 'Oh yes!' the
maid said who opened the door, ''is lordship 'as rooms
'ere right enough, but 'e isn't often in 'em; 'e generally
either calls or sends for 'is letters most days, and once in
a way 'e'll sleep 'ere, but it isn't often. Sometimes I don't
clap eyes on 'im for days together.'

Neither this information nor the fact that his brother's

ideas of 'sapping like the devil' were consistent with
taking the whole afternoon, from lunch on, for amusement, struck Sainty as very reassuring. However, there
was nothing to be done except to write on a card a request
that Arthur would come and see him at his club on the
morrow, and trust that it might be one of the days when
''is lordship called or sent for 'is letters.'

As his hansom bore him eastwards again, he could not
help having his mind diverted from his anxieties by the
rush of London life at five o'clock of a day in the season
unrolled before him like a picture-book. The streams of
vehicles of all sorts flowing in either direction made
progress necessarily slow, and gave ample time for studying their occupants. He was not yet twenty-two, and
had hardly ever been in London; the whole pageant was
absolutely new to him, and it is small wonder if he found
much to interest and amuse him. The great, toppling vans
and omnibuses were interspersed with equipages beside
which the renovated carriages of Belchamber seemed
suddenly rustic and old-fashioned. Little victorias slid
past, bearing beings in shining raiment and crowned with
improbable headgear. Family landaus containing no less
gorgeous matrons, and perhaps a brace of pink-cheeked,
sulky-looking daughters in clouds of blue and white
feathers, or small parterres of roses nodding in the summer
breeze, made stately progress towards the park, or to fetch
papa from his club. One of the prettiest of the passing
girls leaned forward in sudden recognition and touched
her companion's arm, and Sainty found himself respond-
ing to a volley of smiles and bows from Cissy Eccleston
and her mother, which at a touch made him part of the
great, glittering show, and no longer a mere onlooker and
outsider. It occurred to him with a little thrill that it
only rested with himself to come in and take his place
among all these people, the place that was his by right
of birth. Already invitations had poured in, more or less
unheeded, on such an eligible young man. Unversed as he
was in the ways of the world, he knew enough to be aware
that a fatherless peer with a long minority behind him,
an unencumbered rent-roll, and one of the show places

of England, would not be forced to take the lowest room at the various feasts to which all these votaries of fashion were so eagerly pressing.

But this unusual uplifting of his horn was of brief duration. One glance at the little mirrors on either side of the cab in which he rode, and he would have bartered all his advantages for the health and good looks of the poorest of the well-groomed, broad-shouldered youths in shiny boots who trod the pavement of Piccadilly with floating coat-tails and such a happy insolence. At one point where the throng was thickest, Sainty's attention was arrested by a tall and very showy-looking young person in a smart private hansom going in the opposite direction from his own. She was much dressed in the height of the prevailing fashion, and wore what is called a 'picture hat' adorned with a great number of nodding plumes. Her charms, deftly enhanced by art, were of the more obvious order, and she scattered smiles broadcast among the throng of young men, where dogskin-covered hands flew up to many a burnished hat as she passed, enjoying a sort of triumphal progress with the western sun shining full on her flashing gems and dazzling complexion. As the two cabs came almost abreast of one another she leaned back to say something to the man beside her, and with a clutch of the heart Sainty recognised in the slim youth leaning lazily back with his hat tipped over his eyes, who looked so distressingly boyish beside all this full-blown beauty, his brother Arthur.

CHAPTER X

BELCHAMBER's first feeling was that it was a judgment on him for having allowed his mind to wander to worldly frivolities and thoughts of personal amusement. Certainly he had been brought up with a round turn. His next was one of bewilderment as to what it behoved him to do under the circumstances. Ought he to let his mother or Lord Firth know what he had seen? He recoiled with all the force of schoolboy traditions from the idea of telling tales. Had Arthur recognised him? he wondered, and would he come to the rendezvous at the club next day, even supposing that he got his message? He had been on his way to call on his grandmother, and, as he omitted to give the driver any fresh instructions, he presently found himself at Sunborough House. Having ascertained from the porter that the duchess was out, he was turning away when he saw some one signalling to him from one of the ground-floor windows, and Claude came running bareheaded down the steps.

'My dear old boy! this *is* nice,' he said. 'I'd no idea you were in town. I saw you from the window of my room. Come in and have some tea, and I'll tell them to let us know when grandmamma comes in.'

Sainty was drawn affectionately into a large room near the front-door, which Claude explained was his peculiar sanctum. 'It used just to be a sort of waiting-room, and was much wasted, so I got the Pompier to let me have it for mine. That bell rings from his study, so he can get at me whenever he wants me.'

It was a pleasant room, with two high windows draped with some sombre, respectable, woollen fabric. Its original furniture consisted of a large writing-table with a gallery, and a set of green leather chairs, two high-backed mahogany book-cases with brass lattice-work in their doors, and several good old engravings on the walls, the duke's father, mother, and grandfather, after Lawrence, Mesdames Taglioni, and Fanny Ellsler, Count d'Orsay, the Queen on horseback, and the Duke of Wellington. On this severe ground Claude had, so to speak, embroidered a fantasia of more modern objects—little tables, low easy chairs, cigarette-cases, a vase or two of flowers, several books, reviews, and paper-knives, and a vast quantity of signed and framed photographs of all shapes and sizes. With the exception of an eminent man or two, and a few sleek young peers, they all represented beautiful ladies—ladies looking over their shoulders with their hands behind their backs, ladies with sheaves of lilies and baskets of flowers, ladies looking out of paper-mullioned windows wreathed in sham ivy, ladies with children in lace frocks, ladies in ball dress, court dress, fancy dress, or simply what may be called photographic dress, consisting of the sitter's best low-necked gown and a hat, a combination which no one could be expected to believe was ever worn outside the studio. Three large, official dispatch-boxes with paper tags hanging out of their ends stood on the writing-table, and a receptacle like a good-sized dog-basket bulged with letters for the post.

His cousin was so cordial and affectionate, did the honours of his official residence with such charming grace, that Sainty felt impelled rather against his will to tell him of his late encounter. Perhaps if circumstances had not thrown him so immediately in his way, he might not have selected Claude as his confidant; but he desperately needed help and counsel, and here was some one ready with both, some one whom to tell would have none of the grave, official importance of a report to Lady Charmington or his uncle. Warmed by tea and his cousin's enthusiastic welcome, he had not been ten minutes in the room before he had confided to its occupant all his uneasiness and its latest cause.

'Really! Arthur *is* an ass!' was Claude's comment. 'What strikes me first of all is the infernal imprudence of the whole thing. Why can't he go and see the lady quietly, instead of flourishing about Piccadilly in a hansom with her at five o'clock in the afternoon? He's just as likely as not to meet grandmamma or your uncle as any one else, and then all the fat will be in the fire.'

There was a ring of very genuine annoyance in Claude's voice; and Sainty, though he smiled at the aspect of the matter that so characteristically presented itself to Morland as the important one, felt that he had not brought his troubles to an indifferent or unsympathetic person.

'But who do you suppose it is?' he asked, 'and where can Arthur have made her acquaintance? Perhaps it may not be—what I fear; but she looked rather—well, rather——'

'Yes,' said Claude, laughing; 'I should say it was ten to one she *was* "rather." '

'It's no laughing matter,' cried Sainty. 'It was bad

enough when I thought he was only neglecting his work, and just idling and amusing himself; but this makes it all much more serious. But Claude, can't you help? Can you not guess who it might be?'

'Oh, it might be any one of a dozen people,' said Claude indifferently. 'It doesn't so much matter *who* it is,' he added; 'the great thing is to try and get him not to make a fool of himself. You know, dear Saint, it is useless to expect the high moral view from *me*. What you want is that Arthur shan't go and do anything idiotic, isn't it? Well, I'm much more likely to prevent his giving the whole show away than you are, ain't I? You leave it to me; I'll see what can be done.'

It was on the tip of Sainty's tongue to say that the eye which Claude had promised him at Belchamber to keep on Arthur, could not have been peculiarly vigilant; but he did not wish to alienate the one person who might perhaps help him, so he expressed gratitude and a confidence he did not wholly feel; and just then a footman came in to say that ''Er grace had come in, but was dining out, and must rest before dressing, and she 'oped Lord Belchamber would come to luncheon next day.'

'By the way, yes,' said Claude, when the man had left them. 'To-night is the dinner at the French Embassy, and then there is the ball at What's-their-names, and grandmamma must shed her day-skin and give the new one time to harden.'

'What do you *call* her, Claude?' asked Sainty. 'I never feel as if I *could* call her "grandmamma." '

'Oh, I never call her that to her face, *bien entendu*. It was a dreadful question at first. I couldn't call her Hélo as her stepsons do; but I've hit on a lovely plan. I call her "Grace," suggesting facetiously "Your grace," do you see? and it sounds like a cross between a Christian name and a sort of compliment, grace personified, that kind of business. Well, good-night, old chap, if you must go. Don't worry about the little blessing; you had much better let me see what I can do. Right you are. And for the Lord's sake, don't say a word to your uncle or any of 'em.'

'Don't worry,' that was still the burthen of such very various counsellors as Gerald Newby and Claude Morland, and more or less the line his mother took, who was again so unlike either of them; and meanwhile he was expected to stand by and see Arthur drifting to ruin under his eyes. However, he so far obeyed Claude's injunctions as to say nothing to Lord Firth on the subject, when they presently dined together, though his principal object in coming to town had been to ask his advice.

'Have you seen Arthur?' his uncle asked in the course of dinner, and Sainty only said, 'I called at Monkton's and at his lodgings, but I didn't find him.'

'It was a rum idea of your mother's, letting him come to London, but it seems to be working, and so does he. I've asked him once or twice to come and dine, but he hardly ever comes. He says the evening is one of the best times he has for work.'

Sainty had but little chance of private talk with Claude the next day, when he lunched at Sunborough House. His cousin drew him gently to a window when he arrived, while the numerous chance guests were awaiting the appearance of their hostess.

'I've thought of who it very likely was,' he said, with engaging frankness. 'If it 's the person I think, she 's a good girl, and won't do him any harm. You know you can't expect to keep Arthur away from women; the important thing is that he shouldn't get into bad hands, and I'll drop him a hint to be more careful and not to go and *afficher* himself. Hush! here 's our respectable ancestress. Well, Grace, here 's your *good* boy come to see you, to make a change from your bad one.'

Sainty never knew whether it was circumstances or design that made it impossible for him to get another word alone with Claude. He did not feel that Morland's help would be exactly of the kind or in the direction that he wanted, and he was more than ever anxious to see his brother himself, and try and find out just how much was wrong. He went early in the afternoon to a club in St. James's Street, of which he had lately become a member, so as to be sure not to miss Arthur if he should come there.

To his surprise, the porter handed him a letter as he went in, which proved to be a note from Lady Eccleston asking him to dine the same evening. He thought it would be pleasant to accept, but decided to keep it till he had found out if Arthur had any plans for the evening; so he put it into his pocket, and turned into a room on the ground floor, where some of the latest publications were displayed on a long table.

A group of young men who were laughing uproariously over a book desisted rather suddenly on his entrance, as one of them, in whom he recognised the young stock-broker Pryor, looked towards him and whispered something to the rest. They faced round and stared at him much as sheep look at a dog, while Austin Pryor came forward holding out his right hand, with the book still in his left.

'I say,' he said, 'how odd you should come in just this minute! Have you seen this book of your friend Parsons? It's only out to-day, and they say you can't get a copy for love or money. Wasn't he that untidy chap with a fishy eye who was at your coming of age last year? I'm blowed if he hasn't gone and stuck the whole show into his book, only he's made your brother the hero instead of you, he's turned you into a girl, a great heiress with rather jimmy health and a cork leg, who's in love with the villain. But the rest of us are there, even down to poor little me. Your mother, your uncle—oh! and the duchess—he's touched the old duchess off to the life, even to the colour of the gowns she wore at dinner. Well—he's made his fortune. They say he's been offered ten thousand for his next book, if he'll only guarantee two well-known people bein' in it. It's better biz than the House; here am I come away at three-thirty; absolutely nothing doing, I give you my word. I haven't made a fiver this account. Here—would you like the book? I've got to go out, and some one'll grab it like a shot if you don't lay hold of it.'

The other youths seemed to have melted away during this speech, so that when Mr. Pryor, convinced that he had made himself most agreeable, handed him the fortunate novel of the season, and hurried away to gossip about it in as many drawing-rooms as he could work in before dressing-time, Sainty found himself alone with the book in his hand. He sat down to wait for Arthur, and began turning over the pages.

So it was for this that Parsons had wanted to come to Belchamber. Now he understood. As Pryor had said, they were all drawn to the life. 'Well, it doesn't demand much imagination to write a book in that way,' he thought. Presently he came to the passage about the young don, and found he was smiling in spite of himself at Newby's happy confidence that the character could by no possibility have been drawn from him. The portrait was one-sided and most malevolent, but quite unmistakable. A year ago he would have been beyond words indignant at this ill-natured caricature of his friend and hero. Now he could not repress a faint feeling of amusement. What had happened to him in the meanwhile, he wondered; he felt ashamed of his want of loyalty. 'Lord Arthur Chambers askin' for you, m'lud,' a discreet club waiter murmured in his ear; and he remembered with a start that in life as in Ned Parsons' story, the protagonist of the moment was not himself but his younger brother.

'Infernally thirsty weather,' Arthur remarked, as he dropped gracefully into a chair. 'May I have a whisky and soda?—thanks.' Then to the waiter, without allowing Sainty time to answer, 'A large whisky and soda, please, with some ice and a slice of lemon. Well, old chap,' he continued, turning again to his brother as the man departed, 'and what's brought you to town?'

'You,' answered Sainty severely.

'O God! old man, not a jaw,' Arthur pleaded wearily; 'it's too hot.'

'Did you see me yesterday?' Sainty asked suddenly.

'No, old boy—where?' said Arthur, with slightly awakened interest.

'About five o'clock, in Piccadilly. You were in a hansom.'

Arthur flushed crimson all over his handsome face.

'The devil!' he said simply, in a manner which told more plainly than words that he had *not* seen his brother.

'Think of the imprudence of it,' Sainty remonstrated (quoting Claude, rather to his own surprise; it was not in the least what he had meant to say). 'You might just as likely have met Uncle Cor as me, or some one who knew you, and might have written to mother.' He did not like to name Lady Eccleston, who was the person he had in his mind.

'I wasn't doing anything I was ashamed of,' Arthur answered doggedly.

Then there was a little pause, during which the waiter reappeared with a long, clanking tumbler, and the brothers sat and looked at one another gloomily.

'Well?' asked the younger, as he sipped his refreshment.

'Do you often drink between meals?' Sainty asked. 'Are there none of the stereotyped bad habits that you haven't contracted yet?'

'An occasional whisky and soda when one's thirsty doesn't make a man an habitual drunkard——'

After a second pause, 'I suppose you want to know who it was?' Arthur suggested, with another blush.

'I don't know that I do,' Sainty answered. 'It was evident enough the sort of person——'

But Arthur cut him short. 'I won't hear a word against her,' he said hotly. 'Of course she's an actress, and that's enough to make people say deuced ill-natured things; but she's as good a girl——'

'Do you mean to say——' Sainty was beginning, when Arthur suddenly melted, leaned forward, and laid an affectionate hand on his.

'Look here, old man,' he said, 'of course I don't mean that she's immaculate; but she's told me a lot about herself, and I'm sure she's more sinned against than sinning, you know, and all that. And I'm awfully in love with her; you may as well know it first as last. And I can't stand hearing her talked about as if she was just a common woman. What are you doing to-night? I've persuaded her to come to supper with me, and asked some of her pals; will you come to the theatre with me and see her act, and come and meet her at supper? You'll see for yourself how awfully respectable and jolly and all that she is.'

Sainty's mind flew to the little note in his pocket; he would much rather have dined with the Ecclestons, but perhaps it was his duty to go and inspect the syren who had captured his brother, and he was not without curiosity as to a side of life with regard to which he was as ignorant as a girl. 'How can I help him,' he thought, 'if I know no more of his life and temptations than mother does?' And he shuddered to think of the light in which Lady Charmington would view his acceptance of the proffered supper-party.

'You had better dine here with me first,' he said resignedly; 'Uncle Cor is dining out.'

Arthur was so delighted at the ease with which he had brought his brother into line with his plans, and so excited by the anticipation of the evening's amusement, that Sainty found it impossible to get anything out of him as to the extent to which he had been neglecting his work. All mere prosaic questions of that sort seemed to the enamoured swain so entirely trivial that Sainty himself began to wonder why he attached such undue importance to them. Under the influence of what seemed almost like an unselfish passion, Arthur appeared so much more amiable than usual, that he, who had come to lecture, came perilously near remaining to sympathise. He learned that the lady of the hansom was Miss Cynthia de Vere, who was performing in a piece called '*Africa Limited, or the Day of All Jeers*,' a really rattling piece, in which she was perfectly ripping; that she had a not very important *rôle*, as far as words went, which was of course due to professional jealousies, but she was on the stage nearly all the time, and wore some 'clinking' costumes.

'By the way,' Sainty inquired, just as Arthur was about to leave him, 'how did you come to meet Miss de Vere?'

'Oh, Claude introduced me to her, one of the few good things I owe him.'

'Claude!' Sainty bounded. He could only gasp, as the full measure of his cousin's duplicity forced itself upon him.

'You needn't think the worse of her on that account,' Arthur said. 'She doesn't like our slimy cousin; she told me so. She says he's a bad lot, and so he is. Between you and me, I think he's behaved badly to her in some way. She said she'd no cause to love him, but of course I couldn't *ask* her anything about it. Tata, old chap; see you later. I must go and tell a certain person you're coming; she'll be awfully pleased.'

Africa Limited was one of the first of those musical farces which have revolutionised the English stage; it had a great quantity of characters, and no particular plot. The first act took place in England, the second in what was supposed to be Algeria, and was represented by a mixture of the tropics and a pantomime transformation scene. There were any number of songs and dances, that could be introduced or omitted at will, and the time of day was morning, sunset, limelight, or back to high noon, with bewildering rapidity, and a total disregard of the ordinary sequence of the hours. There were a pair of serious and lyrical lovers, who discoursed sentimental ballads and duets; a pair of secondary lovers, more facetious and less sentimental; an excruciatingly funny comic man from the halls, who assumed every kind of disguise for no particular reason; a barbarous potentate, who turned out to be Irish, and the comic man's long lost grandfather; several dancers of *pas-seuls*, and last but not least, a number of extremely handsome young ladies, who did not seem to have much connection with the story, but who turned up in the most unlikely places, always gorgeously dressed, and had each three sentences to say in the course of the evening. It was one of this frolic band whom Arthur shyly indicated to his brother as Miss Cynthia de Vere, and in whom Sainty without much difficulty recognised the damsel he had seen in Piccadilly. Across the footlights and out of the pitiless sunshine of a summer day, she made a striking and picturesque appearance enough. She smiled affably at the brothers, and at several other acquaintances in the stalls and boxes, and took a most perfunctory interest in what was going on upon the stage.

A rather *recherché* dandyism was at that moment the

correct style for young men about town, and Arthur was got up to kill, with a vast expanse of shirt-front illuminated by a single jewel, white kid gloves, and a cane, his fair curls cropped, flattened, and darkened as near to the accepted model as nature would allow, and his face very pink and solemn over his high collar. He went out between the acts 'to smoke a cigarette,' and returned with a new buttonhole and a peculiarly fatuous smile never produced by tobacco.

As they drove to the restaurant where they were to sup, he obliged Sainty with a catalogue *raisonné* of the guests. 'Charley Hunter's coming, and Agnes Baines, the girl next but two to Cynthia, because Charley's awfully mashed on her; Mabel Hodgson, that handsome girl at the other corner from Cynthia; and I had to ask that little cad Harry Atides, because he won't let her go anywhere without him; they say he beats her. Cynthia has such an awfully good heart; she asked me to ask her because she has such a dull life. I don't see why she stays with that little beast. Then there is Elise Balbullier, the French girl—she's awfully amusing and clever; Clara Bingham, one of the chorus girls—she's a pal of Cynthia's; and Colonel Hoby—he knows all the girls, and they like him, and he chaffs 'em, don't you know.'

Some of us not yet in our dotage can remember when it was by no means an easy thing to find a place in London whereat to sup; but about the time that pieces of the type of *Africa Limited* came into fashion, the play-going public discovered that it was unequal to the intellectual effort of witnessing them without the support of two dinners, and the first house of entertainment to cater for this new need was the Hotel and Restaurant Fritz, so called after its enterprising manager. Everything was on a scale of hitherto unprecedented luxury and proportionate expense; the waiters, of every conceivable nationality, wore short jackets and white aprons like those in a French café. A real chef directed an army of myrmidons in the adjoining kitchen. There were shaded electric lights, and little vases of flowers on the tables, among which dignified head-waiters walked like dethroned potentates in irreproachable evening dress, while a string-band made conversation appear a superfluity. A negro in a fez made Turkish coffee at a sort of altar in the midst, and the decorations suggested the saloon of the most expensive Atlantic liner.

The brothers had to struggle to the cloak-room through a crowd of all ages and sexes, the women with fresh powder on their noses pulling out their crushed laces, the men settling their ties and stroking their back hair. Among these latter they suddenly found themselves face to face with Claude. Arthur pushed past him with a sulky nod. Claude jerked his head after him. 'So you've got hold of the culprit,' he said; 'is it all right? have you got anything satisfactory out of him?'

'I have got the most surprising things out of him,' answered Sainty witheringly, looking his cousin straight in the eye.

Claude did not seem to notice. 'I'm waiting for Lady Deans and Lady Dalsany,' he said. 'Women take such an infernal time prinking. Have you seen your cousin Trafford? He's supposed to be supping with us, or rather we with him; but what are *you* doing in this unlikely place?'

'Oh, *I*'m supping in quite a different *monde*,' said Sainty in a low, vibrating voice, which he tried to keep very steady and sarcastic; 'my brother has invited me to meet the girl of his heart. I really must offer you my sincerest thanks for the admirable way you've looked after him for me.' He was swelling with righteous indignation and a consciousness of having driven a nail of incisive bitterness through the counterfeit coin of his cousin's sympathy, as he rejoined Arthur and delivered up his hat to the attendant.

Possibly with some touch of quite new prudence born of his conversation with Sainty, but much more probably with a view to doing proper honour to his fair guest, Arthur had retained a private room, rather, as it appeared, to the disappointment of the ladies, who had looked forward to seeing and being seen in the big restaurant, but immensely to the relief of his elder brother. The table was profusely decked with long trails of smilax and a quantity of those florists' roses that are all of one size and shape and colour, and seem to have been manufactured by the dozen, ready packed in cardboard boxes, having no more suggestion about them of growth by any natural process than the little red silk shades on the electric lights.

Miss de Vere, resplendent in green velvet, with a vast number of diamond ornaments, hearts, stars, crescents, arrows, and even frogs and spiders, pinned into the front of her gown, sat on Arthur's right and between the two brothers. She just touched a string of pearls at her throat, smiling archly on her host, as she took her seat. Long afterwards, Sainty had the opportunity of verifying his surmise that it was a present from that open-handed youth, when, in settling his brother's outstanding liabilities, he came across it in Messrs. Rumond & Diby's little account in company with the claret jug that had figured on the occasion of his own majority.

Seen at close quarters, the fair Cynthia was a little coarse looking, and it seemed to Sainty that a person to whom the art of painting her face must be professionally familiar, ought to have acquired more delicacy of touch. Her eyes were very large, and what the French call *à fleur de tête*; her lips were too full, too red, and seemed to show too much of their linings; and her teeth, which had flashed so brilliantly across the footlights, were less dazzling on a nearer inspection. Her figure and carriage were superb, but her hands, though unnaturally whitened, were not pretty, and her nails were ill-cared for and perhaps a little bitten. She was extremely gracious to Sainty, and evidently anxious to impress him with her *tenue* and the elegance of her manners.

'I met Lady Deans in the cloakroom,' she began; 'isn't she a handsome woman? I *do* admire her. Isn't it odd, her Christian name's Vere, and so's my surname? and we're both so tall. Some one once said we might be sisters, but of course that's nonsense. I know she's a great deal better lookin' than me.'

'It had not occurred to me that you were alike——' Sainty was beginning, but Arthur cut in. 'Rats,' he said.

'You know she isn't a patch on you,' for which gallant speech he was rewarded by a rap on the knuckles from his enslaver's fork. Though he gazed enraptured in her face, she paid him very little attention, and continued to address her conversation to Sainty.

'We had a little supper at my place last night; I wish I'd known you were in town; your brother was there. Oh, all very quiet, of course; only a little soup, and lobster cutlets, and nothing else hot but the fowls; a few little things in aspic, and some plovers' eggs, that's all; but we were very jolly. Straddles came, the famous *comique*, and sang some of his songs and made us roar; and one or two other people sang, and then we cleared away the furniture and had some dancing. We kept it up till four o'clock. I declare I'm quite sleepy; ain't you, Clara?'

Miss Bingham, a little, heavily painted black and red lady, replied from the other end of the table that she couldn't keep her eyes open. 'Lor! we did have fun, though,' she said; 'how was the poor piano this morning, after those boys pouring the champagne into it?'

'Oh, don't speak of it,' said Miss de Vere. 'You know that lovely new drapery I'd got for it, plush and Liberty silk; they completely ruined it. I was really cross. I don't see any fun in spoiling people's things.'

'What a shame!' said Arthur. 'May I give you a new one?'

'No, naughty boy, don't you be extravagant. Why didn't *you* come?' she added, turning to Miss Hodgson, the beautiful statuesque lady who sat on Arthur's left with a fixed smile on her lovely mouth that recalled the hairdresser's window. She was eating a good deal, but not adding much to the conversation. Thus appealed to, she glanced towards the little Greek, still with the same amiable absence of expression, and nodded gently.

'Do you mean I wouldn't let you go?' snarled Mr. Atides.

'Oh no,' she cooed.

'Then why the devil didn't you go? *I* don't know——'

'*Petit monstre*,' murmured Miss Balbullier to Sainty. '*Est-il insupportable! V'là longtemps que je l'aurais planté là si j'étais Mabel.* 'Oby, what is "planted there" in English?'

'Chuck 'im, give 'im the mitten,' promptly responded that gallant officer.

Sainty wondered just what kind of weird irregular regiment could once have been commanded by this blue-nosed veteran, with his dyed moustache and damp, grizzled curls; his hands and eyes were so much older than anything else about him, as to give an uncanny suggestion of magic, as of some imperfectly transformed Faust.

'*Tiens! la mitaine?* I ignore the phrase,' said mademoiselle.

Mr. Atides continued to growl into his plate with a very evil expression, like a dog over a bone, and Agnes Baines, a very pretty fair girl with a pronounced Cockney accent pursued an eager conversation across him with Miss Bingham, as though he were an empty chair.

' 'E's given 'er a tiara,' Sainty heard her say; 'none of your little 'undred-pounders, a real fine one with big stones in it.'

'Isn't Agnes vulgar?' Cynthia murmured to him, very impressive and supercilious from the heights of her superior gentility. 'She's had so few advantages, poor girl! but she *is* pretty, don't you think?'

'They say he's goin' to marry 'er,' Miss Baines continued.

'Your English girls are so kveer,' the French lady remarked to Sainty; 'zay sink of nozzing but gettin' married. To me zat seem so sorrrdid.' As Mademoiselle Elise was credited with having already ruined three young men during the brief period of her sojourn on these shores, without any thought of ceremonial formalities, this sentiment was perhaps not so disinterestedly high-minded as it sounded.

Charley Hunter, who had been vainly trying to attract Miss Baines' attention—though perhaps more of her conversation was addressed to him than he realised—and gnawing his beardless lips at the ill success of his manœuvres, here turned his back squarely on her and addressed himself to Arthur.

'They say they're going to raise the standard; isn't it beastly? as if the damned exams. weren't hard enough as it is.'

'My little feller from Aldershot says they are going to make 'em so stiff that none of you Johnnies will be able to pass unless you jolly well buck up,' remarked Miss Bingham cheerfully.

'I hope you will use your influence with my brother to make him work,' Sainty said, turning to Cynthia; 'it 's very important he should pass.'

'He 's a bad boy,' said Miss de Vere playfully, 'but I'm always at him not to be so idle.'

This speech being greeted with derisive laughter by some of the company, the lady indignantly demanded if they didn't believe her.

'There were no exams. in my day,' cried Colonel Hoby, 'and damn me if I think they turned out less good officers than the damned spindle-shanked, round-shouldered crew of short-sighted asses you have in the army nowadays. They ought to be parsons.'

'Hear, hear! Fieldmarshal,' said Arthur. 'I wish we had you in Pall Mall; there'd be a lot more good fellows in the army than there are, if you were Commander-in-chief.'

Sainty was growing weak with the effort of trying to find something agreeable to say to either of his neighbours. He was oppressed with a sense of the dreariness of the whole function. He had come prepared to be a little shocked, but half hoping for a touch of reckless gaiety. If this was the sort of entertainment Tannhäuser found in the Venusberg, he thought the pilgrimage to Rome must have been an exhilarating change. He found himself almost wishing for the young men who had poured champagne into Miss de Vere's piano, to lend some semblance of liveliness to the proceedings. With its banal, unimaginative luxury and sordid, second-rate chatter, this one excursion of his into Bohemia was as dull as one of his mother's religious dinner-parties. And to think that it was for the privilege of frequenting this sort of society that dozens of young men of Arthur's stamp ruined themselves yearly, on the very threshold of life! Uncle Cor might not be very exciting, but he surely was better company than Atides or Colonel Hoby. But then Sainty was constitutionally unfitted to give its due importance to love's young dream.

CHAPTER XI

SAINTY rather expected a letter with some attempt at exculpation from his cousin; but Claude was evidently aware that in many awkward positions there is no course so expedient as silence. Had circumstances made a meeting with Sainty seem imminent, he might have thought otherwise; but, as things were, having nothing to say, he said nothing, and trusted to time to take the edge off the situation. Sainty composed several very withering answers to the possible letter, but as it never came he had no occasion to send them.

He had not contrived to get a word with Arthur after the memorable supper. 'Hope you won't mind, old man, promised to see Miss de Vere home; only civil,' the boy had murmured, as he slipped into the little hired *coupé* that was waiting. Mademoiselle Balbullier had hinted that a like attention would not be unwelcome from himself, but finding her hints disregarded, had driven off in a hansom with Miss Bingham, laughing very shrilly at some joke that seemed to tickle them hugely.

Sainty returned to Cambridge more than ever persuaded that if anything was to be done for Arthur it must be done quickly. He had for some time had a scheme in his head, which had been germinating slowly, but for it to come to blossom, let alone fruit, he needed above all things the co-operation of Gerald Newby. He therefore made haste to seek his friend and lay his plans before him. He found Newby for a wonder alone.

'So you're back,' Gerald said, pushing the papers together on his desk and pulling the blotting-paper over them, a little trick of his which always exasperated Sainty, who would rather have died than look at anything not meant for him.

'Are you busy?' he asked. 'I've got something special to talk to you about.'

'I'm not too busy to be at the service of any one who wants me,' said Newby. 'Mere college work never seems to me as important as real human needs.'

'Ah! I'm so glad to hear you say that; it gives me a better hope in what I have to say to you.' Sainty had thought so much over the scheme he had to propose—it was so important to him—that now it was trembling on the threshold of utterance he feared lest he should not put it before Newby to the best advantage.

There was so long a pause that the young don came round from his writing-table to a position from which he faced and dominated his interlocutor. 'Well,' he said, 'I'm all attention.'

'First of all about my brother,' Sainty began, with some hesitation. 'You must know that I've found things even worse than I expected; it's not merely idleness and waste of time, as I feared; there's a woman in the case.'

Newby frowned. He had an almost feminine prudery. The fact was he knew very little of such things, and what he did not know always seemed to him dark and dangerous, a subject to be as much as possible avoided in conversation. 'I am very little qualified to advise——' he began.

'Oh! that's not what I wanted your help about,' Sainty assured him; 'at least, not directly; but you know I've often told you how I wished I could get rid of my most unsuitable part in life.'

Newby made an almost imperceptible gesture of impatience, as who should say, 'We are back to that old game, are we?'

'It was not mere talk,' Sainty went on. 'I have thought and thought about it, till I really have evolved something; I have once or twice wanted to speak to you about it, but have been afraid. Why I mentioned Arthur just now, was that a great factor in my desire for a change of life was that I thought I saw my way to helping him, perhaps to *saving* him; and what I've seen in this visit to London convinces me that I've no time to lose.'

'You interest me,' said Newby patronisingly. He went across and fastened his outer door. 'If what you have to say to me is so important,' he said, 'we may as well secure ourselves against interruption.'

'Ever since I was a child,' Sainty began again, 'it has been borne in on me that my brother was as pre-eminently fitted for my place in the world as I was *un*fitted for it. I used to think I was sure to die young, and that so matters would adjust themselves naturally without my intervention. Well—I'm nearly twenty-two, and I seem to get stronger every year. I don't say I'm a tower of strength, but I fancy I'm less likely to die than many more robust men. For one thing, I do no dangerous things. You can understand that the idea is not a pleasant one to me that my one business in life is to keep my brother out of his birthright.'

'It isn't his birthright; it's yours.'

'That's as you happen to look at it; it's not my view. I can't feel as if I had any right to what is only a hindrance and clog to me, and would be such a help to him.'

'But you can't change places with him, however much you may wish to.'

'Legally and physically, no; virtually, yes. For ever so long I've been hatching a pet scheme, but I can't carry it out without your help. I've not the health, the will, nor the intellect necessary; but you would be the ideal person to do it, and you would help and cheer me when I failed.'

'May I know what this wonderful idea of yours is?'

'I can't make him Lord Belchamber—I wish I could; but I can practically give him the position, if I hand over the place and income to him. He would be able to marry some nice girl; he is one of those who ought to marry young. With a healthy, out-of-door life and plenty of innocent congenial occupation, and the influence of a good woman at his side, all that is kindly in him would have room to develop. He is not naturally vicious, only weak and incurably headstrong and obstinate.'

'And what do you propose to do with *yourself*?'

'Ah! that is it; that's where *you* come in. The whole

thing hangs on you.' Sainty looked appealingly in his friend's face. 'I'm half afraid to put it to the touch,' he said; 'I have it so much at heart.'

'I can't give you my views on your Utopia unless you tell me what it is.'

Sainty detected and grieved at the faint sneer in the use of the word 'Utopia.'

'You don't encourage me,' he said.

'How can I, till I know what you propose?'

'I thought we might go, you and I, into one of those East End parishes and start a place something on the lines of Toynbee Hall, a sort of university for the poor, a centre of culture and light and civilisation in the middle of all that dreariness and barbarity; I to find the money, and you practically everything else, with me for your lieutenant to work under your orders.'

Sainty brought it all out with a rush, when once he had come to the point, and then paused breathless to hear how his idea would be received. Newby sat silent for a moment or two; at least he took the matter seriously.

'Have you thought at all what it will cost?' he asked.

'Yes,' cried Sainty eagerly, 'I've gone into all that rather carefully. Say that it costs £20,000 to build the place—it could be done for that, very simple and plain; a big hall to begin with, and perhaps a cloister, and a few sets of rooms like college rooms. After the initial expense I don't think it *could* cost more than £2,000 or £3,000 a year. Of course we should live in the simplest way— there would be no luxury; and gradually I should hope the place would begin to help pay for itself; it wouldn't be a charity, you know.'

'And the land?' asked Newby; 'is that included in your £20,000? You would want a good big plot, for the heart of London, to put up such buildings as you propose.'

'Oh, that could be managed. I might pay for half and raise the other half by mortgage on the property, or even the whole. There need be no difficulty about the money part of it; *I*'d see to that. The question is, will you help? All the rules, all the details of the working of the thing would have to come from you. You would be absolute master. I thought,' he added, a little piteously, 'that it would appeal to you as an opportunity of carrying out some of your ideals. It would, of course, be entirely undenominational; people of all creeds should be invited to explain their views. It might be the beginning, the nucleus of your idea of universal belief and brotherhood.'

The pleading eyes fixed on his face seemed to make Newby vaguely ill at ease. While Sainty was talking he had shifted his position, got up and walked to the window, and sat down again at his desk, on which he drummed a little with his fingers. Now he rose and came back to his friend. There was a touch of embarrassment and something like compunction, as he said—

'My dear fellow, it's impossible, simply impossible.'

Sainty, glancing round the charming room with its air of dignified calm and severe luxury, saw suddenly how sham was its austerity, how real its comfort.

'I am asking a great deal of you,' he said; 'too much, I'm afraid.'

'Don't say that,' said Newby eagerly. 'Don't think I would hesitate at any little personal sacrifice; that is indeed a low view of me. But, believe me, I see the impracticability of the whole thing.'

For a few seconds there was an uneasy silence. The summer breeze from the open windows faintly stirred the pictures on the wall. Voices softened by distance and pleasant outdoor sounds came wafted to them where they sat. It occurred to Sainty that it was not necessary for a young man to 'have great possessions' 'to go away sorrowful' when confronted by the opportunity of the supreme sacrifice for others. No one knew better than he that Newby's way of life would have been far harder for him to give up than his own; and this knowledge lent a great tenderness and humility to his voice as he asked, 'Why impracticable if we are both willing?'

'Take yourself to begin with,' Newby answered; 'think of your people, your mother, your uncle, the duke and duchess—what would they say to such a scheme?'

'Oh, they'd be horrified at first; but I don't think they

would offer any very strenuous opposition to such a simple plan of disposing of me in favour of Arthur.'

'Then, think how *I* should appear in the matter. What would they say of me?—that I had acquired a great influence over you, and then used it to make you devote yourself and your money to the support of myself and the furtherance of my crack-brained schemes. It's ten to one against their even allowing me any sincerity; far more likely they would think my one object was to advertise myself while living at your expense.'

'And do you care so greatly what people say of you?'

'Yes, I do. My dear boy, you are one of the great ones of the earth and can afford to be thought eccentric if you please; but I am a poor scholar—my good name is everything to me.'

'You said once that we could never hope to do anything unless we were prepared to be misunderstood; that no man could really be good for anything of whom the commonplace respectable people spoke well.'

'Good heavens!' cried Newby, with not unnatural exasperation, 'I wish you wouldn't cast snatches of things I may have said in some quite different connection in my teeth.' He made another excursion to the window and stood looking out for a second or two. Presently he turned and said in a much more chastened manner, 'Then there's what I'm doing here. You yourself can bear witness that I am not without influence on a number of young men, an influence you have told me was good. Have I a right to give up my work here, my power of influencing unnumbered young lives towards higher and purer ideals, for a quite problematical chance of doing good to costermongers, and incidentally enabling your brother to stand in your shoes?'

For a few moments neither spoke.

'Then you refuse?' said Sainty almost under his breath. 'Is it quite, quite irrevocable?'

'My dear boy, some day you will see the matter in its true light and will thank me for having saved you from following the will-o'-the-wisp of your own too precipitate philanthropy. The idea is purely fanciful; believe me, it would never work. In the first place, the mortifications, the disappointments, the roughness of the life, would kill you in a year.'

'And if meanwhile my money and my feeble efforts had served to start a really useful work, to launch you on a career of helpfulness, what would that matter? Would it not even be the simplest solution of all? Arthur would then step into the place in which it is so much my object to establish him.'

'Quâ method of suicide the machinery is cumbrous and expensive,' said Newby, with dreary facetiousness; 'and you can't seriously expect me to aid and abet you in committing the happy dispatch.'

They talked much longer, Sainty still pleading for his idea, though without much hope of success, Newby, gaining assurance from the sound of his own voice, pouring more and more cold water on the project and abounding in excellent reason. Sainty could not but see the sense of much that Gerald said; yet he came away from the interview not only depressed and disappointed at the ruthless killing of his cherished scheme, but with an uncomfortable sense of having caught a glimpse of his idol's clay feet, always one of the saddest experiences of life. He felt too a certain closing in on him as of fate; his attempts to mould events or to avert catastrophes had met with singularly little success. Was all struggle useless, then? was it true that we were only puppets in the iron grip of destiny? To a person of his temperament it was only too easy to believe it, yet youth's everlasting assertion of free-will dies hard in our twenty-second year, and it was not without many searchings of heart that Belchamber settled down to the conviction that there was nothing to be done. To say that his brother was never out of his thoughts would be an exaggeration. Happily for us, there is no such thing as complete absorption in one idea. When we have lost all that made life worth having, if we were honest we should own that at certain moments the most trivial of daily preoccupations drove our grief completely out of our minds. There is no evidence to show that the inhabitants of Herculaneum were other than cheerfully busy; and we all pursue a hundred frivolous objects, though lying every one of us inexorably under sentence of death.

In the year that followed Sainty thought much and anxiously of Arthur, but he also thought of many other things. For one thing, the management of his estate was beginning to interest him. Having originally turned his attention that way purely to please his mother, he had gradually come to some appreciation of what he could do for his fellow-creatures over an area for which he was more or less responsible. Whatever his views might be as to the position of the land-owning class, while he held such a position it undoubtedly entailed many duties and responsibilities. Whether his land were eventually to pass to the State or be cut up into peasant properties, as long as it remained his it was clearly better that the people on it should live in well-drained, weathertight houses, than in insanitary hovels; that they should be as far as possible provided with regular employment, educated, amused, kept from the public-house. While Cambridge and his work for the tripos held him, he had thought less of all these things, secure in the conviction that his mother and uncle were giving them careful attention. To tell the truth, he had a little feared to absorb himself in them while he still cherished a hope that his work in life might lie in far other fields, that all this might be Arthur's business, not his. In his immediate neighbourhood there was no very terrible distress to stir his imagination; by the poor on the place Lady Charmington had scrupulously done something more than her duty, and hard as were the lives of the agricultural labourers, at least their lot had fallen to them in pleasant places—their work was done in the pure air of heaven. It was for the huddled, degraded masses of the great cities, and especially of London, that his soul felt the overwhelming, sickening pity which had threatened to drive him out into the wilderness. Now that he personally seemed to be barred from effort in that direction, that his long-cherished hopes of seating his brother in his place had proved quite impracticable, and all the fabric raised by his dreams on that foundation had fallen in ruins about his ears at the blast of Newby's inexorable common-sense, the plain duties that lay immediately around him presented themselves as something to be clutched with an almost despairing intensity. Here, at least, was work ready to his hand, and he promised himself it should be done thoroughly. He absorbed himself in his mother's big ledgers, her detailed and carefully kept accounts of all the workings of the great property, with the same student's passion for mastering his subject that he had brought to his Cambridge studies. Had Lady Charmington been a less conscientious woman, the thought that her power was passing from her might not have been without a sting; but she had talked so much of 'giving an account of her stewardship,' and so often lamented Sainty's want of interest in his own possessions, that, whatever slight pangs she may have had to stifle, she had not the face to express anything but pleasure at his changed attitude. So far, too, he was still her pupil, eagerly learning all she had to tell, and accepting her word as final. It is possible that she took a genuine pleasure in introducing him to his duties, and she may well have been forgiven some moments of pride in displaying to him both the quantity and quality of her work during his minority. Sainty, on his side, began to understand all that his mother had done for him, and his wonder was only equalled by his gratitude.

Lady Charmington's confidence in Arthur's application to his studies began to be shaken about this time by his ignominious failure to pass his examination; and here it was she who turned to Sainty for help—Sainty who, impossible as it seemed, had been right where she was wrong.

'I can't make it out at all,' she would say; 'he seemed to be working so hard. You recollect he wouldn't even come home last Easter; and then in the summer he went off on that reading party.'

Arthur, in fact, after a fortnight at Belchamber—a fortnight during which he had been moody, restless, unlike himself, and had carefully shunned all possibilities of private or personal talk with either his mother or brother —had left hurriedly on a mysterious 'reading party.'

Sainty wrote often to the London lodgings, but seldom got any answers, and doubted whether many of his letters ever reached the person to whom they were written. It became increasingly difficult to pacify Lady Charmington, who passed by a rapid transition from her serene optimism to the depths of the gloomiest apprehension. Sometimes for days she would hardly talk of anything else, expressing wonder, surprise, disappointment, all of which Sainty had more or less to pretend to share, with a sense of deceit when he reflected how little surprised he really was, and how much he could have enlightened the poor lady.

At Sainty's earnest request Arthur came again to Belchamber in November for the shooting, his last visit, as it proved, for many a long day. Sainty argued, remonstrated, implored. 'What was he doing? What did he intend to do? Didn't he *want* to go into the army? He must know he could never get in if he didn't work or pass his exams.' It was all to no purpose. The boy took refuge in a surly silence. He had two such terrible scenes with his mother that for the first time in his life he spent Christmas away from home. 'I'm going to the Hunters,' he wrote. 'If I come to Belchamber there will only be a repetition of the ghastly rows I had with mother in November, and what's the good? I hate rows; jawing never did me any good yet.'

Lady Charmington appealed to her brother. Lord Firth saw Arthur when he came up for the meeting of parliament. Sainty could never learn accurately what passed between them, but his uncle, that most amiable gentleman, said he would not willingly speak to the boy again.

The spring wore away miserably in sickening suspense. Arthur was still nominally working at 'Monkton's,' but several letters had come from the principal of the establishment, complaining of the slackness of his attendance, which had not tended to soothe his mother's feelings.

It was getting on for a year after the supper at the Hotel Fritz, when Sainty, seeing a number of letters, most of which had a bill-like look about them, on the hall table for Arthur, took them to his room to re-direct. He was just about to do so, when he noticed that they had all originally been sent to Monkton's, and had been forwarded from there. The postmarks of some of them were several weeks old, from which it was evident not only that Arthur had not been at the crammer's at all for some time past, but that the people there believed him to be at home. The pen dropped from Sainty's hand, and he sat staring at the envelopes, shuffling them idly from behind one another, as though they were a hand at cards. Finally, shutting them sharply together, he thrust them into his pocket, and went in search of his mother.

Since his defection at Christmas and the failure of Lord Firth to bring the culprit to reason, Lady Charmington had talked much less of her second son; for the most part she maintained a grim and offended silence. Sainty wondered sometimes what this changed attitude might mean. He was certain that she did not think less of Arthur, or worry less about him. Was it possible that she had begun to distrust his co-operation for any reason, and was trying to find out something for herself without his help? Her manner, when he spoke to her on this particular day, was stranger than ever, and she looked at him with a sudden hard scrutiny which chilled him, when he asked if she did not think it might be well for him to go to London and look Arthur up.

'He never writes, and we don't know what he may be doing,' he said. 'I can't let things drift in this way any longer.'

He said nothing of the letters in his pocket. Lady Charmington looked as if she were on the point of saying something, and then decided not to.

'Very well,' she answered quietly; 'how long shall you be gone?'

'I don't know; it will depend on what I find. Mother,' he added, 'don't you agree? don't you think it will be well for me to go?'

Again his mother looked at him as if she would have read his soul; it was the old glance that had made him stammer and look down as a child, the look that said more clearly than words that she thought him a liar. He had never been able to meet it. Instinctively he looked away.

'Go, by all means,' he heard her say, and he knew that her eyes were still upon his face, the eyes of a judge, almost an accuser. 'Go and see what you can do. You may have means of getting at the truth not open to me.'

CHAPTER XII

WITHOUT seeing any one at Monkton's but the servant, or even disclosing his identity, Sainty was able in a very few words to establish the correctness of his surmises. Arthur had not been there for weeks. 'I can get you 'is address, if you'll wait a minute,' the man said; ''e's down at 'is own 'ome; I forwarded some letters to him a day or two back.'

'Oh, thanks; if he's there, I know the address and need not trouble you,' and Sainty turned again to his hansom. He reflected that to find Miss de Vere was to find his brother, and supposed, in his innocence, that he had only to apply at the theatre to learn the young lady's address. But when he presented himself at the stage-door and blushingly demanded it, he was informed that Miss de Vere was not acting at present, and that, in any case, they were strictly forbidden to give the private address of any of their ladies or gentlemen. A letter sent to the theatre for Miss de Vere would be forwarded.

This was an unlooked-for check, and he wondered blankly what he was to do next. He sent away his cab and began to wander slowly westward again; he could think better on foot. He was walking sadly along Pall Mall, when he was passed by a young man with wonderfully broad shoulders and a wonderfully small waist, who paused, looked at him, and finally held out his hand. Sainty recognised Algy Montgomery.

'Hulloa!' said the guardsman, with the smileless gloom of the fashionable London young man. 'Where are you off to? I'm just on my way to call on my stepmother; I understand she says I never come near her. Why don't you come along and see your revered grandmother?'

Sainty had been trying to make himself go and ask Claude for the address he wanted; he had not once set eyes on his cousin during the past year, and to appeal to him again for help was a bitter pill. Think as he would, he could evolve no other way of arriving at his end, and this chance meeting and invitation to Sunborough House seemed like a leading. He would go and see the duchess— what more natural? and if Claude happened to be there, how could he help it?

'All right,' he said; 'I don't mind if I do.'

The pair walked in silence for a few seconds, Lord Algernon trying to accommodate his long stride to his companion's limp.

'Come up to look after your young brother?' he asked presently, through the cigar which he held tightly between his teeth. 'He's making no end of an ass of himself with Topsy de Vere; he never leaves her for a minute——'

To talk casually to a comparative stranger of what was gnawing his vitals was gall and wormwood to Sainty, but he grunted some sort of an assent, and then asked as indifferently as he could, 'You don't happen to know Miss de Vere's address, do you?'

Lord Algy laughed. 'No, for a wonder, I don't,' he said; 'but I tell you who ought to—your precious cousin Morland. I fancy he knew his way there quite well at one time.'

'Oh! did Claude——'

'Got tired of the lady; or perhaps found her rather too expensive (I suspect his grace don't do his secretary particularly well), so passed her on to the little cousin. Sharp fellow, Morland.'

The duchess, whom presently they found having tea in company with Lady Rugby and Lady Eva, had also a word to say of her prodigal grandson. 'Arthur *s'encanaille*,' she remarked. 'He is bad form; he lets himself be seen everywhere with *cocottes*; the young men of to-day have no *tenue*—none. Formerly, yes, I don't say men were any better—they have always been monsters; but they did not throw *ces demoiselles* in the face of the world.'

Lady Eva murmured something to the effect that Arthur was a dear, and dropped a platitude about wild oats.

'Oh, I don't want a boy to be a *merle blanc*,' her mother rejoined. 'Sainty would be all the better if he were just a little naughty, wouldn't you, my child? I don't suppose Algy here, or your own boy, are models of virtue, but there are ways of doing things. By the way, where is Claude? Ring the bell, Algy, and we will see if he is in; he will like to see his cousin.'

Sainty did not feel at all sure that he would, but when Morland presently appeared in answer to the duchess's message, he was as easy and unembarrassed as usual; it was Belchamber who was awkward and ill at ease. There was, perhaps, just a shade of reproachful tenderness in Claude's greeting, an eloquent glance, a silent pressure of the hand, as who should say, 'You may be as cantankerous and unreasonable as you like, my patience with those I love is practically inexhaustible.' At the merest hint from Sainty that he had something to ask him, he carried him off to his own room, and when the request for Miss de Vere's address had been stammered out, produced a little address-book from a locked drawer, and began to search in it with a great appearance of assiduity.

'Here it is—no, let me see, she left there, that's her old address; how stupid of me. Ah! this is it, a flat she took; I remember now. But she's always moving, I don't guarantee that you'll find her there; but they'll be able to tell you if she's flitted again.' His voice was dry and businesslike; Sainty wanted an address, he was trying to help him to it, as he would try to do anything he wanted. Why he had need of it was no affair of his. Claude prided himself on his power of implying much that his tongue never uttered.

He wrung Sainty's hand at parting. 'Good luck to you,' he whispered. '*I* could do no good; may you be more fortunate! And oh! by the way, I wouldn't mention *me* there; I'm not popular in that quarter. Cynthia has taken one of those absurd, unreasoning dislikes to me that half-educated people do, and has set Arthur against me. I suppose she was afraid I might try and get him away from her. It's a bad business. Well, *addio*, and best wishes.'

Oddly enough, Claude was right in his surmise that Miss de Vere might have moved, but Sainty did at last discover her present abode, and arriving there about noon of the following day, found that she had gone to a rehearsal, 'but the gentleman was in.' Sainty was not sorry to find Arthur alone. The boy was at first of course very much on the defensive; the elder brother had to walk most warily among the eggshells of suspicion and susceptibility, but he soon discovered that his coming was not altogether unwelcome. Arthur did not attempt to disguise the fact that he was living with Cynthia; 'he had made her give up her flat, and had taken these rooms for her; they had the whole house, and the people of the house looked after them; it saved the bother of servants; he was answerable for the rent and the housekeeping; naturally he couldn't live at her expense; otherwise she wouldn't take a penny from him, she was very high-minded; it was as much as ever she would let him give her a little present now and then. Anything she made professionally was no business of his; she had gone about a new engagement this morning.'

'But how do you do it? Surely to take a whole house like this on the footing of lodgings is the most expensive arrangement you can make.'

'It ain't done for nothing, I can tell you,' Arthur said ruefully. He was not sorry to unburthen himself a little to his brother. Sainty had had no idea to what extent a young man of family could live on credit in London, for a time at least. By carefully never paying ready money where it was not absolutely necessary, it was astonishing what a lot you could do.

'But what's it all going to lead to?' Sainty asked. 'Do you propose to give up the army, never do anything —just live on here with her from day to day? Even supposing you were me, and had all the money you wanted, would this life satisfy you?'

'I believe you, my boy,' said Arthur heartily.

'It may for a time; it won't, it can't, for long,' Sainty said eagerly. 'And mother? Don't you care about her? Mother's awfully cut up about your not passing your exam. There's another coming on in the autumn; it'll be your last chance. Don't you mean to try?'

Arthur's brow grew dark at the mention of his mother. 'By Jove!' he said, 'you don't know the things she said to me. She *can* let you have it, when she isn't pleased, the mater can.'

'Well, you must admit she had some reason *not* to be pleased,' said Sainty.

'Lots of fellows muff the first time,' said Arthur lamely. 'I've got another try.'

'But are you any more likely to pass the next time? Are you doing a stroke of work for it?' And he narrated to Arthur how it had come to his knowledge that he had not been at Monkton's for weeks. 'I happened on these,' he said, producing the letters he had found in the hall at Belchamber, 'but mother might just as well have found them. She doesn't know yet that you've dropped work altogether, but she must find it out soon. Monkton may write to her any day and ask when you are coming back.'

'Damn it all! I hadn't thought of that.'

'No. You never think of anything half an hour ahead, do you?'

Then Sainty told him how people were talking about him—his grandmother, Aunt Eva, Algy Montgomery (he did not mention Claude). 'Don't you see that in a dozen ways the whole thing may come out to mother at any moment?'

Arthur was very stubborn, took refuge in the reiteration of his devotion to Cynthia and his determination not to be parted from her. Once or twice Sainty almost lost patience.

'You say you *won't* leave her, and you *won't* do this or that or anything you don't choose,' he said with some warmth; 'but what are you going to live on? You own you're up to your ears in debt, and that people are getting impatient. What can you do if mother cuts off your allowance?'

'I'm of age; I've got my own money.'

'Five hundred a year! You can keep up this sort of life so easily on that, can't you? You know you can't touch the principal. I don't suppose the next two years' income would begin to pay what you owe now.'

Arthur looked doubtful; he began to see the weakness of his position. He tried a few platitudes about 'working his fingers to the bone for *her*,' at which Sainty, miserable as he felt, couldn't help laughing.

'You've never done a stroke of work in your life,' he said, 'and you would find it so easy to get employment, wouldn't you? You would be so valuable in a house of business!'

He wisely refrained from any suggestion that the lady's affection might not be proof against the trials of poverty.

Finally, after long argument and entreaty, Arthur was persuaded to say he would go to a new crammer in the country till after the next examination, and would do his best to pass. 'It is no good my trying to work at Monkton's,' he said candidly; 'I should always be bolting back to Cynthia. You can't think how good she is; she's always telling me I ought to work and pass my exams. and please you. Don't try and make me give her up or say I won't have anything more to do with her, or any rot of that sort.'

Sainty, too glad to have carried his point about the work, was ready to promise anything—payment of debts, help in the support of the lady, in short, whatever Arthur liked to demand. 'And first of all,' he said pleadingly, 'you will come down home for a few days before you go to the new place. Poor mother's sore and wretched at the way you've treated her. She doesn't *show* much, but she feels a lot, and you've always been her favourite. Come and be nice to her for a bit before you take up your work again.'

'By Jove! you make me do everything you want,' said Arthur tenderly. Sainty could not help smiling at the thought of how very far this was from being the case, but he was thankful for small mercies. He reflected that he had been lucky in hitting on a propitious moment, when the narrow matters of the house had begun to press rather importunately on Miss de Vere's lover. To grant a favour, accepting the money he needed as a condition, was in every way pleasanter to Arthur than having to sue for help.

Sainty declined to stay and lunch and see Miss de Vere. 'I want to get home this afternoon,' he said. 'Mother'll be so glad to know that you are going to work and do your best to pass; and also that you'll come home for a bit. You haven't been at Belchamber since November, and this is May; I don't think you've ever been away for so long at a stretch before.'

He travelled down to the country that same afternoon with a lighter heart than he had carried for many months, pleased to find he still had some influence over his brother, glad to be reconciled to Claude, and rejoicing in the pleasure he should be able to give his mother in the announcement of Arthur's visit and his promise of industry and reformation. He pondered anxiously on the question how much he need say of the temptations and distractions of London life, to explain Arthur's desire to leave Monkton's and once more try a country crammer's, and concluded that there was no necessity to breathe a word of the nature of the occupation that had kept his brother from working in town. He only trusted other people might be equally reticent. He had telegraphed, before leaving London, to his mother that he would be back to dinner, and as soon as he arrived at Belchamber he was met by a message that she would like to see him at once in her own room. It was in vain that he told himself she was naturally impatient to hear what news he brought; it was with an uneasy foreboding that he approached her door, and he had to pause and brace himself before he summoned courage to turn the handle.

His first glance at his mother confirmed his worst anticipations. She was walking up and down the room, so that her back was towards him as he entered; but the white, set face she turned on him as he closed the door showed him at once that she knew everything. It was terrible to see this silent, dignified woman so ravaged and shaken out of her habitual self-control. Even at that moment he noticed with surprise the curious staginess of her movements and method of speech. It was true, then, that people in times of strong emotion did really behave in this way; and these gestures and phrases which he had always supposed to be pure literary and theatrical conventions derived from something in nature after all.

'So,' she cried, sweeping round upon him, 'I find what I have long suspected was true: my boy, who, if he was thoughtless and a little idle, I thought was a pure-minded, healthy boy, has been degrading himself with loose women; and this has been going on for a year past; it has been common talk; every one has known it; every one but his poor blind idiot of a mother. We must never know anything, of course; our sons may be drifting to perdition, but there is no one who will come and tell a poor woman. People stand by and laugh; I suppose they think it funny; all the godless, indecent, modern books say so. No one, no one will say a word till it's too late, too late to do any good.'

She was in a white heat of rage, tearless, tragic, almost distraught, all the mother and the puritan in her crying out in revolt against the eternal mystery of the flesh, the triumph of the senses in the young male. Yes, in the abstract she knew of it, recognised that men were sinners and full of carnal appetites; but that *her* boy, her child whom she had nursed and tended, whom but a few years back she had held upon her knee, that this pure, bright young creature should voluntarily turn from her to smirch its white raiment in the slough of sensuality—it was not to be believed. If sacred art represented the mother of the one sinless son with seven swords in her heart, what symbol can adequately depict the woes of the mothers of men?

Sainty, with his quick sympathy, divined something of all this in the awful moments that he stood for the first time face to face with his mother. His curious, guarded, sheltered youth, his unhealthy, abnormal perception of other people's feelings, as well as the something feminine and maternal in his relation to his robuster brother, combined to give him a vision of an agony vouchsafed to few of his sex. He saw his mother, his cold, chaste, proud mother, stricken at once in her motherhood, her pride, her chastity, and yet he understood the situation as she could never understand it, as it could never be possible for him to make her understand. His whole heart yearned over her with a pity he seemed to have been specially created to feel in its full force. He made a step towards her with his arms held out, but she turned on him as if she would have struck him.

'And *you*,' she cried, blazing with denunciation, '*you* come to me with a lying pretence of sympathy; you who have talked to me a dozen times of your anxiety about your brother, and seemed at one with me, so unselfishly, nobly distressed about him. You have known of this all along, have aided and abetted him in his infamy. You, who are too sexless and poor a creature to have known his temptations, have helped him in cold blood to his undoing, and with this in your heart have come to me to consult what was best to be done for him. Oh! you were always subtle and sly when you were hardly more than a baby.'

'Mother, mother! for God's sake stop; you don't know what you're saying. What do you mean?'

'Oh! you don't know, do you? Do you deny that you have known this all along? A year ago, didn't you go up and sup and carouse in this creature's company and that of her vile companions? Answer me that. Yes or no? Did you, or did you not? You see, you can't deny it. For all I know, you have been with them often. Is it from her house you have come to me now? to me, the mother of you both!'

'Perhaps I have been wrong, mother, but I don't deserve this at your hands. I have done what I could. I have just come from Arthur. You know he is not very manageable; I have not had an easy part to play. And I have got him to promise to come away; he will come home and——'

'Has he said he won't go back?' She flashed it at him

like a whiplash, and her gesture spoke impatient contempt as he answered—

'No, I can't make him say that, but I hope much from home influences; when we get him here, surrounded by all that will speak to him of his childhood, of all he owes to you——'

She cut him short. 'You temporise with evil. Your arguments are those of the worldly wise.' She was regaining her calm; argument was steadying her, and the old habit of rebuke brought back the judicial tone to her voice. 'There are only two ways,' she said, 'right and wrong. You cannot palter and hold diplomatic parleys with vice. I am willing—I should *like*—to believe that your motives have been good, but I hope you see the harm you have done by your attempts at compromise. Why, oh why,' she broke out again, 'knowing all this, haven't you told *me*? Surely *I* was the person to know, to be consulted on the subject.'

'I wanted to spare you, to save you pain. I may have been mistaken; I haven't seen very clearly what was best, but I hoped to get him away, and that perhaps you might never have the sorrow of knowing. I knew how bitter it would be to you.'

'Oh! this eternal deceit! When will you learn that there can be no question of "not seeing what was best"? My early training of you must have been strangely defective, if at your age you can't tell good from evil. How can it ever be anything but right to tell the truth?'

'It is no new burthen I've had to bear,' Sainty answered, 'to be alone in my knowledge of what was going on. For years I've stood between Arthur and your knowledge of the scrapes he was in.'

'You have, have you! So there has been a conspiracy between you to keep me in the dark. I don't want to be unjust to you; you have not a strong or courageous character; you may have honestly believed you were being kind; but see what has come of your duplicity. Had I known, I might have said a word in season. Arthur would always listen to *me*.'

Sainty thought of the tempests that had raged when

Lady Charmington had said a word in season in the
autumn on a much less ticklish subject, but he forebore to
press this home.

'Well,' his mother resumed, with a certain grim fero-
city, 'I've written now. *I* am not subtle or diplomatic, I
have borne my testimony quite simply and faithfully.'

Sainty's heart sank. He thought of his long and anxious contest, of how hardly at length he had prevailed.
Of his mother's methods of plain dealing he had just had
a specimen; he knew, none better, Arthur's impatience of
the smallest interference, and the spirit in which he would
receive even the tenderest animadversion on Cynthia.

'Mother!' he cried, 'what *have* you said?'

'Said! What should I say? *I* haven't temporised and
beat about the bush. I have said plainly that he was
living in mortal sin, and imperilling his soul; and I've
bidden him leave that woman at once, or never see me
again.'

Sainty sank into a chair and covered his face with his
hands. He saw all he had striven for, all he had effected,
swept away at a touch; he saw too that the mischief was
done, and irrecoverable; there was no good in saying a
word. The despair his attitude expressed must have
touched some tenderer chord in his mother. She came
across to him, and laid her hand, not unkindly, on his
shoulder.

'Pray,' she said sternly. 'Pray to God for help; He
alone can turn this wretched boy from his evil courses.
Vain is the help of man.'

Sainty never knew how he got through the next two
days. He had put a strain upon himself far beyond his
feeble strength; the two railway journeys would in themselves have told on him, but the unresting hurrying
hither and thither in London, the emotion of meeting
Claude again, the terrible nervous excitement of his long
argument with his brother, and then, on the top of all,
when he was worn out in body and mind, the shock of
seeing his mother as he had never seen her, the bitter
disappointment of finding all he had done rendered
useless at a blow, crushed him utterly. He was glad to

take refuge in physical stupor and exhaustion from the bitterness of his own reflections.

In the morning of the third day, when he was gradually coming back to a sense of what had happened, his mother came to his room with an open letter in her hand. Her face was grey and drawn, and she seemed suddenly to have become an old woman. Her voice was hollow and unnaturally quiet. 'Read that,' she said, and tossed the letter on to his bed. Then raising her hand, which shook as she held it up, 'I curse him,' she said, still in that same even, horrible tone. 'Remember that you have heard me curse my son'; and she went slowly out of the room.

With trembling hand Sainty drew the paper to him; he recognised Arthur's schoolboy scrawl. The letter was meant to be very dignified.

'My dear mother,' the boy wrote, 'I have received your letter; I will not notice your insults to a woman I love. You say I am living in sin. Very well, then—so be it. I will do so no longer. I came of age last week and am my own master, and curse me if I'll take it from you or any one. I have to announce to you that I was married yesterday at the registry office in Mount Street to Miss Cynthia de Vere.' He had begun another sentence, 'Till you are prepared,' but apparently thinking anything more would weaken the effect of what he had said, he had run his pen through the words. The letter wound up, 'I am your son,

'ARTHUR WELLESLEY CHAMBERS.'

CHAPTER XIII

No one can live at the height of great crises. After the storm, when the wind has sobbed itself to sleep, the sun comes peeping shyly to count the damage done, the draggled, flattened flowers begin to lift themselves and look about, the fallen trees are sawn up and carted away.

Sainty might take to his bed, and lie there groaning at the wreck of all his hopes and plans for his brother. Lady Charmington might say dreadful violent things, and indulge in the cheap gratification of cursing her son. But sooner or later Sainty must get up and dress, must come downstairs and see the agent and the butler, and his mother must wash her hot eyes and flatten down her hair, must order dinner, and scold the maids, and sit at the head of the table as though nothing were amiss. And it is just this that saves us from madness; the more we have to do, the less time we can afford for sitting down with our sorrow in darkened rooms, the better for us. Kings and business men, and the labouring classes generally, whose work must be done no matter what happens, have a great advantage over leisured mourners. Sainty crept out, battered and disheartened, to face a new world which yet had a great deal in common with the old one. He had to provide himself with a new set of motives, desires, objects in life. But outwardly nothing was changed. The very book he had put down when he left the library to find the letters for Arthur in crossing the hall, was still on the same table with his paperknife laid between the leaves to mark the place.

He never knew how his mother had come by her information. Sometimes he thought of Lady Eccleston, sometimes of the duchess. Her reference to the supper and his own presence at it had suggested a sickening suspicion of a new treachery on the part of Claude, but he finally decided that this was unlikely. A dozen other people might have seen him going in, and gossiped about his presence. Claude had mentioned that he was supping with Johnny Trafford; it might have come round through his Aunt Susie. He did not want to think any worse of his cousin than he need, and he did Claude the justice to recollect that if he never shrank from doing a mean action when he had anything to gain by it, mere purposeless mischief was not in his traditions; indeed, he would rather take trouble to keep things straight. He was not one of those who turned explosive truths loose in the world—who 'thought people ought to know'; on the contrary, on general principles he was all for people *not* knowing, especially awkward facts about their own relatives. On the whole, the causes of the catastrophe seemed to Sainty far less important than the consideration of what, under the circumstances, was left for him to do for his brother.

Lady Charmington, on his screwing up courage to ask if she had any views on the subject, forbade him peremptorily to mention Arthur's name to her.

Lord Firth said the young ass had done for himself irretrievably, but agreed that he couldn't be left to starve. He was much inclined to think, however, that the younger brother's £500 a year, which was all to which he had a legal claim under his grandfather's will, was quite enough for him. 'If you give him any more, he'll only chuck it away.'

'Uncle Cor,' Sainty said, 'what's the good of talking like that? You know as well as I do that Arthur will never live on £500 a year. I see nothing to be gained by pretending that he will. *I* could easily, but *he* never will. And do you suppose I could serenely sit in this huge house, and spend £50,000 a year, and know my brother was in want?'

'Whatever you give him, you may be sure he'll spend double,' said Lord Firth; 'so I should recommend your not beginning with too large a sum; you had better keep something for the debts you will assuredly be called on to pay from time to time.'

'I'd so much rather give him a decent allowance to start with, one that he *could* live on and *not* get into debt.'

'You rebuked me just now,' his uncle replied blandly, 'for not looking facts in the face. Might I suggest that the aspiration you have just put forward is based on a hypothesis quite as visionary as my proposal that Arthur should live on £500 a year.'

Sainty was forced to admit the contention. He wrote, therefore, a letter from which he tried as far as possible to banish all useless recrimination, offering to pay his brother's debts if he would send him the bills, and to allow him a thousand a year; to which Arthur in due course returned a most characteristic reply, beginning with a magnificent declaration that he wanted nothing of people who were not prepared to recognise or receive his wife, and repetitions of his readiness to 'work his fingers to the bone for her,' and ending with a bitter complaint of his brother's meanness in not making him a larger allowance. In due course, however, the bills arrived, and made Sainty gasp; nor did he find when he placed the first quarter's allowance to his brother's credit that it was returned to his own.

There is a certain repose in the fact that the worst which one has dreaded has happened. To some temperaments anxiety is far harder to bear than sorrow, and the mother who killed her baby because she was so dreadfully afraid that it would die, presented only an extreme case of a not uncommon frame of mind.

The sun shone, the birds sang, the early and late summer were not less glorious than usual on the great, well-kept lawns and terraces of Belchamber. The places that have known us do not put on mourning for our departure unless it withdraws from them some fostering care, and Arthur's effect upon a garden was mostly written in broken branches and footprints on the flowerbeds. When people have been more than usually disappointing, we turn with an added tenderness to things, and Sainty, whose regard for his beautiful inheritance had always been sentimentally great, began to take a more intelligent interest in the possessions he had been so anxious to renounce. Since it seemed that he could not shake off his responsibilities, he would embrace them with fervour. He found himself wandering about the great historic house and eagerly learning all he could of the treasures it contained; and he started to rearrange and catalogue the huge library, which had been much neglected and had got sadly out of order. So on finding this a task utterly beyond him without expert help, he imported as librarian a young *protégé* of Gerald Newby from the library of his college, with whom he spent long mornings exploring chests and closets where dusty folios had been ruthlessly heaped together and left to rats and spiders. They made the most wonderful finds of whole boxes of manuscripts, family papers, parchments, letters. Among other things, they discovered one day the original plans on which the grounds had been laid out, signed by Perrault, and though there had been many subsequent alterations, Sainty was delighted to find how much the main lines had remained intact. The orangery with its enclosed garden, the bowling-green by the canal with its formal pleached alleys, and the whole system of waterworks, ponds, cascades, and fountains, were all more or less as the great Frenchman had designed them. Here and there his long, sweeping vistas across the park had been cut by stupid little plantations of conifers, coverts for game, and these Sainty was eager to remove, reopening the grand perspectives. He planned, too, to restore the dignified simplicity of the forecourt, with its great oval expanse of turf and five statues of Flora and the Seasons, according to the original drawing. The statues had been removed and dotted without method up and down the long shrubbery, the great wrought-iron grille and gates carried away to one of the lodges, the turf broken up with flower-beds and terracotta baskets. It would be delightful to put everything back in its proper place.

To these and many other schemes his mother lent an indulgent ear. She had that curious instinctive taste in gardens and houses which so many of her countrywomen combine with an utter absence of the æsthetic sense in all that concerns the fine arts or their own personal adornment; she was quite incapable of real sympathy with his joy in musty old documents and letters, but alterations in the garden were more in her line, and if she did not always think what he proposed an improvement, at least it was natural and normal that a man should take pleasure in his own possessions, instead of wishing to give them away and live in the East End. Sainty consulted her about everything, not merely from long habit of deference, but from real respect for her judgment.

A more powerful bond of union than any alterations in house or garden were certain schemes for the benefit of their fellow-creatures. In their more radical youth Lady Charmington and her brother had started many such, a co-operative dairy-farm, settlements of model cottages, schools, benefit clubs, and a system of old-age pensions that should not lessen the self-respect of the recipients. Sainty's interest in all these matters was no new thing, though he had formerly rather carefully repressed it. Now he took them up with a zeal not even second to Lady Charmington's own. It was not to be expected that he and she should be always in absolute agreement, but on the whole they worked surprisingly well together. There were concessions on both sides. On his they had the ease of long habit, and he was astonished by a quite new tendency in his mother to consult his wishes and defer to his opinions.

Though she never mentioned his brother's name, Sainty had a conviction that she knew by some means or other what he had done for Arthur, and was silently grateful to him for defying her resentment. She helped him to establish himself in the west pavilion, now become un-interruptedly his own, and to arrange his few personal possessions that had come from Cambridge. The old schoolroom became his study; he turned Claude's room into a workroom and place for extra books, with a writing-table for the librarian if he wanted him near him; but Arthur's chamber was left by a tacit agreement as it had always been, and sometimes Sainty would wander in there and look disconsolately on the sporting prints, the school groups, the faded blue cap dangling from a nail, the old Eton bureau decorated by a red-hot poker with its owner's name, a very large 'Chamb' and a very small 'ers,' owing to the artist's miscalculation of the space at his command. Sainty did not want Claude in the old schoolboy quarters, and explained to that accommodating person that he needed more space for his books, and thought his cousin would be more comfortable in one of the many guest-rooms.

By and by other people besides Claude began to occupy these apartments again. There were no regular parties during the year after Arthur's marriage, but gradually Lady Charmington took to asking a few people at a time; his Aunt Susan and her sons, the Rugbies, the Eccles-tons, Alice de Lissac and her step-daughters. His mother even suggested that Sainty should invite some of his own friends, and Newby came several times and was satisfactorily interested in his many undertakings.

'I like to see you taking your proper place,' he said complacently, with the air of an artist contemplating his own work; but the old spring of grateful devotion no longer gushed responsive to Newby's lightest word of commendation. To begin to grow away from a friend is a terrible experience, and few things are harder than to keep up the pretence that no such change is taking place; but when the friend in question has been less the equal comrade than the Gamaliel at whose feet one has sat, the strain of preserving the old attitude is increased to infinity. There is no furniture so encumbering as a fallen idol; we trip over it a dozen times a day. Already the blush of shame had tinged the corner of Sainty's smile at Parsons' lampoon, and now he was constantly to experience similar compunctions. Gerald took a great fancy to Claude and held forth to him unsparingly on many subjects.

'Your cousin is a real Prince Charming,' he would say to Sainty; 'very refreshing, and such quaint views of things, without the university flavour one gets so sick of; he is of immense use to me.'

Morland listened to Newby's lucubrations with an air of grave sympathy, but made fun of him behind his back. Sainty was exasperated all round; he hated Gerald's making an ass of himself, hated Claude's gibes at his expense, hated himself for being amused by them against his will. Cissy Eccleston, on the contrary, was always ecstatically giggling at the young man's witticisms.

The Ecclestons had begun to be a great deal at Belchamber; Lady Charmington seemed to have endless philanthropic projects to discuss with her friend, which needed the latter's constant presence.

'I have asked Lady Eccleston to run down for a few days,' became a recognised formula; 'I want to ask her about the G.F.S. meeting'; or, 'She has got to consult me about the concert at Middlesex House for Lady Stepney's Home for Inebriates; she wants the duchess to be a patroness.' And Lady Eccleston 'ran down,' always taking care to thank Sainty effusively for 'letting her come'; 'I had heaps to talk over with your mother, and it saves such a lot of tiresome letter-writing; it *is* good of you to have us.' In Lady Eccleston's train came Lady Eccleston's daughter, and sometimes a son or two. Sainty had come to have quite a friendly feeling for Tommy; he was such a good soul, so reposefully commonplace, and so unfeignedly happy and grateful at Belchamber.

'You don't know what it is to a chap to get out of that damned London,' he said fervently. Poor Tommy, not being very good at examinations, had had to bow his neck under the yoke of a house of business, for which, after the manner of English boys, his whole previous training had most elaborately unfitted him. Sainty was glad to give him the pleasures which would be no pleasures to himself, and Tommy responded with a sort of wondering gratitude made up in about equal parts of admiration and contempt. Once he rather tactlessly tried to express his regret over Arthur. The Ecclestons were at the moment the only guests, and Sainty said something about its being very dull for him having to go out shooting alone.

'Oh, that's all right,' said Thomas; 'though, of course, I miss your brother. Awfully good chap, your brother. I was deuced sorry he went and muckered the whole show like that. Hard luck on all of you.'

Sainty winced, but he liked the boy for liking Arthur, and silently pressed his arm.

'Beg pardon,' said Tommy, getting very red. 'Stupid of me to say that. The mater would comb my hair if she knew.'

Lady Eccleston indeed was almost distressingly tactful on the subject, stepping round it on elaborate tiptoe, as some people go about a death-chamber.

She and Cissy were full of interest in all Sainty's undertakings. They watched with breathless excitement the works for reinstating the grille and the statues, and allowed themselves to be patiently bored by long readings from some of the old documents which Sainty was editing for publication by the Historical Society.

When there were no other young people in the house,

Sainty felt it no less than his duty as host to try and entertain the young lady, and she was always ready to accompany him on his drives about the place and visits to the
outlying farms and cottages. He thought of himself so
little in the light of a young man for whom a girl could
possibly entertain a warmer feeling than friendship, that
it never occurred to him to imagine any possibility of
objection to these long expeditions, practically *tête-à-tête*,
with only a stolid little groom as chaperon; and indeed
the two mammas smiled very indulgently on them as they
drove off. He showed Cissy all over the co-operative
dairy-farm and explained the system of its working, and
if her remarks did not display a very thorough grasp of
its aims, she listened with the politest attention to his
explanations. Whether the two widowed mothers, when
left alone, confined their conversation exclusively to topics
of external benevolence may be doubted; but anyway
they always seemed to have plenty to talk about, and to
be quite able to spare their children; and meanwhile
Sainty drove along the avenues of the park, or the roads
and lanes of the countryside, with Cissy tucked in beside
him and chattering like a sparrow. The girl had a certain
sense of humour, strictly limited in scope, but diverting as
far as it went. It is true that it mostly took the form of
personal ridicule, and Sainty was rather scandalised at
the frequency with which it was turned upon her mother,
but he couldn't help laughing at some of the revelations.
'And, after all,' he thought, 'she would not make fun of
her if she did not love her; it is the light-hearted thoughtlessness of a child.'

'Mamma is very low to-day,' Cissy said, bursting with
laughter. 'You know, she takes the *Exchange and Mart*,
and is always swopping something or other. I don't think
she does very good business, but she likes the fun of
writing to people she don't know, and the bargaining.
Well, she's got an old black silk gown, quite good still, it
was a good silk; she bought it at Woolland's at a sale (she
goes to all the sales), but she's worn it three seasons and
it's old fashioned, and every creature we know is sick of
the sight of it, so she has been trying to get rid of it in the

Exchange, and what do you think she was offered for it this morning? A goat! Think of us in Chester Square with a goat! Tommy says we can keep it in the back-yard and he'll milk it, and it will save the dairy bill; but mamma is not amused.' And Cissy went off into peals of laughter in which Sainty could not help joining.

This power of making him laugh was the great secret of his pleasure in her society. At most times they might not have had much in common, but after all he had been through, her irresponsible frivolity was very restful. His morbid conscientiousness seemed overstrained and absurd by comparison, and he was ashamed to be frightened by life in the presence of a creature who took it so lightly, displaying such a careless front to the slings and arrows of a quite insufficient fortune. With more humour than delicacy she gave him glimpses of many of her parent's little economies and contrivances. 'I've got to be turned out smart, you know, and we give awfully nice teas, lots of teas—even the little Sunday dinners ain't badly done; but no one dropping in unexpectedly to lunch—no thank you! and if she and I dine out it's cold mutton for the boys and none too much of it. You're awfully good to Tommy; it's just heaven for him being here, poor boy!'

'It's delightful being able to give any pleasure to any one. I have never been able to make any one happy, though I've tried.'

'Oh, come, cheer up! I assure you, you are giving a lot of pleasure to the Eccleston family at this moment; it really is ripping of you asking the whole family. Did you know, by the way, that your mother has said the two boys could come next week when Harrow breaks up, and that we might all stay over Christmas?'

'Yes, of course I knew, seeing that it was I who suggested it. I thought if you had your little brothers here it would not be so dull for you, and my friend Newby will be here, and Claude——' The vivid colour came and went so quickly under the fair skin that Sainty could not be sure if it were Claude's name that called up the faint flush. It might have been caused by the pleasure Cissy's next words expressed.

'Oh, it was you! How angelic of you! As for me, I don't think my young brothers add much to my enjoyment of life, nor I to theirs; besides, I am quite happy in this dear, beautiful place, and going all about your improvements and things with you is so jolly; but I'm awfully grateful to you all the same, and you will be more in mamma's good books than ever; and with mamma, you must know, "good books" is not a mere phrase. She has a red book in which she enters all her friends according to what they have done for her; not an ordinary visitor's-list. She puts down "Lady So-and-So—asked us to her squash, but gave a dance and did not ask us"; or "Mrs. Snooks—dined with us, but didn't ask us back: Mem.—not again till she does," and so on. It's capital reading; if I can get hold of it some day I'll show it to you.'

'Do you mind if we get out at the end of the shrubbery and walk home?' Sainty asked; 'I want to see how they are getting on with moving one of the statues.'

'Oh, do let's! I should love to see Spring (isn't she Spring, the fat woman with the sort of trumpet with the apples? Oh no, of course, Autumn) swinging in mid-air. They had just got the thing rigged up yesterday afternoon when I walked my parent round there. I do hope they haven't got her into the cart yet.'

They visited poor Autumn, whose head was reposing in rather a ghastly manner in a heap of straw on a trolly, while her trunk and cornucopia hung perilously from the pulleys, and her legs still graced a florid Dutch pedestal.

'Isn't she sweet?' Cissy said. 'I do think it's so clever of you putting them all back where they belong. I should never have had the energy to take all this trouble once they were here and established.'

'The worst of it is,' Sainty admitted, 'that now the thing is decreed, I feel almost sacrilegious tearing them from the places where I have always known them. If I had known what a business it was going to be, and what a lot it would cost, I should never have had the courage to undertake it.'

'It must be lovely to have lots of money to spend,' Cissy interjected almost under her breath.

'What I can't understand,' Sainty went on, 'is the frame of mind of the person who spent such sums on *destroying* a good design; he must have disturbed his own early associations as much as I am doing, yet without the same reason for doing so.'

'I suppose he thought he was improving things, just as you do,' said Cissy cheerfully. 'All the things people give such heaps for nowadays are what our grandmothers put in the garrets. Probably the people who come after you will think Faith, Hope, and Charity, or whoever the ladies are, would look much nicer in the park, or on the roof, or at the bottom of the big pond.'

'The people who came after him!' The phrase struck cold upon his ear. Who was there to 'come after' him? Lady Arthur? Good heavens! Sainty shuddered to think what *her* notions of the æsthetic might involve. He had a fleeting vision of Belchamber rearranged according to the standard of taste suggested by the plush piano drapery so fatally baptized in champagne.

This question of who was to enter into his labours and gather the fruits of all that he was doing contained within itself the germ of paralysis. The works for the outward beautifying of the place were the smallest of his preoccupations; but what would his successor care for all his other hopes, his projects for bettering the condition of the 'poor about his lands'? The thought that whatever he might effect would pass with his own feeble and precarious life, and leave no trace behind it, was one of the sharpest darts in the quiver of his familiar fiend.

They walked back to the house almost in silence, Sainty revolving these unhappy thoughts, Cissy, for once, not chattering. Sainty stole an occasional glance at his companion, wondering at her unusual quiet. Her eyes had a far-away look, which gave a great sweetness to her face; he feared to intrude on some tender maiden thoughts which he felt tolerably sure had little to do with him or his concerns. As they came out upon the lawn they saw Lady Charmington approaching from the village, bearing a small, tin-lined basket in which she conveyed cold slabs of pudding to some of her dependants. Cissy waved her muff and ran forward, insisting on relieving her from the burthen which she was perfectly capable of carrying on one stalwart finger. Miss Eccleston's manner to her hostess was the perfection of pretty girlish deference and service, and Lady Charmington's grim countenance relaxed at sight of her.

'Have you had a pleasant drive?' she asked. 'I hope Sainty has taken good care of you.'

'Lord Belchamber has been delightful,' Cissy answered, 'and shown me all sorts of interesting things. We came back by the shrubbery, to look at one of the poor ladies who has had her head cut off. Now I must go and tell mamma we are back. I will leave your basket in the little hall for you, dear Lady Charmington, I know just where it lives.'

Lady Charmington turned to Sainty as the girl skipped away. 'Give me your arm, my son, I am a little tired,' she said. Now Sainty was well aware that his mother was never tired, and would rather have died than own it if she had been. 'Good heavens, mother, aren't you well?' he asked in alarm.

'Oh yes, dear, quite well; but I am getting an old woman. It is a good thing that you have begun to look after things yourself. What you ought to do for me now is to give me a nice young daughter-in-law to look after *me*, and some dear little grandchildren to pet and spoil.'

Sainty was startled; it seemed almost as if Lady Charmington were answering the thoughts that had oppressed him on the way home. He smiled parenthetically at the vision of his capable, energetic mother in the character of the feeble old lady cared for by pious children; nor did he see her 'petting and spoiling' any one.

'I am not likely to marry,' he said. 'With the best will in the world, I might find it difficult. Fairy princesses do not marry the yellow dwarf!'

Lady Charmington's unwonted mildness fell from her miraculously. 'You are almost bound to marry—*now*,' she said, the last word pronounced with a sudden sharp inspiration that told how much the reference cost her.

'Dear mother,' Sainty said gently, 'who could possibly fill your place here? Who would do all that you do, or do it nearly as well?'

'I can't live for ever. As I tell you, I am getting old; already I can't do all that I could. The thought of that woman in my place gives me fever. Do you want her to succeed me—do you?' And Sainty felt the hand on his arm tighten to a clutch.

'We have both got to die before that happens, mother. If you are not in your first youth, you are very strong, and if I am not a tower of strength, at least I have youth on my side; we may both have more vitality than many younger or stronger people.' Alas! that his chances of long life, once so fiercely resented, should have come to be the buckler on which he counted to interpose against the speedy succession of his brother, which in those days he had so ardently desired!

CHAPTER XIV

IT was natural that with other people in the house Sainty should see less of Cissy; he told himself so several times a day, yet the thought was not altogether a pleasant one that she only welcomed his society as a refuge from solitude or Lady Eccleston. The frost had put a stop to the works in front of the house, and a bad chill and sharp attack of neuralgia warned Sainty to discontinue his drives until milder weather. Skating on the big pond became the amusement of the moment, a pastime in which his lameness prevented his joining. Gerald Newby, in a straw hat, spent hours upon the ice, and fell down with Spartan perseverance in his determination to accomplish figures of eight.

'Why is it a necessary part of the make-up of the good young man to wear a straw hat in the winter?' Claude asked; 'I notice that serious youths always do, curates and schoolmasters. Is it a mark of asceticism, as being obviously not the comfortable thing to do, or to give the impression that their brains are overheated with excess of thought?'

Claude, who skated, as he did everything else that he attempted, with elegance and precision, had undertaken to instruct Cissy in the art, and Sainty had to watch them gliding about together, both her hands tightly clasped in his, and even a sustaining arm occasionally flung out when the maiden was more than usually wobbly. It was all perfectly natural; there was not the smallest ground for objecting. Lady Susan Trafford and her sons, Claude's mother, Newby, and Cissy's three brothers were all on the ice the whole time; the pond, though a good-sized sheet of water, was visible from end to end; there were no corners or islands behind which the flirtatiously-inclined could disappear; yet the sight of those perpetually clasped hands became a constant irritation to Belchamber, and it was quite vain for him to reiterate that with her mother and brothers in the house, it was less than no business of his how Miss Eccleston amused herself. 'Had it been any one else but Claude,' he thought, 'he should not have minded.'

It soon became evident to him that he was not alone in the apprehension with which he watched the growing intimacy between Cissy and his cousin. Lady Eccleston, it was plain, viewed it with quite as little favour as he did. Swathed in furs, and with a blue nose, the poor lady fluttered on the bank, in a manner strongly suggestive of a hen whose ducklings have taken to the water. One day, having invited him to take her for a walk, while the hoar frost crackled under their feet in the winding mazes of the shrubbery, she quite unexpectedly unburthened herself to him on the subject.

'I can talk to you, dear Lord Belchamber,' she said, 'as I would to an older man; you are so good, so pure, so unlike the others, and I am so sorely in need of advice.'

'Good gracious! Lady Eccleston,' said Sainty, with hypocritical surprise, 'what's the matter? How can I help you?'

'I'm so afraid you'll think it strange of me to talk to you

on such a subject, but, as I say, you are not like an ordinary young man; you have always been so serious for your age, and then, you know your cousin better than any one; you have been boys together.'

'Claude?'

'Yes, Mr. Morland. How kind of you to understand and help me out; but you *are* so sympathetic, more like a woman in some ways, I always say.'

Sainty was only partially pleased by this equivocal compliment. 'What about Claude?' he asked.

'I will be quite frank with you; you won't misunderstand me, I know. A mother's solicitude; and, after all, what can be more natural? Left so early a widow, and with these young ones to guide and bring up. If my dear husband had lived it would all have been so different; but I have no one to turn to. Tom is a mere boy, really no more help than the young ones. Ah! Lord Belchamber, children are a sad responsibility.'

'Yours seem to be very good ones,' said Sainty.

'You *do* think so? I *am* so glad. Yes, I think they are, but of course I feel a mother is not a judge—her great love blinds her; but they *are* good children, I must say they give me very little trouble. Only the high spirits of youth are always a pitfall. And Cissy—she's a dear, good girl, and we haven't a secret from one another; we are more like sisters. Yet it is for her that I sometimes feel the greatest anxiety.'

'Yes?'

'Some people think her pretty; again, of course, my partiality prevents my judging; but lots of people have told me she was pretty. *Do* you think her pretty?'

'I should think no one could help admiring Miss Eccleston,' said Sainty.

'Ah! that's it. There's no denying it. I can't help seeing it; why should I pretend I don't? The girl does have a lot of admiration; I *do* hope it won't turn her head. She's as good as gold, but London's an awful place. I've done all I can to keep her from all knowledge of evil, and so far, thank God! the child is a thoroughly healthy-minded, pure girl. Doesn't she strike you so?'

'Oh, certainly; but what——'

'You were going to say "What has all this to do with Mr. Morland?" You won't mind my talking to you quite frankly? it *is* such a comfort. Well—any one can see your cousin admires Cissy immensely. And of course she's pleased by his attentions. I must admit he is charming; but *is* he the kind of young man a mother would like to give her daughter to?'

'Have you any reason to suppose your daughter cares at all for Claude?'

'Oh no, no, no! don't misunderstand me; I'm quite *sure* she doesn't. But girls are so thoughtless; the more innocent they are, the more imprudent. If I so much as try to venture a hint to her to be a little more circumspect, she says, "I don't know what you *mean*, mother," and she looks at me in such a way I'm quite ashamed, I really am.'

'Of course Miss Eccleston is all that is delicate and refined, but if you are certain she does not at all return my cousin's partiality——'

'Oh, of that I'm *sure*; she's such a mirror of candour—if she had the very smallest feeling she would have told me—but your cousin is most fascinating, that I must admit, and she *might* get to think she cared. Now, I ask you, who know him so well, *is* he just the sort of man in whose hands a very pure-minded girl with high ideals would be happy? I know my child so well; if she were ever to find out that the man she married had been at all fast, it would simply kill her. And the young men of the day *are* so wicked, or so they tell me. One can't help hearing things *de temps en temps* in London, no matter how much one hates gossip, and *no* one hates it as I do.'

Sainty thought he knew some one who hated it at least as much as her ladyship. He was wondering what Claude really felt for Cissy. In the light of their conversation about Miss Winston, he found it difficult to believe that his cousin was courting a portionless girl with a view to marriage; but he could not catechise him as to his intentions towards every young woman with whom he ever saw him, especially after the scanty encouragement he had met with on that occasion. Were he to answer Lady Eccleston truthfully, there could be little doubt of what he must say; but the thought of acting secret police in this fashion was not agreeable to him.

'You must see——' he began.

'Oh! I do, I do,' cried the lady; 'I see *just* how unpleasant it would be for you to have to say a word against your cousin, and, dear Lord Belchamber, do let me say how much it makes me like you, though to be sure, that wasn't necessary, for I've always said you were my ideal young man. Cissy and I have so often agreed in talking over some of the young men we know, Tom's friends, and the men we see at balls, and others, that there is *no* one quite like you.'

'No, I'm well aware that I am not like other young men——'

'Ah! be thankful you're not, dear Lord Belchamber; the young men of the day, I'm *sorry* to say, are not nice. And thank you *so* much for listening to me so patiently, and telling me *just* what I wanted to know. I can't tell you the comfort this little talk has been to me. You see, I have no one to turn to, and I do think it so sweet of you not to want to say a word against Mr. Morland.'

Sainty wondered a little afterwards just what the information was for which Lady Eccleston was so grateful, for though the interview was nominally sought with a view to consulting him, while he had received a number of interesting confidences, he could not recollect having expressed any opinion at all. Lady Eccleston, however, had apparently found him a satisfactory counsellor, for the next day she returned to the subject.

'You remember what I said to you yesterday about Cissy and Mr. Morland,' she whispered, dropping down beside him on one of the seats in the winter-garden after lunch. 'I'm more than ever convinced she doesn't care for him; it is foolish of me to take fright as I do, but there is just one point I *do* want to put myself right with you about. I was so afraid afterwards you might think—and yet—no, come to think of it, I'm sure you wouldn't; but I should like just to say that I hope you *didn't* think what

I said had *any*thing to do with Mr. Morland being poor, or what the world would call not a good match. As long as he was a good man, and a man of principle, and some one in her own *monde*, I've always said I didn't care who my girl married. No one can say I'm mercenary. My poor dear husband and I married on next to nothing, and there never was a happier marriage. I wish you had known Sir Thomas, you would have loved him.'

Sainty expressed a suitable regret at having missed the pleasure of Sir Thomas's acquaintance. 'Some people,' Lady Eccleston continued pensively, 'some people think I'm wrong. Only last week a dear friend of mine said to me that it was all very well to despise money, but that other things being equal, it was a great power, and that in this age of the world it was impossible to get on without it. I said "You may be right, dear, and I don't deny that for my children's sake I've sometimes wished I had a little more of it, but money isn't everything. It can't give happiness."' And her ladyship raised her eyes to a statuette of Venus in a cluster of palms, with the expression of a dying martyr regarding a crucifix.

'No, Lord Belchamber, if a man's a gentleman and a good man, for me, he may be as poor as—as he pleases—*that* isn't what I fear; but though Cissy seems such a child, she has a very strongly marked character, and intensely deep feelings, and were she to marry a man she could not respect, she would never know a moment's happiness. What she needs above all is a man of strict principles, of high ideals, and with a pure mind and life, and where is such a man to be found? But forgive me for boring you with all this; it can't interest you. George, dear,' to her second son, who passed at the moment, 'are you going skating? Do you know where Cissy is? Is she going with you? I want to speak to her'; and with a little nod of good understanding to her host, Lady Eccleston skipped with her usual amazing agility off the ottoman, and departed with her arm twined about the boy's waist.

Belchamber pondered much on these conversations. 'The ordinary clever man,' he thought, 'who prides himself on knowledge of human nature, would be sure that Lady Eccleston was trying to "hook him" for her daughter, and would, as usual, be wrong. If the lady is not a monument of wisdom, at least I give her credit for not being so obvious as *that*. No; she is treating me, as women always do, as a creature removed from all thoughts and hopes of love, a sexless being set apart like the priest in Catholic countries to be the safe recipient of tender confidences in which he can have no personal concern.' Still he sometimes dreamed (as who may not at twenty-three?) of what life might come to mean if Love should breathe on its dry bones and bid them live; if it were possible that some maid more discerning than her fellows should see with the eye of the soul, beneath his dreary, unattractive exterior, the wealth of love that was waiting like the sleeping princess for the awakening kiss! 'Perhaps I might even have the luck of the unhappy monster in *L'Homme qui rit*, and meet with a blind girl!' Hideousness, even deformity, was no bar to the love of woman, that he knew. He thought of Wilkes, of Mirabeau, of many others who had been more passionately loved than your pretty fellows. Deep in his heart he knew his real disability; it was not his lack of personal beauty, nor even his lameness that was the bar, but his miserable inherent effeminacy. A man might be never so uncouth, so that the manhood in him cried imperiously to the other sex and commanded surrender. 'More like a woman in some ways.' Had not Lady Eccleston said it? There lay the sting. And yet—who could tell? Might not a miracle be worked? Might he not some day find himself face to face with this stupendous, unhoped-for happiness?

He wrote many poems at this time, poems not addressed to any concrete personality, but to that 'not impossible she,' the divine abstraction who should recognise and respond to what lay hidden in his heart. He felt very sure that Cissy Eccleston, with her frank, pagan enjoyment of life and the moment, was not the lady of his dreams. Those little curved lips of hers might seek the red mouth of a lover, but would never bestow the heroic salute that should cleanse the leper, or restore his true form to the enchanted beast. Yet, forasmuch as he had seen so few girls, his Beatrice sometimes came to him clad in something of the outward semblance, the virginal candour and freshness of this sojourner within his gates. He found himself wondering if Lady Eccleston's account of her daughter's ermine-like recoil from all contact with moral impurity had any foundation in fact, or whether this fancy portrait of the girl dying of a stain on the premarital robe of her husband were not as purely fallacious as some of his mother's theories about Arthur. It had been borne in on him that mothers were not always infallible in what concerned their children's characters; he was farther rendered a little sceptical as to the young lady's excessive innocence by some of her own conversation, and notably a certain curiosity displayed with what seemed to him a lack of delicacy on more than one occasion as to his unfortunate sister-in-law.

'Of course one knew all those girls by sight,' she remarked, with engaging candour, 'but I'm not sure just *which* was Cynthia de Vere; it *was* the tall one with the beautiful legs and the rather big mouth, wasn't it? I told Tom so, and he said it wasn't; but I'm sure I'm right, ain't I?'

On another occasion she startled him by the plainest possible reference to the relations of Charley Hunter and Miss Baines.

'I didn't know young ladies knew anything about such things,' Sainty said rather severely.

'They do now,' said Cissy, 'whatever they used to; but I suspect they always knew more than they let on. There was a friend of mine who married Teddie Hersham last season; I was one of her bridesmaids; she was awfully proud of taking him away from Totty Seymour; she used to boast of it to all her friends.'

'I can't bear to hear you talk like that,' Sainty answered. 'It would give people who didn't know you such a wrong idea of you.'

'I'll try not to, if you don't like it; but it isn't easy for me to pretend to be different to what I am.'

'I don't want you to. I only ask you to be true to yourself, and not say things that I am sure are quite foreign to you for the sake of startling people.'

'Well, I must own I do enjoy shocking *you*. You are so awfully proper, you know; but why should you care what I do or say?' she added, with a little arch glance.

'I don't know, I'm sure, but I do. I suppose I—I like you too well not to mind your behaving in a way I don't think worthy of you.'

What wonder if Miss Eccleston found Claude Morland a more amusing companion than his cousin? Sainty was the first to admit the likelihood. He was well aware that Claude would not have offended her by championing her innocence against herself, or have made any difficulties about gratifying her girlish curiosity as to that other world of which she knew so little. The thought of Morland's long, deft fingers delicately removing the bloom from this young creature irritated him unaccountably. Oh no! it was not jealousy; that, again, was what the stupid, knowing people would think; he could never care for this empty-headed little thing in that way, and knew only too well how much more impossible it was that *she* should care for *him*. Only, he did not want her to suffer, nor to coarsen and deteriorate.

He was revolving some such thoughts as these as he walked by himself one day, perhaps a week after his conversation with Lady Eccleston, when he was startled by loud cries from the neighbourhood of the pond, and made all the haste he was able in that direction. The air was certainly milder; there had been unmistakable premonitions of a thaw. He remembered the discussion at breakfast as to whether the ice would still bear, and the eager affirmations of the young Traffords and Ecclestons that it was as sound as ever. Bertie Trafford and Randolph Eccleston had been sliding all over it, and even had stamped in places to see if it would give way; but Mr. Danford, the agent, had come in in the course of the morning to say that it had a damp look about the edges he did not like, and to advise them to keep off it. Sainty had not been greatly interested; the pond, though large, was mostly artificial, and nowhere more than three or four feet deep, and if the boys liked to risk a wetting, it did not seem to him to matter much. Now his thoughts flew to Cissy; he wondered he had not thought of her before, and the next moment he turned a corner, and found himself one of an excited group, the centre of which was Claude, hatless, dishevelled, and very wet, bearing in his arms the inanimate form of Miss Eccleston. Her eyes were closed, and every trace of colour was gone from her face; her lips were blue, and the water ran in streams from her clothing. The boys crowded round, all talking at once, and making a number of foolish suggestions.

'Is she drowned? Is she dead?' wailed little Randolph, and was sternly bidden by George not to be an ass unless he wanted to get kicked.

'What is the matter? What has happened?' asked Sainty, and was conscious of saying the silly thing even before Claude answered with studied politeness, 'Don't you see? Miss Eccleston has caught fire, but we have luckily extinguished the flames.'

Claude was seldom cross, but he hated scenes and emotions and spoilt clothes. 'If some one would help me to get her up to the house it would be some use,' he added; 'and can't any one lend a dry coat to wrap round her? Mine's no good, it's as wet as a sponge. Oh! not *you*, Sainty, *you*'ll catch cold.'

A little way from the house they encountered Lady Eccleston, who had got wind of the catastrophe, and was hurrying to meet them; and Sainty was struck by the change in her manner in face of emergency. Her foolish flightiness seemed to have dropped from her like a garment that an athlete throws off. She had all her wits about her, and gave the most sensible directions. She had her daughter upstairs and in bed between warm blankets in less time than it takes to write it down, and by the afternoon she was able to report to them that Cissy was quite comfortable, only a little feverish and upset by the shock; but she did not think she would be much the worse for her wetting.

Cissy, however, was a most unaccountable time in

getting over that shock. Lady Eccleston expressed herself as amazed that her daughter should take so long to recover from so small a thing.

'Really, Lord Belchamber, I'm ashamed; you'll think you are never going to get rid of us; but the doctor says positively that the child mustn't come down yet. I can't understand it at all, for the chill she has *quite* got over. Of course she had a dreadful feverish cold, and at first we thought it would settle on her lungs, but, thank God! all danger of that seems at an end. Then I ask *what* is the matter? and Dr. Lane says, "It's the shock to the nervous system." But I'm mortified. I really am. Do you know how long we've been here?'

'I don't want to know, Lady Eccleston. I only know we are too glad to keep you as long as you can stay, and I am sure my mother feels as I do about it.'

'Oh! you are too kind about it, both of you! But one has *some* compunctions, you know. And after all your goodness about the boys and all!'

George and Randolph had returned to Harrow, and Tom to his hated office in Throgmorton Avenue, Claude's presence had been once more required by his respected chief, and the rest of the party had melted like the snow that had followed the long frost; but still Cissy lay in a most becoming pink dressing-gown in a small boudoir that had been arranged for her next her bedroom. It took Lady Eccleston days of modest trepidation to bring herself to admit Sainty to these sacred precincts. 'Was she very unconventional? Well, she supposed she was—people always said so—but she was weak where her children were concerned, and Cissy had said, "Why *shouldn't* Lord Belchamber come to see me, mamma?" Not for worlds would she have introduced the ordinary young man'; and then Sainty was once more assured of his 'difference,' his purity, the perfect confidence an anxious mother could repose in him.

'Her brothers are gone, you see, and she misses them so, poor child. And though we are *such* friends, an old woman is dull company *pour tout potage*; and then my wretched throat gives out; I am no good for reading aloud. Now it would be *angelic* of you, if you would read to her a little; *would* you? Oh! *how* kind! She is a perfect baby about being read to; and you are so clever; you will know just what to read; you have such literary taste; everybody says so.'

Thus Sainty found himself installed as reader to the invalid, and spent many hours a day by her sofa. At first Lady Eccleston was always there; then, when they were deep in their book, she would sometimes slip away to her voluminous correspondence or long consultations with her maid over the endless transmutations of her wardrobe. Sometimes Lady Charmington would look in, with a few words of grim tenderness, and lay a large, cool hand on Cissy's hair. Gradually the young people came to be left alone for longer and longer intervals. Belchamber rather wondered, himself, at the relaxation of all watchfulness on the part of their chaperons. 'It is the old story,' he told himself gloomily; 'I am certainly not considered dangerous.'

One day Lady Eccleston was much perturbed at breakfast over her letters.

'I don't know what to do,' she cried, 'it is most unfortunate; do advise me, dear Lady Charmington. There are a dozen things I ought to be in London for. I have a committee on Tuesday; they say they can't do without me; and things seem to be all at sixes and sevens at home: poor Tommy writes that he is most uncomfortable; he says the maids are always out, and he believes the cook gives parties; that there are—what is it? Oh! yes, here— "sounds of revelry by night"; he is always so absurd, poor dear; but it *is* hard on him. I really feel we ought to go, and Cissy is just beginning at last to be a little better.'

'Why don't you run up for a day or two, and do what you have to, attend to your committee, and give an eye to things in Chester Square?' said Lady Charmington. 'Leave Cissy to us, if you will trust us; we will take every care of her.'

'O dear Lady Charmington, I *couldn't*; that *would* be an imposition. Of course she would be ever so much better here, and she is so happy, poor child; Chester Square is so noisy, and of course directly she gets back to London, people will begin to want her to do things, and I shall never keep her quiet. But I simply couldn't; it would be monstrous to put on you to such an extent.'

'Nonsense,' said Lady Charmington. 'It is a thousand pities to take her back to town just when she is getting on so well; a few weeks more of good air and rest will do everything for her; she must come downstairs first, go out for a few drives, before she thinks of a journey. Don't you agree with me, Sainty?'

'Of course we shall be only too glad, if you think Miss Eccleston would not be dull——' Sainty began.

'Ah! dear Lord Belchamber! dear Lady Charmington! how good you both are!' cried the tender mother. 'I am ashamed, positively ashamed, but what can I say? She will be overjoyed. She had to gulp down a big lump in her throat when I told her we must go home; she was so good, she wouldn't say anything, but *I* could see; love sharpens our wits when it is a question of our children's happiness, doesn't it, dear?'

'It is generally not difficult to see through young people,' said Lady Charmington. Sainty was wondering if the necessity for Lady Eccleston's presence in London had arisen out of the letters she had received since she came downstairs, when she could have had the conversation on the subject which had brought the lump into her daughter's throat, but he was too polite to inquire.

The conclusion of the whole matter, as might have been foreseen, was that Lady Eccleston departed to London, leaving Cissy at Belchamber, and the readings were continued with even less supervision than before.

Cissy's literary taste was decidedly undeveloped, and it may be doubted if some of her host's finest reading was not merely an accompaniment to the thinking out of new hats; but Sainty enjoyed immensely introducing a novice to his best beloved authors, and the new sensation of being able to minister to a sufferer, and lighten the long hours of some of their dullness and depression. He wasted an immense amount of care and thought on the selection of suitable gems, passages that should be characteristic and of the highest beauty, and yet milk to the intellectual

babe. Sometimes he almost forgot his listener in the
pleasure of voicing things long dear to himself, especially
poetry, and he read a good deal of poetry. Cissy displayed but little enthusiasm; she always thanked him
very prettily when he finished, if she was not asleep, and
'hoped it didn't bore him awfully,' but she made few
comments, and listened for the most part in silence and
often with her eyes closed. Sainty put down her apparent
indifference to the languor of convalescence. Once, indeed, she startled him by the energy of her appreciation.
He was reading *Maud* to her, and she had several times
disappointed him with a calm 'very pretty' when he had
paused after some exquisite lyric that left him vibrating
like a harpstring. When, however, he came to—

> 'Oh that 'twere possible
>   After long grief and pain
> To find the arms of my true love
>   Round me once again!'

her quickened respiration showed her interest; and at the
stanza beginning 'When I was wont to meet her,' she half
raised herself, saying eagerly, 'I like that; read that bit
again, please; do you mind?' and on Sainty's complying,
she repeated dreamily to herself, as though the words
called up some image that gave her pleasure,

> 'We stood tranced in long embraces,
> Mixt with kisses sweeter, sweeter
> Than anything on earth,'

'Who did you say wrote that?' she asked. 'Oh! of course,
yes, Tennyson,' and with a great sigh she sank back on
her cushions. Then she looked suddenly at him, as though
she feared she had betrayed something, and flushed crimson. 'Go on,' she murmured; 'beg pardon,' and relapsed
into her habitual expression of polite endurance. Next
day she asked him to lend her the book, as she wanted to
copy some of it out.

Sainty was delighted, but surprised.

CHAPTER XV

LADY ECCLESTON's business kept her in London longer than she expected. Each day brought hurried notes from her, full of regrets and apologies, compunction for all the trouble they were giving, but joy that her dear child was in such good, kind hands, and a plentiful supply of a mother's blessings. She was a swift and copious letter-writer, economising time by the ruthless excision of articles, pronouns, and other short words. Tommy always declared that his mother could write two letters at once, one with each hand, and interview the cook at the same time.

Breakfast in bed was the last lingering trace of Cissy's mysterious ailment, by the time her parent reappeared upon the scene.

'What have you done to my little girl?' cried Lady Eccleston in a transport of gratitude; 'she is a different child.' And truly it would have been hard to find a more blooming specimen of girlhood. Indeed, when you come to think of it, six weeks is a liberal allowance of time for a perfectly healthy young woman to get over the effects of a momentary immersion in cold water.

'You have been so kind to my darling,' Lady Eccleston said to Sainty. 'She has been telling me of all your delightful talks and readings; it is just what she needed, a little intercourse with a really cultivated mind. She has always felt the dissatisfaction of the frivolous life of society; there has been the desire to improve herself, the love of reading, but no one to guide her taste, or put her in the right way. Now, if you would draw up a little table of reading for her, tell her *what* to read, and in what order and connection, it would be just everything for her; and perhaps even her ignorant old mother might find a little leisure now and then to profit by your help. One is never too old to learn, you know.'

So Sainty drew up tables, lent books, and marked passages, like the simple little pedant that he was, but without producing any very marked impression on Cissy's fundamental ignorance. Sometimes he wondered if the

girl were not very dull at Belchamber, and how it was
that people who had always seemed to have so many
engagements could spare so much time to one house. It
is true that Lady Eccleston was perpetually threatening
departure, but she was as often persuaded to remain by
the very mildest expostulation that civility demanded.

At last a date was definitely fixed, and Sainty had to
acknowledge to himself that he would miss the charming
companion of his walks and drives. He felt tolerably sure
that he was not in the least in love with Cissy, but he had
come to feel a sort of tender protecting friendship for her,
an interest in her welfare, and a desire to shield her from
evil and unhappiness. Thus, one day, when he had heard
raised voices and rather excited talking as he passed Lady
Eccleston's door, and Cissy had appeared at lunch with
red eyes, he burned to know what was wrong, and if
possible to help and comfort her. Sorrow seemed so inappropriate to this bright young creature; yet, during the
last few days of the Eccleston's stay, the air was heavy
with suppressed tears. It was like the weather when
people look each evening at the clearing heavens and say,
'There must have been a storm somewhere'; an actual
shower would have been a relief. To a person of Sainty's
temperament such a state of things was unendurable.
He could not ask Cissy what was wrong; she who had
been so ready to walk, or drive, or read, seemed suddenly
to have become unapproachable.

One day he watched the mother and daughter returning from a walk. They were talking excitedly in low
hurried voices and with a good deal of gesture; it was
obvious even at a distance that they were discussing no ordinary topics, and what is more that they were having a
decided difference of opinion. Lady Eccleston seemed
to be appealing urgently about something. Sainty saw
her lay her hand not too gently on her daughter's arm,
but the girl threw it off with an impatient gesture, broke
from her, and fairly ran towards the house.

So swift and unexpected was her coming that Sainty
had no time to withdraw, and they met in the hall. Cissy's
face was working, her eyes dry and burning.

'Miss Eccleston—Cissy,' said Belchamber, 'what is wrong? Can I do anything——'

At sight of him she started away like a shying horse.

'Oh, let me alone!' she cried, and hurried upstairs, and Sainty could hear her sobbing as she went. At that moment Lady Eccleston appeared upon the scene, with heightened colour and decidedly out of breath. An indefinable change came over her expression as she saw the young man, a certain exultation seemed to leap in her eyes, to be immediately extinguished in a confusion which had every appearance of being genuine.

'Lady Eccleston,' said Sainty, moving eagerly to meet her, 'what is the matter with Cissy?' He did not notice that in his excitement he had twice called the girl by her Christian name.

'O Lord Belchamber, how unfortunate! I would have given worlds not to have met you just now. Give me a minute or two, I'm all upset.'

Sainty opened the door of the morning-room and ushered the agitated lady in there. His heart was beating uncomfortably; he felt something decisive was going to happen. Lady Eccleston sank into a chair and struggled with emotion, giving vent to a series of little sniffs and hiccoughs, and dabbing her eyes and mouth with her pocket-handkerchief.

'To-morrow we should have gone, and you need never have known,' she said at last in broken accents.

'Known what? I don't understand.'

'I blame myself,' Lady Eccleston went on, not heeding the interruption. 'It was my fault; I ought to have had more foresight and discretion; I see it all now. If Sir Thomas had only been spared it would never have happened; he had such sterling sense.'

'Won't you tell me what's wrong?' Sainty asked.

'I alone am to blame,' Lady Eccleston repeated tragically. 'Of course, I see it now. You are both so young, so pure-minded, so unsophisticated; and dear Lady Charmington has lived so long out of the world; but *I* ought to have seen. Oh! I am inexcusable. But I did hope at least *you* would never know'; and like Agamemnon she once more veiled her grief.

'I might have known, I might have been sure,' she continued after a pause. 'Heaven knows I have enough reason to know how malicious people are, but my belief in my fellow-creatures is incurable. I can *not* bring myself to realise the love of scandal in evil-minded people.'

'Good heavens!' said Sainty, now thoroughly alarmed. 'What can you mean? Surely no one has presumed——'

'People have talked,' Lady Eccleston mourned. 'Cissy being here so long, and my leaving her here, and all. It seems people have drawn all sorts of silly conclusions. I have been asked—— I can't say it; you can guess what; and the poor child has had letters, hints, and congratulations, and all that; you can fancy it has upset her terribly; she is almost beside herself; I can do nothing with her; you saw her just now'; and Lady Eccleston took a little side-glance at Sainty behind her pocket-handkerchief. 'Of course, *I* understand perfectly, and so does she; but I see how it would strike outsiders. Oh! why is one always wise after the event? Now you see why I am so angry with myself.'

Sainty was much perturbed. 'This is monstrous, monstrous!' he cried; 'that she should be annoyed, distressed in this way, is horrible. I hope, Lady Eccleston, you don't think that I have behaved badly, that I have taken any advantage of the confidence with which you have honoured me.'

'Oh dear no, Lord Belchamber; you have been kindness itself, and so has your dear mother. I never can forget all your goodness. I knew how absolutely I could trust *you*; but I ought to have thought, to have remembered. Well, I had hoped and meant that at least we alone should bear the burthen. This is an ill return to make to you for all your sweetness and hospitality. You will wish you had never heard our name.'

'Believe me, I am not thinking at all about myself. The one question is, how is Miss Eccleston to be shielded from any annoyance in the matter? It is intolerable that she should have to suffer.'

'How like you! always so noble and unselfish,' said Lady Eccleston fervently. 'I shall always remember how splendidly you have behaved. I don't blame *you* for a single instant, but I can never forgive *myself*. It is so like me; I am so impulsive. I thought only of the immense benefit it would be to her intellectually, the intercourse with such a mind as yours. I should have recollected there were dangers; that at her age the intellect plays but a very small part beside the heart——'

'Good gracious! you don't mean that she has thought me capable of pestering her with my attentions? I knew well enough that I was only allowed such liberty because —because I was different from other men.'

'No, no; I don't *think* she thought anything of it. *I* should have known that it was only your kindness to a poor little invalid, your desire to instruct a little ignoramus. But Cissy is very young; she may have fancied—— Oh! I don't know what I'm saying.'

Sainty had grown very pale; he had to hold on to a table for support.

'Lady Eccleston,' he said in a low voice, 'you can't mean to imply that Miss Eccleston could possibly care for *me* in that way.'

'Lord Belchamber, this is unfair,' cried Lady Eccleston, starting up. 'You have no right to try and force the child's poor little secret from me. You found me all unstrung after a terrible talk with her, and I have let out far more than I should. I have told you I entirely exonerate you from all blame; I appreciate that your motive was pure kindness. Is not that enough for you? If people have been tiresome and tactless it is not your fault, still less hers, poor girl. I blame *myself*, as I say, more than I can tell you, but that has nothing to do with you. If I have been foolish I am more than punished; but I only regret that I cannot bear *all* the punishment; we never can. The fault or folly, call it what you will, was mine, but much of the price must be paid by my poor innocent child—that is the thought that unnerves me'; and her ladyship once more had recourse to her pocket-handkerchief. 'She has no father,' she wailed; 'her brothers are mere children in knowledge of the world; and I, her mother, who should have shielded her from trouble, in my blind, foolish desire to procure her a little intellectual advantage, have brought on her the bitterest trial of her life.'

Sainty was twisting his stick in his fingers in great agitation. 'It is too bad, too bad,' he said, 'that she should be pestered like this and made unhappy. I would do anything in my power to repair the harm of which I have been the unwitting cause. But if the trouble is, as I suppose, only what stupid people have been saying or writing to her, I don't see what I can do. Poor child! I can well understand how her pride and delicacy must have been hurt.'

'No, no; there is nothing to be done, nothing,' said Lady Eccleston. 'I never meant that you should know; and, Lord Belchamber, promise me one thing: never refer to this to Cissy; she would die of shame, if she thought I had told you. We are going to-morrow; try and forget what I have said, especially—especially——' and she broke off abruptly, and made a stumbling grope at the door-handle, as though she would leave the room.

'Stop a minute, please,' Sainty cried, interposing. 'Don't go. I don't want to be indiscreet, but you said something just now which seemed to hint—— Oh! I know it's incredible; but don't you see, it would make all the difference whether her distress came *only* from the mortification of people having coupled our names, or if it was possible that she could look on me as—as——'

'Say no more, say no more. I understand you perfectly,' interrupted Lady Eccleston. 'You are the soul of punctilious honour. You are capable of any sacrifice, if you thought that even, as you said just now, *unwittingly* you had made a poor girl care for you; but I have not said it and I will not say it. I have pride for her, as I should have it for myself. I would *never* admit it. You are perfectly justified in believing that her distress arises *solely* from what people have said,' and this time the lady, with a magnificent gesture of renunciation, really did get to the door, and left Sainty in a whirl of conflicting emotions.

Was it possible that he had touched the heart of this beautiful young creature? It was inconceivable that *she* should be in love with *him*, and he turned with a pathetic smile to the long glass between the two tall windows. Yet her mother had seemed to hint it. If it were so, then there was nothing simpler than saving her from trouble. A word would do it. But it could not be; the thing was unthinkable. And he fell to wondering if he wished to think it, or not. What was his feeling towards her? Was this protecting, pitying tenderness, this longing to interpose between her and sorrow, was this love? It was very unlike what he had dreamed it to be. But was not everything in life strangely unlike our young idea of it? And ought he to consider his own feelings in the matter at all? If, however innocently, he had led her to think he cared for her, if in her youth and inexperience she had mistaken his friendship, his interest in her studies, for a warmer feeling; above all, if the inscrutable workings of the female heart had led her for some mysterious reason to return it, was he not in honour bound to think only of her happiness in the matter? If a young and beautiful woman had done him this honour, was it for him, him of all people, to feel anything but humblest gratitude? The thought was not without a certain sweetness that a woman had recognised the qualities of his head and heart, to the extent of forgetting his lack of all that women most prized in man, strength, courage, virility. He acknowledged that a man could not have done so, that had the positions been reversed, had he been handsome, vigorous, physically attractive, she ugly, misshapen, unhealthy, no beauties of the soul would have stirred in him the wish to make her his wife. He bowed his head in awe before the greater spirituality of woman; even a thoughtless London girl brought up among worldly surroundings and low ideals was capable of higher flights than the most refined and least carnal of men. And he had presumed to patronise, almost to look down on her, because she had not dulled the edge of her originality with much reading. After all, why did he hesitate? Had he not dreamed of some such possibility as this, yet hardly dared to hope for it? Was it likely that two women would be found willing to overlook his many deficiencies? was not this precisely the one chance of his life? His mother had said she wished him to marry. His mother! Strange that he had not thought of her sooner! He would go and consult his mother; *she* would know better than any one how to advise him.

Lady Charmington listened indulgently to his recital. She did not seem surprised.

'I thought all that poetry reading would come to something of the sort,' she said.

'I can't make out now,' said Sainty, 'whether what is troubling her is anything more than resentment of idle gossip, the natural repulsion of a delicate-minded girl from having her name coupled with a man's.'

'Oh, I suspect it is more,' said his mother. 'But you? Are you fond of the girl on your side?'

'I don't know that I am in love with her, even now, and I certainly never dreamed of the possibility of *her* being in love with *me*.'

'Well, her mother certainly gave you to understand that she was; it is unfortunate if you have made the poor girl care for you, and don't feel you can return it.'

'Good heavens, mother! If it were possible that such a creature had really stooped to love me, I ought to thank her on my knees.'

'I don't quite see *that*; but I should be sorry to have any one able to say you had trifled with her. You see, her mother left her in my charge; and I suppose I ought not to have let you be so much alone together.'

'But surely,' cried Sainty, 'you don't think I am capable of taking advantage of the confidence reposed in me, to— to—— Oh! the idea is ludicrous; you must see its absurdity.'

'I must say you have given the girl every reason to think you liked her,' said his mother judicially. 'I have never seen you show the same desire for anybody's society before; it is not surprising if she mistook the nature of your attentions. Pretty girls are not in the habit of having young men so devoted to the improvement of their minds.'

'I would not "behave badly," as people call it, for worlds,' said Sainty. 'I only can't get over the extreme grotesqueness of its being possible for me to do so. In spite of both you and Lady Eccleston, it still seems to me quite incredible that I should rouse any such feeling in her.'

'There is a very simple way of finding out,' said Lady Charmington.

'But how if in her kindness and inexperience she is mistaking pity, gratitude, affection—call it what you will—for Love? It is possible even (God forgive me for thinking of such a thing!) that the surroundings, the place, the name, the whole business may have acted on her almost unconsciously, and helped her to mistake her own heart.'

'Judge not,' said Lady Charmington, with all the air of one who had never done such a thing in her life; 'I should be sorry to think so badly of the poor child as that.'

'Oh, I didn't mean to blame her. I am sure she would not *consciously* have let such considerations weigh with her; but it seems so abnormal that any woman should feel anything like love for me, that I am still trying to find some explanation to fit the facts.'

Lady Charmington laid her hand on his shoulder. 'My dear boy,' she said 'you are not called upon to understand *her* feelings; what you have got to do is to try and understand your own. It has been the dearest wish of my heart to see you happily married; especially since your brother's behaviour has brought such bitter sorrow and disgrace upon us all. Here is a nice, good girl, well brought up, and I think she loves you. The question is whether you like her well enough to make her your wife.'

Sainty shook his head. 'The question is whether I could make her happy,' he said; 'what have I to give her in exchange for the priceless treasure of a good woman's love?'

Dinner that evening was a cheerless meal. Lady Charmington, never a great talker, was more than ordinarily silent. Belchamber made several attempts to start a conversation on indifferent subjects, and Lady Eccleston chattered feverishly, with one eye on him and one on her daughter, who sat sullen and defiant and ate nothing. Sainty's heart smote him as he looked on her. Whether their two mothers were right or not, he would speak to her after dinner. If she took him, he would consecrate his life to her happiness. If, as he still thought far more likely, their wishes had misled them, and she did not care for him, she had only to refuse him, and her pride was healed. Then, when her friends said, 'We thought you were going to marry Lord Belchamber,' she would only have to say, 'He wanted me to, poor man, but I couldn't do it.' That he was thinking entirely of *her* happiness showed how little he was really in love with her, but that neither affected his decision nor seemed to him to matter in the least.

Lady Charmington was a skilled and experienced knitter, and Lady Eccleston, who kept a bit of property crochet to hook at when she was with other women who worked, became surprisingly interested in the intricacies of the garment on which her friend was engaged. Her voluble inquiries and apologies for her own stupidity kept up a running accompaniment to the click-clack of the needles and Lady Charmington's occasional terse explanations. Cissy had withdrawn to the extreme other end of the long room in which they sat, and pretended to immerse herself in a book. Sainty drew a chair up to hers, so as to interpose the view of his own back between her and the two older women.

'Miss Eccleston,' he said, 'I have got something I want to say to you.'

Cissy looked up from her book. 'Yes?' was all she said. Her attitude expressed only weariness; she did not appear to be at all fluttered.

'You are worried, unhappy,' Sainty went on. 'I am afraid you have been annoyed by people gossiping about your stay here, about the relations between you and me.' He spoke in a low voice, for her ear alone; he was looking into her eyes, trying to surprise some indication of what effect his words had on her. Cissy did not look down or betray any embarrassment.

'I suppose mamma told you that?' she said.

'I can't bear to see you like this, and to know that, however unintentionally, I am the cause.'

'Oh! that's all right; I am sure you meant nothing but what was kind.'

'Miss Eccleston—Cissy, I want to tell you I am quite well aware of the extreme unlikelihood of your being able to care for me. I understand that you should be angry and sore at vulgar people's mistaking the nature of our friendship. I am not silly or vain enough to suppose that you would be willing to marry me; but remember if any one ever says anything more to you about this, your position is quite simple; you have only to say you have refused me——'

Cissy never shifted her calm, level gaze. 'Lord Belchamber,' she said quietly, 'am I to understand that you are proposing to me?'

'I don't for a moment expect you to accept me; I just want you to know, and other people to know, that if you don't it is entirely because you don't wish to.'

'I see; you mean you will make me a sham proposal, on the distinct understanding that I say "no," so that I may have the satisfaction of telling my friends that I might have been a marchioness if I'd liked; but you'd be awfully sold if I said "yes."'

'You know I don't mean anything of the sort,' said Sainty. 'But I know how hopeless it is that a girl like you should care for a man like me, and I wouldn't insult you by supposing that anything I have to offer could make any difference. I don't want to add to your troubles the pain of thinking I had hoped you might accept me and that you have got to disappoint me.'

'Then it *is* a *bonâ fide* offer that you are making me?' said Cissy sardonically; her tone expressed anything but exultation, and though she still looked at him her eyes seemed to be looking at some one else a long way off. 'It's the queerest proposal, I should think, any one ever made,' and she gave a little dry laugh. 'Take care I don't accept it. Whatever you may think, a little pauper like me might well be tempted by what you have to offer, as you call it.'

'I don't like to hear you talk like that,' Sainty said. 'I know it is only a joke, but there are things I don't like joked about. That's the way you used to talk, but you've been so different lately.'

'Lord Belchamber,' said Cissy, 'let's understand one another. If you are making me an offer out of chivalry, that I may have an answer to people's malicious chatter, I can only say I am very much obliged to you; but if you really want me to marry you, I'm quite ready to do so. I can't say fairer than that, can I? After all,' she added in a softer tone, 'quite apart from worldly considerations, I think I might do much worse for myself; you've been very good to me, and you're a much better sort than—than most of the men I've met,' and for the first time she looked away, and gave a little sigh.

Sainty was much moved. 'Cissy,' he said, 'do you really mean that in spite of everything you think you could love me a little?' and he tried to take her hand; but at the touch of him the girl flung herself back into the furthest corner of the big chair in which she sat, and her glance once more crossed his, steel-bright like a rapier. 'Do I understand,' she asked, 'that I have your authority to announce our engagement to our respective parents?'

Sainty stared blankly; he could only nod. Cissy wheeled her chair sharply back, and called out, 'Mamma! Lord Belchamber has proposed to me, and I have accepted him.'

Lady Eccleston was across the room in two bounds. 'My darling, what a way to tell me such a thing! You really are the strangest child. What can Lord Belchamber and Lady Charmington think of you? Dear Lady Charmington, you must forgive my Cissy; she's so excitable, I think happiness has turned her head a little; and mine too, for that matter, for it would be useless to pretend I'm not delighted, only it is all so sudden, so unexpected,' and she clasped her daughter to her heart, and kissed and wept over her in the most approved fashion. Cecilia did not return her mother's kisses; she looked at her with a very queer eye indeed, before which Lady Eccleston's effusiveness drooped a little. She turned to her future son-in-law and held out both her hands. 'Dear Sainty (I may call you Sainty?), I must kiss you too,' she cried.

As Sainty submitted to the threatened salute, it struck him as grimly humorous that it should not be his intended who kissed him, but her mother.

Cissy crossed the room, and picked up the ball of wool which Lady Eccleston had shed in her rapid transit, and by which she was still fastened like a spider to the place where she had been sitting. 'Lady Charmington,' she said, 'mamma has adopted your son with great readiness ; have you nothing to say to me? Are you not pleased?'

Lady Charmington had risen and laid aside her work. 'Of course I am pleased,' she said; 'I have wished, of all things, to see Sainty married ; but, my dear,' she added, something in the girl's manner seeming to strike her as peculiar, 'I hope you are not taking this solemn step lightly; have you examined your heart, and asked God's blessing on what you are doing? Are you sure you love my son enough to be happy with him, and to make him happy?'

But Lady Eccleston was a whirlwind of tears, protestations, laughter, and congratulation; she caught them all up, and swept them away in the current of her rejoicing. No one else was allowed to say anything.

Sainty also had drawn near, and now stood before his mother. She took a hand of each of the young people in hers, and said solemnly 'God bless you, my children.'

At the moment Sainty had a vision of the intensity with which she had cursed her other son, on a like occasion, and thought irresistibly of the fountain that 'sent forth sweet water and bitter.' The context rang in his head like a knell: 'My brethren, these things ought not to be.'

CHAPTER XVI

THE wedding was fixed for the first week in June. As Lady Charmington said, there was no reason for delay, though it must be owned that neither of the young people seemed very eager to press on the date. Lady Eccleston

could not have borne a wedding in Lent, and Lady Charmington had a lingering old Scottish superstition, of
which she was heartily ashamed, against May marriages.
All things considered, the beginning of June seemed
plainly indicated. Everybody would be in town then,
and it was to be a London wedding. Cissy grumbled a
good deal at having to miss the season; but her mother
affected to treat her lamentations as a joke.

'Of *course* she doesn't mean it,' she said, in answer to
Sainty's expression of his willingness to consult Cissy's
wishes in everything. 'You know how absurd my children
are; they always must make a joke of everything, but it
doesn't mean that their hearts are not in the right place;
under all their nonsense, which I never check, for I do so
love to see them merry, they have very serious feelings
about all the big things of life.'

A cousin of Lady Eccleston's, who was married to a
newly-made peer with a large income, and who had never
before shown the slightest inclination to do much for her
poorer kinsfolk, expressed her approval of Cissy's brilliant
match by offering the use of her house for the occasion.

'It is very good of dear Louisa,' said Lady Eccleston,
'and I must own we should have been sadly squashed in
our little *bicoque*. Still, if we hadn't always been *as* sisters,
I couldn't have taken it from her. Poor dear! It is such
a bitter regret to her having no children of her own.
Naturally mine are a great deal to her; and I can quite
understand her pleasure in having Cissy married from
her house. Don't think I'm ungrateful to the dear
creature, Sainty, but I own in my heart I would rather
have had the girl go to her bridal from her own and her
mother's little home; but that is *entre nous*, my dear boy;
I wouldn't hurt poor Louisa's feelings for worlds.'

Sainty found being engaged very different from anything he had read of it. Things seemed so little changed
with him, that he wondered at times if it could really be he
who was to be married in a few weeks. Was it possible
that at a date definitely fixed, and not very far distant,
his whole being was to undergo this tremendous transformation, was henceforth to be linked in closest union

with a creature of whom he knew practically nothing, and that not for a season, like any other circumstance in life, but as long 'as they both should live,' 'till death did them part'? The prospect terrified rather than attracted him.

Sometimes he tried to feel elated at the thought that he was to join the ranks of normal happy people who love and are loved, was to lead about a wife like other men, and hold up his head among his fellows. He told himself that this supremest gift was far beyond anything he had dared to hope. It was to no purpose. He might be flattered, grateful, touched, but he was conscious of none of that blissful thrill that is said to transfigure existence and make a heaven on earth. Sometimes he wondered how it had all come about so suddenly. Everything he had done had seemed not only natural, but inevitable at the time. He had walked into the situation as simply as going in to dinner; yet now there were moments when the thought of what they had both undertaken appalled him. He was as frightened for Cissy as for himself. Did she know what she was doing, what it meant? A dozen times a day he recalled the scene in the library, her hard, unflinching gaze, the mocking tones of her voice. Was that the way that a woman made the 'irrevocable sweet surrender' to a man who had won her heart? If she had made a mistake, if she did not love him, ought she not still to be saved from the fate she had accepted, even at the eleventh hour?

He saw extremely little of his betrothed. He had never had much to do with engaged couples, but he had an impression that they were generally left a good deal alone together, that people and things combined to respect the privacy of mutual love; yet from the day of his engagement it was no exaggeration to say that he had hardly seen Cissy alone for five minutes. It is true that she had not actually left Belchamber next morning; but after their surprising freedom from other claims, both she and her mother seemed now all impatience to be gone, and during the time that they remained, they were mostly shut up in their own rooms announcing the event to a hundred correspondents, or dashing off their thanks for the congratulations that arrived by every post. 'She must really get home, and begin to see about some clothes; there was none too much time, and this was such a bad time of year; just when every one was busy.' Cissy was sure, if she delayed another day, she 'shouldn't have a decent rag to her back, and should have to be married in her petticoats.'

From the day they went to town there began a round of shoppings and tryings-on, of scribbling notes, unpacking, cataloguing, and rapturously thanking for wedding-presents, which, as Cissy was marrying a rich man with a house full of beautiful things, were, of course, far more numerous and costly than if she had married a curate, or a captain in a marching regiment. Then the list of people to be invited to the wedding had to be discussed *ad infinitum*, at first with regard to the size of the house in Chester Square, and after the cousin's offer, to be enlarged, amended, and corrected. With every fresh batch of presents, the number swelled of those whom it was deemed indispensable to ask, till it seemed to Sainty that there was not a stranger in the whole great indifferent city who had not been called in to assist at his nuptials.

He also had come to town, as in duty bound, and was staying with his uncle Firth, but though he spent several hours a day in Chester Square, he found himself horribly in the way there. Lady Eccleston and Cissy sat squashed sideways by the open drawers of their respective writing-tables, like people playing a perpetual duet on two organs with all the stops pulled out. The absurdly inadequate pieces of furniture on which women transact business became so littered with lists, letters, acceptances, refusals, the drawers so bulged with stacks of silver-printed invitations and stamped envelopes, that the little hands with the scratching pens seemed by their perpetual movement to be feverishly preserving an ever narrowing space for themselves, as ducks keep a hole open in a rapidly freezing pond.

Of happy interchange of rapturous feelings, murmured talks in quiet corners, or those long, palpitating silences that lovers know, too blissful to be marred by talk, our engaged couple had no experience. Though Sainty was far too delicate-minded for the mere physical aspects of courtship to appeal strongly to his imagination, it did occur to him that an occasional embrace was not inappropriate between people about to be married; but on the one occasion when he attempted anything of the sort, he had been repulsed with such energy and decision that he had immediately desisted. He had a conviction that Cissy thought him a fool for accepting defeat so easily, but to struggle for a kiss like an enamoured costermonger was repugnant to all his ideas. So he continued to meet and greet his promised bride as though she were the most indifferent of strangers.

One morning at breakfast he asked his uncle if he ought not to make his betrothed a present. Lord Firth came out from behind the morning paper with a bound.

'My dear boy! do you mean to say you haven't done so?'

'Not yet,' said Sainty; 'but I supposed, of course, I should have to.'

'Not even a ring?' asked Lord Firth. Sainty was forced to admit it.

'Why, the very day she accepted you, you ought to have given her a ring; if you hadn't got one fit to offer her, you should have telegraphed to town at once for some. You must get one at once and take it to her; and, of course, you must give her other things too, a tiara or necklace or something really handsome, and a bag or dressing-case. You know the kind of thing. Find out from her mother what she's got, and which she would like, and get the duchess to help you choose things; *she* knows what's what. They must think it very odd that you haven't done it already.'

'There are the emeralds,' said Sainty.

'Of course she'll have them to wear,' said his uncle, 'but you can't *give* them to her, because they are heirlooms. As it happens, the one thing you are rather poor in is jewellery. Your grandmother had a lot, but it was her own, and you may believe she didn't leave any behind her; your mother never cared for it, and never had much. She will probably give your wife, or leave her, what she has; but of course you must see that she has the proper things, and do the thing well. Don't be stingy about it.'

The duchess was delighted to help, and echoed Lord Firth's astonishment at Sainty's dilatoriness in the matter.

'You really are the most extraordinary boy,' she said. 'I'm just going for my walk; we'll go round to Rumond's at once and see what he's got.'

'We've been expecting a visit from your lordship,' said the great jeweller unctuously, 'ever since we heard the happy news. May I be permitted to offer my congratulations on the event? We have always had the honour of supplying your family, and hoped that on such an occasion you would not desert us. I was remarking to Mr. Diby only the other day that I had been wondering we did not get a telegram to go down to Belchamber—either he or I would have been delighted; but you preferred to wait till you came to town: quite right, quite right.'

They were ushered into a little sanctum, where presently on a mat of dark blue velvet were displayed treasures which made Sainty blink, and of which the prices gave him cold shivers down his back. The duchess handled and appraised the gems with the sangfroid of long habit; but her grandson had never in his life had occasion to buy any jewellery, and had not the faintest idea of what such things were worth. To deck the bright curls of a woman with the cost of a hospital, or hang the price of a working-men's college round her neck, seemed to him absolutely vicious; it had a horrible flavour of that life into which he had obtained his only glimpse at Arthur's supper-party—poor Arthur, whom almost alone he would have cared to have near him on his wedding-day, and who he knew would not be there, because his wife could not be asked.

He left the shop with a horrible sense of guilt, and a feeling that the act which in him would be applauded as a fitting generosity was very much in the same category with his brother's prodigalities, not differing in kind, but only so much more blameworthy as it was so much greater in degree. Arthur, he felt sure, would not have hesitated to hang the girl of his heart in jewels, nor have wasted a thought on what it cost, and again he wondered whether his qualms were the result of his well-known parsimony, or one more proof that he was not really in love with her who was to be his wife.

It was soon clear that Cissy did not share his views on these subjects; the evening on which his presents arrived in Chester Square was the only occasion since their betrothal on which she expressed anything resembling affection for him. Her eyes sparkled like the diamonds in her little crown as she tried the things on, and pirouetted about the room with them. She waltzed up to Sainty and dropped him a deep curtsey. 'How does my lord and master think I look?' she said coquettishly; and then in a sudden gust of gratitude she caught his hands in hers, and for the first time bent forward and kissed him. Sainty blushed hotly; this kiss, which spontaneously given would have meant so much to him, was like the stamp on a receipt for cash value received; and it was the last, as it had been the first, of their singular courtship.

As the weeks passed, Cissy grew stranger and more unlike herself. The intervals of feverish gaiety, which had marked the earlier stages of her engagement, became rarer, and were succeeded by fits of gloom and depression that seemed utterly foreign to her nature. Whatever she might be at other times, that came to be the mood in which she invariably received Belchamber. She never willingly addressed him, and there were days when it seemed beyond her power to speak peaceably to him. Sometimes she was so rude that Lady Eccleston would playfully remonstrate, or Tommy would burst out with, 'Hang it all, Cissy, you've no right to speak to Sainty like that. If I was him, I'm jiggered if I'd stand it.'

They had never from the first been allowed many unwitnessed interviews, but now it seemed to Sainty that it was Cissy herself who carefully avoided any occasion of finding herself alone with him, and if ever she could by no means escape, she would take refuge from his attempts at conversation in sullen monosyllables, and sometimes even in absolute silence.

One day he asked her in desperation if she felt she had made a mistake—if she wanted to be released. 'It is not too late,' he said, 'but it soon will be; if you repent of what you have done, if you want me to give you back your freedom, in mercy to yourself, to me, speak while there is yet time.'

'Cissy,' he pleaded, after waiting in vain for any answer, 'if you don't feel that you love me enough, don't do a thing that will ruin both our lives.'

'Do I seem as if I loved you?' she asked brutally.

'So little, that I can't help feeling that the idea of marrying me is repugnant to you. If so, never mind me; have the courage to put a stop to the whole thing; a word from you will do it.'

'Oh! will it? It is not as simple as all that.'

'I will help you in any way I can; I will do anything you want.'

Cissy continued to stare into the fire in silence; she had never once looked at him. 'I don't know what I do want,' she said at last, hopelessly.

Sainty was about to say more, but at that moment, with a great admonitory rattling of the door-handle, Lady Eccleston hurried in, with her arms full of parcels.

'More presents, children,' she cried gaily; 'here, Sainty, come and take this top one off, or I shall drop it. That makes three hundred and seventy-nine. Ouf! I'm glad I've no more daughters to marry.'

'Listening! I thought so,' cried Cissy, starting up, and without a glance at the gifts from which her mother was beginning to remove the wrappings she left the room. At No. 379, fans and smelling-bottles, and even small articles of jewellery, were becoming a drug in the market. Lady Eccleston got very red, but took no notice, affecting to be absorbed in undoing a bit of ribbon that had got into a knot. ' "With best wishes, Mr. and Mrs. Bonham Trotter," ' she read; 'really very good of them. We hardly know them, and I hadn't meant to ask them. It is the seventeenth pair of paste buckles, but they are pretty though not old, and they come in for shoes. Who's this? "Every good wish, Mr. Austin Pryor." What a beauty! It is the prettiest fan she has had; really charming! What *can* this be? A pincushion! "Fondest love from Miss Henrietta Massinger." What rubbish. I wish people wouldn't send all this trash. Give me the green book on my writing-table, Sainty, and let's enter them before I forget it. Three more notes for that poor child to write, and she's tired out; any one can see it.'

'Lady Eccleston,' said Sainty, 'do you think Cissy's *only* tired? To me she seems very unhappy——'

'Tired, my dear boy, worn out; her nerves are in fiddle-strings; I shall be thankful for her sake when it's all over,' and she murmured as she wrote, 'Pair of paste buckles, Mr. and Mrs. Bonham Trotter, 377. Tortoiseshell fan, Watteau subject, Mr. Austin Pryor, 378. Embroidered velvet horseshoe pincush——'

'Do stop writing a minute and listen to me,' said Sainty. 'It's your daughter's happiness that is at stake. Tell me, truly, do you think she loves me?'

'Loves you! My dear Sainty, what a question! *Of course* she loves you,' cried Lady Eccleston. 'Miss H. Massinger, No. 379,' and she looked up with a bright smile, as she rubbed energetically on the blotting-paper. 'Have you been having a lovers' quarrel?' she asked.

'No, no, nothing of that sort; but you yourself must have seen how oddly she behaves. She never will be alone with me for a minute if she can help it; she hardly ever speaks to me, and if I speak to *her*, as often as not she doesn't answer me. It is the queerest way of showing love.'

Lady Eccleston smiled again, a little indulgent smile full of *finesse*.

'My dear child,' she said, 'is *that* all? How little you know girls. Can't you understand that to a girl of Cissy's temperament, so absolutely pure and modest, marriage represents the unknown, the terrible; the prospect of it fills her with a thousand tremors and apprehensions. Believe me, a girl who can approach her wedding-day with calm nerves and a cheerful, smiling face, is either a cow, and has no sensibilities, or else she knows a great deal too much.'

'But she looks at me really as if she *hated* me,' Sainty persisted. 'If she has mistaken her feelings, if the idea is repugnant to her, if she feels that, having once given her word, she is bound, either out of consideration for me, or fear of all the talk, to go through with things, is it not our duty, yours and mine before all others, to save her from herself while there is yet time?'

'Dear modest fellow! Every word you say makes me love you more, and convinces me how exactly you are suited to such a nature as Cissy's; I see how well you will understand her; how patient, how gentle you will be with her. As to her behaviour to *you*, I know; I feel for you a dozen times a day; but you must not doubt her affection. Good gracious! I treated my poor dear husband a thousand times worse when we were engaged. My mother used to say she didn't see how he stood it; but the dear man had endless patience; he never doubted; and he soon succeeded in reconciling me to my fate,' added the lady, with a modest simper, 'when once we were married.'

'Maidenly tremors are all very well,' said Sainty, 'but Cissy's behaviour gives me the impression of a much deeper seated repugnance. Don't, for pity's sake, let her wreck her life if she isn't sure she cares enough for me to marry me.'

'You are generous, considerate, unselfish as ever,' cried Lady Eccleston. 'But trust *me* who know her so well. My dear Sainty, do you suppose if I were not absolutely sure this marriage was for my child's happiness, that I, her mother, who must have her welfare at heart, should not be the first to oppose it?'

After that there seemed nothing more to be said. Still Sainty was not satisfied, and he determined to carry his perplexities to his uncle, on whose sterling commonsense he had often leaned comfortably in boyhood.

Lord Firth looked grave, and pursed up his mouth judicially.

'This is awkward,' he said, 'infernally awkward. Do you mean to say you want to get out of it?'

'Oh no! not for myself at all. I don't say I'm desperately in love; but I don't know that I ever should be. As
long as I thought Cissy cared for me, I was very much
honoured, and ready to devote my life to making her
happy; but as the time comes nearer, I am more and more
convinced that she does not love me. She may have felt
sorry for me; she may have let herself be dazzled by what
she would gain in a worldly way. I don't pretend to understand why she took me; but I am sure she repents what
she has done, that, if it could be managed for her, she
would be glad to be released.'

'Have you told her so? Have you offered to release her?

'Yes.'

'Well, what did she say?'

'She said nothing. When I pressed her she said she
didn't know what she wanted. Then her mother came in,
and Cissy went out of the room.'

'Did you say anything about it to the old woman?'

'Yes; I said what I've just told you.'

'And what did *she* say?'

'Oh, she said girls were always like that, that I didn't
understand them—which God knows I don't—that a
modest girl was always in a funk before marriage, and
that she would be all right afterwards.'

'Hm,' said Lord Firth. 'Well, I'm an old bachelor, and
don't know much about them either; they're queer
creatures. I always vaguely distrust that Eccleston
woman; but I've no reason for supposing she would sell
her daughter, and I must say the girl has never struck me
as being particularly under her mother's thumb. On the
contrary, she's always been rather pert to her when I've
seen her.'

'I can't make it out; it all seems a hopeless tangle,' said
poor Sainty.

'The whole business struck me, when I heard of it, as
being rather rash and ill-advised,' said his uncle. 'If I
had been consulted, I should have suggested you had
better both have been a little surer of your own feelings
before announcing the engagement. I suspected your
mother and Lady Eccleston of cooking up the affair when

I heard of the Ecclestons being so much at Belchamber, but I didn't feel called upon to interfere. It was obviously desirable that you should marry, and if you fancied Miss Cissy, I knew nothing against the girl, though I don't much care for the mother. Besides, you are of age, and capable of arranging your own life without the interference of a guardian.'

'Then you think there is nothing to be done?'

'I don't see what. You say you've offered the girl to break it off, and she didn't seem to wish it, or at least wasn't sure, and that her mother assured you she was only shy. What more can you do? If *you* want to back out, it's another matter. Though it would look very bad so near the time, I suppose it might be done.'

As a last resort Sainty wrote to his mother, though he felt sure what her answer would be; and sure enough Lady Charmington wrote with no uncertain pen. 'If you had any misgivings you had better not have been in such a hurry to propose. Now it is altogether too late to go back on your word. I consider that you are bound in honour almost as if you were already married. It would be abominable to throw the girl over at the eleventh hour, when she has got her things, and all the invitations are out for the wedding. Think of the mortification to her, of the scandal it would cause. People might even say you had found out something against her. It would be enough to prevent her making another match, for every one would know of it, and talk about it.'

Sainty was struck for the hundredth time with the inevitability of his mother's misapprehension. She passed over in silence all question of Cissy not caring for him, which was the one point on which he had insisted, and instantly assumed that his misgivings arose from nothing but the fatal weakness of his character, which made flight his one impulse in face of any decisive act.

Sainty had made his last effort, and proceeded to drift resignedly with the stream. There was just one other person to whom he had momentarily thought of applying for counsel and help, and that was his old friend Mrs. de Lissac; but Alice had behaved rather strangely, he thought, about the whole matter. On first coming to London, he had gone to see her as a matter of course; but though she had made a grand dinner for him and Cissy in honour of the engagement, and had showered magnificent presents on them both, the old cordial welcome was somehow lacking. She seemed ill at ease with him, and had fluttered hastily away from all attempts on his part to talk about Cissy, displaying positive terror if he showed any disposition to become confidential.

Nothing was easier than to discourage Sainty from talking about himself. If his confidences were not met, as Alice de Lissac had always hitherto met them, more than half-way, they died a natural death.

The day of Belchamber's nuptials dawned inevitably in its turn. No convulsion of nature destroyed Lord Firth's comfortable bachelor quarters, or buried the north side of Chester Square in ruins. Sainty got through the morning somehow, in a sort of waking dream, listening abstractedly to Gerald Newby, who had come up from Cambridge at his request to act as his 'best man,' and had much to say on many subjects, from the marriage-service of the Church of England—of some parts of which he strongly disapproved— to the tyranny of custom which imposed the high hat and frock coat, garments neither comfortable, convenient, nor æsthetically beautiful.

Lady Charmington, who was staying at Roehampton with old Lady Firth, brought her mother in for an early lunch as the wedding was fixed for half-past two.

At the appointed time Sainty found himself planted by a great bank of palms and heavy-scented white flowers that made him feel sick. From where he stood the whole great church was visible. Dimly, as through a mist, he could descry his mother, straight and stern, in puritanical drab, beside the huddled white chuddah and nodding plumes of his grandmother, the duchess strapped into a petunia velvet, with a silver bonnet whose aigrette seemed to sweep the skies, his Aunt Eva in a Gainsborough hat, taking rapid notes for the *Looking-glass*, and Claude, slim, cool, and elegant, his beautifully gloved, pearl-grey hands crossed upon his cane, which he had rested on the seat beside him as he stood sideways looking for the bride. Behind them a sea of faces, mostly unknown, of light colours and black coats, of feathers, flowers, and laces, stretched back to where, in a cloud of pink and white, the bridesmaids clustered round the door, holding the great bouquets of roses he had so nearly forgotten to order for them.

The organ boomed, and the knowing-looking little choristers in their stiff surplices went clattering down the aisle followed by a perfect procession of smug ecclesiastics, among whom Sainty caught a fleeting glimpse of dear old Meakins from Great Charmington. Lady Eccleston, emotional, devotional, and gorgeous as the morning, rustled hastily to her place in the front pew where George and Randolph were already nudging each other and giggling. Then the little white-robed boys began to come back, shrilly chanting, and as the choir separated to right and left Sainty could see Tommy, very solemn and as red as the carnation in his buttonhole, and on his arm a vision of soft shrouded loveliness, coming slowly towards him. All the riddle of the future was hid in that veiled figure. How little he really knew what was in the little head and heart under all that whiteness; was it happiness or misery she was bringing him? an honoured, dignified married life, an equal share of joys and sorrows, 'the children like the olive branches round about their table'? or a loveless existence, the straining bonds of those unequally yoked, the little sordid daily squabbles that eat the heart, perhaps even shame, dishonour. . . .? What thoughts for a bridegroom stepping forward to meet his bride at the altar! But who is master of his thoughts?

CHAPTER XVII

THE Duke of Sunborough having only a castle in Scotland, a palace in the Midlands, a detached house with a garden in the centre of London, a shooting-lodge in the north of England, and an old manor-house on the border of Wales, had acquired in his stormy youth a little place in Surrey

some twelve or fifteen miles from town, a villa with terraces and cedar-trees and hothouses and shady lawns
sloping to the river, where, if Rumour may be credited,
there had sometimes been fine goings-on, but which was
now only used on rare occasions for what it has become
the fashion to call 'week-end parties.'

This modest retreat, which would have seemed to most
people a good-sized country-house, had been lent to the
young couple for their honeymoon, and thither they re-
paired, for greater state and privacy, in a large closed
carriage with four horses and postillions, their two new
dressing-bags sitting solemnly opposite to them on the
back seat, while the servants and luggage went by train.

Cissy, attired in the latest fashion and the palest hues,
with a very white face and very red eyes and nose, sat
huddled in one corner and stared out of the window,
occasionally dabbing her features with a little damp ball
of a pocket-handkerchief. From the other end of the long
seat, on which a third person could easily have found room·
between the little bride and bridegroom, Sainty watched
her compassionately. He contrasted the woebegone
aspect and silent aloofness of his companion with the
cheerful garrulity of the same young lady when she had
driven about the country with him only a few months
before. Then, had she seemed depressed or unhappy,
he would not have hesitated to ask the cause of her melancholy, to offer help or at least consolation. Why, now,
was he afraid to attempt to comfort or even to make a
movement towards her? The explanation seemed a
strange one: then she had been an acquaintance, now she
was his wife. His wife! The words struck with a certain
irony on his startled consciousness. It was that half-hour
in church which was to make them 'one flesh' which had
thrust them so far asunder.

At last the silence became unendurable.

'Cissy,' he said suddenly, 'are you very miserable?'

His voice breaking in on the monotonous sounds of their
progress startled himself hardly less than his companion.

Cissy shook herself and raised her head.

'Yes,' she said defiantly, without looking round.

'Because of me?'

'Yes—because of you.'

'Why, what have I done?' There was a relief in speech. If she would only talk, no matter what she said; she might abuse him, accuse him—anything was better than that horrible mute damp woe. But Cissy would not answer.

'Won't you tell me how I have offended you? What have I done that you don't like?'

'You've married me,' she snapped at him.

'Isn't that a little unjust?'

'Most likely it is, horribly unjust. I don't care if it is. I hate myself and you and everybody, and I wish I was dead.'

'Cissy, Cissy,' cried Sainty, dreadfully pained, 'don't say such things.'

'Then why did you ask me?' she retorted; 'why can't you let me alone?'

Sainty told himself if there was ever a moment for patience it was now; so much might depend on what he said next. He made a motion as though he would take her hand, but at that there flashed out of her face a look so evil, such a genuine naked horror as civilisation seldom lets us show. Sainty fell back appalled; he felt that he had seen in her eyes the very bottom of her feeling towards him, and viewed in the light of that revelation the whole hopelessness of their future relations stood momentarily clear before him. He lay back dazed and frightened, thankful as a man to whom lightning has shown the danger of his surroundings, for the friendly darkness that once more veils them from his sight; and for the rest of the drive neither occupant of the carriage said a word.

When at last they drew up at their destination the house was on Cissy's side, and as soon as a bowing servant had opened the carriage door she jumped out before Sainty could offer her any assistance. A little shower of rice that had lodged in the folds of her gown fell pattering from her in the precipitancy of her flight, which caused a discreet grin on the damp, red faces of the postilions and of the duke's under-butler, who had been sent down to help Sainty's valet with the service.

Belchamber caught a glimpse of an inscription framed in laurel leaves stretched across the lintel, of which all that was clear to him were the words 'happy pair,' as he followed his bride into the hall. Here the women who had charge of the house were drawn up together with Cissy's new maid and his own valet.

The housekeeper had embarked on a little speech, evidently prepared with care. 'May I be permitted,' she was saying, 'on behalf of myself and fellow-servants, to welcome your ladyship on this auspicious occasion, and to wish you and the marquis every happiness, and I am sure we shall do our very best to make you comfortable, and his lordship too.' Seeing that Cissy stared at the woman with a dull eye, Sainty came to the rescue.

'I am sure we are both very much obliged to you all,' he said, 'but Lady Belchamber is very tired, and would be glad to see her room, if you will show it to her.' Cissy started at the sound of her new name in the mouth of her husband, but moved off in the wake of the housekeeper, who had dropped from the monumental tone of her welcome into a more comfortable colloquialism. 'I am sure your ladyship *must* be tired—it's a most trying day; and you'll like to see your room, and would you like a cup of tea or anything after your long drive? Dinner isn't ordered till eight, and it's only half-past six. Tea is set out in the morning-room, but it will be quite easy to bring it up to you. I have tried to think of everything, but, of course, anything your ladyship wishes altered ...' Sainty heard her voice growing fainter down the corridor as Cissy and the maid followed her to the staircase. He watched the little procession out of sight and then turned wearily into the first room he came to and dropped with a long sigh upon the gaudy chintz flowers of a comfortable easy-chair. For him, too, the day had been 'trying' in more ways than one.

His man brought him a cup of tea and said that 'her ladyship' was having hers in her room and was going to rest till dinner-time. He had not yet been four hours wedded, and he noticed with shocked surprise the distinct relief with which he hailed the prospect of being free for a little from the strain of his wife's presence. Four hours! The morning seemed a hundred years ago! For the rest of his natural life had he got always to face this mute resentment? And for what? He had not forced her to marry him; indeed, he had adjured her not to. It was unheard of that she should treat him as a criminal; he examined his conscience and found that so far from having anything with which to reproach himself, he had behaved to her throughout with the most scrupulous consideration. Could Lady Eccleston be right, and might Cissy's behaviour be nothing but the natural nervousness of a modest young woman? Were girls always so terrified in presence of the bridal mysteries? If that were all, she might count on his perfect sympathy. No girl could be more of a stranger to all that side of life than he, or approach it with more invincible shyness. In all their talks it had seemed to him that the balance of true modesty had been rather on his side than hers; he had often been shocked by things she had said, but he could recollect no occasion on which any remark of his had appeared to embarrass her in the least.

Tired nature must have come to rescue him from his many perplexities, for he was recalled to consciousness from a doze by the clock striking a half-hour, and finding it was half-past seven, he decided to go upstairs and get ready for dinner. He had no difficulty in finding his room. Through almost the first door on the upper landing he saw his new brushes adorning the dressing-table, his clothes laid out upon the bed. As he turned in, he noticed the sharp click of a key in another door from that by which he had entered, and which evidently communicated with the next room, for behind it he could hear sounds of people moving about, the opening and shutting of drawers and cupboards, and occasionally Cissy's voice speaking to her maid. That he heard all these sounds but indistinctly was presently explained to him. Having changed his clothes he tapped discreetly, and receiving no answer proceeded to turn the handle; to his pleasure it yielded; he had been mistaken then; she had not the distrust of him he had fancied. But his gratification was short-lived; there were double doors between the rooms, and the inner one was quite securely fastened.

'Who's there?' cried Cissy sharply.

'I hope you're rested,' Sainty called in a voice which he tried to make pleasantly indifferent; 'I'm going down, shall I tell them to get dinner, or are you not ready?'

'I'll be down in a minute. Don't wait for me,' she called back, but made no offer to undo the door.

Dinner was not a cheerful meal, when presently Cissy appeared in a smart new tea-gown, and took her place opposite to him. She crumpled her bread and drank a great deal of water, and played with the wine-glasses and her rings and the lace upon her dress. The meal passed almost in silence, the two men gliding softly about and handing the dishes. Cissy ate nothing, and Sainty felt obliged to break and taste a long succession of undesired meats.

'They have given us too much,' he said. 'We must tell that good lady to-morrow that we don't want all these things.'

Cissy assented indifferently.

'You're not eating anything,' Sainty said, after a pause.

'I'm not hungry. I had tea so late.'

Sainty found himself talking to the servants, and asking for things he did not want, to break the oppressiveness of the atmosphere.

If Cissy ate nothing while the servants were present, she made up for it when they had left the room, by piling a whole dish of strawberries on her plate, covering them with cream, and eating them voraciously. Sainty watched her uneasily, with a sudden dread that she might be going mad.

Things were not much more lively after dinner. The smiling housekeeper had explained that she had not had the drawing-room lit up as she thought they would be more 'cosy' in the 'boodwar.' Cissy sank deep in a big armchair, and appeared to be immersed in a novel she had brought with her. Sainty tried to read too, but his attention wandered; his eyes fell first on his companion, the swirl of diaphanous drapery that escaped from the arms of her chair and flowed out upon the floor like water between the piers of a bridge, the little foot in its bead-wrought slipper, the hands flashing with new rings that held the gaudy book-cover like a shield between her face and him. From her they roved to her surroundings. The room in which they sat had been decorated about the year 1860 by Italian artists. Trellised grape vines were painted on the walls, mixed with roses and large blue flowers of the convolvulus family. Birds of gay plumage and highly imaginative butterflies were sprinkled about them, and here and there a plump cupid in a pink loin-cloth stood poised on one foot among the foliage, swinging a basket of flowers. Cupids, indeed, were everywhere; several of them floated round a hook in the sky-coloured ceiling, and made believe that it was not it, but they, who supported the glass chandelier. They crawled in white marble all over the bulging sides of the low, flamboyant mantelpiece. On the French clock above it, a gilt Eros perpetually clasped his Psyche, while from the console between the elaborately draped windows, a biscuit representation of the same divinity held his finger discreetly to his lips.

The note of old-fashioned gaiety which is somehow lacking in our more correct modern apartments seemed specially to fit the place to be the frame of love. Its amoretti and impossible flowers, its white marble and gilding and pale silks, suggested accustomed complicity. In presence of what human kisses had those little ormolu lovers continued their indifferent embraces? What scenes of passion had been multiplied in endless reproduction by those tall opposing mirrors? Perhaps in that very room, Sainty thought, his grandmother might have been tempted towards the breaking of those same vows he had that day taken on himself. He came on her portrait presently in a book of beauty, bound with much tooling in faded crimson calf, which he was idly turning over on the red velvet centre-table. He took it over and showed it to Cissy.

'Look at grandmamma,' he said; 'wasn't she beautiful?'

Cissy took the picture and stared at it with no answering

smile. It seemed to have a curious fascination for her. 'How like!' she murmured. 'How very like!'

'Oh! come,' said Sainty, glad to get her to talk about anything. 'I can't say I think her grace looks much like that nowadays.'

'I didn't mean that it was like the duchess,' said Cissy with a hysterical gulp. 'But don't you see the extra-ordinary likeness to Cl—— to your cousin Mr. Morland?'

Sainty could not have explained why the sudden mention of Claude was displeasing to him.

'He is thought like our grandmother,' he said shortly, 'but he is not nearly so good-looking; the duchess was a great beauty in her youth.'

Cissy did not discuss the question, but she kept the book absently in her lap, and when Sainty had returned to his reading, he could see her turning the pages.

As the long hours wore away, Belchamber became intolerably weary, and he suspected Cissy of being not less so; but when taxed with fatigue, she eagerly repudiated the idea, and professed a tremendous interest in her book. 'I *must* see how it is going to come out,' she said; 'it's awfully exciting.'

Sainty ached all over, but he could not insist. He returned to his own reading, which he found less stimulating than Cissy seemed to find hers. After a while he noticed she had moved into a harder and more upright chair. She was struggling against sleep; in half an hour she had not turned a page of the work she found so enthralling. Finally, towards midnight, he saw the book waving to and fro, the fair head bowed almost down on it. He went softly over to her, and touched her. With a cry she started to her feet; the book fell on the floor with a bang.

'You must go to bed, Cissy,' Sainty said kindly; 'you're dropping with sleep.'

'I'm not tired; I'm not sleepy,' she cried. 'I must finish this—it's so interesting.'

'Nonsense. I've been watching you; you haven't read a page in half an hour; you can't keep your eyes open.'

Her eyes were open enough now, wide and strange, like

those of a hunted animal. She made a gesture with her hands as though to thrust him back. 'I can't—I won't,' she panted. 'You shan't make me. Keep away. Don't touch me.'

'My poor child,' Sainty said, 'what are you afraid of? Do you think I would do anything you don't like? You can't sit up all night. You are dead tired, and must have rest. I won't come near you, if you don't wish it.'

She looked at him but half reassured. 'Do you mean it?' she said doubtfully. 'Can I trust you?'

'I am not accustomed to lie,' Sainty answered. 'Do you think I would take advantage of you by a shabby trick?'

She sighed, and half turned away, then suddenly faced him again. 'It is not enough,' she cried. 'It is not only to-night. You may as well know it first as last. You are odious to me—horrible. I can never—never——'

'Hush, hush!' Sainty interrupted her. 'Take care what you say. You are tired, excited, overwrought. So am I. Go to bed now, in God's name. You know you have nothing to fear. We will talk of this some other time, calmly if we can, but not to-night, not to-night.'

'Yes, now, to-night,' she insisted. 'Why put it off? It's got to be faced, and why not at once? I tell you you are repulsive to me. I can never be your wife in anything but name. I thought I could, but when it comes to the point, I can't do it. It's stronger than me. It's no use.' She spread her hands with the gesture of one who renounces a struggle. On her finger blazed the ring he had given her, and below it shone the plain gold hoop which he had placed there that morning, the outward and visible sign of the obligation she was repudiating.

Sainty staggered as though she had struck him in the face. 'I don't understand,' he whispered. 'If you feel like this towards me, if I am repulsive, loathsome to you, why did you marry me?'

'Oh, it's simple enough,' she answered, with a little cruel laugh. 'You had so many things that I have always wanted, money, position, rank, everything I have been brought up to think desirable. Since I can remember, not a girl has been married among our friends that the first question has not been, was she making a "good" marriage? which meant, was she getting a big enough share of all these things in exchange for herself? No one could say I wasn't. I've made the match of the season. There isn't a girl I know, or a mother, who isn't green with envy of me. You can't say it wasn't a temptation.' And she laughed again hysterically.

'But feeling as you did about me, as you must before the end have known you felt, why in heaven's name didn't you turn back, when I gave you the chance, before it was too late?'

'Do you think I was allowed a minute to think? Wasn't my mother there every minute of the day? At the very time you speak of, wasn't she listening at the door, and didn't she come hurrying in before I'd time to answer? If for a moment I ever forgot the title, and the money, and the jewels, the big house, all the things I'd set my heart on, she was always ready to talk about them, to dangle them before me. If I ever wavered, she would tell me what a slur it was on a girl whose engagement was broken off, how no one would ever believe I had given up all these things of my own free will, how people would say there was something against me, and how I should never marry. There wasn't an oldish poor girl we knew, losing her looks, and still tagging about to balls, and try- ing to pretend she was cheerful, that she didn't remind me of. Never directly, mind you. They were just casually mentioned. O Lord! if I so much as suggested to her that she wanted me to marry for money, she was all virtuous indignation.'

'How ghastly!' Sainty whispered in horror. 'I've read of such things, of mothers selling their daughters, bullying them into marrying men they couldn't love for the sake of an establishment; but I've always thought it was ex- aggerated, not true to life. I didn't think a mother *could* condemn her own child to lifelong misery.'

'Oh, you mustn't be too hard on mamma,' Cissy said. 'She thought she was doing the best thing for me. Re- member she has the very highest opinion of you, and was quite sure you would make an excellent husband; and she knew how much I wanted all the other things. If marriage were nothing but that, nothing but living in the house with a person who was good-natured and never interfered with one, and provided all the good things of life for one, it would be well enough. That is what every one in England always talks to girls as if it were. Mamma would have thought it most indelicate to suggest there was another side. You are made to forget that as much as possible. Oh, of course I *knew*, because I'm not a fool, and girls are not such ninnies as people think them; but I tried to forget, and when I didn't see you, I *did* forget. That was why, when I did see you, I was always so beastly to you; for I'm quite ready to admit I *was* beastly to you.'

As Cissy's terror abated, her engaging frankness began to return to her. Sainty couldn't help liking her for it. He began to be so full of sympathy with her point of view, so sorry for all she must have suffered, that he almost forgot the cruel wrong she had done him.

'Mamma knew I should never be happy with a poor man,' she went on. 'She knew how I cared for all the things you could give me. She was quite right, I *did* want them; I wanted them awfully; I want them still as much as ever: only when it comes to the point I can't give the price. I thought I could, but I can't. Mamma was so far honester than me. She never supposed that once the bargain was made I should hesitate to pay. It's so like me to want things dreadfully, and not to have the courage to do what's necessary to get them.'

Sainty was appalled by her cynicism, even while he admired her straightforwardness. What became of his dreams of romance, of the eye that had seen beneath his unattractive exterior, and loved him for the beauties of his soul? The blue eyes had seen nothing but the sparkling of diamonds. In her vision of married life he had been only the necessary evil, the odious, inevitable condition to which she must submit, if she would have his name and money, as the princess in the story had to kiss the swineherd to get possession of the toys she coveted. Still the princess *had* kissed the herd, and even after all that she had said he thought he would make one last appeal to her. If she realised how much he felt for her, how entirely he understood her unwillingness, how patient, how gentle he was ready to be, perhaps she might be touched, might learn to think of him with something less of horror. To him who had all his life wished for nothing but to make other people happy, it was intolerable to think of himself as the brutal gaoler, the tyrant before whom this young thing paled with terror.

In the eagerness of her explanation, Cissy had come nearer to him. They were standing quite close together, face to face. 'Cissy,' he said gently, 'is it quite, quite impossible? Do you think that if we lived together for a long time, you might in the end get used to me, even come to care for me a little?' But at that she sprang back from him again with an unmistakable gesture of repugnance that said more than words. 'No, no, no—never,' she cried hurriedly. 'I've told you it's no good. I can't help it, my mind's made up. I'd rather give up everything, face anything, for of course I can't expect you to keep me. You can send me back to my mother. Life'll be hell upon earth, but it'll be better than *that*.'

With all his desire to be fair to her, Sainty could not but be struck by her intense egotism, her inability to appreciate any point of view but her own. She was evidently unaware of the brutality of her attitude towards him. To his morbid self-depreciation her undisguised horror of him appeared only too natural. Still, no one likes to be told of these things quite so bluntly.

'You have nothing to fear,' he said a little loftily. 'After what you have said, you may be sure I shall never ask the smallest thing of you. It is a little unfortunate that you didn't make up your mind rather earlier, as you have made it up so irrevocably now. Had you but been as sure of your feelings a month, a week, even twenty-four hours ago, you might have saved us both from what I hardly dare look forward to.'

'I can go home; I had better go home,' Cissy whimpered. Of course the sight of distress melted Sainty at once.

'Don't you see,' he said, 'that to go home now would make just five hundred times the talk and scandal that you felt you couldn't face if you had broken off your engagement?'

'It can't be helped,' Cissy sobbed.

'You have brought us both into a horrible situation,' Sainty answered, 'and I frankly don't see just now what is best to be done; but I'm sure that further talk will do no good just now. It is long past twelve o'clock, and we are both tired out; you can't go back to Chester Square to-night, if you want to ever so much. If I were you I shouldn't get up to breakfast. Good-night.'

Some compunction seemed to seize Cissy as she got to the door. She turned. 'I'm awfully sorry, you know,' she said. 'I suppose, when you come to think of it, I haven't treated you any too well; and—and—of course what I said wasn't very civil, but I thought it best to be honest——'

'All right, all right,' Sainty answered hastily; 'please don't say any more about it.'

As he lay sleepless and uncomfortable on his lonely bed, he wished that the necessity for honest dealing had impressed itself on his wife a little sooner. He thought of the night three years before, when he had lain awake (as he lay now) listening to the sounds that celebrated his coming of age. Somehow the great festal days of his life did not seem to bring him personally much enjoyment.

CHAPTER XVIII

THE Belchambers took possession of their new town-house just in time for the opening of Parliament in the ensuing year. It was only partially furnished as yet, and most uncomfortable; but, as Lady Eccleston remarked with great originality, 'the only way to get the workmen out of a house was to move in yourself.' The first-floor rooms still echoed with shouts and hammerings, but the upper part of the house was more or less ready, and so were the dining-room and some back rooms on the ground-floor, which Cissy had reluctantly decided should eventually be given up to Sainty. It was astonishing how swiftly she had

> 'Shaped her heart with woman's meekness
> To all duties of her rank,'

except the vulgar and obvious one which she would have shared with the humblest of wives. Having once made it quite clear that she was to receive everything and give nothing, she soon ceased to talk of returning to her mother, and Sainty was amazed at the ease with which she adapted herself to the awkwardness of the situation. In her place, he felt sure, he would not have rung a bell, or asked for a postage stamp, but it never seemed to occur to Cissy that there was anything curious in the arrangement; she annexed all her husband's possessions without scruple or hesitation as soon as she discovered that no embarrassing condition attached to doing so.

In spite of her son's entreaties that she would stay with them, Lady Charmington had retired to the dower-house immediately after the marriage, and they had barely returned from their brief and dismal honeymoon in the duke's villa before Cissy began to dispose of everything at Belchamber as if it had all been hers from earliest childhood. There had been some talk of a wedding-journey on the Continent, but Cissy had no desire to prolong the *tête-à-tête* with Sainty, which she did not enjoy. It was England, which she knew and understood, that was to be the scene of her triumphs; and the sight of strange lands had no charms for her compared to the fun of swooping down as mistress on the great house, where she had been an unconsidered little guest, settling which should be her own rooms, having them redecorated according to the taste of the latest fashionable uphol-sterer, and moving into them whatever took her fancy in other parts of the house.

She was so happily busy that she almost forgot to regret the Season, and gave up Ascot without a sigh, contenting herself with Cowes and Goodwood, which she did with great *éclat* from a friend's yacht, while Sainty enjoyed a fortnight of peace and seclusion.

Congenial as she found the task of establishing herself in her husband's ancestral home, it was nothing to the delirious enjoyment of selecting, decorating, and furnishing a big London house, regardless of expense ; and all the time she could spare from entertaining shooting parties in the autumn was devoted to the feverish prosecution of this new delight.

Of course every one agreed that they must have a town-house. The duke and Lord Firth were not less convinced of its necessity than the large circle of acquaintances who hoped to be entertained in it. Even Lady Charmington, while she winced at the recklessness of the expenditure, was partly consoled by the sight of her son taking what she considered 'his proper position in the world.' She consoled herself with the thought that it was her long years of careful management that made all this profusion possible. Sainty must attend the debates in the House of Lords, and though she was rather scandalised by his Radicalism, she reflected that the limited number of peers on that side, since the Home Rule split, made some small office not improbable for him, when the Liberals came in again.

And Sainty, though he cared for none of these things, had no heart to refuse them to the girl whom he had married. The fact was that the more he thought about the matter the sorrier he felt for his wife. For his part, he told himself, he was not made for love, had never expected it to play any part in his life, and was no worse off than he was before. The disadvantage of taking a consistently humble view of one's own attractions is not without its compensations ; thus the wound to his self-love, of which a vain man would almost have bled to death, was to Sainty, who had no vanity and very little self-love, only in the nature of those scratches which smart and feel sore, but rob us of no drop of heart's blood. Life was not perceptibly more unpleasant to him than it had been before, and he had still the same substitutes for a more active happiness with which he had been acccustomed to fill it, his studies, his schemes of beneficence, the management of his property. But this poor child, so well

fitted by nature to love and be loved, whose one chance
of rising above the empty frivolity of her surroundings
might have lain in the enobling influence of a great
passion, for something how much less satisfying than a
mess of pottage had she bartered her birthright, a handful
of tin counters, a paper crown! In spite of what he considered her generosity in taking the blame on herself, he
was more and more inclined to regard her as the victim
of her mother's worldliness, enmeshed like himself in the
toils of that careful schemer. It was not in nature that a
creature so young and fresh should be greatly influenced
by considerations of wealth or rank; he could not think
it. These things had been dangled before her eyes till
she had been dazzled by their false lustre. She was too
innocent, he reflected, to realise to what extent she had
sacrificed all chances of woman's best happiness to gain
them. The question was how to shield her from the
consequences of her own act, to save her from the bitter
repentance only too likely to follow. To do so might not
be permanently in his power; but meanwhile, if she so
keenly desired the undesirable as to be ready to risk the
ruin of her life for it, what was simpler than to give it to
her! Jewels, clothes, a house in town, the means to feed
the thankless rich, the power to walk out of the room
before older women—if these things could make her happy,
as far as they were his to give, let her take them in full
measure. They were freely hers. He had no particular
use for them himself.

Perhaps the spectacle of the ease and gusto with which
she flung herself into her new *rôle* of the great lady was
not without a certain satiric amusement for him.

One day he would find her on the pavement before the
house, attended by Algy Montgomery and a grave professional gentleman who looked the ideal of a racing
duke, while a pair of high-stepping bays were driven up
and down for her inspection. 'Haven't we more horses
than we know what to do with?' Sainty would ask.

'My dear boy!' Cissy cried, 'a parcel of old screws.
Jane Rugby was saying only the other day that we hadn't
a decent pair o' horses in the stable.'

On another she would be busy comparing designs for carriages. 'Those old bathing-machines at Belchamber,' she remarked loftily, 'are all very well for the country; but in my position it would be too grotesque for me to be seen driving about London in them. The duchess has been awfully kind about advising me. It was her idea to send for the old chariot and see if it can't be done up for drawing-rooms. She says unless it has got dry-rot or anything, that a couple of hundreds spent on it ought to make it as good as new; and of course I don't want to waste money on a tiresome thing one would never use on other occasions, if by spending a little on the old one it can be made to do. But I *must* have a decent brougham and open carriage at once; you must see yourself there are no two ways about it. And, come to think of it, you ought to have a brougham of your own. We are sure to clash and want it at the same time, if we try and do with one.'

'Perhaps one of the bathing-machines from Belchamber might do for *me*,' suggested Sainty, not without malice.

'Well,' said Cissy quite gravely, 'I don't know that it mightn't.'

'Who told you of these people?' Sainty asked, examining the neatly painted pictures.

'Oh, they make all the duke's carriages, and *they* are always smartly turned out. Your cousin Claude told them to send me these sketches, and he has promised to go with me to Long Acre to see what they have in the shop.'

Since she married, Cissy had ceased to mention Claude as 'Mr Morland,' and the prefix 'your cousin' was bridging the narrow chasm between that and calling him 'Claude.' Morland was able to be uncommonly useful to the pretty new cousin; not only at the coachbuilder's were his taste and knowledge invaluable, but at the upholsterer's, the *bric-à-brac* shops, the sales at Christie's, and he had even been called on to give his views (and very sound views too) in the more intimate province of the modiste and the dressmaker. Sainty was obviously of no assistance. What could be more natural, if the lady needed counsel in such matters, than to turn to a near kinsman of her husband, and one so well qualified to help? It is true that Lady Eccleston was more than ready to assist her daughter in mounting her establishment on a suitable scale, and would very willingly have accompanied her to the shops, not, perhaps, without a hope of gleaning a few scattered ears on her own account from the harvest Cecilia was reaping with so large a hook; but that unnatural young person seemed to prefer almost any advice or companionship to her mamma's. Ill as he thought of her, for the manœuvres with which she had compassed his union with her daughter, Sainty could not help a secret sympathy with the poor lady, who bore her pitiless relegation to a back place with the smiling stoicism worthy of a Red Indian. The old fiction of the perfect confidence and sisterlike relation between herself and her daughter was still gallantly maintained even to him, and when he reflected what potentialities of tearful complainings she had heroically foregone, he came near to feeling actual gratitude. But he need have been under no apprehension of plaintive confidences; anything natural or direct had long ceased to be possible to Lady Eccleston.

'I cannot have mamma dropping in to lunch whenever it suits her,' Cissy remarked ruthlessly. 'I have told her she must not come more than once a week, unless she's asked.'

'But I thought you said you meant to let people know you were always at home for lunch?'

'So I do; it is a very convenient way of seeing my friends. That's just why I've had to speak to mamma. I should have her here every day if I didn't. And it would bore a lot of younger women, who don't know her particularly well, like Vere Deans or Ella Dalsany, to find her here perpetually—not to speak of the men.'

Sainty did not retort that Lady Deans and Lady Dalsany were not so very much younger than Lady Eccleston. It was no affair of his; and it soon became evident that Cissy's mother was not the only relation whom it bored her friends to meet at her luncheon-table.

Sainty had been brought up in a certain old-fashioned code of manners. His mother, seeing that he was shy and awkward in company, and being not less so herself, had insisted rather unduly on the ceremonial side of social life. He had been taught that hospitality demanded that he should receive and take leave of guests with some form, accompanying them to their carriages, and putting on their cloaks, which the groom of the chambers, who was much taller and unencumbered with a stick, would have done much better. But he was not long in discovering that these attentions were by no means demanded by the ladies of the set into which the duchess and Claude had made haste to introduce his wife.

If Cissy's friends found Sainty tiresome, it must be admitted that he found them no less so. The repulsion was certainly mutual. He wondered sometimes what had become of all the people she had known and liked, and from whom she had received kindness, during the three or four seasons that had preceded her marriage; they seemed to have vanished like smoke. She was absorbed in a little knot of married women, for the most part considerably her seniors, much in the world's eye, and none of them exactly qualified for the *rôle* of Cæsar's wife. Their conversation was extremely esoteric, and the minute fragments of it which were intelligible to him shocked him profoundly. Occasional paragraphs in the papers assured him that 'young Lady Belchamber,' or 'pretty little Lady Belchamber, who was among the most attractive of last season's brides,' was 'very smart' or 'quite in the innermost set'; from which he was fain to derive such comfort as he might. He once ventured to ask Cissy why she never saw anything of the de Lissacs; he had hoped something for her from Alice's influence. 'I thought you and the girls were very intimate,' he said.

'Oh! girls bore me,' she answered; 'and besides, they are not the least in it; they wouldn't have anything in common with the people they'd meet here. Of course with their money they *might* have done anything, but poor dear Mrs. de Lissac has no *flair*, don't you know; she simply doesn't take any trouble. I'll ask them, if you like, some day when I'm having a duty dinner.' And she did.

'Why do we never see anything of you?' Sainty asked of his old friend on that occasion. 'I had hoped that when we came to town we should be much together.'

'Well—here we are!' said Alice, with rather frosty playfulness. 'And you know,' she added more gently, 'how welcome you always are in Grosvenor Square.'

'Cissy is always at home to lunch, you know,' Sainty persisted. 'Why don't you come in sometimes?'

'Lady Belchamber has never told either the girls or me that she was at home to lunch,' said Alice, freezing again, and went on hurriedly to praise the beauty of the house and the taste of its mistress. Sainty looked round him. 'Cissy has a genius for spending money,' he said gloomily. 'Wait till you see the drawing-rooms; these rooms are nothing to the plunges she is making upstairs.' Before Mrs. de Lissac could answer, they were swooped upon by Lady Eccleston bringing Lady Deans with her.

'Dear Alice,' she cried, 'Lady Deans fears you don't remember her; you met at Belchamber. She is going to have a stall at the World's Bazaar, and this is such an opportunity to have a little quiet talk about it. I have been telling Lady Deans that you are one of our *very* kindest helpers, and that you have given the most superb things; a few *really* good things that can be raffled for are such a help, and one can always raffle the same things two or three times over—no one ever knows.'

'Why shouldn't we have a lottery?' asked Lady Deans. 'I mean a *real* lottery, not for sofa-cushions and things, but for money prizes like they have abroad. I'm sure it 'ld catch on.'

'But I thought lotteries were illegal,' Sainty objected.

'Oh! not at bazaars, or for a charity,' cried Lady Eccleston. 'I know dear Father Stephen of St. Radegund's, Houndsditch, told me they had a most successful one for their parish room and made heaps of money. I think Lady Deans's is a lovely idea.'

'Well—it's gambling you know,' said Sainty. 'I suppose you wouldn't allow a roulette table——'

'Why don't you have a Derby sweep while you're about it?' suggested Algy Montgomery. 'You could sell the tickets at the bazaar, and as the Derby won't be for a good couple o' months later you could forget to draw it at all. People would only suppose some other fellow had won, don't yer know.'

Lady Eccleston was enchanted with the notion. 'Dear Lord Algy! *Could* you work it for us?' But Mrs. de Lissac, inured as she was to bazaar morality, was, as a clergyman's daughter, a little alarmed at any connection with the turf. 'How are you getting on with the people for the Café Chantant?' she asked, to change the subject.

Lady Eccleston rattled off a list that seemed to contain every one of any celebrity in the theatrical or musical world.

'And have you got them all?' asked Lady Deans.

'Well, I've written to a good many of them, and one or two have answered,' said Lady Eccleston; 'but I shall pop them all down—their names will look splendid on the programme.'

'But will they come?' asked Sainty.

'Oh *dear* no, they won't come; very few of them will *come*. But some will; I shall make sure of one or two, and we can get some really good amateurs; and every now and then some one can get up and say that Ellen Terry regrets she couldn't manage it at the last moment, or something. We shall let people in for ten minutes at a time in batches; they'll think they just missed some of the best people——'

'Seems to me you *will* "let 'em in,"' chuckled Lord Algy.

'Do you think,' asked Lady Deans, 'there would be any chance of getting Lady Arthur to sing or dance, or anything? I suppose, Lord Belchamber, *you* couldn't ask her for us?'

'But she never *could* sing or dance, or do anything,' interposed Lord Algernon.

'Oh! that wouldn't matter, as long as she would appear. You see, all the story of her marriage and everything made her a celebrity.'

'But it was two years ago,' Lady Eccleston interrupted.

'People have forgotten all about it,' and she deftly piloted the discussion to other projects, so that Sainty was spared the necessity of making any answer to this astounding proposition.

The bazaar in connection with which so many happy suggestions had been offered was one of Society's periodic sacrifices to philanthropy. Certain fair ones, to whom no form of self-advertisement came amiss, were ready to dress up in the cause of charity and display themselves to a wider public than that which usually had the opportunity of admiring them, on the understanding that none of the trouble of organisation should fall upon them, and that the date should be fixed for before Easter, when there wasn't much else going on. On these conditions, Lady Eccleston and a little band of zealous fellow-workers had secured a most imposing list of stall-holders. It was calculated that the suburbs and the Stock Exchange would come in their thousands to see and converse with the ladies whose names and doings Lady Eva Morland made weekly familiar to them in the pages of 'Maidie's Tea Table' in the *Looking-glass*. The proceeds were to be handed to a charity in which a very great personage was interested, and the bazaar was to be opened on at least two of its three days by different members of the royal family. Lady Eccleston was in her element, and running the whole concern. If it was not she who had the brilliant inspiration of making the various stalls represent the countries of the earth and dressing the fair vendors in national costume, at least she took the credit for it. In spite of his mother-in-law's repeated injunctions to him to attend the opening, Sainty had not the slightest intention of doing so. Indeed, he had hoped, by liberal contributions, to get off altogether, but Alice de Lissac had reinforced Lady Eccleston with gentle persistence.

'I think you should put in an appearance,' she said, 'just to support your wife, you know ; it will look queer if you don't, when she and her mother are so much interested. *I* should have thought you would have come to the opening'; and finally Sainty was fain to buy immunity from being present at this ceremony with a promise to visit his wife's stall in the course of one afternoon. It was not till somewhat late on the last day of the three that he brought himself to redeem his given word.

By the time he arrived, the whole show, though brilliantly lighted and to his perception still disagreeably crowded, had become a little worse for wear. The stalls were denuded of half their contents, the air had a vitiated second-hand taste, and a fine impalpable dust, raised by the passing of so many feet, hung like a light haze over everything. Tired, dishevelled girls, looking curiously sham in their fancy dresses by the side of people in everyday garb, and flushed under the rouge that had been thought a necessary part of their costume, moved among the crowd making a last effort to dispose of the remainder of their wares, excited by competition to perilous lengths of flirtation with unknown and rather common young men, with whom on no other occasion they would have thought of exchanging a word.

Sainty was patiently elbowing his way like Parsifal among the flower-maidens, and meditating on the mystery of what was and was not permitted to the London girl, when he was suddenly confronted by Mr. Austin Pryor. Every buttonhole of the young stockbroker's neat frock-coat was decorated with faded vegetation and his arms loaded with a number of quite useless purchases.

'Well, Belchamber,' he began, 'I've got a bone to pick with your wife ; too bad of her, I call it. I'd an awful good time here yesterday with her, and she made me promise to come again to-day and bring a lot of our fellows from the city. I told 'em all how ripping she looked in her Polish get-up, and now they've all come and she isn't here ; she's gone and given us all the slip. Most unprincipled of her, I call it.'

Sainty, while expressing suitable distress at the faithless behaviour of his spouse, was secretly not sorry to be spared her encounter with the gallant Lotharios of Throgmorton Street, when he thought of the fragments of conversation he had already overheard in passing.

'I don't know what has happened to her, I'm sure,' he said politely ; 'I expected to find her here myself.'

When at last he arrived at the lath and canvas pavilion, much bedraped with Liberty muslin and flags, across the front of which a scroll displayed the legend, 'Poland— Marchioness of Belchamber,' he found only the de Lissac girls and another maiden, clad in little hussar caps and dolmans hung coquettishly on one shoulder, resentfully eyeing the ebbing tide of custom, while Alice and Lady Eccleston, aided by her obedient son Thomas, were feverishly tying parcels in the background.

'Have you written on that one, Tommy,' Lady Eccleston was saying, 'Mrs. Brown, Elm Lodge, Streatham? Oh dear, *which* parcel is the big yellow cushion? I am sure that was the one she bought. Well, never mind, this is a cushion anyway, it feels soft; that 'll do. Ah, Sainty, you 've come a little late, dear. Everything is over.'

'What 's become of Cissy?' Sainty inquired.

The young ladies were evidently not in the best of tempers, and this innocent question served to open the floodgates of their wrath.

'Cissy 's gone,' Norah de Lissac said crossly, 'and left us in the lurch. She *said* she was tired, but *I* think she was only bored. When it got dull and shabby and all the nice people had gone it didn't amuse her any more.'

'It puts us in such a foolish position,' Gemma chimed in. 'People naturally come here to see her, and when they don't find her they are not best pleased. One man asked me if I was Lady Belchamber, and when I said I wasn't, he said, "Then which of you is?" Of course I had to say we none of us were, and then he was quite rude and said "Then you've no business to put her name up over the stall." It wasn't at all pleasant.'

Norah took up her parable again. 'She didn't even take the trouble to put on her costume to-day, just came in her ordinary clothes, and of course we looked like dressed-up fools beside her. If she had just sent us word she wasn't going to we wouldn't have put ours on either.'

'Oh, dears, it would have been a great pity,' said Lady Eccleston, emerging from a pile of brown paper with her mouth full of pins. 'You look charming in your dresses; they really suit you better than Cissy; and it would have been so flat if none of you had been in costume, for there really *isn*'t much in the stall itself to suggest Poland, I must admit. I think Cissy really *was* tired, you know ; she has had a hard two days of it.'

'Well, we were tired too,' said the implacable Norah. 'She's not the only person who has had a hard two days. Can't we go home now, at least, and get off these ridiculous clothes?' she asked, turning to her step-mother. Alice looked distressed and murmured something about 'not deserting Lady Eccleston.'

'Oh, don't *think* of me,' cried that lady. 'You and the dear girls go. Tommy and I can soon finish what's left to do. The people are thinning fast, and we've done very well. I *can't* thank you enough for all your splendid help'; and she embraced the whole party with a last galvanic effort at cheerful enthusiasm.

Sainty saw the de Lissac party to their gorgeous equipage, and was just turning away from the door when a small voice at his elbow demanded, 'Shall I please to call the kerridge, m'lord?' and looking down he had a vision of two large appealing eyes and a white kid forefinger pressed tightly to a curly hatbrim. He recognised the diminutive boy who decorated Cissy's coach-box when she rode abroad.

'Yes,' he said ; 'if the brougham is here, I may as well take it. Lady Belchamber has gone home.'

In the course of the drive he wondered why he had taken the trouble to come to the bazaar, and who had been benefited or pleased by his visit.

He had hardly got to his room and sat down to his book by the fire, with a sigh of relief, when a servant came to him.

'If you please, my lord, Gibson wants to know if there are any more orders for the carriage.'

'Not for me,' Sainty answered, his mind on what he was reading. 'Ask her ladyship.'

The man looked surprised and still lingered doubtfully. 'Well,' said Sainty, 'what is it?'

'If you please, my lord, my lady hasn't come in yet.'

'Oh, I think she must have——' Sainty was beginning

but stopped himself. He saw no reason for discussing Cissy's movements with the servants. 'Then you must wait for orders till she does,' he said.

He wondered a little why, if she left the bazaar because she was tired, she had not come home. But after all, Norah's explanation was probably the correct one. She was bored with the whole thing and took the shortest cut for freedom; it was not Cissy's way to allow herself to be bored. 'In any case it is no affair of mine,' he thought, as he turned again to his book.

CHAPTER XIX

AFTER Easter, when Cissy had a morning-room and a boudoir, and the drawing-rooms were practically finished, Sainty entered into undisputed possession of his two back rooms, and spent more and more of his time in them. Only faint echoes of the turmoil in which Lady Belchamber had her being penetrated to that peaceful seclusion. Evening after evening Cissy would dine out with a few of her special cronies and their attendant swains, and go to the theatre or the opera till it was time to begin the round of balls or parties, from which she returned in grey summer dawns, far too tired for there to be any question of her coming down to breakfast next morning. Sometimes Sainty did not set eyes on her for days together. Gradually he slipped back into his old studious life, snatching sketchy little meals from trays, when he remembered to eat anything, and as little a part of the life of the house as if he were in lodgings round the corner.

In May, Lady Charmington came to town, to attend the meetings of the 'Ladies' No Popery League,' of which she was a leading member.

'My mother writes me she is coming to London,' Sainty said. 'Of course she will come to us.'

'Well, she can if you wish it,' Cissy answered; 'but I warn you you're preparing trouble for yourself. She won't like the way we live, and when she doesn't like a thing, she is not always silent and accommodating. She'll expect a family breakfast at 9.15, with prayers at 9. I don't suppose she ever breakfasted in her room in her life. I don't know where *you* breakfast, but *I* certainly shan't come down.'

'I suppose you couldn't, just for the time she's here?' Sainty suggested.

'I'm not such a humbug as to alter my way of life to please her. She may as well find out first as last that I am not cut on her pattern.'

'I think she has pretty well made that discovery already,' Sainty retorted.

'Well,' said Cissy, 'she can come if she likes, and if you want her, but she must take us as she finds us. I told you she wouldn't like it. She'd be a great deal happier at Roehampton with Lady Firth. She could come in to her meetings, and if she wanted to lunch here any particular day, I could always tell people to keep out of the way.'

'You can't say I interfere with you much, or often ask you to do anything to please me,' said Sainty earnestly; 'but when we have a great house here, and my own mother wants to come up, I do think it would look strange for us not to take her in.'

'Well, please yourself. After all, I was only thinking of you. *I* can generally hold my own, but if your mother gets her back up, as she inevitably will, *you*'ll have the devil of a time of it.'

Sainty had presently occasion to prove the accuracy of his wife's forecast. Acting on Cissy's hint, he dutifully appeared each morning to give Lady Charmington her breakfast. The first day, she lingered before sitting down, as though she were waiting for something.

'Won't you make the tea for me, mother?' Sainty asked. 'It's like old times, you and I having breakfast together.'

'You don't have prayers, I see,' Lady Charmington remarked, as she took her seat. 'Or were they earlier? I can quite well come down sooner, if you wish it.'

'Well you see, Cissy never comes down to breakfast,

and, as you know, I am not a great eater, so when we are
alone, I generally have a cup of tea and an egg in the
study.'

'Why doesn't your wife come to breakfast? is she ill?'

'Oh no, she's well enough. But she's out late at parties
and things every night, and I'm glad she *does* rest a little
in the mornings; it's the only time she does.'

'I confess I'm a little disappointed in Cissy,' Lady
Charmington remarked, after contemplating the toast-
rack judicially for a time in silence. 'I never thought her
a very deep or earnest nature, but I did *not* expect to find
her so entirely given up to worldly pursuits.'

'Cissy's young and pretty, and people make a great
deal of her. After all, it's natural at her age that she
should like to enjoy herself.'

Lady Charmington sniffed. 'Enjoyment! People
nowadays seem to think of nothing but enjoyment. We
were not put into the world to enjoy ourselves.'

'Well, most of us fulfil the object of our being pretty
thoroughly then,' Sainty said, 'and yet every one seems
to *want* to be happy; and it is a good deal to expect of the
few who have it in their power that they should voluntarily forego what most people fail to obtain.'

'I don't like to hear you talk like that, my boy; you
don't seem to have a proper sense of your blessings. You
have very much to be thankful for.'

Lady Charmington saw nothing incongruous in finding
fault with some acrimony if things were not to her liking,
but she was always swift to rebuke a complaining spirit
in others.

'Her poor mother, who, if a little too fond of society,
has a very sincerely religious side to her, must be sadly
distressed at her daughter's light-mindedness.'

The thought of Lady Eccleston as a pious matron
wounded by her child's care for earthly matters was too
much for Sainty.

'Why, Lady Eccleston goes wherever a candle's lighted,'
he said; 'or if she doesn't, it's because she's failed to get
an invitation.'

'Censorious, censorious!' replied his mother. 'Who art

thou that judgest another man's servant? You should
watch against that spirit; it'll grow on you.'

Sainty was only too glad to have diverted the precious
balms to his own head, which had been accustomed to
that form of unction for too many years to be easily
broken. He saw his mother off to the first of her meetings
before there was the smallest chance of her encountering
her daughter-in-law, and then betook himself to his own
rooms to read the papers. As he drew near to the fire
that his languid blood demanded in this uncertain season,
his eye fell on the letters he had not as yet thought of
opening. As a rule his correspondence was not exciting.
It consisted mainly of advertisements and begging letters.
The first that he took up this morning had such a family
look of these last, that he opened it with a weary certainty
of his correspondent's need for £3. 5s. 6d. to prevent the
bed being taken from under his sick child; but though
it was written on cheap paper in a hand carefully made
to appear illiterate, its contents were far other than he had
expected.

'Ask your wife where she was on the third afternoon
of the World's Bazaar. A friend.'

Sainty had never in his life received an anonymous
letter, and the experience was distinctly unpleasant. He
shook it off into the fire as St. Paul did the other venomous
thing, but failed to get the poison out of his system so
cheaply. In case it should not work, his nameless 'friend'
took care to repeat the dose, and several other communi-
cations of a like tenor followed the first, but none of them
produced in him the unpleasant sensations of that chilly
May morning, when he stood watching the sparks run
along the blackened paper and the gray ash writhe and
twist for its final flight up the chimney. After a time he
came to regard them as more or less in the natural order of
things, and even ceased to read them; but the writer
showed such skill in varying the address, that in no case
was he able to detect one without opening it. Some
contained but a single sentence, others were much longer,
but all suggested doubts of his wife's conduct, and
recommended a surveillance of which the very notion was

repugnant to him. Of course he could take no notice of
such things. He wondered if he ought to speak to Cissy
about them, only to dismiss the idea as impossible. Still
less could he mention them to any one else. Eventually
he decided that there was but one way to treat an
anonymous letter, which was to behave as if it had not
been received. None the less they stirred in him a vague
uneasiness. The feeling that somewhere about one an
unknown enemy is watching for a chance to hurt, fills life
with an unpleasant sense of ambush. He could think of
no one who had cause to wish him ill. The enmity, then,
must be to Cissy. A disappointed rival? He needed no re-
minder of the extreme unlikelihood of any one's grudging
her the possession of his affections. But how if the rivalry
were for the possession of some one else's affections? That
possibility was not without its sting. For him there could
be no question of jealousy, in the ordinary sense of the
word; but he began to apprehend the possibilities of
scandal, to understand that his acceptance of the anoma-
lous part which his wife had thrust upon him by no means
exhausted her power of injuring his happiness or his
honour; in short, that he was saddled with an obligation
to guard what he did not possess.

Meanwhile he found himself in the no less ironical
position of having to champion her many doings, which
in his heart he disliked, against his mother, with whom
he secretly sympathised. Lady Charmington was far
from having said all her say on that first morning at
breakfast. Cissy's prediction of her disapproval of their
London life was amply verified. Occupied with the
matters that had brought her to town, and going into
a totally different world from her daughter-in-law's, she
was as ignorant as her son of the things that would most
have stirred her wrath; but she found quite enough to
rebuke in the house itself. Cissy's idleness and dissipation,
her late hours, her card-playing, her neglect of her household duties, and the consequent waste and profusion, her
Sabbath-breaking, and the completeness with which she
ignored her husband and her home (not to speak of
her guest and mother-in-law) were each and severally

the subjects of the elder lady's severe animadversions to the offender herself when occasion offered, but far more often to the patient ears of poor Sainty, who had to defend the culprit as best he might.

Another fruitful topic of maternal discontent was Lady Belchamber's failure to provide an heir to the property. This, it may well be supposed, was not an agreeable topic to Sainty, nor one on which he had any ready rejoinders at his command.

'You have been married close on a year,' said Lady Charmington, 'and I see no signs or hope of a child. I said something to Cissy about it one day, and she laughed disagreeably, and said she was glad of it. I asked if she didn't think she had any duty to the family in the matter. I am almost ashamed to tell you what she answered: that a baby was a great tie and a nuisance, and she hoped if she had to have one, it would be at a convenient time of year, when it didn't interfere with things.'

'I don't suppose very young women ever *want* to have a baby,' Sainty said doubtfully, feeling something was expected of him.

'Cissy is not so young as all that. She must be two- or three-and-twenty. I can't imagine any woman marrying and *not* wanting to have a child. I am sure when I married I prayed most fervently that I might give my husband a son.'

'Well, you know, the answer to your prayer was not quite all you could have wished,' suggested Sainty.

Lady Charmington ignored the interruption. 'It is not as though she were not a perfectly normal healthy young woman,' she said, 'for I never was taken in for a minute by all that business of the shock to her nervous system at Belchamber. Constant dissipation, racketing about morning, noon, and night, and tight lacing are not the ways to go about having an heir. I only hope she mayn't do anything else, if she's so afraid that the duties of a wife and mother will cut her out of a party or two.'

'O mother!' Sainty expostulated.

'If she is not going to have any children, what was the use of your marrying?' continued his aggrieved parent.

'We are just where we were with regard to that other woman. *She* has children fast enough! Cissy seems to think she has come into the family merely to have what she calls a good time, and spend the money that I pinched and scraped together for you for so many years. I have *never* seen such sinful waste as goes on in this house.'

Lady Charmington was only putting into words what her son had often, with some bitterness, asked himself. What was the use of his marrying? He had not perhaps quite so crudely admitted, even in his inner consciousness, how much he had been influenced in making up his mind to such a step by the thought of excluding the children of Lady Arthur from the succession to his name and estates, but it had none the less been a powerful motive with him. Had his brother passed his examinations, gone into the army, and in due course married some common-place, unobjectionable young lady, it is more than doubtful if even Lady Eccleston would have succeeded in dragging Sainty into matrimony. For one thing, she would have had to reckon with Lady Charmington as an enemy instead of an ally, which would have put a quite different complexion on the affair. The young man reflected some-times with dumb rage on how his life was turned topsy-turvy, haled from familiar field and woodland to this hated city, that a girl, who was really no more to him than any other, should junket from morning till night with a set of people he could not endure, and squander money, with which he might have benefited millions of his fellow-creatures, on her senseless, unoriginal pleasures. And all for what? Sooner or later the children of his undesirable sister-in-law would sit in his place, and inherit his patrimony as surely as if he had followed his natural bent, and led a peaceful, laborious life remote from all connection with Lady Deans and her playfellows. And with it all Cissy had not even the common decency to avoid the tongue of scandal, as these odious anonymous letters showed him. He really did think she might have spared him that. Day after day he thought of saying something to her on the subject, and always he was prevented by lack of courage or opportunity, or else some unfortunate speech of his mother drove him back into the position of his wife's involuntary champion.

'Cissy tells me she is going away for Whitsuntide,' Lady Charmington announced one day, with the sniff that indicated much more than met the ear in this apparently simple announcement.

'Is she?' said Sainty, anxious not to commit himself.

'Has she not even deigned to let you know?' inquired her ladyship scornfully.

'I think she *did* say something about the Suffords having asked her there.'

'Were *you* not included in the invitation?'

'I really don't know; I never asked. I didn't want to go. I suppose Lady Sufford went through the form of asking me, but she probably knew I shouldn't come. It would be too terrible if I were obliged to go wherever Cissy does.'

'The arrangement seems to suit *her* perfectly,' said Lady Charmington; 'but I can't see why you shouldn't go.'

'It would add to no one's pleasure, and take away considerably from mine,' said Sainty promptly.

'Always pleasure!' cried Lady Charmington. 'The invariable argument! no thought of duty!'

'If a thing which is purely a question of amusement doesn't amuse one, why make a duty of it?' argued her son.

'Well, if it is not your duty to go about with your wife, I should have thought it was hers to stay at home with you. Of course I quite understand that she mentioned her plans to me with the delicate intention of letting me see that she could not keep me beyond next week; but she need not trouble; I had settled to go to mother on Tuesday in any case. She has failed very much lately, and I shall have to be with her more. By the way, I found she was rather hurt that Cissy had never once been to see her since she came to town in February, nor asked her to come in and see your new house.'

'Dear me!' said Sainty, 'I ought to have thought of it. Of course we should have been only too delighted to see granny, if I had only thought she would care to see the house; but she seems always so absorbed in other things, it never occurred to me. It was very stupid of me. I've been several times to see her, but she always talks as if it was such a business to drive into London. I never dreamt of asking it of her. And she says her sight has got so bad, that I wasn't sure how much she would see if she came.'

'She would probably see a great deal that would shock her, as I have,' said Lady Charmington. 'Have you ever calculated at all what this house is going to cost you by the time it is finished?'

'Oh, I've kept pretty good track of the expenses. I've paid for a good deal of the work as it went along. It has all been done much more extravagantly than I thought necessary. Indeed, as far as I am concerned, I shouldn't care if we had no London house at all; but Uncle Cor seemed to think it indispensable, and he doesn't consider that we have done much we need not. He is always afraid that, with my saving tendencies, I shall fail to do myself credit. He needn't be uneasy as long as Cissy is on hand to provide the antidote.'

'There is a great difference between having things suitable to your position and being foolishly and wickedly extravagant,' remarked Lady Charmington.

'Perhaps I have deliberately rather given Cissy her head about this house,' Sainty answered, 'to keep her hands off Belchamber; there was a great deal she was thinking of doing there, but I hope I have put a stop to that.'

'Belchamber!' cried out his mother in horror. 'What could she want to do there? It was always kept in perfect repair; there wasn't a door knob missing nor a tap out of order, and when you came of age there was an immense amount of money spent in cleaning and restoring. I always thought it quite unnecessary her doing up those rooms in that ridiculous way last summer. They looked to *me* more like an improper person's apartments than like anything in an English lady's house.'

'Well, I can't say that I always admire Cissy's taste, myself; there's a little want of knowledge about it.'

Sainty did not judge it necessary to tell his mother how far reaching had been Cissy's plans for the remodelling of Belchamber; he had surprised them by an accident, and had promptly and firmly opposed them. He could not bear the desecrating touch of fleeting fashion on anything so artistically and historically complete as the home of his childhood, and had been glad to purchase its immunity from the threatened changes by larger concessions in the matter of the London house. Perhaps, even so, Cissy would not have abandoned her projects without a struggle, but for the appearance of a most unlooked-for ally to her husband in the person of Claude Morland, who had supervened in the height of the discussion and thrown all the weight of his authority into the scale for the saving of Belchamber.

'Sainty is perfectly right,' he said, with his most pontifical air; 'it would be vandalism. There isn't a more beautiful specimen of its period in England than the great saloon or the Vandyke dining-hall; they are perfect. And the red, yellow, and green rooms, though they are later and not so pure, have a great *cachet* of their own, and are perfectly *de l'époque* as far as they go. No, no, my dear Cissy, it would be a sin. I am all for your using the rooms, and living in them; but, believe me, you mustn't touch them. Do what you like here; you have a clean slate to work on; but don't attempt to "improve" Belchamber.'

Sainty was astonished at the meekness with which Cissy abandoned her cherished schemes, but much too grateful to Claude for backing him up to resent this evidence of his cousin's greater authority. He knew, too, that he owed it to him that the London house, if a little over-decorated and too obviously costly, was, on the whole, harmonious and in good taste.

By dint of unremitting vigilance and almost super-human tact, the date of Lady Charmington's departure had almost been reached without any more serious encounter than a few skirmishes between her and her daughter-in-law; but one afternoon, having heard his mother come in, and gone in search of her, Sainty saw at a glance that a battle royal was raging. Cissy was lolling exasperatingly calm and contemptuous among the piles of cushions she delighted to heap upon the furniture, while Lady Charmington sat stiffly erect, an ominous light in her eye, and a pink spot burning in the centre of each sallow cheek. Her son heard her voice as he entered, and quailed at the familiar tone of it.

'I am well aware,' she was saying, 'that nothing *I* say will have the smallest influence on your behaviour, but none the less I feel it my solemn duty to protest, when I see things going on of which I entirely disapprove.'

'Why trouble, if you are so sure that you will produce no effect?' asked Cissy.

'Because *I* have some consideration for my son's honour, to which you and he seem to be equally indifferent.'

'Oh! His honour!' protested Cissy.

'Yes; his honour,' persisted Lady Charmington. 'When I was first married, a young woman of your age, a young wife not a year married, who received men alone, sprawling about on sofas in that kind of indecent clothing, would have been considered to have lost her character.'

'Mother!' interposed Sainty.

'Oh, it's largely your fault for allowing such things,' his mother flashed out at him. 'If you were more of a man, your wife would never dare treat you as an absolute nonentity in your own house.'

'But what's it all about?' asked Sainty. 'What has Cissy been doing?'

'I'm sure *I* don't know,' answered Lady Belchamber. 'You had better ask your mother.'

'I came in just now,' said Lady Charmington, 'and found her with that flimsy rag she calls a tea-gown half off her back lolling about among the cushions there with Algy Montgomery. I don't call it decent.'

'Why, Algy's a sort of relation, you know,' answered Cissy; 'his stepmother's Sainty's grandmother; it makes him a kind of uncle.'

'Kind of fiddlestick! a good-for-nothing young rip in the Life Guards, of six- or seven-and-twenty at the outside.'

'Do you suppose, if I were doing anything that wasn't perfectly innocent, that I shouldn't have taken jolly good care that you didn't come spying in?' inquired Cissy, with lofty scorn.

Lady Charmington choked. 'It is not my habit to spy,' she cried, 'and I am not accusing you of actual misconduct; but it 's not only to-day that I object to. It 's your general mode of going on. Yesterday you were shut up for ever so long with that vulgar Mr. Pryor, and you drive Claude all over London in your brougham. No honest woman should take any man in her brougham, no matter who it is, that isn't her husband or her brother.'

'Would her grandfather be admissible?' asked Cissy sweetly. 'I must say for a high-minded person who angrily repudiates the idea of spying, you seem to be strangely well informed as to all my movements.'

'Cissy!' expostulated Sainty.

'Well, what is it?' she asked, turning to him politely.

'I have been deceived in you, very much deceived,' Lady Charmington broke out. 'When you wanted to marry my son, you were all sweetness and honey to me; now you've attained your object, you insult me. From the day I arrived here you have studied in every way to let me see I was unwelcome; there wasn't an attention you could have paid me you didn't pointedly omit, or a possible slight that you neglected to put on me. I can well see that a mother-in-law in the house by no means suited your book.'

'Even such a sweet affectionate one?' interposed Cissy.

'Mark my words,' continued the exasperated dowager, 'you will come to grief. You are playing a dangerous game, my lady. You have no conscience, no principle, no sense of duty to restrain or save you. If you forget God and go after your own vain amusements from morning to night, you will assuredly make shipwreck in the end.'

'Well, at least you will have the satisfaction of thinking it was not for want of being warned.'

'Your sarcasms will never prevent my speaking my mind. I have seen nothing in this house against which I do not think it incumbent on me, not only as the mother of your husband but as a Christian woman, to bear testimony—luxury, waste, riotous living, and indelicate behaviour. I am going away, and I know you will be glad to be rid of me, but I couldn't have reconciled it to my conscience to go without speaking.'

'I must say that you have eased your conscience very thoroughly, and most agreeably. Is there anything else your sense of duty impels you to mention before you go?'

At this, Lady Charmington fairly lost her temper. She strode over to Cissy, and Sainty flung himself between them, afraid that she was going to strike her. 'You little minx!' she cried. 'You little selfish, vulgar minx! You have lied and wheedled your way into this family, and grabbed all you could lay your hands upon, and what have you done in return? The one thing that was asked of you, to bear a child, and give the house an heir, you have most lamentably failed in doing.'

Cissy sprang to her feet, a curious evil look on her face, and for a moment the two women looked into each other's eyes. 'Oh! in the matter of a baby, take care I don't astonish some of you yet,' she cried.

CHAPTER XX

'But you will come to *my* ball,' said the duchess with decision. The 'but' was in answer to Sainty's assertion that he did not go to balls. '*Vous vous faites ridicule, mon enfant.* That you shouldn't accompany your wife everywhere, that I can see; it would be silly; but equally it is not right never to be seen at all. People ask if anything is wrong with you that you can't appear, if you are half-witted or have fits.'

'It is very kind of them to occupy themselves with my affairs,' said Sainty. 'I shouldn't have supposed that most people remembered that I exist.'

'But it is perhaps as well they *should* remember it sometimes,' said his grandmother, with a significant glance at Cissy.

'I should have thought the one form of entertainment

from which a lame man might have been held excused was a dance,' Sainty persisted.

'Ah! there are dances and dances,' replied the duchess. 'This is not a dance *où l'on dansera*, it is a serious entertainment. I don't say it will be amusing; I don't give this kind of thing for my own amusement or for other people's; there will be ministers, public men, royalties; *enfin* a solemn thing, and you are of the family. You must come, mustn't he, Cissy?'

'Oh, certainly, if you wish it, dear,' Cissy answered lightly. 'I should think it would just suit him. He will find people to whom he can talk about the housing of the working classes. You know how I always *love* coming to Sunborough House, but not to *this* kind of thing; you have said yourself how it bores you.'

Sainty smiled at his wife's complete assumption of equality with his grandmother, both in age and position. He couldn't help reflecting how enchanted Lady Eccleston's daughter would have been a short year ago at the prospect of attending the function of which she now spoke so slightingly as being for the uninitiated.

'Well, you will both come, like good children,' said the duchess easily. 'We don't live only to amuse ourselves, you know.'

And so it came about that Belchamber found himself attending the ball in question, and very much lost in that glittering throng. At first he had been amused by the show, as he might have been by a scene in a pantomime. The pompous men, bearers of great names or high positions, stuck about with orders, the indecent bejewelled women, the lights, the flowers, the music; it all made an effect of some gorgeousness, with the really stately beautiful house as a background. But after an hour or so he became aware of a sense of intolerable weariness. He had taken it for granted that he and Cissy would be entirely independent of each other, and that after he had shown himself to his grandmother and the duke, and amused himself for a little while with the pageant, he would be free to depart whenever it pleased him; but to his astonishment Cissy had remarked that she had no intention of staying late and she would be very much obliged if he would take her home in his brougham. 'I want Gibson early to-morrow morning,' she explained, 'so I don't want to take him out to-night, and I haven't been in bed before three one night this week. We can just show ourselves, and then slope.'

Once at the ball, however, she seemed to find it less dull than she had anticipated, for Sainty several times caught sight of her dancing, which she had announced that she certainly should not do, and had quite failed in his endeavour to get speech of her to tell her that he would walk home and leave the carriage for her. The night was fine and his own house not five minutes away. Any one but Sainty would simply have gone and left his wife to find it out. But this was a course which his invincible conscientiousness forbade his taking. As he hung forlornly about, hustled by the people who crowded in and out of the rooms, he thought that surely no sound in nature was so ugly as that of a quantity of human voices all talking at once and endeavouring to dominate each other. He came presently on Mrs. de Lissac, who always soothed his exasperated nerves; but after all he need not go to a ball to see *her*. 'We could have had a much pleasanter talk in your house or mine, without having to try and outshout a hundred other people,' he said.

'I never can quite get over the strangeness of being here at all,' Alice answered. 'It always seems rather like a fairy story to me, when I think of my very simple bringing-up at the rectory, that I should come to rub shoulders with all these grandees.'

'It is a fairy story in which you have certainly been the good fairy,' said Sainty warmly. 'I can't tell you the difference it has made to me having you in London to come and talk to sometimes.'

'It is dear of you to say that. I like to think that to you I am not the rich woman and possible subscriber or hostess, but just your old govey that you loved when you were a little boy. Sometimes, dear,' she added, with a timid look of great tenderness, 'I fancy you are not much happier now than you were then.'

Sainty passed the back of his hand wearily across his eyes. 'Happy,' he said; 'is any one happy? Think of the lives that are being led within a mile of us to-night; can any one be happy with the cry of those millions in his ears? Certainly not these people with their eternal desperate pursuit of amusement who are afraid of being left for five minutes in company with their own thoughts.'

'Poor boy! you certainly are *not* happy or you would not be so bitter. It is dreadful to think of those poor people. I often wonder if we have a right to be so rich when there are so many starving; but my dear husband says this is Socialism, and if we weren't rich we couldn't give away so much, and certainly he is very generous; and he says that all these things that I feel as if it was wrong to spend so much on give employment to lots of poor people to make, who would be out of work if there were no rich people to buy things.' She brought out this time-honoured piece of argument with such a triumphant pride in her spouse's wisdom that Sainty thought of nothing less than combating it.

'There is one form of happiness that *you* ought to enjoy in perfection,' he said, 'that of being and doing good.'

Alice blushed. 'Oh, you mustn't call me good,' she said; 'but I was going to say, if there is a lot of misery and poverty, I'm sure there has never been so much done towards relieving it as nowadays.'

'The "World's Bazaar," for instance,' said Sainty.

'Well—yes, dear—that and other things. And I'm sure if, as you say, being and doing good makes us happy, you ought to know it too.'

'I!' cried Sainty. 'Whom do I make happy?'

'Oh, you are always doing kind things for people, and see how happy you make your wife.'

'My wife's happiness is very much independent of me; indeed, I am rather the principal drawback to it.' The words slipped out almost before he was aware. Even to this kind old friend he had never spoken of his relations with his wife, and this seemed neither the time nor the place he would have chosen to do so. Mrs. de Lissac looked pained, but she took advantage of his little outbreak to say, 'I have sometimes wanted to speak to you about your wife, but have not quite liked to. I think you and she should be more together. You leave her too much to herself. She is very young and pretty to be so independent, and perhaps a little thoughtless.'

'Talking of Cissy,' Sainty interrupted, 'can you tell me where she is? As a beginning of acting on your advice, you see we have come into the world together to-night, and I am actually waiting to go home till she is ready.'

A sinuous young lady, clad in a sheath of some glittering, shimmering blackness, turned at the words and held out her hand. 'How d'ye do, Lord Belchamber?' she said 'I don't believe you remember me. Are you asking for Lady Belchamber? I saw her not five minutes ago with Mr. Morland.'

With a start Sainty recognised Amy Winston. The unrelieved black of her dress, and of a long pair of gloves that were pulled up to her elbows, lent a baleful pallor to her face and neck, and above her brow there shone in her dusky tresses a single diamond star which, if real, was a very remarkable ornament to belong to a single woman said mainly to support herself by the manufacture of magazine tales and occasional verse. At sight of this siren good Mrs. de Lissac fell back into the crowd, while the young man to whom Miss Winston was talking, after a half glance at Sainty, made off not less hastily, so that they were left facing one another.

'I remember you perfectly, Miss Winston,' Sainty said, 'although we have not met very lately. You were kind enough to say you had seen Lady Belchamber. I wish you would tell me where I should find her; she wanted to go home early to-night, and I think may be looking for me.'

'She didn't appear to be,' replied the young woman, with the faintest suspicion of insolence; 'nor, I must say, did she seem in any particular hurry to get home. She was going into the garden with *le beau cousin*. Didn't you know the garden was lit up? it is one of the great features of the Sunborough House parties. Let 's go and look for them.'

Sainty couldn't well refuse. He was thinking how much more indecent a very low-necked bodice was on a thin woman than on a fat one.

'Wasn't that Ned Parsons who left you just now?' he asked, as they made their way towards the staircase.

'Yes. He has become very fashionable since his book was such a success; he goes everywhere now. By the way,' she added, with a little laugh, 'I suppose that's why he bolted at sight of you; he thinks you haven't forgiven him for the liberty he took with your coming-of-age party.'

'I should have thought he had quite as much reason to fear my grandmother; yet I find him at her house.'

'Oh, well—a great ball like this is hardly being at people's house, you know; it doesn't count. But as a matter of fact he and the duchess have quite made it up. They met at Lady Eva's, and the duchess prepared to crush him. "I hear, Mr. Parsons," said she, in her most regal manner, "that you have put me in a book." "Who can have told you such a thing?" Ned asked, with touching innocence. "The duchess in my book is old and ridiculous; how *could* she be meant for you?"'

Sainty couldn't help laughing. As they emerged into the cooler and less crowded garden, his guide waited for him, to come up beside her. Hitherto she had preceded him, worming her way through the crowd with a deftness bred of long habit, at which Sainty marvelled, and talking lightly to him over her shoulder.

'One doesn't often see you at this sort of thing,' she said.

'It is only the second ball of my life,' Sainty answered. 'You were at my first too.'

'Ah! the famous ball immortalised by Parsons. Is it possible that it can be three years ago?'

'Nearly four now.'

'Good heavens! so it is. How old we are all getting! Your wife was there too; it was the year she came out. How little any of us thought what was going to happen, except perhaps dear Lady Eccleston. I shouldn't wonder if *she* had an inkling even then.'

Sainty did not like his companion's tone, but hardly

knew how to resent it. He had hoped by a rather stiff silence to intimate his want of appreciation of her particular form of humour, but she continued to chatter quite unabashed by his unresponsiveness.

'Cissy is quite a success,' she continued; 'it is astonishing how quickly she has caught on. I don't know any one who has more admirers, unless perhaps it's Mrs. Jack Purse, and she's been much longer on the scene of battle.'

'And who may she be?' Sainty asked, hoping to divert the stream of Miss Winston's malevolence from his own vegetable patch.

'Lord Belchamber, where *have* you lived? I wish she could hear you; she'd die of it. Why, Mrs. Jack is smartest of the smart. She knows hardly any one but Jews and royalties. I was quite astonished to find her at the Suffords' at Whitsuntide. Hylda Sufford said she couldn't imagine why she came to her, but I think the Guggenheim's party for the prince falling through had something to do with it.'

'My wife didn't tell me she met you at the Suffords'.'

'Oh, I don't know how I came to be asked, but I was.'

'And did you amuse yourself?'

'Oh, we had great fun. One night we all dressed up for dinner. Hylda was a harlequin and Ella Dalsany the columbine.'

'Do you mean to say that Lady Sufford came down to dinner in tights before the footmen?'

'Gracious, yes! And Gladys Purse was Mephistopheles and Lady Deans Marguerite; but we all thought Cissy had the best idea.'

'And what was that?' asked Sainty nervously. He had neither asked nor received any account of the Suffords' country-house party.

'Why, she just put on her best frock and all her diamonds, and said she was the Traviata.'

Sainty was not sure that this inspiration of his wife's exactly appealed to him. He walked in gloomy silence.

'Didn't she tell you about it?' asked Miss Winston. 'She had a tremendous success. Mrs. Jack, with her red legs and cock's feather, was nowhere. Cissy has one

immense pull over Gladys Purse as far as the younger
men are concerned. It's terribly expensive to admire
Mrs. Jack; whereas a charming but impecunious youth
like Claude Morland gets many little advantages by the
way from his devotion to his pretty cousin.'

In spite of an effort to keep her talk on the level of
impartial ill-nature, Miss Winston could not quite help a
touch of scornful bitterness in her mention of Claude.

Scattered images had been loosely grouping themselves
in Sainty's brain as she talked, half-forgotten incidents
of his coming-of-age party, the softly opening door, his
encounter with his cousin in the sleeping house, his
examination of Claude as to his feelings for this same lady
—it seemed to him that he began to detect a certain
method in the apparently purposeless gossip with which
she was favouring him. And then, blinding in its sudden
illumination, there flashed across his mind the recollection of the anonymous letters. Here was the key to their
authorship thrust suddenly into his mind. He felt the
quick, instinctive recoil of a man about to tread on something nasty, and then a sort of shuddering pity for what
the creature at his side must have suffered. None knew
better than he how they were wounded who put their
trust in Claude Morland. He wanted to turn and hurry
from her, or at least to find something that should stop
the flicker of her evil tongue. He found nothing better to
say in the shock of the moment than 'Do you think you
ought to talk to me so about my wife?'

Sunborough House has, for the heart of London, a
relatively large garden, which being cunningly illumined
with Chinese lanterns and little coloured lamps, the next
day's papers were already reporting that the effect was
'fairy-like.' Despite these beauties and the somewhat
chilly allurements of an English summer night, only a few
of the most flirtatiously inclined had been persuaded to
drag their expensive skirts over the sooty London grass,
and Sainty and his companion had the further end of the
enclosure, which they had now reached, practically to
themselves. As he made his feeble protestation, they
came, round a tree, upon the glass doors of a sort of little

summer-house which backed up against the high railing that divided the garden from the Park.

Miss Winston gave one glance into the lighted interior. 'I think we are *de trop* here,' she said, turning to Sainty, and, slipping nimbly from his side, she vanished in the soft shadows of the shrubbery. Almost at the same moment the door was opened from within with such suddenness that Sainty, who had not the agility of the fair Aimée, could only save himself from being struck by throwing himself back into the angle formed by the tree and the railing, and in this small space he now found himself made a close prisoner by the open door, which was firmly held in position by the broad back of a man, as he could see through the glass. He reflected that his position was not a dignified one, that as the inmates of the summer-house were evidently leaving it, he had only to stay quiet till they were gone, and then push the door and follow them at his leisure; and they need never know how nearly he had been tricked into playing the spy upon them. Miss Winston had evidently counted on finding her quarry there (perhaps from personal knowledge of his cousin's habits), and had hoped that she could so excite his jealousy that he would not be able, once there, to resist the temptation of looking. He had no doubt as to whom he would have seen, even before he recognised Claude's voice. He was relieved to hear that there was nothing lover-like in it. Morland spoke in brief, business-like tones through which pierced a scarcely disguised note of annoyance. 'Then you won't see him?' he said, pausing against the door, evidently continuing some discussion they had been having.

'I daren't,' Cissy answered. 'I'm sure it would kill me.'

'Then you must do the other thing; there are not two ways about it; and the sooner the better. If you're right, you've no time to lose. But are you quite sure?'

'Oh yes, quite. I wasn't at first, but I am now.'

'It's cursedly unfortunate——'

They spoke low, and as they moved off he could hear no more.

Sainty pushed the door, and stepped out from his temporary prison. Of the fragment of dialogue that he had overheard he did not understand a word; indeed, he did not pay it any particular attention at the time; he supposed it to refer to some of the many plans the two were always discussing. He was accustomed to Cissy's use of needlessly strong language. 'I should simply die of it' was a common phrase with her for expressing dislike of the most trivial things. It was not till months after they were spoken that the words came back to him with a new significance.

He followed the retreating figures up the garden, his feeling one of relief at the failure of an ill-natured plot of which he had been meant to be the victim. Miss Winston's motive was not difficult to guess. It all seemed like something in a novel or play, curiously theatrical and unlike life; but at least the *dénouement* had been essentially undramatic.

When he reached the front hall, he found Cissy already cloaked among the group of people who were waiting for their carriages.

'Where *have* you been?' she said. 'I've been looking everywhere for you. I told you I wanted to go home early. I thought you must have gone.'

'I was looking for you,' Sainty answered. 'I was told you had gone into the garden, so I went there after you; but we must just have missed.'

In the brief transit to their own door neither spoke. Sainty was wondering if he ought to say anything to Cissy of the ill-will that was dogging her footsteps, to put her on her guard against evil tongues. A woman in her exceptional position could not be too careful to furnish no weapons to scandal. Yet it was not only Miss Winston's vengeful jealousy that had warned him to look after his wife. Had not kind little Mrs. de Lissac tried to suggest that he left her dangerously unguarded? Even the duchess had hinted the advisability of his being more with Cissy. It was evident that she was being talked about. Cissy herself seemed to provide him with just the necessary opportunity for speech, so difficult to find in their

divided lives. To his surprise, instead of going immediately upstairs on arriving at home, she followed him
into his rooms on the ground-floor. His study, though of
Spartan simplicity compared to the rest of the house, had
the indefinable pleasant air of rooms much lived and
worked in. Everything in it was meant for use, and daily
used. Books seemed to accumulate round Sainty like
some natural growth. The one lamp with its plain green
shade lighted the comfortable litter on the big, serviceable writing-table, and on another table near it was the
humble appliance by help of which, as in his college days,
he sometimes refreshed himself with a midnight cup of
tea if he was working late.

'How cosy you are in here,' Cissy said, looking about
her. 'I must have spent five times as much on my boudoir,
but with all its silk walls and cushions and frills and
furbelows it doesn't look as homey as this.'

'You're never in the house for long enough to do more
than scratch off a dozen notes,' said Sainty, 'unless you
have people with you. Nothing ever looks like a home in
which people don't live.'

'I think it's the books,' Cissy went on. 'They are
wonderful furniture. I really must get some.'

She lingered, wandering about the room looking at one
thing and another. 'What's this for?' she asked, coming
to the old kettle with its lamp.

'Sometimes I like a cup of tea if I'm working. It's a
bad habit I got into at Cambridge.'

'How shocking for the nerves, my dear,' cried Cissy,
with a lifelike imitation of old Lady Firth. 'Well, you
might have a decent-looking kettle and teapot. I shall
have to give you one. Do you mean you could make a
cup of tea now, this minute? What fun! Do make me one.
I'm cold and famished. It will be lovely.'

Sainty obediently set about lighting the spirit-lamp and
preparing the demanded refreshment. He was not a
little puzzled by this latest caprice of his wife.

Cissy went to the door, and called the butler. 'You
needn't sit up,' she said. 'Give me a candle, and then put
out the lights and go to bed.' She came back, and flung

herself into an armchair, her summer wrap of satin and lace billowing foamlike round her.

Sainty, as he made the tea, was wondering how he could introduce the subject on which he wanted to speak. It was not once in six months he would have such an opportunity. He must not let it slip. And yet he was unwilling to sermonise when for once she was in so friendly a mood. He brought the cup of tea to her, and stood looking down at her as she gulped little teaspoonfuls of the hot liquid.

'You have never told me anything about your visit to the Suffords',' he said.

Cissy looked up suddenly. 'What about it?' she asked distrustfully.

'I mean about dressing up for dinner and all that. Was it amusing?'

'Oh, *that!*' said Cissy indifferently, but with an air of relief. 'I didn't suppose it would amuse you to hear about such nonsense. Who told you?' she asked, with a return of suspicion.

'Miss Winston. I met her to-night. I hadn't seen her for years.'

'That's a nasty cat,' Cissy remarked with conviction. 'She hates me.'

'Oh, you know it?'

'Know it? Of course I know it. Why——' She seemed to think better of what she was going to say, and checked herself. 'What did she say about me?' she asked.

'She spoke in a way I didn't like,' Sainty answered. 'For some reason that woman is your enemy, and I wanted to tell you to be on your guard against her.'

'Oh, thanks, that's all right. I'm not afraid of Aimée Winston,' and she smiled a little cold smile at her own thoughts.

'Don't you think,' said Sainty, with some hesitation, 'that you are a little imprudent sometimes? a little careless of appearances? that, in fact, you rather give a horrid woman like Miss Winston occasion to take away your character?'

'Oh, my character!' said Cissy lightly. She had set

down her tea-cup, and was pulling off her long gloves, and rubbing her round white arms softly over each other.

'I think, you know,' Sainty went on, 'you are beginning to be talked about a little. It was not only Miss Winston, but some one else, a nice woman, who——'

'Mrs. de Lissac, for a fiver!' interjected Cissy. 'There's another woman who don't love me, though not for the same reason.'

'Well, it *was* Alice, as it happens,' Sainty admitted; 'but she only said the kindest things, that you were too young and pretty to be left so much to yourself. You know even the duchess implied that I ought to be seen with you sometimes.'

'Well,' said Cissy imperturbably, 'why aren't you? It seems to me that it is *you* who are failing in your duties, according to all these ladies, not me.'

The coolness of the retort took Sainty's breath away for the moment.

'But you know,' he stammered, 'that there is nothing you would like less. I have never pretended to any right to control your actions. You know you are free to amuse yourself as you like. All I ask is that you won't compromise yourself, won't get talked about, and—and all that.' He ended rather lamely. He half expected an outburst. To his surprise she leaned towards him, and laid her hand very gently on his.

'Don't you think,' she said, and her voice was kind, 'that you *are* rather to blame perhaps? If I *am* talked about, isn't it partly your fault? Can I help it if other men admire me?' She had unclasped her cloak, as the tea warmed her, and now, as she rose, it slipped from her and fell into the chair. She was standing very close to him, a beautiful woman, her beauty enhanced by everything that dress could do for it. Her breath was on his cheek, the faint heady fragrance of her garments troubled his nostrils, the dazzling fairness of her bare shoulders was close under his eyes. He drew back a little, bewildered. 'I don't understand,' he murmured. 'I have tried not to annoy you. You remember what you said. After that I naturally could not trouble you.'

Cissy sprang suddenly away, and caught up her cloak. There was in her movement something of the recoil of a spring that has been forced too far in one direction and has suddenly escaped.

'Ah, no,' he heard her whisper, 'I can't——' and then aloud, with a sudden scornful flash, 'No, *of course* you can't understand,' she said. 'Heavens! it's nearly three . . . and I, who meant to go to bed early. There's a fate against it. Give me my candle. Good night—or what's left of it.' She hurried past him, almost snatching the candle from his hand. The feeble flicker of it had vanished from the great well of the staircase, while he still stood in the doorway dumbly wondering.

What had she meant? Was it possible that she repented of her cruelty, that she wished—— For a moment it had seemed so. Yet he could not believe it. Vividly he recalled the night of their wedding, her agonised repetitions that she never could be his. And yet her following him to his room, her words, still more her looks. He stood there long irresolute, wondering if he were losing a great opportunity. Once he started to go and seek her. He looked up at the skylight far above, where the first faint coming of morning was making a pale twilight. He listened, but in all the silent greyness of the big house he could hear no sound but the innumerable ticking of clocks. A breath of chill discouragement seemed to steal down to him where he stood. He had a vision of the grotesque figure he should cut, misled by his own fatuity, and meeting closed doors, or the half concealed impertinence of a waiting-maid, and slowly he turned back into his own rooms and shut the door.

CHAPTER XXI

From the time of their coming to London it had required no effort on their part for the Belchambers to be very little together, but after the ball at Sunborough House, Sainty was aware that they avoided each other. On the rare occasions when they met, he was conscious in his wife's manner of a more thinly veiled contempt, while on his side he felt a shyness with her which was the beginning of dislike.

There was something almost frightening to him in the absolute quality of her egotism. In the scene of which he had been a horrified witness between her and his mother, Lady Charmington had by no means displayed a conciliatory courtesy, but if she had been rude she had at least lost her temper in a thoroughly human manner—she had *cared*. Had Cissy shown heat in return, he could easily have understood it. What revolted him in her attitude was the complete indifference as to what her mother-in-law thought of her, or whether they were on good terms or ill. The way in which, when she wanted nothing more of them, people simply ceased to exist for her, seemed to him monstrous. She had summarily declined to make any overtures towards peace, alleging, not without justice, that she was the injured party. 'Lady Charmington had insulted and abused her in her own house, and she had taken it with the meekness of a lamb. She really could not see what there was for *her* to apologise about; she was quite ready to *accept* an apology if her mother-in-law wished to make one'; but that lady, oddly enough, showed no signs of any such desire. She had departed next day without so much as seeing Cissy again, merely mentioning to her son before she left that he would probably suffer the curse of childlessness, as a punishment for his wife's behaviour and his own inability to guide and chasten her.

So the young couple drifted more and more apart, Sainty realising with a terrified fatalism the extent to which this creature, at once so hard and so capricious, who bore his name and spent his money, yet had never been his wife and had become almost a stranger to him, had it in her power to injure him irretrievably.

After the duchess's ball he received no more anonymous letters, which confirmed him in his theory of their authorship. Miss Winston, having played her trump card in the disclosure she thought she had made to him, evidently judged it useless to continue the letters which were meant to lead up to it. One day, however, the post brought him an envelope which, at first sight, he made sure was the beginning of a new series. He was on the point of destroying it, unopened, when he was aware of his own coat-of-arms and crest gorgeously emblazoned on the back, and a closer inspection proved that the illiterateness of the handwriting was not feigned but perfectly genuine. It was from Lady Arthur, and contained the unwelcome news that his brother had been ill, more seriously than she had at first imagined, and a request that he would come and see him. 'He won't make the sign,' she wrote, 'and I expect he'd be very angry with me if he knew I was writing, but all the same I know it would be a comfort to him to see you. He's worrying about money matters. You see, being so ill has made him think if he was to die what would become of me and the children.' It was put rather crudely, but Sainty admitted that it was a legitimate cause for solicitude, and hailed this proof that Arthur was taking thought for others. Even if it were the others who were taking thought for themselves, a poor woman could not be blamed for wishing to secure the future of her helpless offspring. He decided that he must go down and see his brother. He was sorry Arthur had been so ill; he never remembered him ill in his life, since the measles and chicken-pox of early childhood.

Sainty did not judge it necessary to say anything to Cissy about his expedition; it required no diplomacy on his part to conceal any of his movements; if he should be absent for a week, she would neither know nor care, and he found by consultation of Bradshaw that he could go and return in the long summer day. It was a relief to him that he need not spend a night in the house of kinsfolk whom he did not receive in his own. The situation was awkward and unpleasant, and when he thought of all that Arthur's marriage had made him do and suffer, it must be confessed that he approached his brother's home and wife with invincible repugnance.

The Chamberses had taken up their abode (of course in a hunting country) in an old vicarage from which a victim of shrunken tithes had been glad to move into a smaller house. Arthur had added new and magnificent stables that had cost Sainty a pretty penny before they were completed. The house itself might have been transplanted bodily from the heart of Belgravia. It was of such commonplace and uncharacteristic architecture that even the process known to Lady Arthur as 'Smartenin' the old place up a bit' had failed materially to disfigure it. It was approached through all the dignity of a lodge gate and 'carriage sweep,' which swept round a mound of damp laurels opposite the front door, and deposited Sainty at a small Ionic portico of stucco pillars. Having confided his name and business to a dingy man in a shiny dress-coat who opened the door to him, Belchamber was told "'is lordship was expecting of 'im, and would 'is lordship please to walk this way,' and followed the butler upstairs to Arthur's room. He smiled to see how exactly the interior of the house corresponded with his anticipations: everything was modern, ugly, expensive, and already shabby. A great litter of caps, gloves, sticks, and hunting-crops encumbered the hall, together with a female garden-hat ornamented with huge red bows and faded muslin poppies. A strong smell of cooking pervaded the staircase, and from some of the many open doors came the sound of women's voices in dispute, and high above all else the shrill wailing of a baby.

It was with a conflict of feelings that Sainty found himself once more face to face with Arthur, whom he had not seen since his fruitless attempt to detach him from the woman who was now his wife. They had parted as boys, they met again as married men, and with no particularly happy experiences behind them. Sainty noted with pained surprise how much of his brother's good looks had been what the French call 'the devil's beauty.' That boyish freshness was gone for ever, and the face had gained nothing of manly dignity in its place.

The young man was sitting propped with pillows in a big easy-chair, arrayed in a gorgeous silk dressing-gown. His recent illness had given him a pinched, bluish-white look about the nose, but the colour had set and hardened on the cheek bones, and the eyes had a tired, shifty look. The beautiful curls were already worn a little thin at the temples, and an absurd little fair moustache seemed to be ineffectually trying with its waxed points to conceal the two lines that ill-temper had traced beside the nostrils.

'Very good of you to come,' he said, as he held out his hand.

'I'm so sorry to hear you've been ill. What was it?' Sainty asked, as he sat down beside him, struggling with a lump that would rise in his throat.

'I fancy I've been pretty bad,' Arthur answered. 'Some superior form of mulligrubs. I don't believe the damn fool of a doctor knows quite what *was* the matter. I think he was frightened himself. He gets into corners with Topsy and whispers, till I want to break his head. I've pulled through all right, but, of course, another time I mightn't, you know, and that's what I wanted to see you about.'

There was no suggestion that he wanted to see him for any other reason. They met after two years of absence and estrangement, and after what seemed a very fair chance that they might never meet again. The elder brother was husky with emotion, the younger as unmoved by any thought of their common past as though it were his solicitor whom he had summoned to the discussion of a matter of business.

His coldness reacted on Sainty, and helped him to steady his voice as he answered, 'Your wife intimated in her letter that you were troubled about money matters.'

'That's it. You see, as long as I live I've got this cursed pittance. A fellow can't live like a gentleman on it, but at least we don't starve. But as the missus pointed out to me, if I was to hop the twig, there'd be just nothing for her and the kids; so I made her write and tell you I was ill; I thought I owed it to her. She grumbles a good deal, and she's a damn bad manager, and we have our rows, but she's not a bad sort of an old girl. Last winter she went without a pony for her shay, so as I could keep another hunter. Now that was rather decent of her. I'm not very partial to the kids myself; it's unbelievable how they yell; but I shouldn't like 'em to be left in the gutter, you know.'

'Do you know me so little, Arthur, that you could suppose if anything happened to you, I shouldn't provide for your wife and children?'

'Well, you were never a particularly free parter, you know, old man, and then you didn't approve of the connection. How was I to know?'

'Of course, in case of your death, I should continue the same allowance to your widow.'

'Would you now? Well, *that's* all right. But I say, suppose *you* were to kick? you're not so remarkably strong, you know, yourself.'

'In that case, your boy comes in for the whole thing, and of course the trustees would make a suitable provision for his mother.'

'Oh, gammon! we don't count on that, you know. What's to prevent your having children yourself? By the way, isn't Lady Belchamber showing any signs yet?'

'Er—no; as a matter of fact—not——'

'Well, she'd better look sharp, or we shall begin to indulge unholy hopes. But, bar chaff, you couldn't put it in writing, could you, about the allowance going on in case we were both to what the papers call "join the majority"?'

'If it will be any comfort to you I can, but I should think you could trust me; and in case I should ever have an heir, I promise at once to add a codicil to my will, providing for your children.'

'Well, let's have that in writing too; then there can't be any mistake about it, and Topsy'll let me alone. She's got her damned old mother with her (she's an old vulgarian, I tell you), and the two of 'em have nagged my life out of me about this. I never will have old Mother Mug here, but I was going to town for a lar—on business, if I hadn't been taken ill, and so I said she could have her to keep her company while I was away, and I'm blowed if the old devil didn't turn up, just the same.'

'How do you like this place on the whole?' Sainty asked.

'It isn't bad in the winter; just between two packs, you know; and one or two of the people round have given me some shooting. But at this time o' year it's simply infernal; not one blessed thing to do. As I told you, if it hadn't been for this cursed illness, I was going to town for a bit; if I didn't get away now and then I should rot and burst.'

'Is there nobody you see or like in the neighbourhood?'

Arthur winced. 'Well, you see,' he said, 'most of the huntin' lot go away in the summer, and the regular county sort of set ain't particularly lively; and then the women jib a bit at Topsy. One or two of 'em have called, but not many. Our parson and his wife toady her freely; they ain't particular as long as she's my lady, and will give 'em money for the school treat. I assure you she's becoming quite the charitable, religious lady; nothing else to do, poor girl. But most of these county women are a damned stiff-backed lot; they ain't like Londoners.'

At this point in the conversation the dingy butler, who looked like the 'heavy father' of a not very prosperous travelling company, came to say that 'lunching was served, and Lady Harthur Chambers 'oped Lord Belchamber would do 'er the honour to come down.' He also brought Arthur's meal on a tray, over which the invalid let fly a volley of curses: 'the napkin was dirty, the soup was cold, the bread was stale; he could take it back to the damn cook and tell her, —— her, if she couldn't send up a decent basin of broth to a sick man, —— her, and —— her, she'd better —— well go.'

To this rolling accompaniment, Sainty got himself out of the room, saying he would come up again after lunch, and was conducted by the seedy retainer into the presence of his sister-in-law, who received him with much state.

The three years that had elapsed since their last meeting had not treated Lady Arthur more kindly than her husband. They were in her case three years considerably nearer to the term of youth. In the days of the supper at the Hotel Fritz she had been a decidedly handsome young woman, if a little over-florid. In the interval she had grown more florid and less handsome, and suggested an impression of having run to seed. A growing tendency to corpulence was resisted by violent compression, with disastrous results to the complexion, imperfectly corrected by a plentiful application of *blanc de perle*. Her attire was gorgeous beyond the needs of the occasion, but left somewhat to be desired in the matter of tidiness, and exhaled a heavy scent of musk that made Sainty feel sick. She presented him to her mother, a terrible warning of what she was on the highroad to become. This lady was a shorter and twenty years' older edition of Lady Arthur, more coarsely painted, more frankly vulgar, more consentingly fat, and she wore an olive green wig of Brutus curls.

'Do you like the country, Mrs. de Vere?' Sainty asked, as they sat at meat together in heavy silence.

'Muggins,' the lady corrected, with a giggle. 'De Vere was Maria's—I mean Cynthy's—stage name.'

'My *Nong de Tayarter*,' said her daughter, with a warning look at the dingy man, who was handing the potatoes with an air of forced abstraction.

'Well,' said Mrs. Muggins, 'I was connected with the profession myself when I was young; there's nothing to be ashamed of in it. It's an art, and nowadays very highly considered. But you was askin', my lord, if I liked the country. For a little visit like this, I don't say, but to live in, year in, year out—no thank you. It may be all very well for them that were born to it, but give me London. I like to see my fellow-creeturs. I should think Cynthia'd die of the mopes in this place. I should, I know, if I was her.'

'It isn't very lively,' assented her daughter.

'I can't think whatever you find to do all day,' said the elder lady.

'I have my children,' said Cynthia, with the air of a Cornelia, 'and I'm getting quite interested in the village and the poor people.'

'Well, it wouldn't amuse *me*,' said her mother. 'I call it cruel of your brother, my lord, to keep her mewed up in a place like this. Such a winter as she's had. It's all very well for him, 'untin' five days a week, and shootin' with Squire this, that, and the other, but what fun does *she* get out of it, poor child? Their stuck-up wives don't even come and see her, and the moment the 'untin' and shootin's over, my lord was off to London and New-market, if he hadn't been took ill. He was hardly here a week last summer. Does he offer to take *her*?—not him, not if he knows it.'

'Three weeks at the sea was all the change *I* got last year,' said Lady Arthur.

'And *that* I had to make you insist upon, or you wouldn't have got *that*,' chimed in mamma.

'It was more for baby's sake than my own,' said Cynthia; 'the child needed sea air.'

'Dear little Arthur was baby then,' explained Mrs. Muggins; 'the second little dear wasn't even expected. Now there's two of 'em they'll want a change more than ever.'

'You have two children?' Sainty said. 'Are they both boys?'

'Both of 'em,' assented Lady Arthur proudly. 'Poor as we are, there's many people would be glad of my two little boys, or even one of 'em,' and she pointed this delicate allusion by a side glance at her mother, as who should say 'I had him there.'

The ill-concealed hostility of these people, the way they abused his brother to him, his sister-in-law's hint at the want of ease in their circumstances, all combined to make Sainty's visit thoroughly uncomfortable.

'What's been the matter with Arthur?' he asked, to change the subject.

'Eating and drinking too much,' responded Mrs. Muggins readily. 'And so I told him. "Arthur, my boy," I says to him "you mark my words: you're digging your grave with your teeth."'

Lady Arthur simpered. 'It's rather awkward to talk about insides to gentlemen,' she said; 'but it was of that nature. The doctor said he had had a narrow squeak of—what was the word?—perrynaitis, or perrytaitis or something. I told him he couldn't expect ladies to remember his long Latin names, but it was some kind of inflammation from what he said.'

'What she don't tell you,' put in the irrepressible Mrs. Muggins, 'was how she nursed him. Three nights she never went to bed nor had her clothes off her, and, as often as not, sworn at for her pains.'

'I only did my duty,' said Cynthia nobly; 'but I hope I shan't often have to do the same again.'

'What she wants,' said Mrs. Muggins, 'after being shut up so much, and the anxiety and all, is a good change. Why don't you come up and stop with me a bit, when I go back, and see the theatres and the shops? The spring fashions are very pretty: sunshades are very tasty this year, I must say.'

'I do want a new sunshade,' Lady Arthur admitted, 'and for that matter, lots of things; but Arthur don't care *how* I'm dressed *now*,' and she removed a discoloured tear with the untorn corner of an imitation lace handkerchief.

As they were leaving the dining-room, she detained Sainty a moment to whisper in his ear, 'Has Arthur spoken to you about what I wrote?'

'Oh yes,' said Sainty, 'we have talked about it. I assured him that would be all right.'

Lady Arthur looked relieved. 'What should I have?' she asked.

'Oh!—er—the same as now,' Sainty gasped.

'You'll think me very mercenary, I fear,' said his sister-in-law, with an attempt to climb back into the grand manner from which she had so swiftly descended. 'I don't care for myself, you know; I've worked for my living before, but a mother must think of her children; even a bear will fight for its cubs.'

The 'cubs' were presently produced, of course. The baby was a mere bundle of lace and ribbons; but the elder child, who appeared to be nearly two, and had been most carefully combed and starched and decorated for the occasion, was set upon two chubby legs within the door, and stared stolidly at his uncle. Sainty tried hard to see something of Arthur in the little boy who would probably be his heir, but the younger Arthur was a most unmistakable miniature edition of Mrs. Muggins, with the same prominent eyes and hanging lower lip, and even his 'oiled and curled Assyrian locks' suggested a sort of childish imitation of the Brutus wig. His grandmother was fully aware of the likeness, and evidently thought it must be a cause of unmixed gratification to Lord Belchamber.

'He favours our side of the family,' she said proudly, 'and, though I say it that should not, a handsomer little picture of a cherub I don't think you'll easily find.'

'Give uncle a sweet kiss, dearie,' said the proud mother; but on Sainty's stooping to receive the embrace, the amiable infant set up such a piteous howl, in which the baby promptly joined, that both children had to be conducted into retirement.

'I think,' said Sainty, 'if you'll let me, I'll go up and see my brother again for a few minutes. I see I must be leaving in about half an hour, if I am to catch the afternoon train up. I told the fly to come back for me.'

'Well, if you *must* go,' said his sister-in-law, 'there's no good pressing you to stop. I'm afraid the lunch was not what you're accustomed to. No doubt you have a French cook and every luxury, but *we* have to cut our coats according to the cloth, you know. I may not see you again before you go, I'm going to take mamma for a bit of an airing. I hope Lady Belchamber is well. She has no children, I think.'

'Well,' said Arthur, when Sainty returned to him, 'what do you think of old Mother Mug? *She's* a beauty, isn't she?'

'She seemed to think you were a little inconsiderate about your wife, that she needed a certain amount of change and amusement; and, indeed, that poor woman must have a dull life, so very different to everything she has been accustomed to.'

'No doubt the pair of 'em have been abusing me finely, and, of course, you take their part. What the devil's she got to complain of, I should like to know? Haven't I made an honest woman of her, and jolly well muckered my own life by doing it? I suppose she expects me to give up the little fun I do get, and take her to London and show her round. Don't you marry your mistress, old man. You can take it from me, it isn't good enough. But there!—you *are* married, and you haven't got a mistress.'

Sainty did not escape without the usual demand for money, which Arthur irritated him by calling a loan.

'What's the good of talking like that?' Sainty said. 'You know you haven't the slightest intention of repaying it. As you are always rubbing it into me that you can't live on what I give you, is it likely that next quarter, or next year, you will be able to save the amount you require out of the same insufficient allowance?'

'You don't suppose I enjoy having to ask you for every dirty penny I want?' retorted the invalid sullenly.

'Then why don't you try to live within your income, and then you wouldn't have to?'

'I must say you always make it as unpleasant as possible.'

'Well, don't let's wrangle about money; I give it just the same. I'll send you a cheque. Good-bye, and I hope you'll soon be better.'

'And these are the people who are to come after me!' Sainty said to himself bitterly as the train took him back to London. He had a vision of Belchamber, his beloved Belchamber, overrun and ravaged by these barbarians; of Cynthia 'smartenin' the old place a bit,' with the aid of Mrs. Muggins's suggestions as to what would be 'tastey'; of Arthur cutting down the trees and selling the books and pictures to buy more horses and lose bigger bets; of that unattractive child with its stiff curls and goggle eyes coming in turn to make final havoc of the ruin its parents had left. And it was for this end that he had given his name, his future, his honour, into the keeping of a beautiful, parasitic creature without heart or conscience, who obeyed no law but her own imperious appetites!

CHAPTER XXII

ALTHOUGH Belchamber had become a very different place from the home of his childhood, it was still a relief to Sainty to get into the country. It must be confessed that the parties with which Cissy delighted to fill the house were extraordinarily unexacting in the attention they demanded from their host, so that he was able, as in London, to lead very much his own life, undisturbed by his wife or her guests. Except at dinner, or in occasional passage meetings, as he slunk from the library to his own sacred quarters in the western pavilion, he seldom met any of them.

Moreover, the young couple were, for the moment, nearly alone. Most of the society which Lady Belchamber specially affected was either at Cowes and Goodwood, or devoting a fortnight to the care of its property and the reception of its schoolboys before the annual round of Scottish visits. Sainty had been passingly surprised at Cissy's decision to forego a very gay house-party in Sussex, and return quietly to Belchamber at the beginning of August. The young woman did not seem to be in her accustomed health; indeed, she admitted she was quite done up, and needed rest; there had even been a talk of 'waters.' She had begun to be not quite herself before they left London, and then there had been the curious incident of her fainting at her own party.

Quite early in May, before Lady Charmington's unfortunate visit, Cissy had announced her intention of giving some kind of entertainment, but the difficulty of deciding on what form it should take, and the impossibility of finding an evening when it would not interfere with something else she wanted to do, had combined to defer the execution of the plan till nearly the end of the season. She found it so much easier to go to parties which other people had the trouble of arranging than to take the trouble to arrange one for herself, that Sainty had begun to hope the whole thing might fall through, when she suddenly fixed a date, called in Lady Eccleston to assist her, and telegraphed to Roumania to offer a fabulous sum to a celebrated violinist, who had not been heard in England that summer. By eking out this star with the only two expensive singers who had not yet left the opera, and rigorously excluding from her invitation-list any one to whom it could be a pleasure or excitement to be present, she managed to have a very brilliant and select little gathering indeed, which, but for the unfortunate *contretemps* above mentioned, would have been an unqualified success. The right dowagers were slumbering in the front row, the right younger people were jostling and chattering in the doorways, the talented performer was executing his most incredible calisthenics, when Sainty, jammed into a far corner of one of the big rooms, became aware of a bustle and commotion near the door of the boudoir. People moved and heaved and whispered, and ceased to bestow even a perfunctory attention on the music, which came rather abruptly to an end. He saw Claude Morland elbow through the crowd with a bottle and a glass, and some one near him said 'Lady Belchamber has fainted.'

Among the many duties thrown unexpectedly on him by the catastrophe, appeasing the anxiety of the guests and soothing the susceptibilities of the artists, he was startled by the speech, accompanied by a meaning pressure of the hand, with which Alice de Lissac took leave of him. 'I am *so* glad,' she whispered; '*now*, I feel sure all will come right.' Enlightenment as to her meaning came most unexpectedly from his mother-in-law next morning when he inquired of her after his wife's health. Lady Eccleston, who had been the last to depart the night before, arrived at an amazingly early hour, and after a long visit to her daughter was still able to appear in Sainty's apartments almost before he had finished his breakfast. She was evidently in high good-humour and began by embracing him tenderly.

'How did you find Cissy?' Sainty asked. 'I haven't sent to ask after her yet for fear of disturbing her. She seemed quite worn out last night; I think she has been doing much too much.'

'She is not *ill*,' said Lady Eccleston, with a world of meaning. 'I will not allow that she is *ill*.'

'I am glad to hear it,' said Sainty. 'I thought she looked very seedy last night, I must say.'

'She will admit nothing,' continued her ladyship. 'I think I have told you *how* delicate and reticent she is on certain subjects. Even to *me*, her mother, and you know we have always been like sisters, she will tell nothing. Do you know what I think? she will tell no one till she has told *you*. That's it; you may be sure that's it. She will run no risk of your hearing it from any one but her. For heaven's sake don't let her know I have even hinted at anything——'

'What *do* you mean, Lady Eccleston?' Sainty gasped, a supposition of which only he knew the full grotesqueness beginning to dawn on him.

'Dear, sweet, innocent Sainty!' cried Lady Eccleston, in a transport of archness. 'You and my girl are made for one another. You are like a pair of child-lovers in a fairy-tale. I have told nothing, remember that; I will tell nothing. I will not rob dear Cissy of the joy of announcing it herself. Besides, as I say, I can only conjecture; she has absolutely refused to admit it.'

'Dear Lady Eccleston,' cried Sainty, in great perturbation, 'I can't pretend to misunderstand you; but, believe me, I think you are wrong. I am sure—I am *almost* sure—it cannot be as you suspect.'

Lady Eccleston shook her head and pursed her lips mysteriously. 'A mother is not deceived,' she said. 'But recollect I have told you nothing. Cissy would never forgive me. I will not even congratulate you till *you* tell *me*. Meanwhile I shan't breathe a word, not a word. Trust me'; and she again folded her son-in-law to her heart. 'It was the one thing wanting to our happiness,' burst from her, as it were involuntarily, as she hurried away, leaving Sainty too much bewildered to protest.

Two days later they went into the country. Cissy was certainly not feeling well. She asked Sainty if he would mind going sooner than had been settled; she thought rest and country air would set her up. No, she wouldn't see a doctor; there was nothing wrong with her. 'I'm just knocked up with being on the go, morning, noon, and night, for months.'

'Your mother suggested the weirdest explanation,' said Sainty.

Cissy flushed crimson and then grew so pale that he feared she was going to repeat the performance of the night before.

'Mamma really is a bigger fool than I thought,' she said hotly. 'I didn't think she would have had the idiotcy to carry that nonsense to *you*. What did you say?'

'What could I say? I told her it was impossible, but she would listen to nothing.'

'Of course it's impossible! no one should know that better than *you*.'

On the afternoon of his first day at Belchamber Sainty ordered his little cart and drove as in duty bound to pay his respects to his mother. He had not seen Lady Charmington since she had left his house in wrath, and though he had written to her several times he had received only the briefest and coldest answers. It was not, therefore, with any very pleasing anticipations of the coming interview that he set out to visit her.

It was one of those perfect, cool autumnal days which English people mistake for summer. The open spaces of the park were dappled with pleasant temperate sunlight like the flanks of the deer that fed there. Hundreds of rabbits squatted in the familiar glades or tilted themselves hastily into covert as he passed. Never had his home looked lovelier or more peaceful, or appealed more strongly to him. The woods and coppices called to him with a thousand voices, and his poor heart, starved of all human emotion, answered as only the lonely and despised among her children can answer to the great cry of Nature the universal mother.

Then, as he drove along the smooth green alleys, there came to him the recollection of his brother and of the woman his brother had married. Ever since his visit to them Sainty had thought much about his sister-in-law, and had striven in his own mind to do her justice;

terrible as she was to him æsthetically, he was forced to admit that she was a better sort than her husband. She did think of her children and do her duty by them according to her lights, whereas Arthur thought of no one but himself. After all, were Cissy's ideals in life, except superficially, much less vulgar than Lady Arthur's? He sometimes wondered if it were not better to have been frankly improper before marriage and settle down into an irreproachable wife and mother, than to be a frivolous little worldling, refusing to live with her husband, and lending numberless occasions to the tongue of scandal.

Argue as he would, and rigidly impartial as he strove to make his mental attitude, the thought of his successors poisoned the beauty of the day for him and blotted out the sunshine. It was vain to tell himself that Cynthia's standard of personal conduct was higher than Cecilia's. Her ghastly veneer of gentility shocked his taste more than even her mother's frank vulgarity or Arthur's callous selfishness. To think of her and her shiny-faced babies at Belchamber was to profane his most sacred associations.

He soon found that he need not have doubted his mother's welcome. She received him with what, for her, was almost cordiality. On the rare occasions when Lady Charmington assumed a staid and humorless jocosity, she was wont to affect a Scottish accent and manner of speech, and Sainty noted with surprise this mark of unusual hilarity. 'Come ben the house, man,' she remarked; 'the sight of ye is good for sair een.'

'How pretty you have made everything,' said Sainty. 'Your borders are lovely. There is no one like you for a garden, mother.'

Lady Charmington looked round her with a certain pride. 'Yes, I think I've improved the place,' she said. 'Do ye know these late-flowering delphiniums? this is the only kind that blooms as late as this. I thought at one time my hollyhocks were going to have the disease, but I've brought them through it.'

'They are lovely; and how beautiful these roses are.'

'That's the pink Ayrshire; it's not so common as the white. You know the big bush in the corner of the west wing, I brought it from Scotland with me soon after I married; these are some cuttings from it I took a few years ago, and last autumn I moved them here; haven't they grown?' Thus talking on safe subjects, they entered the house, where Sainty's admiration was claimed and freely given for various ingenious arrangements and improvements.

'And how's Cissy?' asked Lady Charmington presently, a certain subdued excitement in her look and manner.

'It is very good of you, mother, to ask after her so kindly,' Sainty answered. 'She doesn't seem to me very well; she's a little knocked up with all her gaieties, I think, but she won't admit there's anything wrong with her which a little rest and country air won't set right.'

'Wrong with her! certainly not; what should ail her?' cried Lady Charmington, with the same curious air of meaning more than she said.

'I hope,' Sainty began awkwardly, 'that you won't remember her rudeness and bad behaviour to you last May; it would be terribly painful to me to have you on bad terms with one another. I quite admit she behaved shockingly to you, but I hope you will overlook it. I feel sure if you will come and see her you'll find her ready to meet you more than half-way.'

'I bear no malice,' said Lady Charmington, with bewildering good-humour; 'and indeed I could find it in my heart to forgive her at this moment worse things than a little incivility to myself.'

'That's very kind of you,' Sainty said; 'but why specially at this moment?' He was beginning to feel uncomfortable.

Lady Charmington leaned forward and looked sharply in his face.

'Is it possible you really don't know?' she said. 'You are the queerest couple I ever came across. I made sure you had come here to announce it to me, and I didn't want to take the wind out of your sails by letting you see that I knew it already.'

'Know what? announce what?' cried Sainty. He was beginning to divine his mother's meaning; his mind reverted to his conversation with Lady Eccleston. Why did all these women persist in mocking him with congratulations on the impossible as though it were an accomplished fact? 'Have you heard from Lady Eccleston?' he asked, with apparent irrelevance.

Lady Charmington pounced on the implied admission. 'Oho! So you are not quite as ignorant as you pretend! But why should you try to keep it from *me*, when you must know it is the bit of news which it would give me more pleasure to hear than anything in the world?'

'Dear mother,' said Sainty, 'do you suppose if I had any such news to tell as you seem to imagine, that I shouldn't have rushed to you with it? But it's not so. It can't be so.'

'But why shouldn't it be so?' asked Lady Charmington.

'Believe me, it's impossible,' Sainty was beginning, and then he recollected that he couldn't tell his mother *why* it was impossible. 'I don't know what's come to everybody,' he said lamely.

'Why did you ask if I had heard from Lady Eccleston? It shows you guessed what I meant.'

'Because she too has run away with the same idea, and when I told her that she must be mistaken, she only became more positive.'

'You see,' said Lady Charmington triumphantly, 'her own mother thinks so, and *she* ought to know.'

'But really, really, I feel sure you are all wrong. I don't want you to build on this, mother, because I know what a disappointment it will be to you.'

'Do you mean to say your wife is not going to have a baby?'

'I certainly think not; she said herself her mother had been talking nonsense. Did she tell it to you as a fact, in so many words?'

'Lady Eccleston's style is sometimes a little involved, but I certainly took her letter to mean—— Oh yes— there's not a doubt of it; she *can't* have meant anything else.' Lady Charmington turned over a pile of letters on her writing-table, and selecting one began to mumble through it. 'Um, um, London emptying fast, just on the wing myself, cannot go till I've found some one to read to my dear blind . . . um, um, um. Ah! here it is: "I cannot refrain from giving you a hint of the great news. I know how it will rejoice your heart. But don't betray me till the dear children tell you themselves. I should not say a word about it, only they are both so absurdly reticent and sensitive; it is quite possible they may neither of them mention it. Dear Cissy was almost angry with me; she tried to make out I was mistaken, but a mother's eye! you and I know when . . ." Well, we needn't go into all that; but you see, her mother's convinced.'

'Well,' said Sainty, 'I can only set on the other side that Cissy denies it herself.'

'How about her being taken ill at the party?' It was evident that Lady Eccleston had gone into details.

'People may faint without being in that condition,' protested Sainty; 'no one should know that better than I. Believe me, you are all building too much on that momentary loss of consciousness, which may as likely as not have come from tight lacing.'

Lady Charmington shook her head impatiently. 'Her mother says she has never been known to faint before in her life; and any one can see with half an eye she has always laced . . .'

After this the conversation languished perceptibly. It was obviously futile to go on discussing the prospects of an heir, when the parties principally concerned agreed in denying that there *were* any prospects. Lady Charmington, 'convinced against her will,' was very much 'of the same opinion still'; but balked of the topic on which she burned to dilate, she resolutely declined every other which her son brought forward. Sainty's well-meant efforts to extract information on local or farming subjects were killed by the stony indifference she opposed to them, so that he presently took his leave, without obtaining more than a very qualified and doubtful agreement to his suggestion that she should come and see Cissy.

At first the pertinacity of their two mothers in attributing miraculous offspring to Cissy and himself had seemed only a peculiarly galling mystification. Sainty never knew at just what moment a horrible solution of the puzzle had begun to suggest itself to him as possible. Had he fought against the conviction from the first, or did it come to him slowly and insidiously as his mother marshalled the reasons for her belief against his repeated denials? He could put his finger on no point in time when the suspicion had flashed into his brain; but by the time he reached his own door again, it seemed to him that there had been no hour of his unhappy married life when this terror had not sat grinning behind every trivial incident. He determined to see his wife, to know the worst at once. He asked for her, but learned she was out. 'Her ladyship had gone driving late, after tea, and had not come in yet.' He had no chance of speech with her through the evening, but when at last she went to her room, he followed boldly, hardly waiting for the answer to his knock before entering the room.

Cissy had thrown herself on the sofa, and the loose sides of the tea-gown she had worn at dinner had a little fallen back. At the sound of the opening door she started up, and drew her draperies so swiftly about her that Sainty could not be sure if he had noticed or only imagined a slight change in her figure.

'You!' she cried.

'Yes,' he said, in as steady a voice as he could. 'I want to speak to you, and I could find no other chance of seeing you alone.'

Their glances crossed and he read in her eyes a confirmation of his worst suspicions. Still he must be sure, must hear it from herself. She had looked startled, almost frightened, as she faced him, then her face took on a dogged, sulky expression.

'Well?' she said.

'I went to see my mother this afternoon,' Sainty began.

'Your mother,' Cissy broke in. 'Oh! *she's* been making mischief.'

'On the contrary, she was all amiability and delight, ready to make it up with you, to forgive everything "at this moment," as she said.'

'That's very kind of her; but why?'

'She was bursting with congratulations and excitement; she had had a letter from your mother.'

Lady Belchamber muttered something very unfilial about her parent. 'And what did *you* say?' she inquired.

'I? What *could* I say? I said they were both mistaken. That you had told me it was not true; and of course it isn't—it *can't* be; I don't need to be told that.'

He was pleading against his own certainty; from the time he came into the room, he knew what he should hear before he left it. Yet with his whole heart he was begging her still, if it were possible, to deny the shame that had come upon his house. He stood mute and suppliant before her, and she looked at him almost pityingly. Then with a little discouraged gesture she turned away and sat down again on the sofa.

'It *is* true,' she said quietly. 'You may as well know it first as last. In any case I couldn't conceal it much longer; and now that mamma has guessed it, she will have told it to at least fifty people already. She little knows what she's doing,' she added, with a hard laugh that jarred on Sainty's overstretched nerves.

He had been sure of it, had known it. Yet now that the words were spoken, that the fact confronted him, admitted, undeniable, irrevocable, he staggered with the blow.

'You are going to have a child?' he gasped.

She nodded, and for all answer threw back the covering she had pulled across herself.

'But it is not mine.'

'Yours!' impatiently. 'How should it be?'

'Good God!'

There was a silence. Sainty moved restlessly about, as agitated as though it were he who was making the confession. Cissy was far the more self-possessed of the two. She sat upon her sofa watching his agonised motions with a faintly inquisitive distaste, as a person of imperfect sympathies might observe the contortions of some creature he had unwittingly injured.

'I suppose,' she said presently, 'you want to know whose it is?'

'No, no!' cried Sainty shudderingly. 'That least of all. For God's sake don't tell me!' and he made a step towards her as though he would have choked back the name he feared to hear.

Cissy stared. 'Queer!' she ejaculated.

There was another pause. A clock struck midnight, and was echoed loudly or faintly by others near or distant. Sainty counted the strokes, and was conscious of irritation when one began before another finished and embroiled his counting.

It was again the woman who spoke first, and the question was characteristic, severely practical.

'What are you going to do about it?'

'I don't know—I can't think. Give me time—give me time to think.'

Cissy looked at him with undisguised contempt. '*I* should know what to do,' she said. After a while she added, 'Of course I can't stay here now.'

'I don't know—I don't know,' Sainty kept repeating. 'We must do nothing in a hurry. Think of all it means, all the consequences.'

Cissy shrugged her shoulders. 'It seems rather late for that,' she remarked. 'Besides, we can't keep it to ourselves indefinitely, you know.'

'At least give me to-night to get my ideas into some sort of order,' Sainty pleaded. 'You can't be surprised if this is rather a shock to me, can you?' he added, almost apologetically.

Cissy laughed. 'I wonder if any man ever took this announcement in just the same way?' she said.

CHAPTER XXIII

To Sainty, sitting alone in his old room in the western pavilion, it seemed that there was no bitterness left untasted. Far into the night he sat, his elbows on the table, his head buried in his hands. At first all seemed mere chaos and horror; he was stunned and could not think. But for the haunting consciousness of misery, he could almost have fancied that he had slept. Gradually, however, definite images began to emerge from the bewildered trouble of his brain.

What was this thing that had come on him, through no fault of his own? He had done no wrong, snatched no forbidden pleasure; it was those other two who had sinned and enjoyed. Why must he be pilloried with them, share the scandal and the punishment? He, with his morbid shrinking from publicity, to have his private life turned inside out to the scorn and laughter of the vulgar! He knew well enough how little sympathy he had to expect; in all times and countries had not the betrayed husband been a butt for mirth? He wondered why. It seemed hard to him that of the three characters in the eternal drama of adultery, it should always be the one innocent person that was selected for satire. Surely it was the most elementary justice that punishment should fall on him who injures his fellow, not upon the injured. Yet of they three, who would suffer most? He, without a doubt, who had the greatest capacity for suffering. He saw, as in a dream, the dingy scene of the divorce-court, the headlines in the papers, his name dragged in the dirt. He pictured to himself the long martyrdom of cross examination, the bar pathos, the bar wit; he knew how he should flinch and writhe at the stake.

In his case, moreover, the situation was complicated by the coming child. He had not only to proclaim his dishonour to the world, but must lay bare to every grinning idiot the grotesque story of his married life. If the husband whose rights had been invaded was absurd, what of him who had not even been able to obtain those rights. And he must stand up in open court and tell this thing of himself, he who felt the mere idea of marriage too sacred for spoken words! The cruel irony of it all! Was there no other issue but through that horrible, sordid ordeal? What did men do in his position? What was the *beau rôle* for the injured husband? He thought of Dumas's '*Tue-la!*' and wondered how it would have advanced matters if he had murdered Cissy, supposing he had the strength and courage to do it. It was only to shift the scene; another court, an added horror, but the same publicity, the same scandal, the same story to tell, the same agony to undergo.

He almost regretted the foolish old fantastic code of honour which would have made it incumbent on him to challenge the seducer, and as likely as not be killed by him. Death *might* have been a solution, but there was no such easy way out of the situation as that. The hand that had done him so much wrong would not render him that supremest service.

Hitherto he had succeeded almost without conscious effort in keeping the inevitable third in this grim trio almost an abstraction. Yet he remembered how passion-ately he had refused to know, when his wife had offered him the name of her lover. Now the figure was beginning to take shape against his will; a tall figure with a false air of slenderness, a figure that by the languid grace of its movements counteracted the slight tendency to heavi-ness in the hips and shoulders. How well he knew that back, the sinuous curves of the waist, the sidelong, per-suasive droop of the head; he had seen it walking away beside Cissy on the afternoon of their very first meeting. It had been pressed against the glass door that held him an unwilling witness on the night of the ball at Sun-borough House. How clearly the impressions came back to him, the dusky garden speckled leopard-wise with lanterns, the lithe, shimmering blackness of the figure at his side trying to instil the doubts he would not harbour, the swift swing back of the door, the words so clearly over-heard, that then had held no meaning for him. Still it was only a back, he had not seen the face, the gentle, kindly, sly, mocking face. He pressed his icy fingers tight against his hard, straining eyeballs, as if he could shut it out, that face he would not see. Not *he*! not he of all men! Had not his mother mentioned other men with whom her impru-dence was compromising Cissy? Oh! but that back was unmistakable. And then the voice! low and soft, but so distinct; he could hear it, could hear the words, counsel-ling the horrible meanness of which he had so nearly been the dupe. He understood *now* the secret of her mysterious behaviour in the library that night. Surely such baseness was unbelievable; even Cissy had recoiled from carrying out the scheme.

For one brief moment he wished she could have done it —that he might have been deceived. 'I need never have known!' he cried, and his voice speaking aloud in the silence of the night startled him like the cry of a creature that is being killed.

He raised his head and looked about him. The candle he had brought had burnt almost to the socket; he rose and lighted two others from it, and blew it out. The chill of the fireless summer night made him shiver, but there was that which lay so cold about his heart that he welcomed the physical discomfort as almost a relief. He moved about the room for a little, but soon tiring, went and sat down again.

The same procession of black thoughts kept up their weary circle through his head; round and round he followed them, yet came no nearer any light, nor any decision of what it behoved him to do under the circumstances. Was this the end of all his dreams, all his sacrifices, all his endeavour for others, all he had hoped to accomplish? Was everything to go down in this whirlpool of a disgrace greater even than that which Arthur's marriage had brought upon them? It was Arthur's marriage that had been the origin of all his troubles. Oh yes, he saw it clearly enough now; however he had deceived himself at the time, he had married, had taken on himself the most sacred obligations, for no object but the mean one of excluding his brother. Perhaps this was his punishment.

He saw what a puppet he had been in the hands of two strong-willed women, an instrument to satisfy the vulgar ambitions of the one, the angry revenge of the other. What a failure, what a dreary failure he had been all through! For years he had had but one thought, one object in life, to steer Arthur past the rocks and quicksands of youth, and anchor him safe in the harbour of property and responsibility, and with what result? What had come of all his plans, his careful tact, his delicate manipulation of his mother and brother? Arthur's marriage afforded a comment of grimmest irony on his efforts in that direction. Since then, as ardently as he had once longed to renounce his birthright in favour of his brother, he had striven to preserve it from that contaminating touch, to keep that brother's wife from sitting in their mother's place; and, once more, with what result? To instal in the innermost shrine of all he held most sacred a woman no less wanton than her sister-in-law, only without her redeeming qualities and the excuses of her early training, one who would make his home a wilderness, his name a by-word! Shame, then, shame either way, and nothing accomplished!

It is not to be supposed that he thought these things out for himself, coldly, sententiously, in order, as, for the sake of the reader, they have to be written down. They were the residuum of all sorts of wild and whirling fancies, flung up at him, as it were, out of a seething cauldron of black wretchedness, which was rather sensation than thought. Not once, moreover, but a thousand times, did each and all of them appear and vanish in a kind of witches' dance to his weary brain, without perceptible sequence or connection. He seemed somehow to be outside his own consciousness, to sit and watch these images, as, one by one, some demon held them up for his tormenting, yet all the while every nerve in him tingled with the apprehension of how intimately they were part of himself.

As he sat gazing stonily at despair, there came a soft stirring of the stillness, a murmur, a breath; then from without, a faint chirping.

'. . . as in dark summer dawns,'

he quoted mechanically, and was aware of a vague irritation that he could not remember the beginning of the line.

'The earliest pipe of half-awakened birds
To dying ears, when unto dying eyes
The casement slowly grows a glimmering square.'

He looked. The chintz curtains that veiled the windows were growing ghostly and transparent. It was the dawn.

All through the night he had sat with his trouble, yet the morning found him as helpless and undecided as ever.

'To dying ears, when unto dying eyes,' he repeated dully. Ah! if it were but that! Death! how easy to die! What a rest, what an escape! It was life, not death, life with its hideous decisions and responsibilities that he had got to face.

The candle flames became more spectral as the light slowly broadened, the light of a new day, the day in which he would have to make up his mind, to take a line, to *act*. There was no way out—none. Once more he was confronted with the inevitable, the pitiless future coming every moment nearer, with all it held of suffering and shame, the fruitlessness of all his efforts, all in vain, in vain!

Then suddenly, as if some voice had spoken, came the question 'Why?' Why need it be in vain? The solution, after all, lay ready to his hand. He had only to hold his tongue. It was all so simple. 'Their strength is to sit still,' he thought. Why, among all that had passed through his wretched head, had this never struck him? He had wished for a child to bar his brother and his brother's sons from the succession. Well! here was the child, his wife's child, born in wedlock, legally, lawfully his. Who could ever say it was not? No one but they two, and of their silence he could be tolerably sure.

At first he put the idea from him with horror. It was a cheat, a fraud. He, with his fastidiously high standard of conduct, to cozen his brother out of his inheritance by a shabby trick. Impossible! The thing was impossible.

He got up, and put back the curtain, and stood looking out into the silence of the growing morning. Over opposite to him, the grey sky was beginning to flush with palest rose, in which the last stars were growing dim; but as yet the great quadrangle lay all in black shadow, out of which the restored statues stood vaguely up like shapes of evil menacing the eastern glory. No, no, no. Better the talk, the scandal, the publicity of the divorce court, than to stand convicted before the tribunal of his own conscience. Whatever else went down in the shipwreck of his life, let him at least keep his self-respect. 'What did it profit a man to gain the world, and lose his own soul?' Yet how often in the old days, in his talk with Newby, had he inveighed against the selfishness of the Puritan idea, which would make the saving of one's soul the object of conduct. Surely the only rational motive was the consideration of how one's acts affected others. In the present instance who would be the worse for his silence? No one would be hurt or disappointed. These people did not expect to succeed; they had given up all hopes of it when he married. Had they not told him so themselves? On the other hand, there was his mother, his mother who had done so much for him. He remembered how he had found her, when she had first learned the truth about Arthur, and terror mixed with his grief at the mere conjecture of what she might say and do with the marriages of both her sons thus ending in shame. Their talk that afternoon had shown him how much her hopes were centred in the birth of an heir to Belchamber. The mere prospect had blotted out the very recollection of her quarrel with Cissy, and Lady Charmington was not a forgiving woman. His fear of her had always gone hand in hand with his love of her, and both made him wince at the thought of her disappointment. Had he the right to bring this fresh blow upon her, who had suffered so much, merely to salve his own conscience? After all, had he any self-respect to sacrifice? Was it possible for him to have a meaner opinion of himself than he had always entertained?

At that moment the sun topped the mass of the eastern wing, flooding with light the broad spaces of grass and gravel at his feet, and casting a long ray over the tall, stately *façade* of the beautiful house. And at the thought of all that was symbolised by that pomp of hewn and fretted stone, the aristocrat that lurked so deep within him, so overlaid with fine theories of brotherhood and equality that he was unconscious of his very existence, stirred and claimed his own. 'For the credit of my house,' he murmured uneasily, as he turned away from the window.

He did not yield at once, or without a struggle, but he knew from the first that it would come to that. From the moment the idea leaped full-grown like Athene from his brain, it was fully armed to meet every point that had distressed him. He feared scandal. There need be no scandal. He shrank from the ignominy of a divorce case. There need be none. Did the thought of unveiling to the public eye the bitter humiliation of his married life revolt him? Here was a means not only of secrecy, but actual disproof. Did it break his heart to think of inflicting such a blow upon his mother? He had only to be silent to crown her dearest wishes, and make her the happiest woman in England. Had he married, enduring all that marriage had brought him, that he might keep his sister-in-law and her children from the heritage of his name and home? Here, too, was the one thing necessary for that end. And to attain all these desired objects there was nothing to do, no word to say, no lie to tell. He had only to let things take their course. It was the line of least resistance, so easy, so fatally easy!

To a man of his character and disposition, what a temptation, what a terrible temptation! He was weakened by his long vigil, the little stock of vitality that he could ever call to his assistance worn almost to a thread with watching and misery. He knew he should give in. To all the arguments in favour of it, what had he to oppose but one poor little scruple of personal honour?

He wondered if his wife had known what he would do before he had thought of it himself? Had she traded on her certainty of his cowardice? At such a suspicion, he almost grew strong again; but no—she had seemed to entertain no doubt that he would repudiate her. He fancied she had even felt a certain relief at the prospect of being rid of the semblance of a connection with himself, and the freedom to claim openly the protection of the man whom, in her way, she loved. If so, here was another argument in favour of silence. By it he could thwart and punish her.

He wandered into his brother's old room, next his own. Here the drawn blinds made still a glimmering twilight, and lent an unreality to the familiar objects. He went and looked at the old school photographs. There was one of Arthur in a group of the cricket eleven, which had always been his special favourite. The figure stood squarely on its legs, the brawny arms bare to the elbow and crossed upon the chest, a boyish grin lighting the handsome face, from which the cap was pushed back by the strong upward spring of the hair above the brow. It was the image of youth, and life, and happiness. Long he stood motionless before it, and then he bent forward and pressed his poor, pale lips to the cold glass. 'Arthur,' he whispered. 'My little Arthur, you are dead, and so is your miserable brother who loved you so. You are no more that brutal, querulous egoist that I saw the other day, than he is the wretch who can stoop to crime to rob you.'

Distant sounds showed him that the household was beginning to be astir. Before his man came to wake him he must have removed the signs of his long vigil. He returned hurriedly to his own room, once more drew the curtain across the window, extinguished the lights, and hastily undressing himself, crept into bed. Already the sense of having something to hide stung him with a terrible self-contempt. He had caught sight of his drawn, haggard face as he passed the mirror. It was the face of a coward.

He did not leave the pavilion all day. He sent word he was ill. That at least was true enough, but late in the evening, as he was lying on the sofa in his study, there came a knock at the door, and Cissy entered. Though perhaps a shade paler than usual, nothing in her appearance suggested a guilty wife come to hear her sentence.

'I have come to return your visit of last night,' she said, as she stood looking down on him.

Sainty groaned and hid his face. At sight of her, the desire to brand her as what she was almost conquered, where conscience and sense of honour had failed—almost, but not quite.

Cissy kept her indifferent pose, playing with the ornaments she wore.

'Well?' she asked at last. 'Have you made up your mind yet?'

'Yes.' His voice came muffled and strange.

Lady Belchamber started. 'What are you going to do?' she demanded, with slightly quickened interest.

'Nothing.'

There was a pause.

'Do you mean to say,' she asked at last, 'that you are going to acknowledge the child?'

'Yes.'

She turned away from him with a half-stifled exclamation. Was it relief or disappointment? he could not tell. After a time she flung a word over her shoulder: 'Why?'

'Because it happens to suit me,' he said doggedly.

The silence was broken by the little laugh he hated.

'I suppose I ought to be very grateful to you,' she sneered.

Sainty sprang from the couch. 'I have ceased to expect gratitude or any other kindly feeling from you,' he blazed out at her; but his wrath fell as quickly as it had flared.

Her puny disdain was powerless to hurt him, merged in the measureless ocean of his self-contempt. There would be lies enough, acted, looked, and lived, if not spoken. At least to her there need be no pretence of an attitude; if not with an accomplice, with whom may one permit himself the luxury of being honest?

'After all, why should I scold at you?' he said wearily. 'You have nothing to thank me for. Don't suppose, if I stoop to this incomparable baseness, that it is with any thought of pleasing *you*.'

Cissy stared at him, cowed by the dim apprehension of a tragedy she was incapable of understanding; and it was not without a certain satisfaction that he saw in her eyes the vague terror of the incomprehensible beginning to permeate her habitual scorn of him.

CHAPTER XXIV

THOUGH the birth of an heir to the house of Belchamber might naturally be supposed a festive occasion, it brought little satisfaction to those principally concerned. It is true that Lady Charmington talked broad lowland for weeks; nor was Lady Eccleston, who kept a supply of conventional sentiment always on tap, likely to be wanting at such a time; but in spite of every grandmotherly effort to impart a correct sense of rejoicing, a certain flatness attended what should have been such an auspicious event. Cissy, entirely preoccupied by terror of physical suffering, insisted that her confinement should take place in London, where she would be within reach of the best professional aid, to the extreme disgust of her mother-in-law, who had decided that Belchamber was the appropriate scene on which the newcomer's eyes should first open. Sainty, being appealed to, expressed the most complete indifference on the subject; he said he didn't suppose it mattered to the baby where it was born, or that it would be likely to retain the smallest recollection of the event. 'It will be a great disappointment to everybody,' Lady Charmington remarked. 'Besides, it will mean your not being here at Christmas. How do you expect your people to rejoice in the birth of an heir, if you slink away and let it happen in London, like anybody else's child?'

'How do you know it will *be* an heir?' Sainty said. 'Why shouldn't it be a girl?'

His mother disdained to notice such a preposterous suggestion.

'It ought to be here,' she kept repeating.

'*I* wasn't born here,' Sainty said.

'That was quite different; Belchamber wasn't our home in those days. Your father and I hardly ever came here in the old lord's time; for that matter, they weren't here much themselves. Besides, I wanted to be with my mother; there is nothing to prevent Cissy having *her* mother with her here; things are very different for *her*

from what *I* had to put up with. I should like to have
seen my mother-in-law allowing me to be confined in her
house! but your poor father felt it very much.'

'Well,' Sainty said at last, 'you can settle it with Cissy;
if you can persuade *her*, you're welcome to; *I* never can,
and in the present case I don't care to.'

Every allusion to the coming event was the turning of
a sword in his heart. His mother's restrained eagerness
was not less terrible to him than Lady Eccleston's loud
jubilation.

He never knew if Lady Charmington availed herself of
his suggestion that she should appeal to Cissy. Certainly,
if she did, it was with no success, for long before there was
any possibility of the child making its appearance, Lady
Belchamber removed to London, taking her parent with
her. Cissy, as usual, when frightened or needing help,
turned to her mother, for whom, as we know, she cherished no very profound respect at other times; and Lady
Eccleston was not even permitted to return to her own
house in Chester Square, but must take up her abode
with her daughter, who considered it a great concession
if she allowed her to go out for an hour's shopping. It is
not to be wondered at if mamma became a little important under the circumstances, and gave herself airs in
writing to the other dowager, who must have hated
having to stay and eat her heart out at Belchamber, with
no hand in what touched her so nearly.

Poor Lady Charmington abounded in strange, recon-
dite lore, and gave much advice which was a little out
of date at the stage proceedings had reached. 'On no
account let her mother coddle your wife,' she wrote to
Sainty. 'If she wants a son, make her take exercise and
not be too luxurious or over-eat herself.'

Every day the letters came, advocating a Spartan
régime; but the messages never reached their destination.
Sainty would have cut his tongue out sooner than address
a word to Cissy on the subject, who, none the less, produced in due course an infant of the desired sex.

Lady Charmington hurried up to Roehampton, and
actually dragged poor old Lady Firth into London to

visit her great-grandson. The old lady, who had become nearly blind, and now hardly ever left her own fireside, peered curiously at the baby through two pairs of spectacles.

'I don't know who he is like,' she said. 'You *have* a look of your father, Sainty, but you are *more* like our family; this little lamb isn't like either. No, certainly not a bit like *you*, nor yet like your wife, who is so fair. I don't know, I'm sure, who he takes after.'

'Does it matter much, grandmamma,' Sainty asked, 'as long as he is strong and healthy?'

His mother turned on him promptly. 'Oh! *you* never think anything matters. Can't you even take an interest in your own first-born son?'

'Come, mother, it doesn't follow that I take no interest because I don't think it matters who he looks like,' Sainty protested meekly.

He had several occasions to curse the propensity common to the whole female sex, when brought into the presence of a newborn babe, to hunt down and fix a likeness for it to some one or other of its kinsfolk. It seemed as though the one important thing to do for the little Lord Charmington was to determine this vexed question of resemblance. The child was of a marked type, too, with long-lashed dark eyes, and an unusual quantity of very black hair, as far removed from Sainty's sandy insignificance as from the delicate fairness of his wife.

At last the matter was set at rest quite unexpectedly, and Sainty breathed more freely. The duchess, who had come to town for a little Christmas shopping, called to inquire after Cissy, and requested to be shown the baby.

'*Eh bien! vous voilà père!*' she remarked, looking rather quizzically at her grandson, as he piloted her upstairs. 'My compliments! And how is Monsieur Bébé? Is he pretty, at least? brown or blond, a Chambers, a Bigorr, or,' with the faintest pause of indescribable insolence, 'an Eccleston?'

Belchamber took dexterous advantage of opening doors, giving warning of steps, and such small attentions, to avoid giving any direct answer, but he might have saved himself the trouble. The eternal topic was at once brought up by the monthly nurse, as she proudly displayed her charge.

'We can't think who he is like, your grace,' she said, folding the flannel back from the tiny face. 'Just look at his beautiful great eyes, and did ever you see such a head of hair on a babe?'

Sainty could have throttled her. 'That's the one thing every one seems to think of,' he said rather testily.

'Like?' said the duchess. 'There can be no question; he's like *me*. You know the miniature of me as a little girl —the child is the image of it.'

Sainty started; he had so entirely forgotten that her grace was ever dark, that the resemblance had escaped him, but once pointed out it was salient. He felt like a criminal who discovers that the detective he has been dodging is on the track of some one else. After all, she was *his* grandmother too!

'Of course!' he cried, 'how stupid every one has been not to think of it.' And the next time the unwelcome subject was mentioned in his presence (by his mother, who had been showing the precious infant to Alice de Lissac), he said quite naturally, 'Oh, we've settled *that* question. He's just like the miniature at Sunborough House of the duchess when she was a child.'

Lady Charmington, who loved her mother-in-law no better than Cissy did hers, was most unwilling to admit the likeness, but could not deny it; and there being no doubt that baby derived his appearance from the member of the family she least wished him to resemble, was in future as averse as her son could desire to all discussion of what had occupied her so much.

Lady Eccleston, on the contrary, who loved all great people, was enchanted to point out the likeness to every member of her huge acquaintance. 'Isn't he like the *dear* duchess?' she would cry. 'It is *so* clever of him to have picked out the most beautiful of all his relations to take after, bless him!'

As time went on, the shortlived interest in the hope of

the Chamberses rapidly waned. The bonfires in his honour had hardly burnt themselves out before this poor little scion of a noble house found himself in as much danger of being altogether neglected as if he had been of quite humble birth. Lady Charmington returned to the country, and Lady Eccleston, having provided a grand nurse and nursery-maid with unimpeachable testimonials out of one of the most aristocratic nurseries in the land, gradually allowed herself to be re-absorbed by her numerous avocations, social and philanthropic.

Cissy has been most inadequately represented if it need be stated that the very last person to trouble her head about the poor little thing was its mother. She was entirely at one with the fashionable *accoucheur* who attended her, in his opinion that to nurse the child would be far too great a strain on her constitution. After the briefest period of seclusion which the same authority could be got to say was sufficient for her own restoration, and a flying visit to the seaside, she seemed to have but one object in life, to make up by extra assiduity for the weeks she had been compelled to sacrifice from the engrossing occupation of amusing herself. If before she had been much out of her own house, she was now hardly ever in it. The only limit to the number of her engagements was the fear lest she should be betrayed into doing something that was not 'smart'; and even with this important restriction, they were far too numerous to admit of her having any time to bestow upon her son.

As for Sainty, he hardly ever saw her. In so large a house, with a perfectly mutual desire to keep apart, it was not difficult to avoid meeting. He had had one necessary interview with her after the birth of the boy, in which he had told her some very plain truths.

'You may as well understand the situation quite clearly,' he said. 'In return for the various things you enjoy as a result of being believed to be my wife, I have hitherto asked nothing of you; after what has happened, I would not take it if you offered it on your knees. I made just one condition, which you have not thought fit to observe, that there should be no scandal; to avoid it,

I have sacrificed my last shred of self-respect. Don't, therefore, think that you can count on a like cowardice on my part in the future. I pretend to no sort of control over your actions. What you *do* is of no consequence to me; but on just this one thing I *insist*: I must never hear you talked about, and, above all, there must be no repetition of this—this occurrence.'

'I see,' said Cissy. 'Having by hook or by crook got the heir for which you and your mother were so anxious, you have no further use for me, and will seize the next opportunity to get rid of me.'

Sainty looked at her a moment, so antagonistic, so hard, so insolent in her youth and beauty, to which her late recovery lent a character almost ethereal. Bitter as her taunt was, he could not deny its substantial truth.

'Precisely,' he said, and left her without another word.

While Cissy immersed herself in social frivolities, Sainty was trying to find in work forgetfulness of the child he was ashamed to remember. He devoted long hours to humble toil and study, of which the only result would be a paragraph in the report of some learned society, read by no one but its own members. He attended the debates in the House of Lords with unparalleled assiduity, and came to be a familiar figure in the gallery on important nights in the other House. The scarcity of Radical peers gave him an extrinsic value for the leaders of his party, while his patience, powers of work, and known interest in all schemes of beneficence, marked him as specially designed by Providence to serve on Parliamentary Committees.

There was one important point of difference between the couple. While Cissy's absorption in her favourite pursuits was quite natural and genuine, and she found no difficulty whatever in forgetting her maternal duties, it was only by consistent effort that Sainty succeeded in shutting out the recollection of his shame. The image of the baby, with its tell-tale dark eyes, was perpetually between him and the page he was writing or the pamphlet on which he was trying to fix his attention.

As we know, his rooms were on the ground-floor of the

London house, while the nurseries were up three flights of stairs; it seemed impossible that any echo should penetrate from them to his study, yet he was always fancying that he detected faint sounds of crying from the upper regions of the house. Sometimes he would stop in his work and listen, and then, convinced that his imagination had played him a trick, turn again to his reading or writing, only to be haunted by this illusive wailing as before.

One day in the early spring, the child being then some three months old, this impression was more than usually persistent. At last, exasperated by his inability to fix his mind on what he was doing, Sainty pushed away his papers and went out upon the back stairs to listen. This time there was no question of imagination. Perhaps some door usually closed had been left open, but whatever the explanation, there was no doubt that a most real and material lamentation, such as the human infant alone is capable of producing, was echoing through the house. He returned to his table and sat down again. 'I suppose babies of that age always yell,' he said to himself, and he recalled Arthur's complaint of that tendency in his own offspring. Why, of all people in the world, need the baby's crying make him think of his brother? The recollection of that stucco rectory in the shires, where the birth of the little Lord Charmington must have aroused anything but enthusiasm, made him start and tremble like a felon.

For a moment he fancied the noise had ceased, but a second visit to the landing convinced him such was not the case. He looked at the clock. It was almost time for him to go down to Westminster; he would go out and walk a little first—sometimes he thought he did not have enough fresh air—it would do him good. He put away his papers, gathered together some loose sheets of notes that he wanted, and left the room.

What made him turn to the stairs instead of the front door he never quite knew. Some occult power seemed to draw his feet. He couldn't go out to do battle for the children of the poor with that lamentable wailing ringing in his ears, and make no inquiry into what ailed the child under his own roof.

He had not mounted to these upper floors since he had conducted the duchess thither, but if he had been in any doubt about the room, the cries, which seemed to redouble in force as he drew nearer, would have been a quite sufficient guide. Through the wide-open door Sainty could see the interior of the nursery before he entered. Lady Eccleston had given the rein to her grandmotherly fancy in the provision of all things needful and luxurious for the young heir. He was at least sumptuously lodged; the walls were gay with sanitary illustrations of juvenile literature from Miss Greenaway's charming designs; buttercups and daisies sprinkled the window hangings; everything streamed with pale blue satin ribbon, and the very powder-box, of choicest ivory, had the mystic word 'Baby' slanting in turquoises across the lid. But nothing was ranged, or ordered, or in its proper place. The costly little garments so lavishly provided were tossed about with careless profusion, damp cloths trailed over the floor, a common enamelled saucepan for heating the child's food had been set down on a lace robe, and half-washed-out feeding-bottles mingled on the table with the materials from which the nurse had evidently been manufacturing a new hat for herself.

The room was bare of human presence save for the emitter of the howls, who was lying alone in his cot, roaring himself purple in the face. He had kicked himself free of his wrappings, and his poor little legs were quite cold to the touch. Without attempting to cope with the complication of integuments, Sainty loosely pulled the coverlet over the child, and then looked with horror and anxiety at the convulsed face. What was to be done? 'Don't!' he said imploringly, in no particular expectation of being understood, but from a general instinct to say something. '*Please* don't!'

Whether the sense of a human presence was of some comfort to the baby, or it was only startled by the sound of an unfamiliar voice, it is certain that it intermitted its screaming, and slowly unpuckering its face, allowed the

hidden eyes to appear. They were all wet and shiny with
tears, their long lashes glued into points like a series of
tiny camel's-hair paint-brushes.

Sainty wondered if he dared wipe them. 'It can't be
comfortable to have one's face all slobbered over like that,'
he thought, and taking out his handkerchief began, as
lightly and tenderly as he could, to remove some of the
superfluous moisture that seemed to exude from every
feature. The baby, far from being sensible of this attention, showed unmistakable signs of being about to resume
its lament. Sainty swiftly desisted from his endeavours,
and once more implored its forbearance.

The baby, with its face all made up for a fresh howl,
paused suddenly when, so to speak, half-way there, and
once more opened its eyes. It stared solemnly at Sainty
and Sainty stared back at it. What dumb interchange of
intelligence passed between them it would be hard to say,
but presently a faint, windy smile flickered across one side
of the baby's face leaving the other immutably grave.

Sainty was transported with gratitude; he nodded and
smiled repeatedly at the baby and tried to think of
pleasant noises to make to it. One of the little hands had
broken loose from under the coverlet and was beating the
air—sparring at life with the aimless hostility of infancy.
Very gingerly Sainty laid his forefinger against the palm,
and instantly the absurd fingers closed round it and held
him prisoner.

Long he stood beside the cradle gently swaying the
hand that held his own back and forth and contemplating
the baby, which, soothed by the rhythmic movement,
seemed inclined to sleep. Since it ceased crying, its face
had become a much pleasanter and more normal colour,
and, as the suffusing crimson died away, Sainty could
notice how the poor chin was chafed and red where
it had rubbed on the wet, unchanged bib; the tiny nails,
too, were edged with black, and surely, he thought, a
carefully tended baby ought not to smell as sour as this
one did. It was being borne in upon him that the child
was neglected, a thought which made him not less
indignant that he could not feel wholly without blame in

the matter. True, the child was not his, but by acknow-
ledging it he had accepted responsibility; he knew far too
well how little reason there was to expect that its mother
would occupy herself with such matters to think of shel-
tering himself behind the plea that it was her business. It
was monstrous that the sins of its parents should be
visited on this helpless creature. The queer little claw
still grasped his finger, and he was still swinging it and
crooning gently, when the nurse hurried into the room
and was visibly taken aback at sight of her master. At
once she was voluble in explanation and excuse.

'That was the worst of these girls, you never could
trust 'em; her back wasn't a minute turned that that
Emma wasn't off to her own affairs. She hadn't but just
stepped downstairs to give the orders herself about his
lordship's milk, which, it was surprising, with all these
lazy servants in the house, never *could* be sent up at the
right time, and had particularly told the girl not to leave
the room for a second till she came back . . .' with much
more to the same effect.

Sainty grimly eyed the artificial roses she was whisking
out of sight with clumsy dexterity, in her attempt to bring
order out of chaos, with one hand, while with the other she
made playful passes at the baby, crying 'Did he?' and
'Was he, then?' and 'Nana's here, precious.'

Neither Sainty nor the baby was in the least taken in by
this transparent comedy.

'I think this child is not properly looked after,' the
former said sternly.

'Not looked after!' Nurse was outraged in her finest
feelings. 'Not looked after! She didn't know what his
lordship meant. She was never away for a minute all day
and often up half the night with the little darling; not
that she grudged it, not she; she was well aware it was
but her duty and what she was paid for, but it *was* hard
after all to be told she didn't look after the dear child, and
she did think no one who hadn't done it had any idea
what it was to be with a young infant at night. . . .'

And just then the peccant underling returning from her
own private expedition in neglect of her duty, she made a

diversion by falling on her and smiting her figuratively hip and thigh in a frenzy of righteous wrath.

The baby's official guardians having for the time being returned to their posts, Sainty did not judge it necessary to remain and enter into details in which he might easily betray his ignorance. Having made his sweeping indictment and seen his heir restored to tranquility by a bottle, he returned to his own neglected duties, feeling a little as if the Lord Chancellor might address to him some of the scathing reproaches he had just heard flung at the head of Emma.

He tried to immerse himself in his usual employments, but, do what he would, he was haunted for the rest of the day and far into the night by the vision of the piteous, dirty baby left to howl by itself in the midst of its luxurious surroundings, and felt the cold clasp of the tiny fingers growing gradually warm and moist upon his own.

CHAPTER XXV

THE interview last recorded between Belchamber and his heir was to have momentous consequences for both of them. The principal gain was at first to the baby, as the immediate result was the dismissal of his neglectful attendants. Cissy, for her part, first delicately expressed surprise at Sainty's interesting himself in the matter at all, and then adopted the simple plan of refusing to believe a word against the nurse, whom she eventually passed on to another young mother, with as strong a recommendation as she had received of her, adding in explanation: 'My husband took a dislike to the woman, and so, of course, she had to go.'

Lady Eccleston was full of concern and astonishment. 'I *can't* understand it,' she cried. 'Lady Quivers gave her the very *highest* character, and before that, she was four years in the nursery at Branches, first as nursery-maid and then as under-nurse, and I went to see dear Lady Olave myself, who couldn't say enough about her. I *can't* think she would really neglect the darling.'

Sainty repeated his experience, and 'Go and see for yourself,' he said. 'The child is ill-cared for; he isn't even kept clean.'

Grandmamma went to inspect, and returned declaring the angel was as neat as a new pin. 'You can't, no matter *how* careful you are, prevent their dear little chinnywinnies from getting a wee bit chapped if they dribble much,' she said.

'No doubt he was clean enough after my unexpected visit,' Sainty answered; 'but I assure you *I* didn't find him so; his hands were dirty and nothing about him was fresh. I don't know much about babies, but I'm sure they ought not to smell so nasty. He was hungry and cold too, poor little chap! and left all alone to yell himself into a fit.'

'Nurse declares she wasn't gone five minutes; she was dreadfully distressed that you should have found the child alone. I feel sure one can trust that woman; I can always tell by people's faces and the way they look at one; and Lady Quivers said she was *so* devoted to her last, and I know it was a very delicate little thing.'

For once, however, her son-in-law was inexorable. 'The woman may have been all you say when she came,' he said; 'but it is not surprising if the best of nurses grows neglectful when the mother sets her the example.'

This was taking the matter to very unsafe ground, where Lady Eccleston felt that it behoved her to walk warily. 'I *can* want nothing but the darling baby's good,' she said hastily. 'I hold no brief for nurse, and if you are dissatisfied with her, dear Sainty, of course she had better go, though I don't see what precautions we can take more than we did in getting this one.'

It was Alice de Lissac who finally discovered a successor to Lady Quivers' treasure, and imported a pet lamb from her mother's bible-class at Great Charmington to act as nursery-maid.

Once the treasure was gone, the other servants abounded in evidence which more than justified her removal, though they would apparently have had no difficulty in reconciling their consciences to perpetual silence had she remained. It transpired that it was her frequent habit to administer narcotics to her unfortunate charge, in order that she might fulfil evening engagements of her own, from which she had sometimes not returned till the small hours of the morning; yet when Sainty felt it his duty to impart this information to her new employer, he was very civilly shown the door, with profuse thanks, but a polite intimation that his interference was not required; from which he was forced to conclude that Cissy was not as exceptional among fashionable mothers as he, in his ignorance, had imagined.

He carried the child off to Belchamber, where he knew that Lady Charmington would keep a lynx eye on the new nurse and her acolyte, and where, indeed, it soon began to improve visibly in condition.

Since its mother seemed to be without the common instincts of the animal kingdom, he imposed it on himself as a duty to see that the poor little creature was at least warmed and fed, and not poisoned with drugs. The duty was at first rather a painful one, involving as it did a constant recollection of what he would fain forget; but, as the months went by, like other things originally taken up from the sternest sense of responsibility, it came to have for him a decided interest.

It has been somewhat cynically said that to be under an obligation to a man is the beginning of dislike; be that as it may, there is no doubt that any one to whom, in a world of frustrated effort, we have been able to do a tangible service, establishes thereby a distinct claim on our gratitude. 'This,' we say to ourselves with a pardonable glow, 'is our work; here is something accomplished, some one better or happier for our existence.' And it is impossible not to have a kindly feeling towards the person who has procured us such a pleasing reflection.

Sainty found his mind constantly running on his small charge; he dwelt with pleasure on the prospect of seeing it; he even began to make excuses for more frequent visits to Belchamber, where it was astonishing how often his presence and personal supervision seemed to be required.

In addition to the baby, there was now another person

there on whom he had the pleasure of knowing he had conferred a benefit; he had rescued his brother-in-law, Thomas Eccleston, from the hated thraldom of the broker's office, and placed him with his agent, Mr. Danford, who was beginning to feel, as age stole upon him, the necessity for help in managing the huge property.

The good Tommy, his legs permanently gaitered, his honest pink face burnt to a healthy brickdust colour, and his hands hardened by much congenial outdoor labour, was as happy as a rabbit in a vegetable garden. To initiate this neophyte into his duties, and at the same time keep things smooth between Danford and the pupil in whom his jealousy could not but scent a possible successor, called for many visits from the master. Sainty made time for them gladly, half ashamed to admit even to himself how much the new tenant of his old nurseries had to do with his alacrity. It surprised him to find how eagerly his eyes would scan the walks and lawns for the distant gleam of white in the perambulator.

Week by week, and month by month, the little life was expanding and developing like an opening flower in the sunshine, and Sainty noted the changes, watching with reverent awe the miracle of the dawning intelligence. He brought wonderful toys, heads in fancy costume that could by a turn of the wrist be made to gyrate on a handle to a feeble lute-like accompaniment; wonderful parti-coloured acrobats in the attitude of St. Andrew on his cross, who shook their extended limbs with a great tinkling of bells; white, furry animals that emitted strange squeaks when pressed in the abdominal regions.

It must be confessed that the toys left the baby rather cold; sometimes he looked at them with solemn and contemptuous eyes, sometimes with an indulgent smile; more often he swept them from him with a downward sabre-cut action of the right arm. Whatever he did seemed to Sainty an indication of unusual capacity. He thought with a pang of fierce hatred—was it envy? was it contempt?—of the men who begot such marvellous beings, and grudged an occasional moment from their low toils or pleasures to glance impatiently at them and order

them from the room. Of a mother who could bring forth
a child and leave it to take its chance of life or death in
the care of hirelings, he dared not trust himself to think
at all.

A hunger of paternity possessed him. How he could
have adored a child of his own! His own! Was this child
not his own? To whom did it rather belong? the father
who disowned, the mother who neglected it, or to him
who had tended and cared for it, and was learning to love
it? And the crowning wonder of all was that the child
was learning to love *him*. It was not a merry baby—'a
solemn, wise-like thing,' the nurse called it—looking out
upon the world with grave, mysterious eyes, and that
peculiarly detached, far-off expression that belongs only
to babies and cats; but at sight of Sainty the rare smile
never failed to light up the little white face, the legs would
jump and kick against the nurse, the arms held out for
his embrace.

A baby's partiality has as little cause or meaning as its
aversions, and it is as unreasonable to be flattered by the
one as to be hurt by the other; but a man must be of
a sterner temper than our poor Sainty to resist a certain
mild elation when a little creature hurls itself into his arms
with such confident self-surrender. To him, moreover,
the novelty of the experience made it doubly dear. His
mother had doubtless loved him in her own grim way,
because he was her son; others, as his uncle, had pitied,
or done their duty by him; others again might have paid
him attention for what they hoped to obtain from him;
but never in the course of his existence could he remember
that any living thing had been simply attracted to him by
the magnetism of his own personality; and no one can
suspect a baby of any complexity of motive. So, when his
coming was greeted with jubilant laughter and dancings
and outstretched arms, a warmth crept about his heart,
and he owned to himself with humble gratitude that out
of what had seemed his greatest affliction had come the
best happiness his life had ever known.

Of course he did not arrive at this height of devotion all
at once; it was the growth of many months, and every

time he came to Belchamber, the little tendrils wound themselves more closely round his heart. At the end of the session, he established himself there with a more joyful sense of home-coming than he had known for years.

To those who have experienced how rich in possibilities is the intimacy of a baby of six months, it were unnecessary to describe it; they who have not would hardly credit it, however cunningly set forth. There is something intangible about it that must necessarily evaporate in the mere attempt to put it on paper. Sainty fell into the habit of having the child almost constantly with him; often it slept on the sofa in his study, or in its perambulator under the great cedars while he read or wrote beside it, and the sense of its nearness at once soothed and stimulated him; even if it woke, it was so gentle and quiet that it hardly disturbed his work.

He abandoned his little cart in favour of a larger open carriage in which the nurse and baby could accompany him on his drives. Not infrequently they would start by way of the dower-house, where Lady Charmington would be a willing addition to the party. Sainty and his mother were brought very close together by their common worship of the child; at no previous time, and on no other subject, had her son been in such constant need of the good lady's advice. Exactly what the baby had suffered at the hands of the 'treasure' remained in doubt, but certainly its internal economy was none of the strongest, and many changes of diet had to be tried, which its two guardians discussed by the hour. Then it began to cut its teeth exceptionally early, with all the usual accompaniments of heaviness, loss of appetite, and restless nights. Without his mother's rocklike common-sense to lean upon, Sainty would have worked himself into a fever of anxiety; her experience of the frailty of his own early days was of inestimable comfort to him.

'I tell you, this child is a tower of strength to what you were,' Lady Charmington would say. 'I've been up night after night with you when you were teething.'

'But was I as hot and restless as baby?'

'Hot and restless? I should think you were! twice as

bad, and croupy into the bargain, which this child, thank God! hasn't a symptom of.'

So Sainty took heart, and when, after a time, he was made to feel with his finger two tiny white points in the red gum, this also seemed to him an almost supernatural achievement on the part of one so young.

He had come to regard the precious infant as so entirely his charge, that he did not bestow much thought upon its recreant mother. Cissy had started on a round of visits at the end of the season, hardly going through the form of inquiring if Sainty thought of accompanying her. It was a shock to him to find how completely she had gone out of his existence, when she presently announced that she was coming to Belchamber; she had spent a day or two there, before going North, to get some country clothes and give her maid a chance to repack, but had not seen the baby more than two or three times, nor appeared to take any particular interest in what was being done for it. It never occurred to Sainty as likely that she would in any way occupy herself with the child or its relation to him; it was therefore no small surprise to him to discover, before she had been many days in the house, that it was a distinct irritation to her to see them together.

The first time she found it under the cedars with him, she inquired, with a perceptible shade of annoyance in her voice, where the nurse was, and why she hadn't taken it out.

'Baby generally spends most of the morning with me here if it's fine,' Sainty said. 'The doctor likes him to be in the open air as much as possible, and it gives nurse a chance to do various little things for him.'

'Nonsense! it's her place to be with him; she'll get utterly spoilt if you do her work for her; she has got a girl in the nursery. If she can't manage, she had better have another. There's no earthly reason for you to do nursery-maid.'

'I like having baby with me, and *this* woman doesn't neglect her duties; at least she doesn't leave the child alone, when he's *not* with me, like the one your mother got for him.'

'You were always unjust about that poor woman. Ah! here you are, nurse. You had better take baby and walk him about. You shouldn't leave him here to worry his lordship.'

'Begging your ladyship's pardon, my lord partick'larly *wished* for the child to be left with him,' retorted the nurse, as she wheeled the perambulator viciously away, quivering with suppressed indignation.

'You see the results of your spoiling that woman,' Cissy remarked. 'If she's going to be insolent to me she'll have to go.'

'No—by heaven! I'm hanged if she shall,' Sainty burst out. 'She's devoted to the child, and takes very good care of him, and he isn't very strong. It would be monstrous, after never giving him a thought from the time of his birth till now, if you undertook to sack the people who *do* look after him, because you considered they didn't sufficiently kowtow to *you*.'

'It's precisely what you did to her predecessor.'

'On the contrary, I sent her away because she neglected him, which was, no doubt, what gave you a fellow-feeling for her.'

'Oh! well, don't let me interfere between you and your *protégé*. I don't even pretend to inquire what terms you are on with her; but I must confess I can't see what particular pleasure you derive from the constant presence of another man's child.'

'Hush!' Sainty said, casting a swift, frightened glance around to see if any one was within earshot. 'Be careful what you say. Remember the child is *mine*. He has got to be mine. Your remark was in your usual excellent taste, but on that particular subject you will have to forego the pleasure of wounding me. If you are so fond of reminding me that I am not his father, you will say something one of these days before others that you will regret.'

It gave him a horrible sense of complicity to be obliged to entreat her discretion, a feeling that, bound by their guilty secret, let them hate each other as they would, they dare not quarrel. Probably Cissy was not less aware of this necessity than her husband, for though her object remained the same, she altered her tactics. She would try to keep the child from him by little underhand manœuvres, sending it out when she thought him likely to want it, and even going so far as to take it with her when she drove; but she did not risk another face attack.

Sainty, on his side, did nothing to provoke an encounter. He saw the child not less, but as it were by stealth, and this introduction of a slightly clandestine element into their intercourse only heightened his love for it. Not that it required any great exercise of tact or ingenuity to evade Cissy's notice. Lord Charmington would have fared ill had he been dependent on the fitful attentions of his mamma for care and comfort. Even the amiable desire to deprive her husband of his one pleasure could not make a domestic character of Lady Belchamber. She was much away, and when at home constantly surrounded by guests who absorbed her attention. It was only at rare intervals that she found any leisure to bestow on the separation of her husband and her child.

She had a trick of arriving when least expected, swooping suddenly into visible space like a comet, and, like a comet, followed by her train; though to speak of her appearances as comet-like gives a false impression of something periodical and calculably recurrent, whereas no one could foretell when Cissy might take it into her head to entertain a party, which seemed to be her only idea of the uses of a home.

Once, when he thought she was safely launched on a round of country-houses, Sainty had asked his old friend Gerald Newby, for whom she entertained no great regard, to pay him a visit. They were at tea on the lawn, when, preceded at a short interval by a heralding telegram, her ladyship descended on them with a few friends, and the announcement of a further contingent for the morrow.

Lady Charmington had come over from the dower-house, and Tommy had dropped in for tea and to play with his nephew, about whom he was almost as weak as Sainty.

No one looking at the group under the cedars would

have guessed that he was witness of anything but the most delightful scene of domestic felicity. The stately ancestral home, the superb trees, the great stretches of smoothly mown turf, the young married couple with their baby between them, surrounded by all that wealth and great possession could give, the adoring grandmother, the loving uncle, the admiring friends, the glow of flowers, the cheerful, intimate little meal, all combined to make the picture complete. It appealed strongly to Newby, who beamed indulgently on the party.

'Our dear Sainty appears in a new and most amiable light,' he said; 'I am not accustomed to see him as Kourotrophos. It is the epithet applied to Hermes in his character of the child-tender,' he added explanatorily to Cissy, who looked rather blank.

'I can't think why nurse doesn't fetch baby,' that lady remarked; 'or, for that matter, why she brought him down at all. I've always told her not to when any one was here. Whatever one may think of one's own children, one has no right to bore other people with them.'

'*I* asked to see the child,' said Lady Charmington, the light of battle waking in her eye.

'Mother had settled to come over before I knew you were coming,' Sainty said quietly. 'When I got your telegram it was too late to stop her, and as she had come on purpose to see baby, I couldn't refuse to send for him. No one need bother about him; he will be quite good with me.'

'Dear little man!' said one of the ladies who had come with the fond mother. 'I'm so glad you didn't stop him, Lord Belchamber. I love babies. I've been trying to think who he reminds me of. He's not a bit like you or Cissy.'

'We think him like my grandmother——' Sainty began.

'I never could see that he was so like the duchess,' Lady Charmington cut in.

'To *me* he's the image of Claude Morland,' remarked the luckless Tommy.

There was a sudden hush that may have lasted some five seconds ere it was broken by Newby inquiring, 'What has become of your charming cousin? I liked him so much, and hoped I might meet him here.'

'We see very little of Claude now,' Lady Charmington responded. 'He never seems to come here. I suppose he finds other places more amusing. He was glad enough to come in old days.'

'I fancy,' said Sainty, 'as the duke gets older that he is more dependent on him. He very seldom gets away.'

He had, in fact, for some time been conscious that Claude came much less to the house than formerly, and was acutely aware of a like consciousness in Cissy, though each was careful to say nothing about it to the other.

'By the way, that reminds me,' said Lady Charmington to Sainty. 'I had almost forgotten. Alice de Lissac writes she is coming to her father for a little, and she is very anxious to see baby. May I bring her over some day?'

'Why should Claude remind you of Mrs. de Lissac?' Cissy asked with a little laugh, her desire to score off her mother-in-law getting the better of her prudence. 'I never knew they had much in common.'

'Only because Alice says in her letter they have seen a good deal of him lately. He seems to have been several times to Roehampton; and mother mentioned his coming in to see her one day with one of the girls.'

'Morland's a deep 'un,' ejaculated Tommy. 'Shouldn't wonder if he was after one of the heiresses. Those girls'll have a devil of a lot of money. The mater was always egging me on to be civil to 'em. Do you remember the World's Bazaar, Cissy? Oh my!'

'I wonder if he can be thinking of Gemma,' said Lady Charmington thoughtfully. 'Alice doesn't *say* so, but——'

'It 's not true,' Cissy burst out; then, seeing awakened curiosity in several surrounding pairs of eyes, she added more indifferently, 'I know Claude well enough to feel sure he would never be attracted by that black Jewess.'

'He might be by her blond sovereigns,' suggested Tommy.

Cissy became suddenly solicitous for the comfort of her

guests. 'I am sure you want to see your rooms,' she said.
'Wouldn't you like a bath after that dirty journey?' and
swept them into the house.

'Cissy don't seem to fancy the idea of Morland being
sweet on the dark lady,' Tommy giggled. 'She used to
flirt with him herself once. I remember mater——'

'Tommy,' said Sainty, 'do, like a good soul, ask nurse
to fetch baby.'

He felt sick and frightened. The contrast between the
appearances of life and the ghastly things that were so
thinly overlaid by them suddenly appalled his spirit.
Almost unconsciously he picked up the baby, and clasped
it closely to him. It was on that same spot, and on much
such an afternoon, that he had first seen Cissy five
years before. With the clearness of a picture thrown on a
screen, he saw her standing as she had stood that day with
Claude beside her, her girlish beauty bathed in soft,
golden light, and recalled the prophetic pang with which
he had watched them turn away together under the
baleful gaze of Aimée Winston. As he sat holding their
child to his heart, the permanent dweller in his cupboard
seemed to grin out at him with a more than usually fiendish
malignity.

CHAPTER XXVI

ONE morning early in October, Thomas Eccleston
appeared in his brother-in-law's study with a shade of
distress deepening the habitual ruddiness of his open
countenance.

It has already been intimated that Sainty cherished a
very real affection for this young man, holding a character so manly and direct to be little short of miraculous in a
child of Lady Eccleston.

'What's the matter, Tommy?' he asked. 'You look
perturbed. Have you and Danford been coming to
blows?'

'Oh no, Danny's all right; it so happens I'm rather in
his good books just now. But the fact is, I've had rather

a queer letter, and I didn't quite know what to do about it, so I thought the simplest thing was to bring it to you, though it 's not by any means what he intended me to do.'

'Who 's "he"? Danford?'

'No; I tell you it 's nothing to do with him.'

'To begin with, then, who 's your correspondent?'

'Well, if you want to know, it 's your brother.'

Sainty started. 'Arthur? What *can* he want of you?'

'I think the best way would be for you to read it,' Tommy said, holding out the letter.

Sainty hesitated a moment, then took it and read:

'DEAR ECCLESTON—I expect you'll be rather astonished at hearing from me, and still more at what it 's about. The fact of the matter is, I want you to do me a good turn. I was awfully glad to hear my brother had got you at Belchamber, and it suddenly occurred to me you would be just the chap to do what I want. To cut a long story short, I want to come to Belchamber. I suppose it 's very undignified of me, but I'm badly in want of a little amusement, and I thought if they were going to have a shoot, and it wasn't a very big party, you might suggest to your sister to pop me in as one of the guns. You may think it funny that I don't write straight to my brother, but I know he'd be infernally sniffy, and say I had no proper pride; and Cissy always seemed a good sort, and so did you, and I thought between you, you could work it for me. I know they won't ask Lady Arthur, and I don't ask it of 'em. At first I was afraid she mightn't take it kindly, but she 's been all right about it; she says she don't want to go where she isn't wanted, but don't mind my going without her. Do you think you can work it through your sister? Do, if you can, and oblige yours ever— A. W. CHAMBERS.'

'Oh! *how* like Arthur!' Sainty murmured, as he refolded this characteristic letter.

'I thought,' said Tommy, who had been watching him uneasily as he read, and fiddling with the things on the writing-table, 'that it was better to come straight to you than to go to Cissy about it.'

'So it is, and I'm very grateful to you, dear boy, for all

your loyalty'; and Sainty laid a thin claw in Thomas's large red hand. The sub-agent pressed it fervently.

'What had I better say?' he asked. 'It puts me in such a deucedly awkward posish, don't yer know.'

'Of course he had no business to write to any one but me,' Sainty said. 'Well—you needn't answer; I'll write to him myself.'

Tommy looked much relieved. 'Hope I didn't do wrong,' he said doubtfully.

'On the contrary, you did more than right,' Sainty said warmly.

'Shall you ask him?' Tommy ventured, after a pause.

'I can't say straight off; I must talk to Cissy about it, and' (with an ill-concealed tremor) 'to my mother.'

Cissy made no objections. Arthur was a pleasant, good-looking fellow, and a man you could ask without his wife was as good as a bachelor. Rather to Sainty's surprise, Lady Charmington was not less willing. She hardly ever mentioned Arthur. Since the day when, livid and furious, she had solemnly cursed her younger son, Sainty could almost count on the fingers of one hand the times when she had spoken his name; but when, with some trepidation and much uncertainty, he approached her on the subject, he was met quite half-way.

'Unto seventy times seven,' she remarked, 'the Scripture tells us we must forgive. That woman I will *never* receive, but as long as he is willing to come without her, I see no reason you shouldn't have him at Belchamber; and —and—you may tell him I am willing to see him too, if he likes.' And Sainty read in the sudden suffusion of the hard eyes, the tale of the poor woman's long, silent yearning for a sight of her favourite son.

So Arthur had his wish, and came once more to Belchamber. There was, no doubt, a certain awkwardness in the situation, and Sainty was surprised and touched to find that, though he certainly felt it much the most, Arthur was not without a perception of it, too. He was decidedly subdued during the first days of his visit, and Sainty's ready sympathy went out, as usual, to any one who was ill at ease. Had Arthur been in his accustomed mood of complete self-satisfaction, he would have felt less tenderly towards him, but seeing him so humbled and brought low, on the footing, as it were, of a guest and poor relation in the home of their common childhood, was almost more than he could bear.

Perhaps Arthur intentionally rather accentuated this note, conscious of the effect it would have on his brother. He would pointedly ask leave to do the most obvious things. 'There's a spare gun in the gun-room,' he would say; 'the keeper says he doesn't know whose it is. Should you mind if I took it, old chap? I've only one here, and it got so hot yesterday I could hardly shoot with it.' Or it would be, 'Tommy and I are going to practise a bit; may I use this old bat? I fancy it must once have been mine, but I'm not sure.' Or, 'Would it be convenient for me to have a horse this morning? I was thinking of riding over to see the mater.' Formerly, whatever the house afforded was as freely his as Sainty's. If he was not the owner, he was something more than an ordinary heir, and guns, bats, and horses were so emphatically his natural property, that it was unthinkable his asking permission to use them.

On the first morning of his visit, the brothers had wandered out together, and Arthur had commented on the new arrangement of the forecourt.

'You've fetched all the old statues out of the shrubbery, I see,' he said. 'What did you do that for?'

Sainty explained almost apologetically, that it was an attempt to return to Perrault's original plan.

'Is it so long since you were here?' he said. 'I had forgotten——' Then, as the other remained silent, gloomily sucking at his pipe, 'I'm afraid you don't like it,' he suggested meekly.

'Oh! well, of course, it's none of *my* business. I must say I think they looked better where they were, but I'm not much of a judge. Naturally, don'tcherknow, I liked 'em where I've always seen 'em. I can't bear changes in the place.'

'I'm sometimes half sorry I did it, myself,' Sainty admitted. As he spoke he was aware that the moment had come which he had been dreading ever since his brother's arrival, the first appearance on the scene of the baby, who was being taken out for his morning's airing.

'And so this is the son and heir, is it?' said Arthur. 'Hulloa! little 'un, how do you do? I'm your uncle. You look very solemn, but it would be more natural if I did. You don't know the difference your small existence makes to me and mine.'

The baby, as usual, at sight of Sainty, began making demonstrations of welcome, doubling himself forward over his restraining strap, and giving vent to a note like that of the nightingale, which is conventionally represented in print as 'Jug-jug-jug,' and a cry of 'A-da, A-da-da, A-da,' which was a sort of sound of all work with him for the expression of his varying emotions.

'He wants his dada,' said the nurse, eager to display her charge's precocity, and, at the same time, gratify her master. 'He says "Dada" quite plain, my lord, and it's the first word he's said.'

'It's a wise child that knows his own father,' said Arthur jocosely.

Sainty could not restrain a hasty glance at him, but he was evidently innocent of any special or personal application of the often-quoted adage.

They walked on for a little beside the child, Sainty resting one hand lovingly on the edge of the little carriage, the baby squirming round and looking up into his face, wrinkling its nose and gurgling to attract his attention. When their ways divided, the parting was not effected without a burst of protest from the infant, which Sainty soothed and diverted as skilfully as the professional attendant.

'The little beggar seems to like you,' Arthur remarked. 'I don't remember either of mine ever yelling for *me*.'

'You have probably never taken as much notice of them as I do of baby.'

'You were always a kind of old granny; you'll probably spoil that brat. Have you done anything to the stables since I was here?'

Once received, the prodigal brother came several times

to Belchamber in the course of the winter. He liked the luxury, the magnificence, the good food, the gentlemanly licence of the conversation, the fine horses to ride (he soon ceased to ask if he might take one), better than the shabby gentility of the stucco rectory, the half-trained grooms, the half-lame hunters, the half-refined wife of his own home. It sometimes seemed to Sainty that he almost forgot he was a husband and father at all, and there were not wanting among the ladies of Cissy's surrounding some who were quite willing to help him to this pleasing oblivion.

'I like Lady Deans,' he would say confidentially; 'she 's rare sport, and there 's no nonsense about her; she don't care what she says, and you haven't got to think twice about what you say to *her*. Now if I were to say half the things to Topsy I say to her, she'd bridle and shy and look as sour as if she'd been brought up by a bishop. And when you think—oh my!' and the sentence would end in a long puff of cigar smoke, or the burial of the speaker's nose in a tall whisky and soda.

Arthur was a decided success with the members of the softer sex. The story of his romance cast quite a halo about him, and the very few mothers of grown-up girls who were tolerated in that gay company felt almost tenderly towards a detrimental who had put it out of his own power to marry their daughters.

As for Cissy, she and her brother-in-law got on capitally. She pressed him to come whenever he liked, partly, no doubt, because she divined that his presence was a constant unhappiness to her husband. The sight of him in juxtaposition with the baby kept a keen edge on all Sainty's feelings of remorse; nor was Arthur likely to be restrained by a fastidious delicacy from all allusion to the change which the birth of an heir had made in his own position. His remarks on the subject were not always in the best possible taste; he affected jokes about the Babes in the Wood, referred to himself as the 'wicked uncle,' and 'wondered Sainty was willing to trust him in the house with the precious infant.' Such pleasantries, of a slightly sub-acid jocularity, went through and through Sainty in a way that the speaker could neither have guessed nor intended; he probably thought, on the contrary, that he was taking his blighted prospects with an easy amiability which did him infinite credit. He was not indeed without certain touches of kindliness towards his nephew. 'When he gets a big boy, you must let his poor old uncle teach him to ride and shoot,' he would say. 'We must make a good sportsman of him, and you know *you* won't do much in that line for him, old man.' Sainty wondered if he wanted the boy to be a sportsman. His personal hatred of taking life extended itself to this nurseling of his affections. Must those tiny fingers be taught to curl round a trigger, that innocent heart learn to find its pleasure in slaughter and destruction? Yet he desired all forms of perfection for his darling; he hated to think of him at the same disadvantage among those with whom he would have to live as he himself had always been. He would have him strong and brave and daring, trained in all arts and exercises that became a gentleman; for instance, there could be no doubt that a certain proficiency in horsemanship was desirable for the ideal youth, but he recalled with horror his own early efforts to attain it, and shuddered to think how he should tremble, when, in course of time, the child came to an age to face these dangers.

He began to see how ill-fitted he was to be the trainer of a young man. Hitherto he had imagined himself only as a nurse of callow infancy, shielding the little one with his greater insight and sympathy from the misunderstandings that had made his own childhood unhappy. Somehow he had fancied the child would be like him, timid and shrinking, needing protection; but now it struck him that there was no reason why it should resemble him at all, and he recoiled with sudden terror from the thought of what unlovely qualities the offspring of two such parents might have inherited. How would he be able to bear seeing the treachery of the one, or the hard egotism of the other, reproducing itself in the being he loved best in the world? Had he the firmness needed for correcting such tendencies? Could he ever steel himself to the necessity of punishment?

On the other hand, it was hardly to be desired that the little boy should grow up on his pattern. He was not so conspicuous a success in his position that it was an object to educate a successor on the same lines. He began to understand the kind of problems his own bringing up had presented for solution to his mother and uncle; he remembered how futile had been the efforts of these two strong natures, with all the advantages of example, to instil into his feeble soul a more virile attitude towards life, and the sum in proportion of what difficulties he would have to encounter in a like endeavour was not a hard one to work out. If Lady Charmington, absolutely sure of what she wanted, and with her bull-dog tenacity of purpose, had failed so lamentably of her object, what kind of a creature would he turn out, assailed by a hundred doubts, fears, and indecisions, and desiring simultaneously quite irreconcilable ideals?

He recognised that the child had become the chief preoccupation of his life, its health, its food, its education—for he already tormented himself with questions that, by their very nature, could not have to be faced for years to come; and the more he troubled himself about the little thing, the more he loved it, the greater his love grew, the greater grew the desire to do his duty by his charge, the greater the anxiety as to what that duty might be.

So far, however, his troubles were only those common to all parents and guardians who took their responsibilities somewhat morbidly ; his special self-torture began where theirs left off. When all was said and done, the thousand dangers that dog the steps of youth safely passed, the pitfalls on either hand successfully avoided, the boy trained to all perfection of manly virtue and delight—what then? To what purpose, and for what end, should he have fashioned this splendid creature? To be the means by which he was to rob his nearest kinsfolk of their birthright! If his remorse was constantly awakened by Arthur's presence, and the things that he said, it yet addressed itself less to Arthur than to the child. It was not so much the injury to his brother and his brother's children that was becoming an hourly torment to his conscience, as the injury to this innocent accomplice in making him the instrument of wrong. Was that, then, the best that he could do for the son of his heart, the being who was daily becoming more and more the centre of his existence, dearer than are the children of their loins to ordinary fathers, to use him as the unconscious weapon of his own fraud? There was no way out, no turning back; he could not now disavow him if he would. The crime was committed, irremediable, to go on breeding injustice, perpetuating wrong to the last chapters of the history of his race.

He saw in imagination the little boy passing from childhood to youth, from youth to manhood, growing tall and strong and beautiful, in his turn marrying, and begetting children to become links in the long chain of falsehood and carry on the consequences of his lie. And he would have to live and watch this happening, always alone, always in silence, with no one to whom he could unburthen his heart. There would only be two who shared his knowledge, and to neither of them could he say a word on the subject, though hideously, eternally aware that they knew, and were watching with himself. And then a new terror assailed him. When a secret was already the property of three people, could he be certain that no breath of it would ever reach the person principally concerned? He had plenty of experience of how recklessly Cissy could talk on occasion, what rash and terrible things the desire to wound could make her say, and he trembled lest in some fit of sudden anger with her son, some momentary loss of self-control, she might turn and crush him with the story of his birth. The word once spoken could never be recalled; he saw the poor boy coming, white and stern, to ask him if this thing were true, and felt by anticipation the agony of his own inability to deny it. A dozen times a day he lived through the misery of that confession, and watched the love and respect die out of those dear eyes, as his unwilling hand dealt the final blow. Perhaps it would be some fair growth of young romance, the prospect of an innocent, happy marriage with a good girl, that he would have to blast with that terrible avowal. He heard himself condemning the boy to sterile loneliness or the devious byways of illicit love, to make a tardy reparation, and restore the stolen heritage to its rightful owners.

These thoughts were with him day and night; they went to bed with him, and got up with him; they followed him about the place; they sat with him beside the sleeping baby, and looked at him out of its great solemn eyes when it woke. Truly 'the Lord his God was a jealous God,' that fastidiously high standard of conduct and personal honour, his one sin against which was to be 'visited upon the children, unto the third and fourth generation.'

And then on a sudden the end came, and he learned the futility of his crime and his remorse alike. The poor little life that had been to him a source of such happiness and such self-torture came to an end as independently of any act of his as it had come to its beginning. It may have contained from the first the germs of some mortal disease, or perhaps the practices of its former nurse had left behind more fatal results than any one suspected. It is probable that too rapid teething had something to do with it. A baby's life is at best but such a newly kindled flame, feeble and unsteady, that a puff of wind will make it flicker and go out. The whole thing did not take a week. The child was flushed, heavy, restless, as it had so often been before. 'He is cutting another big tooth,' the nurse said. 'It's no wonder he's a little fractious, poor lamb! It's the third in a fortnight.' Lady Charmington was appealed to, and repeated, for the twentieth time, her comfortable assertions of how much more Sainty himself had suffered during the same anxious period; by constantly reassuring her son with them, she had finally almost persuaded herself that the baby was as strong as she wished it. She declared it was ridiculous to send for the doctor. 'Have him, if you like,' she said; 'but I know just what he'll say. Baby has been exactly like this so often, and each time you always think it is something dreadful. Nurse knows exactly what to do for him, don't you, nurse?'

On the third day Sainty grew restive, and sent for him all the same. The doctor, if not as well satisfied as Lady Charmington, yet seemed to think there was no particular cause for anxiety. He detected a little sound in the bronchial pipes, and asked if the child could have got a chill in any way. 'It might all very well come from the teeth,' he said. 'The little fellow is feverish; you had better keep him in for a day or two.'

He came once or twice more, a little uncertain, very non-committal; and then, one day, there was a swift, unexplained rise of temperature, a convulsion or two, and, before even Sainty, with his genius for prophesying disaster, had fully realised the danger, all was over in this world as far as the baby was concerned.

CHAPTER XXVII

'My little boy, my poor little boy! You were conceived in sin, and your birth was a lie. Your father never owned you, your mother never loved you. It was left to me, who should have hated you, to tend and cherish you. It was little enough that I could do for *you*, but God only knows what you have been to *me*. It was no fault of yours, my baby, but my misdoing, that would have made your innocent existence an injury to others. I might have known that you could do no harm, that you would go away before your life could wrong them.'

Sainty was murmuring broken phrases, his face bowed upon the face of the dead child. The tiny coffin, almost like a toy, was supported on two chairs facing each other, and on a third chair beside it he had sat almost continuously since the room had been put in order and the people turned out of it. His mother had said it was bad for him, but, with that single exception, there was luckily no one who cared enough to try and take him away, and so he had remained, hour after hour, steeped in the great quiet that surrounded that little figure.

The pale, diffused daylight came sifted through the lowered blinds, giving an unreal look to common objects, turned suddenly useless, and ranged against the walls. Sainty himself had helped to order the room, and to deck it with flowers. He would allow no heavy fragrance of white, funereal blossoms, but all the greenhouses of Belchamber had been ransacked for the unseasonable roses of winter, and to this day the smell of roses brings back to him the little white waxen face, barred with its black-fringed lids, at which he gazed so long in those sacred hours of communing with the dead.

It was his first experience of death. His father had died when he was a mere baby, and both his grandfathers in his early childhood; since he had been able to reflect or remember, he had never lost a friend. It struck him as strange that he, who had tasted so many sorrows, should have had no experience of this, the supremest and commonest that man is called upon to bear. It was different from any other trouble he had ever known, deeper, more awful, more hopeless, yet somehow for that very reason more bearable too. There was no element of meanness in it, nothing petty or small. Such grief was large, calm, august, and above all very still; in presence of this perfect peace he could not strive nor cry. Shelley's words about the Niobe came back to him as he sat there, and he kept repeating them to himself, 'Her tender and serene despair.' Despair, then, was 'tender and serene'; how true it was! He was not even very unhappy. The consciousness of the aching void in his life would come later; but, for the moment, the bitterness of parting was lost in the relief of seeing his darling free from the suffering it had been torture to watch and know himself powerless to allay. He understood why David had arisen and washed his face and taken food, when they told him that his child was dead.

The baby's hands were folded, and held a bunch of violets; and as he bent over them, laying his parched lips upon their marble coldness, the comforting promise seemed to steal down to the sources of his being, that at last, far off, after all the fever and the pain, this rest on which he looked was waiting for him, as for every one.

. . . .

A discreet tap on the door jarred the silence like a drum-beat, and Sainty went across and opened it. A servant stood there wearing the decorous expression of those officially connected with mourning which is not a personal grief to them.

'Her ladyship has been inquiring for you, m'lord,' the man said, 'and the post has come. I have put your lordship's letters on your writing-table.'

Sainty came out into the passage, and locked the door behind him, slipping the key into his pocket. 'You can tell her ladyship she will find me in my study,' he said; 'or if she prefers, and will let me know, I will come to her.'

He wondered what Cissy could have to say to him; he felt a sure foreboding that it would be nothing he should care to hear. What more was there for her to say to him henceforth, for ever?

He went to his study in the old western pavilion and sat down at his writing-table; it was heaped with a great pile of letters; the morning's mail had been added to those which, yesterday, he had had no heart to open. They would have to be gone through some time, he supposed; it was a task he could not well leave to his secretary. Why not attack them at once while he was feeling calmed and strengthened? He drew a few towards him and nerved himself for the ordeal of reading them. He thought he knew so well what they would contain, yet in the very first that he took up he found matter quite unexpected, which even at that moment arrested his attention.

'DEAR OLD SAINTY,' he read: 'I don't at all like the idea of intruding my happiness on your grief; but I equally don't want you to hear of it from any one but me, which you would be sure to do if I didn't write at once. And first let me just stop and tell you how awfully sorry I am for you and Cissy losing your little boy. I can't bear to think of you with your sensitive nature. The only thing to be said is that it was better than if he had been older, when you would have missed him so much more; you can't personally have seen very much of him at that age.

But to come back to myself. I hope I am the first to tell you (as you are almost the first that I have told) of my engagement to Gemma de Lissac. You who know my Gemma, and the admirable woman to whom she owes so much, will realise without any words of mine what a lucky fellow I am. I need not say I am tremendously in love, and absurdly happy. Mr. de Lissac has been most awfully good about it, and very generous. Of course, a wretched pauper like me could never have married a girl who hadn't got something. For myself, as you know, my wants are few, but I couldn't have asked Gemma, who has always had every luxury since she was a baby, to give up all she has been accustomed to, especially her thousand and one good deeds. Mr. de Lissac wants me to chuck my P. S.-ship and go in for parliament, and the duke has been very kind in promising his help. Forgive such a long letter about myself when you are in trouble, but happiness is always egotistical, and I can't help hoping that mine won't be indifferent to you. As I have written you such a yarn, and have so many letters to write, will you please tell Cissy, with my love, and ask her to forgive my not writing to her separately. I haven't written to Aunt Sarah either, as I think Mrs. de Lissac is writing to her. Wish me joy, old man. There is no one whose good wishes I shall value more. Your affectionate cousin, CLAUDE MORLAND.

'*P.S.*—I don't offer to come to the funeral. I know you'll feel just as I should about it, and want to keep it all as quiet as possible.'

Sainty read the letter through twice. He had hardly finished his second perusal of it, when the door opened, and Cissy stood before him. She was dressed in hastily improvised mourning of incongruous showiness. The black clothes enhanced her fairness, and accentuated the slim girlishness of her figure, but her face had no youth in it, and her eyes glittered with an unnatural brightness.

'You wanted to see me?' Sainty asked.

'Yes,' she said. 'I have got something to say to you, and I may as well say it first as last.' Then, as he stood waiting in silence to hear her, 'You and I have got to have an explanation,' she added.

'Is it the moment, with the child lying dead in the house?' Sainty asked, with a gesture of protest.

'Yes,' she said eagerly, 'it is just that I wanted to speak about. As long as he lived, I have stayed for my child's sake.'

Sainty gave a convulsive laugh. 'You have done a great deal for the child's sake!' he said.

'Now,' she went on, 'I have no reason for remaining. I have come to tell you that after the funeral I am going away. I can't keep it up any longer. We hate each other, you know we do. Life together has become intolerable.'

'Life together!' Sainty repeated. 'Do you call it life together? To me it seems that we could hardly be more apart. In Kamchatka I should not be further from you.' And indeed she seemed so far away, that he felt as if his voice could hardly reach her; he wondered how she could ever have affected him for pain or pleasure. He looked at her across a chasm in which lay the dead child.

'And where do you propose to go?' he asked indifferently.

'I shall go to the only man I have ever really loved,' Cissy said dramatically.

'I thought we were coming to that.' It all seemed no business of his, not to affect him in any way; he even felt a little sorry for her under the blow he was going to deal her. He found himself casting about in his mind for the best way of telling her. How strange that that letter should just have come (or was it, perhaps, not wholly a coincidence?), that he should have selected that hour for opening it, that it should have been the first one that he had read! He still held it in his hand, and without saying anything he moved it so that the writing might attract her attention.

'What have you got there?' she cried, turning suddenly very white. 'Let me see it. Is it from Claude?' She sprang upon it, and snatched it from him before he could give it to her, and he heard the two sheets rattle against each other with the shaking of her hands.

'There is a message for you in it,' he said, as he turned away. He did not want to pry into her misery. He felt no exultation, only a sick, contemptuous pity, pity in which there was no love.

Presently, hearing her give a sort of hoarse cry, he looked round. She had sunk into a chair, with one arm laid along the table, her other hand, clenched, rested on her knee. The letter had fallen on the floor. She sat looking straight in front of her, and her mouth moved as if she were speaking, but no sound came. She had evidently forgotten his presence altogether. She was frightening like this, her lips drawn back a little from her teeth, her face set in a grimace that made her almost monkey-like, ugly as strong emotion always is. After a time she began to beat on the edge of the table with her hand. 'Blackguard! Blackguard!' she kept repeating under her breath.

Sainty was longing for her to go and leave him alone with his grief. The presence of this other misery which, by the nature of the case, he could do nothing to soothe only aggravated his own; it seemed to bring him down to earth, to drag him back to the sordid and base, from the regions to which he had risen in the chamber of death. What had he to do with this woman's fierce resentment, balked of her earthly passion, he who had been so near the borders of eternal peace?

He went over to her and spoke very gently. 'I think we should be better apart,' he said, 'each with his own sorrow. We can do nothing to help each other.'

She seemed hardly to understand what he said, but she nodded dully and rose, and he held the door open for her to pass.

It was nothing to him, he reflected, whether she went or stayed, whether she played out the dreary farce of their married life to the end, or broke away to follow her own devices. The shame, which had seemed so unendurable that he had bartered his personal honour to avoid it,

appeared to him now as a thing of no importance. He
wondered how he had ever cared about it. Let her go,
in heaven's name, if she had a mind to! He almost
wished that she would, but he knew in his heart that
Claude's letter had done its work; there would be no
more talk of her going. He stooped and picked up the
crumpled papers, smoothing them out and looking at the
beautiful, neat little handwriting, not an erasure, not a
correction. Whatever the writer might say of haste and
want of time and pressure of correspondence, that letter
had not been written in a hurry.

'It 's so complete,' he said to himself; 'the last touch.
Nothing was wanting but this.' He found himself almost
admiring the absolute quality of his cousin's villainy, so
rounded and finished, with no loose ends.

In a few seconds his mind flew back over all the stages
of his connection with Claude, the first coming to Belchamber of the large, pale boy, with his dreamy eyes and
curious fascination, the old Eton days, his baleful influence on Arthur, the story of his connection with Aimée
Winston, the double treachery of his behaviour about
Cynthia. . . . But when he came to the part Morland had
played in his own married life, his imagination shuddered
and winced, he could not, dare not, think of it. 'And now,
to crown all, this——' And his hand struck the pages
with their rippling, conventional expressions of happiness
and affection, their bland pretence of sympathy offered
and demanded. For a moment the room swam round
him, and he had to clutch the table for support. Could
he let this thing be? Ought he to allow this girl to be
sacrificed, and not make an effort to save her? But
almost simultaneously he recognised the futility of any
such attempt. He thought of Gemma, conceited, headstrong, self-confident, and at the same time superlatively
sentimental, and imagined the reception he should meet
with if he were to tell her the man into whose hands she had
just surrendered her existence was—what? The lover of
his wife, the father of his child. How could he tell this
thing, and that he had known it and accepted it in
silence? No wonder Claude had dared to write as he did;

he knew well enough that from Sainty at least he was safe from all attack.

Should he have to answer, to thank, to congratulate, to 'hope they would be happy,' to send gifts? At least he would not have to go to the wedding; his mourning would save him from that—his mourning for the child of the bridegroom! He felt a wild longing to get back to that upper chamber where all these mad thoughts were stilled. What had he to do? The letters. Why should these people steal the little time he had left to be with his lost darling? With a sigh of ineffable weariness he sat down once more, and hastily tore open two or three. The same little phrases recurred in all. 'Sincere condolences,' 'heartfelt sympathy,' 'God's will,' 'Consolation where alone it may be found.' He remembered employing some of them himself on like occasions. Why make these attempts to plumb the unfathomable? As well smear ointment on a door behind which a man lay wounded.

As he turned over the heaps of still unbroken covers in search of a handwriting that promised at least the relief of tears, his eye was caught by one unfamiliar, yet not unknown. He took the letter from the rest and held it poised upon his palm, trying to fix the memory it recalled. The anonymous denunciations of his wife? Ah! no, that was impossible. Yet as he broke the seal he realised why his only other sight of this writing was associated with that time. It was from his sister-in-law.

'DEAR LORD BELCHAMBER,—I know you have never liked me, and did not approve of your brother marrying me; but though it is little kindness or notice I've ever received from you or yours, I am a mother myself, and I know what it would be to me to lose either of my little darlings; and so I feel I must write a few lines of condolence with you and Lady Belchamber in your great sorrow, for I really do sympathise with you in the death of your dear little boy. I know you think me a common, grasping woman, but I don't give a thought to any difference it may make to us, and, as Arthur says, what is to prevent your having others? I have a *heart* (indeed it was me made Arthur write and offer to come to

Belchamber without me, and he'll come to the funeral too). I'm not really a bad sort, and can feel for your loss. With sincere condolences to you and Lady Belchamber, I should like to sign, Your affectionate sister-in-law,

CYNTHIA CHAMBERS.

'*P.S.*—I have ventured to order a wreath sent, which please accept.'

AFTERWORD

How many people have read *Belchamber* today? Of the few who have read it, how many, besides myself, have carried about scraps of its wisdom and wit, its tact and its bitterness, for the last thirty years? The description in it of the converted Jew "who instead of not attending the synagogue now stayed away from church"; Cissy Eccleston and her mother "squashed sideways by the open drawers of their respective writing-tables, like people playing a perpetual duet on two organs with all the stops pulled out"; Sainty's grandmother, the duchess: "the little of her grace's dress that was visible above the line of the tablecloth was of a delicate peach-colour"; the cameo of Edwardian gaiety preserved in, "Lor! we did have fun, though, how was the poor piano this morning after those boys pouring the champagne into it?"; Cissy's row with her mother-in-law and the baleful, "Oh, in the matter of a baby, take care I don't astonish some of you yet," with which she concludes it; the kindly, vulgar note from Lady Arthur which concludes the book itself and puts the last polish on its irony—all these scraps have lain about in my mind among scraps from accredited authors like George Meredith and Thackeray, they have borne the test of time, and the novel from which they are taken has become, so far as one reader is concerned, a classic. Here is *Belchamber* reprinted. Re-read, it exercises its old power. Perhaps it is a classic after all. Anyhow, let me empty yesterday's champagne out of the poor piano, and cautiously try a few notes. The instrument cost a good deal to begin with—that is indisputable.

Howard Sturgis was born in 1855, in London, of American stock. He grew up in affluence, he was educated at Eton and Cambridge, adopted no profession, and was well placed for observing the airs and graces of the great—a foreigner in a front seat. His friend Henry James, equally well placed, fidgets in the seat slightly, and registers at moments a gratified awe as the procession passes, but Sturgis sits very quiet; socially he was always at his ease, he had nothing of the flustered immigrant about him, and he could mock at the "errors in the Fourth Dimension" often made by his less fortunate compatriots. His father, Russell Sturgis, was for many years head of a great banking-house in this country, and this naturally brought him into contact with the eminent. After his father's death he resettled close to Windsor in a smallish house, Queen's Acre, which he wrote "Qu'Acre" and pronounced "Quaker." Here he completed a change which to us in our storm-tossed age may not seem a dramatic one, but it appeared significant enough at the time: the change from fashionableness to bookishness. There had always been a strong literary bent in him—and indeed in his family, for his brother Julian was a prolific novelist—and now that he was independent he lived more exactly according to his desires. He took to writing himself and he produced three novels, *Tim* (1891), *All that was Possible* (1895), and *Belchamber* (1904). His friends liked *Tim*, but some of them disapproved of *All That Was Possible*. *Belchamber* pleased neither them nor the world at large. Sturgis was a domestic author, of the type of Cowper—he wrote to please his friends, and deterred by his failure to do so he gave up the practice of literature and devoted himself instead to embroidery, of which he had always been fond. His life wore away in quiet occupations, and in hospitality to interesting people and to the young, family servants looked after him or grew old in his service, invalid dogs tottered about, he lost much of his money, he became ill, and at the age of sixty-five he died in his own house. Not a thrilling life, nor according to some theorists an admirable one. A life that was only possible at a particular epoch in our civilization.

The most authoritative account of him is to be found in

Mr. Percy Lubbock's sketch of their mutual friend Mary Cholmondeley. There is also a chapter in Mrs. Edith Wharton's reminiscences, some reference in A. C. Benson's Diary, and some further detail in the preface contributed by Mr. Gerald Hopkins to the 1935 edition of *Belchamber*. I went once to Qu'Acre myself—years ago—I don't remember much. A novel of my own had just been published, and Howard Sturgis' urbanity about it rather disconcerted me. He praised very neatly, and conscious of their own crudity the young are not always reassured by neatness. He has been compared to a clean, plump, extremely kind yet distinctly formidable old lady, the sort of old lady who seems all benignity and knitting but who follows everything that is said and much that isn't and pounces and scratches before you know where you are—pounces on the present company and scratches the absent. After lunch I made a little slip. My host led me up to the fireplace, to show me a finished specimen of his embroidery. Unluckily there were two fabrics near the fireplace, and my eye hesitated for an instant between them. There was a demi-semi-quaver of a pause. Then graciously did he indicate which his embroidery was, and then did I see that the rival fabric was a cloth kettle-holder, which could only have been mistaken for embroidery by a lout. Simultaneously I received the impression that my novels contained me rather than I them. He was very kind and courteous, but we did not meet again.

His friends called him "Howdie." He was of medium height and rather heavily built, and he gave a general impression of softness though not of timidity. His most remarkable feature was the strong growth of brilliantly white hair. The forehead was tall and narrow, the eyes soft and rather prominent, the moustache heavy and well trimmed, the complexion delicate, the voice grave and low. As to the character, kindness and malice, tenderness and courage appear to have blended, as they occasionally do with the highly cultivated.

He was a bit of a muff and far, far, far from a fool. He was at the mercy of life, yet never afraid of it, and almost his last words were "I am enjoying dying very much." He loved his friends. Piety towards the past and the departed was very strong in him—the sort of piety which Henry James has illuminated in *The Altar of the Dead*. Finally—but need this be underlined?—he was most intelligent and probably quite unshockable. One gets at moments an impression from his books that he is waiting for people to catch him up, and that they have not done so yet.

Tim is an Etonian meditation rather than a novel. The hero, a delicate, sensitive, skinny little boy, falls in love with a friend four years older than himself, and his devotion only ends with death. Tim is well drawn, and of the nature of a first sketch for the finished portrait of Sainty in *Belchamber*. Carol is a wish-fulfilment rather than a living youth, and too blue and gold and pink to be real. Both boys go to Eton—for Sturgis was in the thrall of his own school and class, and could no more imagine a gentleman not going to Eton than a servant not dropping an "h." More interesting than the main relationship is the reaction of the other characters towards it: their irritability and jealousy over an emotion which they do not share or direct and cannot understand. Tim's father is admirably done in this respect, so is Carol's fiancée, and Sturgis already shows himself expert in the less amiable detours of the human heart. Death—which in his later work was to be less accommodating—comes in here as a god, at the suitable moment, to explain and to reconcile. It is a wistful, "pretty" book, unlikely to find favour in this hard-boiled age, but it can still be read with pleasure if read indulgently, and it was written to please.

If *Tim* is a meditation, *All That Was Possible* is a *tour de force*. It records "a summer in the life of Mrs. Sibyl Crofts, comedian, extracted from her correspondence." She has been the mistress of a man who has discarded her, as generously as his circumstances permit, and now she has come to a remote valley in Wales, to shut herself up from the world. The neighbours suspect her of immorality and the Henshaws, the chief family of the district, cut her. She writes about it all to a friend in a civilized, amusing way. Then, among her indifferent comments and pleasant accounts of the scenery, a new emotion enters: she is falling in love with Robert Henshaw and he with her. The situation is handled by Sturgis with great subtlety: he is already a competent novelist who knows what he wants to do and how not to overdo it, and he works up step by step to his rather conventional *dénouement.* Sibyl had supposed that Henshaw wished to marry her—surely to a man of his strict morality no other relation could be possible—and all her delicacy was bent on preventing him, since it would hinder his career. But she might have saved herself the trouble: he had never though of her for a wife! "I had looked on him as an angel—a redeemer—and he had regarded me as something pleasant but wrong, a temptation of St. Anthony, to be resisted if possible; and when resistance became irksome, to be yielded to, and enjoyed in secret.... There was no thought of lifting me; he would come down to me in the mud, and we would lie there contentedly together." She is not angry with him and being intelligent she realizes that a secret liaison is all that is possible from his point of view. But she loves him too much to explain her own, and slips away one night, when he thinks he is coming to her arms.

> O that 'twere possible
> > After long grief and pain . . .

These lines from *Maud* provide the emotional undertone to all three books. The heart is never appeased. Perhaps Sturgis was not quite free from self-pity, and when he comes to draw the character of Sainty, he seems tempted to load the dice against him in order to demonstrate how badly the game of life goes. He may have had happy relationships himself, but he never allows them to persist between his characters. However, happiness is a very difficult thing to do in art, and what novelists have put it across convincingly? It only arrives through music.

He must have learnt much when writing *All That Was Possible*. A novel told through letters is a severe exercise; monotony threatens on the one hand, inconsistency on the other, and here both are avoided. There are no positive faults in the book, and many technical merits: that it is profoundly moving or interesting cannot be claimed. It is unlikely ever to be read again, and for this reason some account of it seemed desirable.

Fortunately there is no need to give an account of *Belchamber*. Thanks to this reprint, the reader can judge for himself, and all I need do is indicate the world which he may expect to enter. It is a long novel. Sturgis, having learnt his craft and consorted with other practitioners, is about to employ it for a double purpose: he will display his matured view of life, and he will depict the aristocracy. The aristocracy are a favourite subject for writers today; in our general breakup they have become museum-pieces. But this American approached them with no awe, he used them because he had observed them with his parents as a young man. As a result, his lords and ladies are easy and convincing: he seems to have got the hang of them externally, and he has animated them within by his experience of human nature. Even Sainty, the misfit, remains an aristocrat; he is bored by his class yet never ceases to belong to it. And his painted grandmother, his grim mother, his cad of a cousin, his manly uncle, his rotter of a brother—they belong to it too, swimming round and round in an aquarium whose glass seems unbreakable. (The action takes place in the early 'nineties, before the death-duties have done their work.)

As at a charity bazaar, the aristocracy is supported by some side-shows, such as dear Alice Meakins the governess, a Thackerayan dear, who marries rich and reminds us of the existence and the ineffectiveness of virtue. And there are the Ecclestons, spongers, who provide the fatal alliance. And there is Gerald Newby, the young Cambridge don. Gerald is the most highly finished product of the author's observant malice; he comes before us as a being not indeed perfect, not immune from faults, yet not unworthy to be mentor and hero to the Marquis of Belchamber. Alas, Gerald's faults increase, and by the time of the coming-of-age party, he is focussed as a snob and a prig. His subsequent appearances are a nightmare, one dreads to see his name on the page, and this is all that fate has offered poor Sainty by way of a friend.

Sainty himself is the crux. He is on the stage the whole time. Does he hold it? Believing that he does, I rank *Belchamber* high. Henry James complained to A. C. Benson in the Athenaeum one evening that Sainty was a "poor rat" and the book a "mere ante-chamber," but James was a poor critic of any work not composed according to his own recipes, and he was particularly severe on novels by his friends. Sainty is not a rat. He can be dignified and even stern. His tragedy is only partly due to his own defects: he really fails because he lives among people who cannot understand what delicacy is; at the best they are dictators, like his mother, and miss it that way; at the worst they are bitches, like his wife. As a scholar and quiet bachelor he would have made a success of his career. And Sturgis, writing away at Qu'Acre, must have enjoyed precipitating himself into perilous surroundings and returning in safety to dedicate the results to a friend. "The world," he says, "is like a huge theatrical company in which half the actors and actresses have been cast for the wrong parts." He himself had not been cast ill, but there is a fascination in imagining misfortunes, which he did not forgo, and which helped him to create his hero.

At the appointed time Sainty found himself planted by
a great bank of palms and heavy-scented white flowers
that made him feel sick. From where he stood the
whole great church was visible. Dimly, as through a
mist, he could descry his mother, straight and stern, in
puritanical drab, besides the huddles white chuddah
and nodding plumes of his grandmother, the duchess
strapped into a petunia velvet with a silver bonnet
whose aigrette seemed to sweep the skies, his Aunt
Eva in a Gainsborough hat, taking rapid notes for the
Looking Glass, and Claude, slim, cool, and elegant, his
beautifully gloved, pearl grey hands crossed upon his
cane, which he had rested on the seat beside him as
he stood sideways looking for the bride. Behind them
a sea of faces, mostly unknown, of light colours and
black coats, of feathers, flowers and laces, stretched back
to where, in a cloud of pink and white, the bridesmaids
clustered round the door, holding the great bouquets
of roses he had so nearly forgotten to order for them.

The organ boomed, and the knowing-looking little
choristers in their stiff surplices went clattering down
the aisle, followed by a perfect procession of smug ecclesiastics, among whom Sainty caught a fleeting
glimpse of dear old Meakins from Great Charmington.
Lady Eccleston, emotional, devotional, and gorgeous
as the morning, rustled hastily to her place in the front
pew where George and Randolph were already nudging each other and giggling. Then the little white-
robed boys began to come back, shrilly chanting, and
as the choir separated to right and left Sainty could see
Tommy, very solemn and as red as the carnation in his
buttonhole, and on his arm a vision of soft shrouded
loveliness, coming slowly towards him. All the riddle of
the future was hid in that veiled figure. How little he
really knew what was in the little head and heart under

all that whiteness; was it happiness or misery she was bringing him? an honoured, dignified married life, an equal share of joys and sorrows, "his children like the olive-branches round about their table"? or a loveless existence, the straining bonds of those unequally yoked? Its little sordid daily squabbles that eat the heart, perhaps even shame, dishonour...? What thoughts for a bridegroom stepping forward to meet his bride at the altar! But who is master of his thoughts?

The above extract will give some idea of the documentary value of *Belchamber,* of its pictorial quality, and also of its method: the paragraphs of narrative with psychological stings in their tails are typical. It is a melancholy and disastrous story, and yet it exhilarates, for the disasters grow out of one another so naturally that the reader is delighted as by the spectacle of some rare if monstrous growth. When Sainty's brother marries a chorus-girl he thinks that the depths of family shame have been reached, but his own marriage, necessitated by the misalliance, has yet to come, and then the consequences of that marriage...until he actually gets to feel that Lady Arthur is not so bad a sort, after all, whereupon the book closes. No prizes have been handed out, no palms, no butter, and doubtless it is this refusal to compromise which has damaged *Belchamber* with the general public. If it had portrayed a good woman or her spiritual equivalent, a moral victory, the sales would have been higher.

On some such note as the above—a note of hardness—it seems most courteous to take leave of this brilliant, sensitive and neglected writer. He did not care for the applause of outsiders. He wrote and he lived for his personal friends.

—E.M. FORSTER
1935

OTHER NEW YORK REVIEW BOOKS CLASSICS*

** For a complete list of titles, visit www.nyrb.com or write to:
Catalog Requests, NYRB, 1755 Broadway, New York, NY 10009-3780*